THE
ANIMAL WIFE

ELIZABETH
MARSHALL THOMAS

POCKET STAR BOOKS

New York   London   Toronto   Sydney   Tokyo   Singapore

The author is grateful for permission to quote the following material:

"Caribou Woman," from folktales told by Maria Suessi.

"The Fox Wife" and "The Wild Goose Wife," from *The Way of the Animal Powers,* by Joseph Campbell. Copyright © 1989 by Harper & Row Publishers, Inc. Reprinted by permission of the publisher.

"Jenshih, or the Fox Lady," by Shen Chi-Chi, from *Traditional Chinese Tales,* translated by Chi-Chen Wang, Columbia University Press, 1944.

Map and kinship chart by Leslie Evans

A Pocket Star Book published by
POCKET BOOKS, a division of Simon & Schuster Inc.
1230 Avenue of the Americas, New York, NY 10020

ISBN: 0-671-73323-0

First Pocket Books printing July 1991

10 9 8 7 6 5 4 3 2 1

POCKET STAR BOOKS and colophon are trademarks of
Simon & Schuster Inc.

Printed in the U.S.A.

To Steve
Lorna
Robert and Stephanie
Joss and Ramsay
Ingrid, David, Zoë, Margaret, and Ariel

He heard the tock-tock sound of a caribou walking, and he saw, through the trees, a woman dressed in fur. Her hair was brown and her eyes were almost yellow. When she saw him, she startled. So he stood up very slowly and greeted her gently. Already he had fallen in love with her.

—"The Caribou Woman," northern U.S.A.

She then remained with him, and when they had lived together a number of days, the man detected a musty odor about the lodge and asked what it might be. She replied that the odor was hers and that if he was going to find fault with her because of it, she would leave. Throwing off her clothing, she resumed her fox-skin, slipped quietly away, and has never served any man since.

—"The Fox Wife," Ungava District, Labrador

It was the children who first saw him coming. They ran and told their mother, who was incredulous, for they had flown, she thought, much too far for him ever to reach them. She refused to come out to see him, and when he walked into her tent, she feigned death. He took her out, buried her, covered the grave with stones, went back into the tent, and pulled down his hood in mourning. However, his wife, alive, broke out of the grave, strode into the tent, and began pacing about, when he took up his spear and killed her. A great many geese came down around him, and he killed them. But his two boys, meanwhile, had fled.

—"The Wild Goose Wife," Smith Sound, Greenland

Yin grieved when he heard the sad news and asked what had brought about her death. "She was killed by some dogs," Cheng answered. "But how could dogs, however fierce they may be, kill a human being?" Yin asked. "But she was not human," came the answer. "Then what was she?" Yin asked in astonishment. Then Cheng told him the story from beginning to end, much to the amazement of his friend. Later when they indulged in reminiscences of Jenshih the only thing they could recall about her that marked her from other women was that she never made her own clothes.

—"Jenshih, or the Fox Lady," China, A.D. 750

CHARACTERS

Group from Woman Lake summering at the Fire River:

> BALA, headman of the group at the Fire River
> AAL, Bala's sister
> EIDER, Pinesinger's mother
> PINESINGER, kinswoman and co-wife of Yoi

Mammoth hunters from Narrow Lake summering at the Hair River:

> *The owners of the hunting lands:*
>
> > SWIFT, the headman
> > MARAL, Swift's half-brother
> > KIDA, Swift's younger brother
> > ANDRIKI, Maral's younger brother
> > KORI, Swift's son
> > AKO, Maral's son by Lilan
>
> *Their in-laws:*
>
> > MARTIN, Waxwing's husband
> > WHITE FOX, Kida's brother-in-law

CHARACTERS

The women:

RIN, a widow, Swift's half-sister
WAXWING, Rin's daughter
ANKHI, Rin's niece
ETHIS, Ankhi's sister
YOI, Swift's elder wife
TRUHT, Maral's elder wife
LILAN, Maral's younger wife
JUNCO, Kida's wife
HIND, Andriki's wife
PIRIT, Andriki's young daughter
FROGGA, Maral's infant daughter by Lilan

Group from the Char River summering with the mammoth hunters:

GRAYLAG, the headman
TIMU, Graylag's son
TEAL, Graylag's wife, Yoi's aunt, daughter of Sali Shaman
MERI, Yoi's niece, White Fox's wife
RAVEN, Graylag's nephew, White Fox's father
BISTI, Raven's wife
THE STICK, Graylag's stepson

Some others named herein:

THE LILY, a large male tiger
MUSKRAT, a captive woman
SALI SHAMAN, a famous female shaman from the Fire River, dead many years
KAKIM, an orphan from the Fire River, dead a few years

Kinship Chart

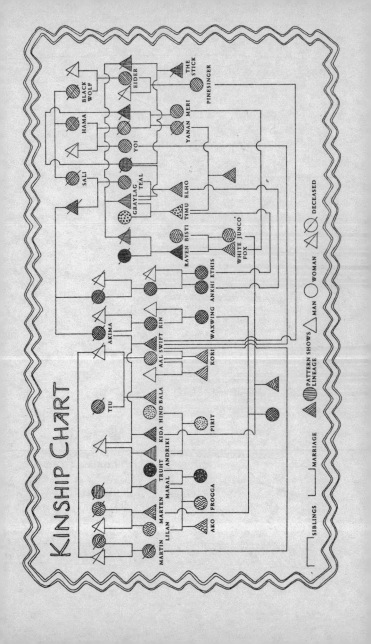

SIBLINGS   MARRIAGE   ◉ PATTERN SHOWS LINEAGE   △ MAN   ◯ WOMAN   ◁ ◅ DECEASED

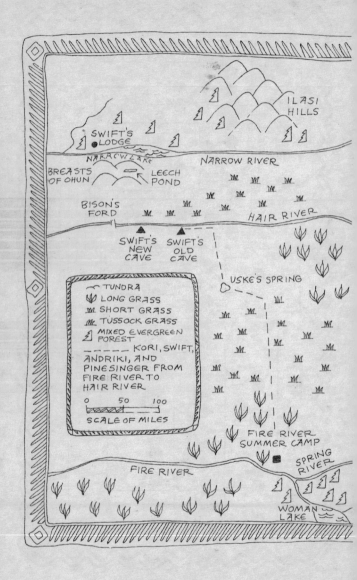

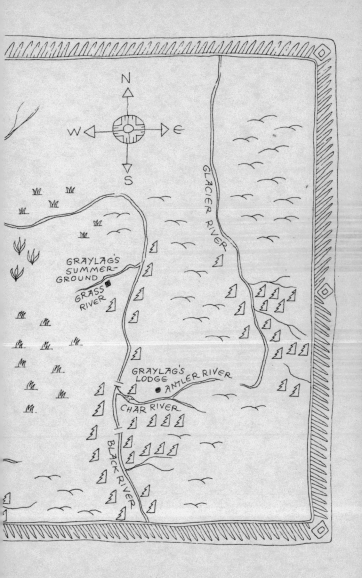

THE
ANIMAL
WIFE

PROLOGUE

MY FATHER HAD FOUR WIVES, BUT STILL HE LOOKED AT women. He said they looked best in the fall, after eating well all summer. By fall their ribs no longer showed, their skins were smooth, their hair was glossy, and their arms and legs were round. And in the fall, before the river froze, they bathed in groups in the shallow water by day, when people could see them. "Do as I did," Father once told me. "Marry as many as you can."

At the time, his advice surprised me. I thought of all the mammoth ivory and other presents he had given to his four groups of in-laws, and of the trouble the four women had caused him.

Father was a shaman and a headman. He owned the hunting on both sides of the Hair River from the southeast where it leaves the Black River all the way northwest to the range of hills called the Breasts of Ohun, where on Narrow Lake he had his winter lodge. Father was a strong and famous hunter who killed more meat than his people could use. He was a feeder of foxes!

So he was important, which made his wives important. With the meat and gifts he gave their kin, they should have been satisfied. But they were never satisfied. His first wife died, and my mother, his second wife, divorced

1

him. His third wife was quarrelsome, and his fourth wife deceived and disappointed him. He had no peace because of women, so when I heard his advice about marrying many of them I thought he was teasing.

Not so. He meant it. Father didn't seem to mind the troubles. He liked women, and he knew I would too.

When I was very young, I lived as all children do, always with women. Whatever my mother did, I also did. I almost thought I was a woman. I knew my body was different, but that didn't worry me.

One of the earliest things I remember is a summer evening by the Fire River, where the women were bathing. The sun, round and red, was lowering itself into the grass on the horizon, and the frogs in the river had begun their pulsing song. They reminded my mother to sing too, and she got me to join her. The song was low and rhythmic, like the frogs'. We sang:

> Tell my mother he is coming,
> My husband, the heron, is coming.
> Tell my sister he is coming,
> My husband, the heron, is coming.
> Tell my children he is coming,
> My husband, the heron, is coming.

On and on, for all the kinfolk. The name of the song is "The Frog Woman's Song." The other women joined and we all sang, my mother's voice high above the rest. Sitting on the bank in a frog's position, I sang gladly, with all my heart, not noticing that the song was a warning.

Ah, my mother. Her name was Aal, and in those days she was a big, strong woman. I remember sitting between her knees at night beside the women's fire, leaning against her body, listening to her voice through her chest. In the company of other women she spoke very freely about my father and even about my uncle, her brother. Often what she said made the other women laugh at the men. As I grew older, too old to nurse or to lean against her, I realized that the songs she sang and the things she said about my father and uncle showed bitter feelings, and I saw that she held much against these men.

THE ANIMAL WIFE

By the time I could reach my right hand over my head and grasp my left ear, something about women worried me. I could feel their hidden anger and their secrecy. The men I knew were open like daylight, proud and public. What they thought they said frankly; what belonged to their bodies was there in front, complete; and the things they owned could all be seen—the meat, the hunting lands, the camps and lodges, and the firesides at the camps and in the lodges.

But women were closed, like darkness, quiet and private like shame or night. Their thoughts were unspoken and their bodies held mysteries—they could bleed in secret without harm to themselves, and no one knew whose children they carried. On their rumps they wore rows of raised scars, the marks of Ohun, reminding the world that what they owned was of their bodies or could not be seen—the unborn children, the lineages, and the firesides at the Camps of the Dead, the Camps of the Spirits, where our spirits join our lineages, where the elders of our lineages give our spirits to birds, who return us to our kinswomen, who give birth to us again. All this belongs to women.

When I grew up, I wanted them. That is Ohun's plan. I forgot my mother's anger and her secret songs, and found I liked and trusted women. Also, some of them liked me. One, a girl my own age named Pinesinger, was willing to meet me in a willow thicket by the river when my uncle's people came together with her father's people on our summergrounds. After that, the kind of things that happened to Father began happening to me. So my story is the story of women, of my father's and of mine—they who made a trail I couldn't help but follow, like deer in fresh snow.

1

MY FATHER WAS NAMED FOR A BIRD—THE SWIFT—BECAUSE
he was born in winter, when the Bear wants us named for
animals. I must have been born in some other season,
because my name is ordinary—Kori. I was very young
when my mother divorced my father and took me to live
among her people on the Fire River. I don't remember
the journey. She must have carried me.

The first time I remember seeing my father was at the
Fire River when I was almost grown. My mother's
brother and his people, together with my stepfather's
people from lodges on Woman Lake, were camped on
the north bank of the Fire River where it winds out onto
the plains. The whitefish were running, and on the
day Father came the new crescent of the Strawberry
Moon rose just before daylight. That afternoon, while
we were resting at our fires or in the grass shelters we
had built to keep off the wind and the biting flies, I
heard someone say, very quietly, that two men were in
sight. We all stood up, and our men reached for their
spears.

The grass on the plain was long and soft. Under the
wind it moved quickly and easily. Because the day was
warm, the air was also shuddering, wobbling. So much

was moving that we couldn't easily see the faraway shapes of the two men. But we watched as they got nearer, one behind the other. They were strong, not tired, and they came fast.

After a while they stopped to lean their spears against a wormwood bush. This was good, since it showed they weren't coming to fight us. We looked at each other, happy about that. Soon we saw their faces. They were men of the mammoth hunters. Their hair was soft and pale, the color of grass or of a lynx's fur, and they were bearded. One of them wore no decorations on his shirt or trousers, but the other wore fringed sleeves. He also wore a necklace made with an amber bead and the eyeteeth of a large meat-eating animal. Of the two, he seemed to be the elder, and he walked first.

From afar his eyes searched the faces of the people waiting for him. He smiled, then laughed, then called out, "Bala! I'm here! Are you well?"

What was this? Bala was our headman, my mother's brother. But almost everyone, even people who weren't his kin, spoke to him carefully, thoughtfully, calling him Child of Tiu, or else Uncle, showing the respect that everyone felt for him. Almost no one called him just by name, just like that: Bala. I looked up at him and saw that he was squinting, trying to see the face of this new man. "Is it my brother-in-law?" he asked himself, starting to smile.

The two men hurried to us, and soon were hugging the men of our camp, who crowded around them, laughing and shouting as grown men will when they meet after a long time. Most of the women watched from a distance. My mother, I noticed, slipped away from the others when she saw who had come, and sat on her heels by our grass shelter, her eyes hard, fixed on the face of the man with fringed sleeves.

In time the younger of the newcomers glanced at Mother, then nudged the other, the man in fringed sleeves. "There's Aal," he said, pointing at my mother with his lips and chin. The man in fringed sleeves turned slowly for a look at her. When their eyes met, he nodded a greeting. For a moment she stared hard; then, raising her chin, she looked away. The man in fringed sleeves turned back to his welcome.

Soon Mother stood up, smoothed her trousers, and passed her hand over her braid. Then she came quietly to Uncle Bala and touched his elbow. When he bent his head, she put her lips to his ear and whispered something.

But Uncle wasn't a man for whispering. "If you don't want to be near him, go!" he said aloud. "How long has it been since I shared my fireside with Swift?"

Mother turned on her heel and strode away, and I stared at the man in fringed sleeves. Even before I'had heard his name, I had guessed he was my father.

For the rest of the afternoon, my father and the other stranger sat on their heels in the cleared, ash-covered space in front of Uncle's grass shelter, where most of the men and boys of our camp crowded together to look and listen.

The other stranger was Father's young half-brother, and his name was Andriki. He was almost as tall as Father, but still quite young. I noticed that the eyes of both men were pale, like my eyes. Most of my mother's people had dark eyes, or good eyes, as Mother called them, something she and her kin shared with reindeer and other good animals. As Mother often said, pale eyes were found on lions and other bad animals. So it made me happy to see pale eyes on two such good, tall, strong men.

The fringes on Father's sleeves, like feathers on a bird's wing, showed that like the birds he belonged to the air, which meant he was a shaman. And the fat, curved teeth in his necklace were a lion's! Anyone with lion's teeth in his necklace would seem sure of himself, but Father was very sure of himself. His half-brother treated him respectfully. So did Uncle Bala and the Fire River men.

Uncle threw fish on the coals, to roast for his guests. While the smell of cooking blew down the wind, many of the women joined the men at Uncle's fire to hear my father talk about some of the people he had left behind. Uncle Bala asked first about Father's third wife, Yoi, who had been born here at the Fire River. Among us lived many of her kin and members of her lineage. So far, said Father, she had had no children with him. Otherwise she was well, and, said Father, she sent her greetings to all the people. A murmur of pleasure went through the little crowd at these words. The people at Bala's fire remembered Yoi well.

What of her two nieces? the people asked. Those two were last seen at the Fire River when their aunt went north to marry Father. The elder of them had died, said Father, but the younger was married. She lived at his lodge, and she too sent greetings to the people of her lineage. We murmured again, not all of us as loudly. These nieces had only visited us once, years before. I, for one, didn't remember them.

Father also talked about his journey. For almost the length of a moon, he told us, he and Andriki had followed a mammoth trail that led from the Hair River across the plains to the place where, in the fall, mammoths crossed the Fire River on their way to a winterground. At the start of their journey, Father and Andriki had seen many bison. Then they had seen reindeer and horses, but nothing after that until they were within two days' walk of the Fire River. Why? There was no water on the plains.

Father and Andriki had dug milkroots, which they had squeezed for the juice. They had eaten dry berries still clinging to the bushes from the summer before, they had snared bearded partridges and ground squirrels, and they had killed and eaten an old male lion whom they had caught following them. Once they had found hyenas on a saiga and had taken the carcass. I listened carefully to Father's stories of the things they had eaten, seeing in my mind's eye how I might find food if I should ever make so long a trip.

When the fish had been eaten and the two men had wiped the fish fat and the black of the coals from their faces, my father began to talk of lineages. He praised the lineages of the Fire River, saying that good and strong people came from them. This pleased all of us, as Father seemed to be talking of our lineages. Then he praised the

lineage of a woman who had lived here long ago, a
woman who had been a famous shaman. Some of the
women then reminded Father of people who belonged to
the old shaman's lineage. Father smiled. He knew.
Wasn't Yoi, his third wife, who now waited for him at the
Hair River, of this lineage?

Who cared? Women own the lineages, and as far as I
knew, only other women wanted to hear about them. I
wanted to hear more about the long journey across the
dry plains. So did the other boys who had crowded in to
listen. But we were disappointed. People began to talk of
marriage gifts. Then Father reminded the adults of some
carved ivory beads he had given to Mother when he
married her, and a long discussion of these beads began.
We lost hope of hearing anything more interesting. When
the shadows of the bushes grew long over the plain and
the sun set into the lines of clouds on the horizon, the
adults were still talking of marriage gifts.

But not to me. My body was at Uncle Bala's fireside,
squeezed between two of my cousins, but my ears were
trying not to hear. Instead I was concentrating on a
daydream of the springtime, of something that happened
near a camp we had shared with people who were now
camped upriver. I was in a willow thicket, watching the
girl named Pinesinger kneel on the trousers she had just
taken off, about to go down on her elbows in front of me.
Over her shoulder she was watching me. Two rows of
raised scars, the marks of Ohun, led my eyes across her
pale, bare rump, which at my touch went rough with
gooseflesh.

I was torn from my daydream by Uncle Bala's voice,
now almost exasperated. "How can we return your
gifts?" he cried. "Years have gone by. Your gifts have
been given away in other people's marriages. We can't get
them back. You should have spoken sooner!"

"So that's how you think," said Father sadly.

"I'm reminding you of what happened," cried Uncle
Bala.

"But now a way should be found to make things right,"
said Father. "After all, you got your sister back. I have no
gifts and no woman."

"But you're married to Yoi!"

"Yes, for many years, but Yoi is childless," said Father. "And her lineage, like Aal's lineage, is from here."

"What can I do about your women?" asked Uncle Bala. "How are they my responsibility?"

"How not?" asked Andriki.

"Who caused this childlessness and divorce?" asked Uncle Bala. "Was it me?"

"Didn't your sister divorce my half-brother?" asked Andriki. "How can your lineage shrug off the blame?"

"Why did my sister have to leave?" asked Uncle Bala. "Doesn't she say that my brother-in-law mistreated her?"

"No one mistreated your sister," said Andriki. "She mistreated herself with her quarrelsome ways. Her disposition ended the marriage."

"Then shouldn't my brother-in-law have spoken sooner?" Uncle Bala cried. To Father he said, "Wasn't Kori a baby when you and my sister divorced? Haven't the gifts you gave for Aal been carried far away? What's done can't be undone. You ask too late. Look at Kori."

Father's eyes widened, and he looked around at some of the other boys. I realized he thought that one of them was me.

"Not them," said Uncle Bala, touching my shoulder. "This one is Kori."

Father turned, and for the first time he seemed to see me. For a moment he said nothing. I saw gray hairs in his beard and at his temples, and many lines around his pale blue eyes. He stared, bland and knowing, like a lynx. Our eyes met. "Kori." The lynx face nodded a greeting.

"Father," I said.

That was the first day of Father's visit. At night he and Andriki slept beside Uncle Bala's grass shelter and, when the air grew cold, got up to warm themselves by Uncle's fire. But because my cousins and I had been too busy listening to the men to gather fuel for the night, there was nothing but a ball of dung to burn. I knew this because I had moved my sleeping-skin from Mother's shelter to Uncle's.

When I saw Father and Andriki hunched over the

tiniest of coals and heard them talking softly about firewood, I got up and offered to get fuel for them.

"Are you Kori?" asked Father. In the dark, he hadn't recognized me.

"Yes, Father," I said.

"Thank you, Kori. We'd like to warm ourselves."

So I walked through the starlit camp, among the shadowy grass shelters, and wherever I saw someone awake at a fire, I asked for fuel. Soon people had given me a handful of branches and several balls of dung, and these I brought to Father. Then the fire burned up, and the two men smiled at me as if inviting me to sit with them. So I did. The three of us sat quietly at Uncle's fire. Then, as I looked at Father and Andriki in the firelight, it almost seemed that I belonged with them—as if three of us from Father's lodge were visiting Uncle Bala's fire.

2

ALL THE NEXT DAY FATHER TALKED WITH UNCLE BALA AND the Fire River men. At night Father talked privately with Uncle Bala, and after Uncle Bala went to sleep, Father talked even more privately with Andriki. All that time I stayed near them. When they talked, I sat behind them, listening. When they ate, I ate. When they went out on the plain to urinate, I went to urinate too. Sometimes my mother or my stepfather would call me to do something —to gather fuel, perhaps—but I pretended I didn't hear and wouldn't obey.

By morning of the second day Andriki was calling me Botfly. It made me sad, that nickname, since my mind's eye saw a botfly hovering, unwanted, near the leg of some animal. Yet nickname or no, I didn't stop following my father, even though all he did was talk.

The second day was like the first—people talked about lineages and marriage gifts. Father insisted that the Fire River people had already gotten all there was to get—they had been given presents for my mother, then they had gotten my mother back, and then they had been given more presents for her by my stepfather's people. Father had nothing.

Uncle Bala insisted that the Fire River people no longer had the gifts given by Father's people. Nor did they have my mother anymore, because she had married my stepfather. Worse, my stepfather's people hadn't given many gifts, because the marriage was recent and the marriage exchange was still incomplete. So it was really Uncle Bala's kin who now had nothing.

Sometimes, to emphasize what he was saying, Uncle Bala would offer to give Mother back to Father. Also for emphasis, Father would seem to agree. "You know I want your sister," he'd say.

"You'll have her," Uncle Bala would cry. Then he would call to Mother, but of course Mother wouldn't come.

Everyone knew that both men were just pretending. Even I didn't think that Father really wanted Mother, any more than Mother wanted him. And I didn't think Uncle expected her to answer his calls.

But in the late afternoon, when Uncle happened to call her as she was passing by, Mother surprised us all by striding up to Father, her nostrils flared with rage. This time, with her hand hiding her mouth so that Uncle Bala couldn't see what she was doing, she pursed her lips to form a ring around her tongue, the sign for shitting anus. Father's eyes flew wide at the awful insult, and he started to stand up, as if he meant to lay hands on Mother. But Andriki grabbed his arm and jerked him down. "Be easy, Brother," said Andriki.

"Respect my in-law!" cried Bala to Mother, having guessed what she had done. But she was striding away, her glossy braid and the fringe of her belt swinging, while on her hip her baby in his sling gave us a look which seemed to say that even he wanted nothing to do with Father.

Why was Father pretending? What really had brought him so far to visit Uncle Bala? That night in Uncle Bala's firelight, when I was sitting hidden in Father's shadow, so close I could feel the warmth of his body through his deerskin shirt, Father held up his fingers and counted off his wives. "Martin was my first wife," he said. "Martin died. Your sister, Aal, was my second wife. Aal divorced me. Your kinswoman, Yoi, is my third wife. Years have passed, but Yoi is as childless as she was when she came to the Hair River. And I am her third husband." Father grasped his little finger and shook it in front of Uncle Bala. "So I need another wife. Do you keep gifts without giving a woman?"

A woman! So that was what Father was after. I was quite surprised. But Uncle Bala seemed to have known all along. "Do you mean that the gifts you and your kin gave for Aal should be part of the new marriage exchange?" he asked suspiciously. "Because our people won't agree. I might be satisfied, but the others won't be satisfied."

"We will give new gifts for Eider's Daughter," said Father. Again I was surprised. He was naming a woman, someone whose respect name Uncle Bala knew but I did not. Father added, "Although I'm sure your people won't expect too much, after all that's happened to me at the hands of your women. But more ivory is waiting at the Hair River for you and your kin. And this." Father took off his lion's-tooth necklace. "This for my new in-laws. Look at the bead."

He handed the necklace to Uncle Bala, who let it dangle from his fingers, barely glancing at it. I looked at the huge eyeteeth pried whole from the skull of a lion, teeth as long as my hand and pointed at both ends, sharper and shinier at the fang than at the root. Beside the teeth the carved amber bead seemed unimportant. But over the bead ran Uncle Bala's thumb.

"The amber should please her people," said Uncle Bala.

"Good," said Father.

"But she's not here," Uncle Bala went on.

"No," said Father.

13

Uncle laughed, now relaxed and easy. The tightness between him and Father seemed to be gone. "We haven't seen her people lately. They must be camped upstream, since they haven't passed us going downstream. We'll send someone for her."

"Everything is good, in that case," said Father.

Early the next morning, even before the first gray light, I heard Father's voice in the darkness. "Are you tired of fish, Bala?" he asked. "Shall my half-brother and I bring you meat?"

In the distance a lion who had roared a few times during the night suddenly roared again. We listened. "Everyone likes meat," said Bala.

It was the quietest time of day. In the east the morning star, the Hunter, was just beginning his stalk across the plains of the sky. Father and Andriki stood up, took their spears, and walked off into the mist that still lay by the river. I followed.

We had not gone far before Andriki looked back at me over his shoulder. "Kori is following us," he told Father.

Now Father stopped and turned. "Let him," said Father. "Isn't he my son?" To me he said, "What's that in your hand?"

It was my spear. I looked down at it. It must have seemed like a toy to Father, because the point was made of sharpened bone, not flint or obsidian or even greenstone, since these good stones were not found nearby. In fact, the adults traveled far to find their heavy spear-stones, then struggled to carry them home. After so much work, no adult would give spear-stones to a young person. But what could I say to Father if he didn't know this already? Looking up from the spear, I met his pale eyes. "It's sharp enough, Father. I can use it," I said.

"Well then," he said, "if you know how to hunt, go ahead of us and find something!" So I went ahead of them, pushing quietly through the soft grass, moving carefully around the bushes, trying to watch for everything at once and not to make noise. All the while I was afraid that one of them would see game before I did, which would shame me.

Before long, in the shadow cast by the rising sun, I noticed the tracks of a lion—probably he who had been roaring. I thought I knew him—the headman of a pride of lionesses who usually stayed far downriver but sometimes bothered us by coming quietly at night to look at us in our camp. His tracks were so big that no matter how often I saw them, they always startled me. Without speaking, I pointed to them.

Father and Andriki looked at the tracks rather scornfully. "Do the men teach you fear, here at the Fire River?" asked Andriki.

His question stung me. Had he taken my showing him the tracks as a sign of fear? "No!" I answered.

Andriki pointed ahead of us so that I would keep going. I looked to the west, into the sky that was filling with daylight. There ravens were circling, looking down at something. Suddenly it came to me what they were circling, and where I could take my father and Andriki to find meat. Where lions are eating, people say, ravens are the smoke of their campfire.

Father and Andriki seemed to be waiting for me to move. Carefully I began walking toward the ravens. After we had walked a while, Andriki poked me with the tail of his spear. I looked back at him. He made the hunter's handsign for question. Watching his face to see how he would take my answer, I made the handsign for meat. His eyes widened very slightly, just enough to show surprise. I found this satisfying. On I led them, more slowly now, easing myself forward over the sparse grass, staying far away from the bushes.

The ravens had vanished. I walked toward the place where they had been. At last, half hidden by a distant thicket of juniper, I saw them again, now sitting on the rack of red bones they had been circling. I stood still, trying to see and hear everything. The lion might be with this carcass, perhaps in the juniper. In fact, I thought I smelled him.

Looking carefully into the grass to be sure no other lion was hiding near us, I cleared my throat. "Uncle," I began, "we're here!"

My words woke him! From the juniper I heard a short,

sharp grunt, a startled cough. "Waugh," said the lion, as a person might say, "By the Bear!"

We listened while the silence grew. Now the lion was also listening. Soon we heard a clap of sound, the buzz of many flies all jumping suddenly into the air. The flies had been chased off the carcass by something that moved in the bushes.

I felt the skin crawl on the back of my neck. Wanting the lion to think of standing bravely in the open, not to think of creeping, of stealth, I steadied my voice and said loudly, "Look at us, Uncle! We won't surprise you. Be easy. We respect you. Hona!"

Now something moved on the far side of the juniper, and slowly, showing us the side of his body, the lion walked into sight. His eyes, round and pale in his dark, scarred face, looked straight at us. "You see us, Uncle," I said, keeping in my voice a firmness and a calmness I didn't feel. "You are one. We are three. We have spears. Go now, and we won't hurt you."

Carelessly, as if to show that he was ignoring us, as if to show that he was leaving anyway, the lion took himself to another thicket, farther away. There he threw himself down. Ough! But in the grass we saw the top of his head, his round ears. He was still watching.

"Thank you for the horsemeat, Uncle," called Father politely. "Brother, help Kori get the meat while I keep my eyes on this lion. If he changes his mind, I want to see." So Andriki and I used our knives on the horse, then made a bundle of the meat and marrow bones with twine from my hunting bag.

"My in-laws may be content to wait like women, watching animals eat meat while people eat fish," said Father proudly as we were ready to leave, "but my son knows what men do."

Glad of the praise, I didn't want to say that Father was wrong about his in-laws waiting like women, watching animals eat. They didn't have the patience. To save wear on their brittle, hard-gotten spearheads, our men often took meat from lions, especially from this lion. In fact, this particular lion had come to expect being stoned and insulted if a group of people found him alone on a carcass. By now, when he saw people, he seemed glad to get up and go away. But if I had told this to Father, he might have changed his mind about my bravery, so I smiled and said nothing.

On the way back Father again told me to lead. This pleased me too. As we walked he called out, "You did well."

This pleased me most of all. "Thank you, Father," I said, speaking without turning, in the hunter's way.

"How did you know there was only one lion?"

"Because he called all night but no one answered. Because his wives do his hunting before they do their hunting. Because his meat was old. Did you hear the flies on it? There were too many to have come this morning. Last night those flies slept on that meat."

Behind me, Father was quiet. We walked on, the day growing warm and the smell of grass rising. In time I heard the river. We were almost in camp. Now again Father spoke to me. "Kori!"

From his voice, I knew that he was standing still. I stopped and turned to face him. "Yes, Father?"

"Have you no better spear?"

This question surprised me. If I had a better spear, I would have brought it. But, "No, Father," I said.

Father stared at me, frowning. "Why won't your uncle give you a flint? Why does he waste your hunting?"

I didn't know why, so I said nothing. Soon I began to feel uneasy, held tight by Father's eyes.

"By the Bear!" he said at last. "Come here, Kori."

So I did. Still staring at me, he reached into his hunting bag, pulled out a great, heavy flint, seized my hand, and brought the flint down into it so hard my palm stung. But as I clenched my fist tightly around the heavy stone, my heart filled with a fierce, glad feeling. "Father! You have given me a flint!" I said.

"Yes, my son," said Father.

A few days later, while Uncle Bala was cooking fish for the three of us—Father, Andriki, and me—as we lay on our backs looking at the half moon in the afternoon sky, Father said, "The longest days will soon be here, a good time to travel. Our home is far. We will leave when my wife comes. We'll take Kori."

Oh, I was happy! I jumped to my feet, seeing in my mind's eye the wide plains, the open woods, the great Hair River, and the corpses of huge animals.

"Sit down, Kori," said Uncle. "The fish is almost ready to eat."

"I'm going to make my pack!"

The men laughed. "You don't need to make your pack just yet," said Uncle. "And your mother? What of her?"

What of her? I was old enough to decide for myself where I would go or stay. I hurried to Mother's empty grass shelter and took my winter clothes—my parka, my outer trousers, and my moccasins—from the bush where I kept them. No one saw me. My deerskin sleeping-skin, my spear, and my hunting bag (with the flint inside it) were already at Uncle Bala's fire. Before Uncle Bala's fish had quite finished cooking I had tied all my things together into a pack, and I was leaning on this pack, pulling the fishbones out of my teeth, when I heard Mother screaming on the far side of camp. Word of my plans must have reached her.

In no time my stepfather came striding up to Uncle Bala's fire, his belt in his hand. Without greeting the men or showing any politeness, he thrashed the belt against the ground, raising a cloud of dust and ashes, and roared, "Go home, Kori!"

Sometimes in the past I had had whippings from Mother, whippings I liked to think I hardly noticed. But never had I been punished by my stepfather. His rage was frightening. I started to my feet.

But Father put his hand on my shoulder and pushed me down. To my stepfather he said, "Kori stays with me."

My stepfather turned and left, looking worried. Later he came back with six of his kinsmen. They stood in a half-circle over Father and Andriki, all talking at once, insisting that Father would not take me.

Father and Andriki stood up. I saw how, if the argument became a fight, we were greatly outnumbered. Father must have seen this too. Yet very carefully, very slowly, he rubbed his hands together as if to heat the calluses a spear makes on one's palms. He meant to hint that he wouldn't run from fighting. But his tone of voice was pleasant. "Must Kori stay here as a guest of his lineage?" he asked. "Or shall he come to the Hair River, where together with me, my brother, my half-brothers, and their sons he will own the hunting?"

My stepfather had no answer for that. He was not my kinsman anyway, just someone who was speaking for Mother.

"Kori can decide for himself," said Uncle Bala. "Well, Kori—your mother or your father?"

"My father," I said.

"Then you must tell your mother. Go on. Go do it."

So I went. I found Mother all red in the light of the setting sun, sitting by her fire in front of her grass shelter, cracking the shinbone of the mare I had taken from the lion. Without a word she looked at me sadly, handing me the broken shin. I took it and licked out the marrow. "You're leaving," she said.

"But not now," I said. "Not until Father goes."

Mother looked at me steadily, planning her words as if she hadn't heard mine. At last she spoke. "On the bank of the Hair," she said, "you will find a huge, dark cave where many people spend the summer. I used to spend the summer there too. We were there when I bore you. I went out to the plain where no one would see me and I hid myself in a thicket. I hid from the lions. There were many lions. I crouched down out of sight and hung on to the thickest branch of one of the bushes. I bit the branch so I wouldn't scream. I was there all day, until sunset, without help or safety or water. At last I bore you, in a river of my blood. And then I carried you back to the safety of the cave. I took care of you. I fed you. These fed you." Mother opened her shirt and showed me her breasts, the nipples now hung with drops of milk for her new baby.

"Mother, I know that—" I began, but she interrupted me.

"Don't speak! I'm speaking," she said. "In winter, when there was no food, you ate the food of my body.

Even when I starved, I had milk in my breasts for you. And wherever I went, I took you. When your father divorced me I brought you to my people, thinking that you would be with me when I grew old, that you would hunt and give me meat, give back to me some of that life and food I gave to you. But I see I was wrong. You're going." She pressed her lips tight and looked at me with huge eyes.

Childishly, I began to cry. I couldn't help it. "Please, Mother," I said, "Father wants you. You could still come. Please change your mind. Nothing is settled. It's not too late."

"I won't live with your father," said Mother. "Let him remarry. I feel sorry for his wives. I feel sorry for you. You won't like it at his home on the Hair River."

"Why not?" I asked. But Mother shook her head. She wouldn't tell me.

I finished the marrow and laid the bone on the fire. We watched it without speaking until it flamed. Inside the grass shelter, on Mother's deerskin bed, the baby began to cry. For the first time that I could remember, Mother didn't go to him. As if she didn't hear him, she turned to look at the sky in the west, where the low red sun was filling the clouds with fire. She said, "You will go and I will stay. But we will meet again, Kori. Not on the summergrounds or wintergrounds of any man, but there in the west, where we will eat the sun by the fire of our lineage—yours and mine, but not your father's—with our elders in the Camps of the Dead."

After dark, at Uncle Bala's fire, I had to unfasten my pack to get my sleeping-skin, and I saw how I had been too eager to leave, too hasty. But even after all that Mother had said, I had no thought of not following Father. My pack might sit untied for a while, but it was ready.

Yet as I lay waiting for sleep, I saw in my mind's eye a single fire far out on a plain, lit by evening light. Small, but with a long shadow, my mother sat alone beside it. The thought made me so sad that again I couldn't help but cry. Perhaps Father heard me. In the dark I felt his hand on my arm. "I think your mother wants you to stay," he said. "You don't have to come with us this year. You can wait for another year. There's plenty of time."

"I won't wait," I told him.

Soon after that, one day at noon, when all of us were resting in the shade of bushes or in our grass shelters, someone noticed that to the east of us people were in sight. We all stood up to see a group of men, women, and children coming toward us in single file. No need for these people to put their spears in the bushes! Even from afar we knew them. They were our kin, part of the group with whom we had spent the spring. Surely in their group was Father's woman. Surely they were bringing her to him!

Somehow my stepfather had crept up behind me. "Ah, you Kori," I heard him say. "Go get wood. Your mother wants to cook fish for these people. Don't pretend you can't hear." So I had no choice but to do as he said, and was out of camp when the newcomers walked in.

When I came back I found them eating fish around Uncle Bala's fire. They had taken off their shirts to enjoy the cooling breeze, and now were sitting on their heels or lying propped up on their scattered packs, loudly laughing and talking with the people of our camp and throwing fishbones in every direction.

In the middle of the group was Father. Facing him, with her back to me, sat Pinesinger, she whose bare rump I still saw in my dreams, she who had given me so much pleasure in the willow thicket in the spring. At first I was puzzled by the sight of her. I couldn't understand why she had come.

Her fine, strong body was naked to the waist, but otherwise she seemed to be wearing wedding clothes. An ivory pin held her braid to her head, her trousers were new, and the beaded tops of her knee-high moccasins were made of urine-bleached leather. All this I saw, but my mind didn't want to know what I was seeing. My tongue seemed to stick to the roof of my mouth. I hoped my eyes weren't popping.

"Kori! Come and greet my wife," called Father.

At the sound of my name, Pinesinger's head snapped around for a look at me. I thought she seemed startled, even frightened, at the sight. Then she caught herself and looked at me with the dignity of a grown woman waiting for a child's greeting. She had become my stepmother. In a stepmother's way she spoke to me formally. "Greetings, Aal's Child," she said.

That night, for the first time since Father came, I didn't sleep near him. Pinesinger and her people were guests of Uncle Bala, and to watch Pinesinger together with my father was too much for me. Nor could I bring myself to go back to my mother and stepfather. Instead I chose my mother's sister's fire and carried my sleeping-skin there. My aunt and uncle took little notice of me, so I lay down near them.

I couldn't sleep. My thoughts would not leave Pinesinger. My body ached to have her again, while my heart ached at the thought of her with Father. How had he gotten betrothed to her right in front of me without my knowing? People had called her by her respect name, Child of Eider. But who was Eider? Pinesinger's mother was called Dai Dai.

My aunt and uncle began to whisper in their bed. "What's that noise?" asked my aunt.

My uncle laughed. "It's nothing," he said. "Just Kori panting."

So my aunt laughed too, then sighed with contentment as she settled herself in her deerskins with my uncle. But he now wanted to make fun of me. "Why are you breathing so hard?" he asked. "Are you thinking about a woman? Think about a man!" I heard my aunt trying to stifle her laughter.

But the question of Eider was puzzling me so much that their jokes didn't hurt my feelings. "Aunt?" I asked.

Her laughter still clung in her voice. "Yes, Nephew?" she said.

"Who is Eider?"

"Why, she's the woman who just came. She's Pinesinger's mother. Is that who you mean?"

"But that woman is called Dai Dai."

22

"Oh! Ha! Dai Dai!" cried my uncle.

"Ah! Kah! Kah, kah, kah!" shrieked my aunt. "Go to sleep, Kori! Let your poor mind rest! Whoever heard of naming someone Dai Dai?"

So I saw the reason for my confusion. I had known Pinesinger's mother by a children's nickname. I was deeply ashamed.

3

WE LEFT UNCLE BALA'S SUMMERGROUND WHEN THE STRAWberry Moon was almost full. Taking our direction from the sun, we walked straight north from the Fire River. There were no landmarks in that huge sweep of grass. There were no trees, just bushes, and no hills, just clouds like mountains on the horizon or in the dome of the sky. There was no trail. Our legs made their own trail where the grass stems broke, and the larks and sparrows that perched on the grass flew up as we hurried by. The nights were very short. Each evening lasted so long that dawn almost overtook it. We had all the daylight we needed, and we could walk as long as we liked.

I don't think we traveled fast enough for Andriki, who worried aloud that we would reach the Hair River too late to hunt mammoths. But we traveled too fast for Pinesinger. All day she lagged, and when we stopped in the evening to gather whatever we could find on the plains to burn for fuel, she would drop her pack and say she was too tired to help us. As soon as we had cleared a space and used our firesticks to start a blaze, she would drop herself down to the bare ground like an animal and lie with her braid in the dust. Very soon, from the rise and fall of her rib cage, we would know she was asleep.

She would wake up later to eat, and then to cover herself with her own sleeping-skin. She didn't yet share Father's. And she would complain. I soon began to see her as Andriki saw her, not as the beautiful woman who would never be mine but as a bother.

One night as we sat on our heels around our fire, cooking strips of meat from a bison's carcass that we had won that same day from a group of hyenas, Pinesinger woke from her nap weeping. She turned her dusty face so the firelight showed us the streaks of her tears.

"What now?" asked Andriki.

"I dreamed I was at home," she whispered. "I dreamed I was with my mother. We sang. We ate cloudberries. But it wasn't real. I'm here alone."

"Alone?" cried Andriki, leaping to his feet. "I'll show you you're not alone!" He jumped over the fire, and soon we heard him in the shadows, snapping the branches of the little bush we were planning to use for shelter. He came back with a long switch, which he lashed back and forth so that it whistled, then thrust into Father's hand. Folding his legs, he bumped himself down on his haunches and said, "Every day this woman complains. She lags. She makes us wait. She won't work, and she won't sleep with her husband. Instead she dreams of food that grows far away. Is this how she repays the gifts we promised her kinsmen? Use that switch to teach her how to act when she lives with us!"

Pinesinger began to sob loudly, as if Father were already beating her. But Father placed the switch on the fire. "Be easy, Brother," he said. "My wife is young. Where she sleeps and what she dreams needn't worry you. When we find our people, the women will comfort her. Until then, we'll let her be. Did we need a woman's help on our way to visit Bala? Do we need a woman's help on our way home?"

Father looked at Pinesinger and said quite gently, "Now see how you annoy us, Wife. Don't make trouble on a long trip." He waited, perhaps to see whether she would apologize for the trouble she had caused, but when she looked down at her hands and said nothing, he nodded as if he understood her silence and handed her some strips of roasted meat.

Perhaps Pinesinger didn't like the trip between the Fire River and the Hair River, but I liked it more than any trip I had ever taken before. Although at first I sorrowed for Pinesinger once in a while, the more she sulked and complained, the less it bothered me that she was Father's and not mine. Anyway, my long-ago doings with Pinesinger seemed small compared to traveling with Father and my uncle. I woke every morning looking forward to the day's events and went to sleep sure that I had never been so happy.

For one thing, I had never been so far from home. Well, of course I had made almost the same journey long ago, when Mother brought me across these plains after she divorced Father. But I had been too young to remember. The only traveling I remembered was the traveling of Uncle Bala's people between their wintergrounds at Woman Lake and their summergrounds on the Fire River, a trip we took each year regularly, spring and fall. I knew every step of the trail. My mother, my stepfather, and my Uncle Bala always made sure I carried something heavy. "You're grown now," they would say. "You're not a child, to carry a child's load." Unless I was staggering, unless my knees were bending and shaking, the adults would think my load was too small.

But with Father, besides my hunting bag with my firesticks, my knife, my childish spear, and the good flint Father had given me, I had only to carry my sleeping-skin and my winter clothes. With Father, I wasn't in a group weighed down by heavy things and children. With Father, I was free, like a hunter, a man with other men— followed, to be sure, by one of Father's women, whose goose-pimpled skin my mind's eye saw no more.

I grew especially fond of Andriki. I think he couldn't help but feel how much I admired him—I was in awe of his strength and courage, and of his skill at hunting too, ever since I had watched him stalk a marmot on a bare, short-grass plain. I know I should have called him Uncle, since he was Father's half-brother. But he was so much younger than Father and such a friend to me that I almost forgot he wasn't my own brother, and I caught myself calling him by name. He was too young and far too easygoing to correct me.

No longer did he call me Botfly, but instead he found reasons to praise me. He admired my eyesight, my fast pace, and my willingness, and he liked all my stories. No one from the Fire River would have listened to me tell these stories, since the people there had already heard them from better storytellers many times before. But to Andriki the stories were new.

I couldn't hear enough of his stories. My favorite was about a man, Wolverine, who found a bulb under a juniper bush. This is such a funny story! The bulb is really another man, Weevil, who has taken the form of a bulb so he can sleep without having anyone bother him. "A bulb!" says Wolverine. "I'll eat it!" So he does. Later Weevil wakes up in the dark. He's in Wolverine's stomach, but he doesn't know it. "It's night! Where am I?" says Weevil. Then Wolverine says, "I'm alone, but I hear a man talking. Where can he be?" Here's the best part—Weevil keeps asking where he is and Wolverine keeps looking around, looking around, wondering where the voice is coming from. At last Wolverine takes down his pants, squats, and passes Weevil out as a turd. A turd has no eyes, so he can't see! Now Weevil speaks in a little high voice. He says, "I've gone blind!" Of course he's blind—he's a turd! And when Wolverine hears his turd talking, he grabs up his pants and runs away.

This was Andriki's best story. Even now I have to laugh when I think of Weevil rolling around like a maggot, not realizing what has happened to him! Every night I made Andriki tell the story, until one night Father said he had heard it too often. So Andriki couldn't tell it anymore.

But there were other things to talk about. Father and Andriki told me of their summergrounds by the Hair River, and of the dry, deep cave in the wall of the ravine, a cave so big it could hold all their people and still have room for more. Father told of a wide trail that led from the plain down the wall of the ravine, a trail used by mammoths coming to drink in the river. This the mammoths did in summer, whenever the meltwater pools on the plain dried up. Hunters could hide themselves at the rim of the ravine and roll stones down to frighten the mammoths, so they crowded each other off the trail and fell onto the rocks in the ravine below. Almost always some of the mammoths broke bones, especially leg bones. That was the good thing, said Father. Most mammoths won't walk on a broken leg. People could spear the injured mammoths, or if they were afraid, they could just wait until the mammoths died of thirst, and then the people could eat their fill and get ivory and more ivory, enough for all their marriages.

Father and Andriki also told me of their winter lodge. When the Hair River left the ravine, it went far across a wide plain, then into a low, wide valley full of birch trees. If you crossed the river there, crossed a wide heath, and went north until you came to the hills called the Breasts of Ohun, you would find a stream flowing west on its way to the Hair. On the stream was Narrow Lake, and on the north shore of that lake was Father's lodge.

Because the lodge was not very old there was still firewood near it, still rather easy to find. Also there was food. To the northwest stretched a low, wide-spreading heath where spikeberries ripened in the fall, just at the time the people came back from their summergrounds. Red deer, reindeer, horses, and bears also came to eat the spikeberries and then to spend the winter, the deer and horses pawing for food on the heath, the bears asleep in holes. So the people ate meat. "A good place," said Father in our camp one night as he sat with his elbows on his knees, shading his eyes from the firelight. "Our place. Mine and all my father's sons'. Our men share it, and now you too will share it, Kori. We'll be there soon."

Thinking of us, the men of Father's hunting lands, sharing the lodge and the winter hunting, I stared into the flames, letting the flickering light carry me to the snow-covered lodge with a fringe of thin white birch behind it and the pair of pointed hills rising behind the birch trees: Ohun's breasts. In my mind's eye it was a clear, cold evening, and Father and Andriki and I were carrying deermeat home.

In a way I wanted to reach the camp, but in a way I did not. For one thing, I was enjoying the travel. But also, perhaps I felt a little shy when I thought of meeting the rest of Father's people. After all, I didn't know them. Wouldn't things change when there were many of us, with everyone wanting to talk to Father, and perhaps his other children there?

I thought of such things late at night. Then I would get up and sit by the fire. If someone else was awake too, we would get to talking, and I would forget whatever thoughts had worried me.

Father and Andriki had started our trip carrying full waterbags. They used the Fire River style of waterbag—an uncut skin pulled off a musk deer over the head, as if the skin were its parka. Bulging with water, these skins looked like musk deer again. At first I was glad not to have one to carry, because a bag of water is almost as heavy as a bag of rocks. But after a few days we had drunk most of the water, and we grew thirsty. By then we were far from the river, out on the plain, where there are no springs or streams. Then I would have been glad to carry a waterbag. Instead we dug milkroots, if we could find the vines that grew from them, and squeezed the bitter liquid from their pulp. My palms smelled of it. Once we killed a bison calf and drank her milky rumen and her clotting blood.

By traveling fast, Father hoped to cross the plain leaving a straight track. If we were sure of reaching the Hair River, it wouldn't matter if we went thirsty for the last few days. But because Pinesinger was slowing us down, when the tenth day came we were no longer finding milkroots but we were still far from the river. We were thirsty. So we turned west and made for a large pool, which Father said was fed by a spring and never dried, or not until the Moon of Fires.

One evening we came over a rise of ground and found ourselves at the edge of a very wide, round, shallow hollow. In the center, a pool reflected the sky. The many broad paths leading to the pool were soft with trampled dung; they were the paths of mammoths and other grazing animals who lived on the plain. For a great distance around, the grass had been chewed to its roots by all these animals. Small brown snails waited on the muddy banks, and frogs floated in the shallow water, their eyes out, watching us, their arms and legs spread. We decided to camp for a few days.

I will always remember that spring and its pool. I see it in my dreams. The corpse of a mammoth who had died the summer before lay by the water. On the evening we arrived, we saw it from afar, like a huge, gray, moss-covered boulder lying on the grass. The dead mammoth's hairy skin had dried and shrunken tight to its bones, and its corpse was hollow. Beginning at the rump and belly, where the skin was thinnest, animals had eaten their way into the carcass.

We walked up to it, thinking to eat some too. Stooping very low, we put our heads inside the cave of the body and looked around. The undersides of the ribs and hips and spine were scraped bare. Lions and hyenas must have lain inside that mammoth, eating their fill, but long ago. No one could eat now, since the scraps that were left were as hard and dry as wood. A foul smell and a dim red light filled the body, the smell from the old decay and the light from the red, setting sun shining through the dried skin. Fox scats lay by the thighbone, and I saw how the carcass made a very good den, where a fox could hide from those he hunted and from those who hunted him.

"Here's Kori's lodge," said Andriki, teasing. "I'm going in." Bending low, he did.

Father laughed. "Why not?" he said, crowding in behind Andriki. I followed, and we all squeezed inside, laughing and shoving each other—all but Pinesinger. I sat on a rib, with my back against Andriki. For fun, he made the low, rumbling call of a mammoth. The call boomed, quite frightening and very strange, in that close space.

Looking out through the rear of the carcass, between the mammoth's stiff hind legs, I saw the long legs of Pinesinger walking away from us. Father also saw her.

"Where are you going, Wife?" he called firmly, his stern voice sounding rather unexpected coming from inside a carcass.

But Pinesinger didn't answer. Perhaps she hadn't heard him. Instead she circled the pool, vanishing for a while from our view of her through the rump of the mammoth and reappearing later on the far side of the pool, where she stripped and waded in. In the golden sunlight of the very late afternoon, she sat on her heels to dip water over her arms and shoulders, her breasts and belly.

In silence we watched her. Wet and shining in the red sunlight, leaning forward between her long, folded legs, with her hair twisted up on the top of her head so that her neck seemed delicate, she was very beautiful. I suddenly felt foolish, squeezing with grown men inside a stinking carcass, doing something silly for no real reason, just because we hadn't done it before.

Perhaps Father and Andriki felt foolish too. Without a word they clambered out of the opening in the belly, straightened up, and began to look around as if they had always been serious, always purposeful, ever since we had come. Father pointed out a good camping place in one of the small thickets of larch that stood on the rim of the hollow. We didn't want to camp beside the pool, of course, because of the animals that would visit it in the dark. In fact, the light was already fading. "Hurry, Wife," called Father. But Pinesinger was slowly washing her legs, ignoring him.

The thicket we chose had been used by people before. Long ago someone had cut brush and laid it, butt ends toward the center, in a ring. Once this would have helped a little against lions. Now the brush was old and broken, and lay almost flat. Even so, it was better than nothing at all. And we could cut more if we liked.

"Whose place is this?" I asked Father.

"Isn't it mine?" he answered.

"Who cut the brush? You?" asked Andriki.

"Yes, but Bala sometimes comes here. He would have cut brush too, since he doesn't like lions." Father laughed.

THE ANIMAL WIFE

Andriki looked carefully around for lion sign, since a thicket such as this, overlooking a pool where horses and bison must come to drink, is chosen by lions for the same reasons it is chosen by people. He soon found a lion scat, which he broke open and sniffed, then threw far away. "Very old," he said. So we made our camp while the daylight lasted, pulling grass, breaking more branches to add to the ring, and glancing often at Pinesinger, who by now was washing her hair.

The moment camp was finished, Father strode off to speak to Pinesinger. In the distance he stood beside her. It gave me a strange feeling to see them together in the late, slanting sunlight, he clothed and standing, leaning slightly forward as if talking to her earnestly, she naked and squatting on her heels, seeming to ignore him and wringing out her hair.

Suddenly he seized her arm and pulled her to her feet. In the great distance, she laughed! She laughed and tried to fight him. He lifted her up and danced around with her. She laughed again, her arms around his neck and her wet hair flying. They were playing! As if I had been caught watching what I should not have been watching, I felt my face grow hot.

Andriki too felt shame. Gruffly he pointed out to me a distant dark green bush that could only be a fireberry. "Go there," he said. "Perhaps you can find a few of last year's berries. I'm going to set snares." So, as the evening star, the Hind, began to pick her way across the fading sky, Andriki went one way and I went another, leaving Father alone to play with his woman.

Daydreams of Pinesinger began to creep into my mind as I looked for the berries. Soon I could no longer stop my thoughts of her naked body, or of my father's naked body, for that matter—shaming thoughts not right to think.

4

WHEN I CAME BACK TO OUR CAMP IN THE LARCH THICKET, I found Father and Pinesinger, now wearing her trousers, sitting very close. During the day we had dug a large tuber, and this Father had split and placed on the coals of the campfire. But the tuber was burning. Father and Pinesinger had been too busy to watch it and only noticed it as I walked up. Father leaped up, kicked it out of the coals, and seizing a stick, beat the fire out of it.

Just then Andriki came into camp. As his glance took in the burned food, he sat down stiffly, trying to hide his disapproval. I was embarrassed, since I saw no way to behave toward the broken black food without drawing attention to what had started the trouble. So no one spoke. The chunks of smoldering root filled the air with the smell of charcoal. None of us would eat much that night.

Soon Father took Pinesinger by the arm and led her to his bed, already unrolled in the furthest thicket. I glanced at Andriki to see how he felt, and saw that his face was stern and angry. His back was to Father and Pinesinger, and although he couldn't help but overhear their low voices, he seemed not to listen but scowled at the pool and the plain.

Suddenly his face came alive. He touched my arm. I looked where he was looking and saw animals moving, about half as far to the east of the pool as we were to the north. We saw only their legs against the pale, short grass, since their dark bodies seemed to melt into the darkening sky. They were coming to the water. Andriki made the handsign for horses, then for spear. He got his spear, I got mine, and we crept toward the horses, bending low so our shapes wouldn't show against the sky.

Near the water, we crouched down for a look around and saw that the shadowy horses had moved farther away. The stallion was being very careful. So were we as we stalked—careful not to surprise a lion or to move into a lion's ambush.

Just then an idea came to me. Catching Andriki's eye, I made the handsign for carcass. He saw at once what I meant—we could hide inside the mammoth's carcass. Sooner or later the horses would have to come near it if they wanted to drink.

We made our way to it and crept inside. Andriki was very pleased with me—he clapped my shoulder and shook his fist with delight. Here we could hide in some kind of safety. We could even move a little without being seen. Andriki made the handsign for wait, eased himself out again, and came back with a ball of mammoth dung. This we rubbed on ourselves, to hide our odor. Then, crouched inside the carcass, reeking of mammoth dung, peering out between the hind legs or through the slit in the skin of the belly, we waited for the horses to come near.

It was very hard to see in the gloomy, murky light between dusk and night. The daylight was gone, but the night was not yet clear. In this gloom we heard a sudden rush of wings and many birds calling—a flight of sandgrouse had come to the pool. What good sense, I thought. They drink now, before the owls come out but when the hawks can no longer see them. Then I heard a squawk and flapping wings. Something had caught a sandgrouse after all. Perhaps they weren't so sensible. If they drank in the heavy dusk every night, a fox could know just where to find them. For that matter, so could I. I planned to set a snare in the morning.

Inside the carcass the air was very close and warm, smelling of death and the dung we had rubbed on ourselves. After the sandgrouse left with their rush of wings, I heard only Andriki's breathing and the soft creaking of his clothes when he changed his position slightly. He peered out the slit in the belly, and I peered out the rear. I saw stars reflecting on the water, but nothing else. To my great disappointment, the horses had gone. Something had frightened them. Nudging Andriki, I made the handsign for horse. Andriki peered through the gloom for a while, then answered with the sign for gone or finished. But he also made the signs for wait and animal, and I saw that his thinking was like my thinking: if we waited long enough, something would come near us.

So we waited. The gloomy dusk cleared and the stars shone brightly. The pale earth reflected their light like snow. Nothing moved. Now and then a frog called from the pool, but otherwise everything was quiet. I had almost forgotten Father and Pinesinger, who seemed very far away.

Andriki nudged me. He was listening. Then I heard something—stones rolling under an animal's feet. Soon we heard a bush breaking. Only a rhino makes such noise. My teeth clenched as if to bite back my fear. Somehow we had missed the fact that a rhino drank here. We hadn't noticed footprints or scrapes. I hoped he didn't blunder into the carcass. When I dared to peek out, I saw that it was not one but two rhinos, a mother and her calf.

They had come to drink, but something was stopping them. Near the pool, they stood facing the plain. In time they turned their rumps to whatever it was and drank noisily, and on the plain a hyena called. So, hyenas too! I saw two silhouetted heads and four large open ears, dark against the dark sky. Eyes on the rhinos, the hyenas slipped toward the water.

This bothered the mother rhino, who suddenly spun around and rushed them. Calmly the hyenas waited, stepping aside at the last moment so that she lumbered between them. They joined each other at the edge of the pool, where they drank, then waded in. Perhaps they wanted to swim or wallow. Perhaps they had hidden a carcass in the water and wanted to pull it out again. Whatever their plans, the rhino stopped them. She bounced herself around the edge of the pool to chase them, sending starlit drops of water flying with every step. The hyenas cantered away and stopped at a distance, then waited quietly for her to forget about them. But now the little rhino wanted to chase them. He was faster than the mother, and more purposeful. She had only wanted to scare them; the little rhino wanted to catch them. They saw this and left.

Much later the rhinos left too, making a noise like two boulders rolling down a hill. We could still hear them far away on the dark plain, breaking bushes and kicking stones.

Suddenly Andriki became very still. I thought he had stopped breathing. Soon I felt him jabbing me desperately with his thumb. "What's wrong?" I whispered.

His answer was to seize my head, clamp his hand over my mouth, and point my face toward the slit in the mammoth's belly. Right beside the carcass I saw what had made him suddenly go quiet—the four legs of a lion.

I froze, staring. I had never seen a living lion so near. I could smell it, even over the smell of the carcass and the dung. My first thought was to run, but that of course was impossible. My next thought was to attack the lion. But with what? A spear? If he should come into our cramped space, our spears would be too long. We hardly had room to move, let alone to aim a spear. With Andriki's hafted ax? Andriki's ax was in camp, in his pack. With Andriki's knives? Earlier he had put one into my hunting bag so I could help cut up the horse we were here to kill. I groped for this knife and felt the edge—not very sharp, more for rubbing back and forth to make a cut than for stabbing. Was it better than nothing? I wasn't sure. The lion wouldn't like having a knife rubbed back and forth on him. So my third and best thought was to sit perfectly still and pray to the Bear not to let the lion notice us. Andriki, I realized, was doing this already.

After a while, rather slowly, the lion lowered his rump to the ground. The tip of his tail now lay within my reach. An awful thought came to me: what if I pulled it? *Ai! Kori!* cried a voice in my mind. *Has fear made you crazy?* I stared at the tail where it lay in the starlight, until at last the lion stood up again. Then I saw eight legs. Two lions.

They passed close to each other, rubbing their chins on each other as lions will. We heard them purring.

We saw more legs—three lions. A pride was gathering. Out the rear opening of the carcass, against the pale earth, I saw a fourth lion passing, then a fifth, going to the water. We heard the tongues of lions slapping the water —three slaps, a rest, three more slaps—then we heard quarrelsome growls like thunderclaps. And then came a noise so loud it was almost beyond hearing. On and on it went, louder than thunder, robbing me of my senses, stopping my breath. Andriki and I seized each other when the noise started and fell back limp when, after a trembling grunt, it ended in silence so deep I could hear my heart. A lion had roared.

The roar left us deaf and weak. While we tried to gather our wits so we could think straight, two lions began to grunt as if they wanted to roar again. Soon they roared together. We were stunned by the time they finished. Our ears just didn't work. So the silence was almost worse than the terrible roaring. The silence grew large, and with it my fear. At last, very carefully, very slowly, I put my head low and peeked out the slit in the carcass's belly. All around me large, pale shapes were moving back and forth. I drew back so I wouldn't be seen.

In fact, there seemed to be nothing to do but keep still and wait. I thought, *If the Bear wants us to live until morning, we will.* Even so, I saw myself being torn apart, my arm here, my leg there. I remembered Father's necklace with a lion's eyeteeth, each tooth as long as my hand. Such teeth would go right through my skull and meet in my brain, right through my chest and meet in my heart. A voice in my mind said, *Think of something else,* but I couldn't do it.

So we sat still while the night wore on, our muscles crying with cramping pains, our eyes stinging with sweat. Sometimes a lion would roar in the distance, filling us with hope that the pride had gone. But sooner or later a nearby lion would answer.

At last it came to me that the lions might never leave.

Why should they? After all, this pool wasn't like the river, which had more drinking places on its banks than anyone could count. This pool was the only place to drink for many days' travel in every direction, and for this good reason the lions must have claimed it long ago. It was their camp, where they needed only to wait near the water until the animals on the plain grew bold with thirst.

Then a thought came to me which made me feel very ashamed that we could have been so simple, so stupid. Whatever had made us think that in a place like this we would find horses at night, or bison, or saiga, or deer? Such animals surely drank here, but in daylight, when they could see. No grazing animals would come blindly at night into the lions' camp! It was we who had come blindly.

And at home in camp was how the lions acted. Not caring who heard them, they snuffed and rumbled, snarled, scratched, and roared. A big male noticed our trail of scent—he squirted urine on our footprints, then scratched backward to scatter the earth—but he must have decided we had traveled on. He wouldn't have dreamed we cared so little for our lives that we would spend a night in his camp.

The next thing we knew, the lions were leaving. One moment we heard them snuffling near us, sometimes purring together, sometimes threatening each other, and the next moment I looked out and saw them walking quickly away.

Then all around us we saw mammoths. A herd was drifting by as quietly as smoke. Just as quietly as the moon, which was lifting itself from the grass on the horizon, they cast their huge reflections on the surface of the pool. At the water, though, their silence ended. The calves squeaked and squealed while the females rumbled and screamed. All drank noisily, then the calves rolled and played in the water while the grown females splashed their breasts and bellies and behind their ears like people rinsing themselves after a tiring day.

Suddenly the carcass began to shake. In panic, I must

have tried to scramble out, because Andriki seized me. I struggled, but he held me tight. Then in the gap between the hind legs of the carcass the tip of a mammoth's trunk appeared—a hairy tip with two holes like mouths, wet, shining in the moonlight, holes that in a moment let fly a burst of hot, grassy air.

Still holding me tight, Andriki clamped one hand over my eyes so I wouldn't see the trunk and the other hand over my mouth so I wouldn't shout. But he needn't have bothered. Through cracks between his fingers I watched that great trunk, as thick as a man's leg and many times longer, probing delicately as it searched for us, stretching its twin mouths to let loose another blast of air within a handbreadth of Andriki's dung-rubbed moccasin. I felt no fear. Inside my body, my spirit had fallen into a faint, knowing we were as good as dead. I waited for the powerful mammoth to pull us out where she could smash us to paste.

But no. Slowly her trunk withdrew. Slowly she moved it up between the legs, until we couldn't see it. Then over our heads we heard a long, slow scratching as her trunk dragged over the carcass's dry skin. For a little while the trunk scraped gently on the carcass, then it slipped off. Then, as quietly as they had come, the mammoths left. When we dared to peek out, they were gone.

We saw the black pool still rippling, with the moon making a straight path on what was left of the water. We knew better than to leave, so we sat, cramped and very tired, to wait for daylight, which we saw was not far away. Andriki put his arms on his knees and his head on his arms and dozed.

But I was too excited to sleep. We had been frightened, it was true, but in spite of everything no harm had come to us. We were alive! Not only that, we were still hunting. Or I was—I could do anything! Jokes came to my mind so that I almost laughed aloud. My mind's eye saw me telling the story of this night to Pinesinger.

Pretty Pinesinger! In fact she was lying with Father, caring nothing about our danger. Nor would she care later. No—when she heard of our trouble, she would laugh at us. So ran my thoughts as I watched the moon's path on the water, when suddenly, to my surprise, I saw the moon's path ripple. Ah? Something was stirring the water. I saw one, two, then five shapes, animals with long necks, animals with their heads bent, drinking. The horses had come back! "Andriki!" I whispered, shaking him. "Quick! Your spear!"

So Andriki and I, spears in hand, eased ourselves out of the carcass, looked for danger in both directions, then crept toward the horses, bending low and stepping so carefully that our footsteps made no sound. Or almost no sound. Suddenly the stallion raised his head and looked right at us. We froze, but not in time. The horses turned, already running. But in the instant they showed us their sides, our spears flew at the nearest, a mare.

Andriki's spear hit her in the neck, and my spear pierced her heart. She screamed, then ran bucking, then fell. The stallion turned to scream an answer and might have come back to help her, but she was dead. With a moaning sigh, her breath left her and her body relaxed. Dead by my spear! I couldn't believe the size of her. She was a mottled yellow mare with a short black mane, huge and fat—enormous!

"Get your spear, quick," said Andriki, busily working his own spear free. "Her scream could bring the lions."

I tugged at the spear, sure that at any moment lions would walk out of the gloom to take the mare from us. "We could hide her under the water," I said.

"Good," said Andriki. "Let's tie her feet before she stiffens." With twine from our hunting bags we did this, then took off our trousers and moccasins and together, with much effort, dragged her under the water.

"She'll swell up," I said.

"Take her deeper," said Andriki.

"Maybe the lions are already eating somewhere else," I said as we pulled.

"Maybe," said Andriki.

"What next?" I asked when the mare's body was hidden under water.

"Don't you want to get back inside the carcass?" joked

Andriki. I laughed. He grew serious. "This is a bad place at a bad time," he said, looking at the eastern sky, where gray light was showing. "Let's get away from here and build a fire. When the daylight is strong, we'll go to camp."

So we dressed ourselves and walked a way in the milky gloom just as the larks began singing. Then we stopped and rolled a fire with Andriki's firesticks in some tinder I took from my hunting bag, piling on grass until we had a good fire going. Because we hadn't bothered to make a clearing for it, the fire was soon caught by the morning wind and spreading freely over the plain. Father saw it, mistook it for a signal, and came to us, followed at a distance by Pinesinger.

During the night, he told us, they had heard the lions roaring. Later they had seen the huge round eyes of several lions just beyond their firelight. While the lions had walked back and forth, Father had showed them his spear and told them how badly they would be hurt if they came nearer. The lions had left after a while.

It made me think, that place did. Many mammoths had drunk during the night, but by dawn the pool was full again. It even had a trickle of water running out of it, like a little stream. But unlike a stream, the water soon vanished into the air or sank under the ground.

That place was named for a woman: Uske's Spring. I didn't know anything about Uske, but I felt sure the pool had been there since the world began. The water had a taste to it—almost bitter. Father said it was known to cure illnesses. Many things about that place were unusual, different. A child begotten there could be a shaman, said Father.

But soon we realized that Father had begotten no child that night. Fear of the lions must have made Pinesinger deaf to Father's coaxing. Having been so close to the lions, Andriki and I could understand her feelings, but Father didn't seem to—he seemed disappointed and impatient with her.

Even so, he was pleased with me because of my

hunting. As a result, on the following night I saw something very strange, something I had never seen before, a thing that belonged to the world of shamans and spirits, a thing of the air.

5

"CHILD OF AAL, YOU MAKE ME PROUD," SAID FATHER TO ME as we worked our knives under the skin of the wet yellow mare. "You had enough nerve to spend the night beside the only drinking water for many days' walk, and you killed this horse with that child's spear. When a son does well, people praise the father. So you do right to do well. One day people will call you Strong, a feeder of foxes, a man of meat, as people now call me!"

We had dragged the water-soaked mare to a clump of bushes on a windswept rise of land from which we could see in all directions, especially to the west, where, tiny in the distance, the lions seemed to be stretched out to sleep. The west wind blew in gentle gusts from them to us, each gust stirring the great cloud of odor that rose from the carcass. Father had chosen to butcher there so he would know if the lions learned of us.

His praise made me very happy. I said, "Thank you, Father."

For a little while Father sat smiling to himself, as if in his mind was the thought of people praising him and me. Then he took his knife to the mare again. Suddenly he looked at Pinesinger, who was sitting on her heels watching, tense and angry. "Wife!" he called. "Come help us."

This seemed to annoy Pinesinger. She jumped to her feet. "Help you?" she asked. "Help you what? Why are we sitting beside a pile of meat? What if the wind shifts? There are five of them, at least. There are four of us. What will we do if they come here? Will we fight them? Let's take the best of the meat and pack it before they take all of it and us too! Hi! You want to kill us?"

"We'll pack the meat," said Father, sounding cool. "But not now. Now we're going to cut it into strips. We'll cook some. And you will help. Bring your knife."

"Bring my knife? I'll bring it back to the Fire River where the men have sense!"

For a moment Father watched her thoughtfully. Then he stood up, walked over to her, grasped her upper arm, and pulled her to her feet. He took her jaw in his hand and tipped her face until their eyes met. He smiled. "Do as I ask," he said. So she did, as if she had heard danger in his voice, although his smile and his tone showed none.

Far away, sleeping more deeply than people ever sleep, the lions lay limp on their sides, or flat on their bellies with their hind legs spread, or balanced on their backs with their legs loose and open, their bellies to the sun. But by now kites and ravens had noticed the meat and were flying down to steal a share, calling noisily as they do when they see food. One of the lionesses raised her head, listening. I mentioned this, but only Pinesinger seemed to hear what I said.

Andriki wanted to cook the liver. Whipping his firesticks out of his belt, he held the female stick under his foot and whirled the male stick in the little vulva. In no time the female stick made smoke, then fire, which Andriki fed with grass, then dung and twigs, then branches, then the liver, which caused the rising smoke to curl like a cloud with such a delicious, heavy smell that our mouths watered.

One of the lions sat up and sniffed the air. Then all the lions got to their feet and began to move toward us, showing us that there were not five of them but eight. Pinesinger began to weep. "Don't turn and run," warned Father, picking up his spear. But how could we stand off so many lions? They came quickly. When they were near, they began to trot. We backed away, trying to fix them with stares, trying to speak to them firmly, to tell them that the meat belonged to us, not to them, but they came steadily until they were almost at the meat. Then, with a loud roar like a thunderclap, one lunged toward us. If she was trying to scare us away, she succeeded. We turned and ran, overtaking Pinesinger, who had ignored Father's warning.

At a great distance we stopped to watch the sad sight—the big yellow bodies close together around my mare, now with her legs waving as the lions tore at her. Near them our fire burned brightly. We saw from the way the smoke rose straight and freely that the liver was gone.

I thought we would leave Uske's Spring, but in those days I didn't yet know Father. He pointed out that lions or no, we would find more animals here in a single day than we would ever find on the open plain, and that we should hunt rather than leave. The lions wouldn't bother us again for a while, because thanks to me, their bellies would soon be full.

When Pinesinger heard this she sat down and stared at the horizon, speechless with anger at Father. At last he noticed her and began to tease her gently. We saw that he wanted to coax her into a better mood. When Father wanted something, it was hard to deny him. Soon she gave him an unwilling smile.

Andriki raised his chin to beckon me, and I followed him across the short grass of the plain toward a line of brush that could hide a herd of horses. It seemed that we were to take ourselves away again, to leave Father and his new wife alone. Before we stepped into the bushes, we looked back to see them sitting side by side. It made me sad to think how easily Father forgave Pinesinger, and how easily he could tempt her.

So Andriki and I spent the rest of the day wandering over the plain, digging and eating onions and other bulbs as we found them and sleeping in a juniper thicket when we knew the lions were asleep, while the sun was in the top of the sky. Here and there we found horse tracks and horse dung, but never horses. Every time I thought of Father and what he and Pinesinger must have been doing, I also thought of the lions eating my horse, and I tried to put Father and the lions out of my mind, since all of them, that day, were taking something from me. Father may have thought that the plain around the water was crowded with animals, but Andriki and I found none, and when the sun was low in the sky we turned back, stopping once to dig onions for Father and Pinesinger.

As our eyes searched the grass for the hollow round leaves, we saw an unexpected thing—charred sticks and a few fire-blackened stones, right at our feet. We almost stepped on them. An old campfire! We bent low to look closely. No tracks were there, and no ashes; they must have been washed away by last winter's melting snow. Among the sticks we found a bit of flint shaped like a blade, but much smaller, as if someone had made a spear to kill a bird. We searched some more, and in a tuft of grass we found a strange thing without meaning, a sinew string tying together two broken pieces of a branch. That in itself was not very interesting. What made it strange was that the branch had been peeled and horse's teeth and feathers were dangling from it. What was it?

I looked at it from all sides. It wasn't anything. Yet someone had made it. It seemed to carry something foul around itself, something to do with spirits. Looking troubled, Andriki took the thing from me and put it in his hunting bag to bring to Father.

I was glad to find that Father and Pinesinger had not spent the day in complete thoughtlessness. They had cut juniper to make a high brush fence that would keep the lions from walking up to us at night (although not so high that a lion could not jump over). Also they had gathered wood and built a fire.

Father's forehead wrinkled at the sight of the horse's teeth and feathers we had found. "What is this?" he asked Andriki. But Andriki didn't know. Father and Andriki talked for a while about what the thing might be for and what people might have made it, but they knew of no one who had been here. If the people were from the Fire River, they would have visited their relatives among

Father's people at the Hair. If they were from the east, from the Black River or the Grass River, they especially would have taken time to visit Father, since Father's group and their groups had recently gone to great trouble to tie themselves together, to share hunting. There had been an exchange of women. Never would these people stay on Father's hunting lands without first visiting him to tell him, lest secrecy lead to suspicion and misunderstanding, to a break in the carefully made ties. So surely the people who had camped here had been strangers.

Soon an angry tone grew in Father's and Andriki's voices. Strangers, like lions, came to do harm, they said. The ugly branch seemed proof of the strangers' bad intentions. "We should hunt those people down," said Father. "They must be animals to stay here without making themselves known. I'd like to hear them tell me why they think so little of us."

"You won't find them," said Andriki. "They were here long ago. Perhaps they were traveling far. Perhaps they were homeless. Anyway, the camp wasn't used long. And there weren't many of them; they needed only one fire."

"Yes, but who were they?" said Father.

His question, of course, could not be answered. As for me, although I had sometimes met people I didn't know, I had never met people nobody knew. I had never met a real stranger. I tried to imagine what one would look like, but no image came. Were they men or women? Young or old?

Strangers! I remembered hearing of an evil man from Pinesinger's lineage who long ago had gotten one of his kinswomen pregnant and then had run away to escape the family's anger. His kinswoman had died bearing the child, but the kinsman-lover was said to have lived for the rest of his life almost as a slave among strangers in the west who spoke like animals. He couldn't understand them. They didn't understand him. But only people who didn't understand his evil would have let him stay. Perhaps those were the people whose horse teeth and feathers we had found.

I thought to ask Father, but suddenly he threw the peeled branch over the fence and turned to Pinesinger.

"We must watch over my woman," he said, catching her braid. "The strangers would steal her." Her head bent from Father's grasp, Pinesinger laughed, glancing at me from the corner of her eye to learn how I took his playing.

Andriki sighed. I saw that he too might feel jealous of Father. "No doubt," he said gloomily, which made Pinesinger look from me to him, teasing and satisfied.

"How is it that you worry about strangers?" she asked Father gaily, showing that while we were gone they had found a way to make light of their differences.

"They would take you away," said Father.

"Wouldn't you bring me back?" Pinesinger laughed. Father gave her a wide, delighted smile.

The air seemed heavy with the doings of Father and Pinesinger. What they had been up to while Andriki and I were gone, they would surely continue as soon as it was dark, expecting Andriki and me to ignore them. How could we ignore them? Some of us had to listen for the lions. Like a fox in fox-mint, Father had grown silly over Pinesinger. It was shaming.

But I suppose I would have sat there, staring at my feet, if Pinesinger had not complained about food. "Is this all?" she asked when I put onions for each of us into the fire.

"Yes," I said.

"You came back before dark with nothing but onions? Where is the meat you said was so plentiful?"

It was Father who had thought that meat would be plentiful. I looked at him now, to see if he was going to let Pinesinger annoy me. It seemed that he was—everything she said pleased him. "I killed meat this morning," I said carefully.

"But you lost it," she said. "Robbed by animals. What did you do all afternoon?"

"I? What were you doing, that gives you the right to ask?"

The anger in my voice surprised everyone. Pinesinger looked at Father, waiting for him to correct me.

"Watch your tongue, Kori," he warned. "Is it for you to decide what your stepmother asks?"

"I'll ask whatever I like," added Pinesinger.

"Then ask him," I said, pointing with my lips at Father. "He's listening to you. I'm not."

"Kori!" said Father.

"Father!" I said. "You're letting her provoke me."

"She'll do what she likes, and you'll respect her," said Father.

"I won't," I said. "I killed a horse, but you lost it. I brought onions, but this stepmother isn't satisfied with onions. What does she want of me?"

"Meat," said Father.

I could hear from his tone that he was joking, trying to slow the anger that was growing between us, but for me his joke came too late. "Then I'll bring meat," I said, standing up and taking my spear from the juniper fence.

"Will you!" said Father. "From where?"

"From where I got it last night. I'm going to the pool." No sooner were the words out of my mouth than I hoped Father would stop me. I didn't want to spend a night alone.

But Father was looking at me with admiration. "Good!" he said. He turned to Pinesinger. "My son is fearless," he told her. Then I had no choice but to go, so I went.

In the long shadows of bushes that crept across the plain, I tried to keep to the lowest ground, so my outline wouldn't show against the sky. I tried to watch the wind to see where my scent might be flying, and I tried to look for lions behind every patch of wind-tossed grass. And I tried to walk carelessly, to seem indifferent to danger, as long as I was in sight of camp. But on that evening of all evenings, I remembered a saying: "A lion can hide in clear air."

At last, from afar, I saw the dried husk of the mammoth carcass with its long hair moving against the setting sun. It made me think how much time must pass before dark, let alone before morning. Then I knew my fear was coming, and I breathed deeply, trying to calm myself, so I would think clearly, so I would feel steady, with my fear pushed down.

Only frogs were at the pool in the evening light. Fresh

tracks showed that a herd of bison had come and gone recently. As I scanned with half-shut eyes the rim of the great hollow that held the pool, I saw against the distant, moving grass the smooth, round stillness of the head and ears of one of the lions. Keeping low, I tried to make my way to the carcass without his noticing me. Perhaps he was watching something else or just gazing at the air, as lions will. His head and ears didn't turn to follow my movement.

By the pool I rubbed mammoth dung in my hair and under my clothes between my legs and in my armpits. Then I looked into the carcass to be sure nothing was hiding there, and saw only the arch of the ribs, the huge gray spine, and the dim light shining through the dried skin. I crept inside.

Soon I felt hungry and uncomfortable. I couldn't sit up straight, but I didn't dare lie down. Why had I come here? If I had sense I'd start back to camp while the daylight lasted, working out an excuse for myself along the way.

I soon gave up this idea. Why was I even thinking of leaving? The person I would have to face was Father, who thought me brave. If I went back, my show of fear would shame him. Also, I would shame myself in front of Pinesinger. I couldn't do that. I would have to stay. *If you aren't ready to be here,* I said to myself in my mind, *then get ready.* I put my arms across my knees and laid my head on my arms. What would happen would happen. I hoped I could accept whatever the Bear sent me.

During the long, dim twilight, the lions walked heavily to the pool. The expressions on their blood-darkened faces seemed serious and important. Just like people, the eight of them spaced themselves evenly along the edge of the pool. Crouching low, letting their eyes roam as they drank, they slowly splashed their tongues against the water.

Before the lions left, the sandgrouse flew down among them to drink, as they had the night before. Flight after flight came, the little grouse crowding at the edge of the pool as if the excitement of their thirst was so great they had lost all caution. The high, loud murmur of all their anxious voices and the heavy rushing, rushing of their wings felt like blood pulsing in my veins, like madness in my head. But as suddenly as the first flight had come, the last flight flew away. In the silence the birds left behind I heard the lapping tongue of only one large animal.

To pass the time, to try to think of something other than fear and hunger, I looked around at the inside of the mammoth carcass, which I could see quite well in the last of the daylight. Had the mammoth been a male or female? The sexual parts were gone, but by the lower front leg was the dry husk of a breast. A female. Above my head were her arching ribs. Right where I was sitting her heart had beaten. I wondered what had stopped her heart. Surely no animal, not even a lion, would think of attacking a full-grown mammoth. Only a person would do such a thing, and then only in a safe way. But out here on a plain, where the mammoth could fight back? No person would dare. Had the mammoth died of old age? I could see through her hollow neck to the edge of her lower jaw, where huge stained teeth lay in or near their sockets. Some teeth were worn, but all looked useful. She hadn't died of old age. Could she have died of sickness? I didn't know.

I looked at her left hind leg, lying on the ground. Around the outer part of her leg skin still clung, showing how wide her foot had been, like the stump of a big tree. But from the inner part of her leg and foot, from the knee to the toes, her skin had been torn away. Here small animals, perhaps foxes, had picked out her flesh and cleaned her bones. As I stared at these bones, it came to me that their shape was familiar, although until last night I hadn't seen the bones of a mammoth's foot before.

Then suddenly I knew—her foot was like mine! It was like a huge human foot, the ankle bones, heel bones, the arch and toes, lying inside a clumsy mammoth moccasin. As if wearing moccasins stuffed with grass, she had walked on tiptoe, with her heel making the fetlock, her toes pressed down on the round pad that was the sole of a mammoth's foot.

Then I looked at her front foot. The bones were not quite as clean as the bones of her hind foot, but foxes had picked the flesh through her wrist and down into her foot. Then I saw that it was not a foot but a huge hand that had carried her weight, a hand with a cupped palm and five spread fingers. She had balanced herself on the tips of her fingers, just as a person might if walking on all fours.

I looked around at the inside of her, up at her ribs, back at her hips. Near where I was sitting, her unborn mammoth children, about as big as I was, would have curled. For a long time each one would have lain there, then been born, then gone. It gave me a strange feeling.

When the dusk was very thick, another mammoth, a bull, came silently to the pool. I guessed he was there because I smelled him, and I thought of his great weight poised on his toetips and fingertips. No wonder he moved so quietly. Later I heard him spraying himself. Much later I heard him sigh, and later still I heard him flicking a few drops of water around the surface of the pool. For him too the night was passing slowly. In full darkness two herds of cows and calves came to drink and rinse their bodies. Perhaps the bull had been waiting for them; he eased himself in among them, then left with one of the herds.

The rhino came. Perhaps I was dozing when the hyenas stole up for a look at me. I felt them rather than heard them—the hairs prickled on my arms, and I opened my eyes to see, dark against the darkness, a hyena's blunt snout in the opening in the carcass. Was the Bear guarding me? The hyena drew back. He didn't come in.

At last came the dead, still part of night, when nothing moves, everything is quiet. No bird called; no frog disturbed the water. Even the air was still. I fell asleep and dreamed that something was sitting beside me. I wasn't afraid—far from it, I slept peacefully. I dreamed that day was coming, and in my dream I woke up. Then I saw that the light was not from the sun but from the last thin crescent of the Strawberry Moon just lifting over the horizon, red in the mist over the pool. And the person beside me was Father. He was sitting on his heels with his knees tight against his body in the small space, and he was watching me. I must have started. He pointed with his lips to the far side of the pool, where something was moving.

In my dream I grew very excited—the start of a hunt, when the game is in sight. Carefully I crept outside. Father quietly followed me. We stood up. The trails, the water, and the grass were dark in the shadowy, moonlit haze. I saw that the animals across the pool were horses—the same little herd of the night before, now with a mare missing. In single file they moved up to the water. Then some of them dipped their mouths, while others kept watch nervously. I knew they were remembering what had happened to them the night before. They were thinking about me.

Then I saw that something else was standing among them—a human figure, a small woman, her body naked, her head and shoulders hidden under thick, loose hair. While the horses took their places at the water's edge to drink, she turned her pale face toward me. She alone seemed to see me. The horses and the woman were very quiet. I heard only the drops of water falling from the horses' mouths when they raised their heads.

Soon the woman dropped to one knee and, bending low, put her lips to the water and drank too. Then the horses left in single file through the moonlit haze, their shapes growing thin as they moved deep into the mist. In silence, the woman followed the horses as the grass and the distance swallowed them.

In my dream a drifting scent of sweat reached me, telling me that the horses were made of warm flesh. But the woman? The sight of her had kept me standing still, made me forget my spear and all about hunting. Who was she? I looked around to ask Father. Then the calling of a curlew woke me, and I saw the hazy, slowly brightening sky. Father wasn't there.

In camp I found people ready to travel. Pinesinger was sitting on her pack, looking impatient. They had been waiting for me. We soon left, going slowly, looking carefully for the lions. Andriki led us, watching the brush ahead. Behind him came Pinesinger, who kept watch to the right. I came next, watching to the left, and behind me came Father, keeping watch behind, where most likely we would see the lions.

When the day grew hot and we were far away, I slowed my pace so that Father and I fell behind the others. I wanted to tell him my dream.

He listened calmly, and when I had finished he said, "Just so. It's a strong place, Uske's Spring, a shaman's place. The animals go there. People go there, just as we did. Birds go there. And spirits go there. All go there to rest and drink. Our trails meet at Uske's Spring."

By then it had come to me that the woman I had seen was Uske. I said so. But Father said, "Uske is another name for Ohun. The woman with the horses was a spirit—maybe one of the people whose camp you found, maybe just a horse."

"The yellow mare I killed?"

"Who knows?" said Father.

Well. All day as we walked I thought of Uske's Spring and the things I had seen—the horse's teeth and feathers left behind by strangers, the huge hands and feet of the mammoth, and the dream-woman who might once have been a horse. We had seen much there and might have seen more if we had stayed. So it was sad to leave, but how could we not? Pinesinger wanted to leave, and at the time Father's love for her was so great that he couldn't refuse her.

6

WE WENT NORTH FROM USKE'S SPRING TO THE HAIR RIVER, going straight, taking the shortest way to water. Father's cave and all its people were several days' travel downstream from the place where we came to the Hair. If Father, Andriki, and I had been traveling without

Pinesinger, we would have kept right on going. But Father was feeling very thoughtful of Pinesinger, who had rolled around noisily with him in his bedding every night since we had left Uske's Spring. For that, of course, he was grateful. He made us stop at the river to let her rest.

We spent an afternoon there. We stripped and scrubbed ourselves with sand, then undid our braids and washed our hair. The fast water foamed over us and carried our filth downstream. Out on a sandbar we picked lice from each other's drying hair. It was very nice there in the sun, sheltered from the wind by the sides of the ravine. Dragonflies hovered over the water, and herds of black and yellow butterflies crowded at the water's edge, slowly fanning their wings and drinking. Lapwings stood idly on the sandbar, and two families of brown geese floated in the eddies, watching us. My skin felt cold and clean.

On the riverbank we turned our clothes inside out to let the sun heat them, then rubbed and brushed them with juniper to scrub the lice out of the seams. Sunset found us naked on the bank beside a little fire we had made from a cedar tree cast up by the spring flood. There were mosquitoes, but when these began to bite we rinsed ourselves and the biting stopped. We ate our fill of sedge root, snails, and watercress, and also divided one frog killed by Andriki—nothing, really, just a few little bones to suck. The sun went down to show the new moon already high—the Long Grass Moon, very thin but strong and very bright.

There is always food along a riverbank during the Grass Moon. By the Hair, the brambles at the top of the ravine had huge, juicy black berries on them. Mother used to call these dewberries. Father and Andriki called them brambleberries. By day we walked among the brambles, picking and eating as we went, and in the evening we climbed down the ravine's steep side to dig sedge root and to sleep by the water. In some places the side of the ravine was so steep we stayed away from it, lest it crumble or lest we miss a step and fall to the rocks below. In other places it sloped so gradually that game trails led down it, trails used by mammoths and bison, saiga, reindeer, roe deer, spotted deer, and horses, lions, hyenas, dholes, and foxes—all the animals of the willow scrub near a river and all the animals of the open plain. Father and Andriki were very proud of this. There was no hunting land like their summer hunting land, the south bank of the Hair River, they told me and Pinesinger.

One day near the end of our journey, Father talked of the people we would find at the cave. We were walking into the wind, following a game trail along the edge of the ravine. Father went first, then Andriki, then Pinesinger, then me. To pass the time on a long day of walking, I kept my eyes on the steady back-and-forth swinging of Pinesinger's hips and my mind on the memories stirred by it. Pinesinger knew it. Every now and then she would wiggle herself like a gosling.

Father couldn't turn his head because he had to watch where he was going, but he talked as he strode forward, and the wind blew his words over his shoulder. He wanted us to know about his people before we met them.

"I and my brothers are the sons of one man by two wives," he began. "My full brother is Kida, much younger than I. Andriki's full brother is Maral, who is older. I am the eldest. I am the headman of everybody. With our kin and our in-laws, we two pairs of brothers and our sons use these high plains by the Hair, which are the summergrounds of more grazing animals than anyone can know.

"Maral and I found the cave where we live in summer. Before we used it, lions used it. When we found lion sign, we gathered fuel and filled the cave with fires. When the lions tried to come in, they found too much smoke and too many coals, so they knew people had taken the cave and they went away.

"Soon after, even people far away heard how we were killing mammoths near this cave. They heard of the meat and the ivory that came from those mammoths. Everyone who knew of the cave envied us because we owned such good hunting.

"My brothers and I had already started marrying our

wives. We found women at the Fire River, also at the Black River and later at the Char River. Men from those places wanted to join their groups with our group, because of our meat. And we wanted to join with their groups. Our summer hunting is the best anywhere, but our wintergrounds are the same as anyone else's—sometimes the animals take shelter in our woods, and sometimes they don't. If they don't, we starve. That's why we made sure to marry women from places with good winter hunting.

"Now we have in-laws who share our hunting lands, and in return we share their hunting lands. Now if there are no animals on our wintergrounds, we go to our in-laws. They take us in. My marriage to your mother, Kori, let us hunt on Woman Lake, but Woman Lake is far. My marriage to my wife Yoi lets us hunt on the Char River. The Char is also far, but it is better. So that we could be well tied to the Char, my two nieces married the two sons of the man who owns the hunting there. Today his people sometimes spend the summer by the Hair. We give him ivory."

Never before had I heard so much about Father's people. Never before had I given them much thought. As I listened I worried, wondering what all the people would think of me, and how I could remember anything from the tumble of names that Father soon began to call out over his shoulder. I knew I wouldn't remember any.

Or so I thought until Father, now not so far ahead of us that he had to raise his voice, spoke of a girl named Frogga. "She's the daughter of my half-brother Maral with his second wife," he said. "Her lineage is mostly from the Grass River. She'd make a good wife for you."

A wife! And I had been thinking I wouldn't remember the names of Father's people. Frogga's name didn't leave my mind from then on. A wife!

"Soon after her birth," said Father, "Maral and I began to speak of a marriage between you. We could have promised her to someone from the Black River, it's true, but we don't want to give away all our women. We asked ourselves where else we would find someone for you. My brothers and I got wives from the Fire River, but you couldn't—most of the unmarried women there are in your lineage, thanks to your mother and her kin. Well. Now that you're here, we can speak of the marriage with Frogga more seriously. Maral favors it."

We walked along in silence for a while. Father seemed content. He had finished speaking and strode forward, looking calmly this way and that. I felt on fire. I was forming in my mind the image of a beautiful girl with a long braid of black, gleaming hair. But Andriki seemed to be struggling with doubt. "You've forgotten Aal," he said at last.

"Aal? What about her?" said Father.

"She may not agree."

Father turned his head for a quick, reproachful glance at Andriki. "You may not know it, but I've already spoken of this marriage to Bala. Bala favors it too. Anyway, he has nothing against it."

"Yes, but Aal," insisted Andriki. "She's not the same as Bala."

"What are you getting at?" asked Father.

"Well," said Andriki, "Bala must have told her of your plan. As we were leaving, she said she thought it senseless to betroth young people far ahead of marriage. She said if death took one of them, the other people could never agree how to undo the betrothal exchange. Gifts would get mixed up, and no one would know who owned what. I wondered at the time why she said such a thing to me."

"Well," said Father, "it does sound as if Bala told her."

"She's the mother. She'll want a large gift," said Andriki. "Will Maral be able to find one for her?"

Father was silent for a time. He walked steadily, his eyes on the trail, but his thoughts must have been busy. At last he said, "Aal wants something. So her words have something hidden in them. She usually means more than she says."

"You know her best," said Andriki.

Father thought some more. "It's her necklace," he said at last. "Did you see it?"

Andriki thought for a while. "I saw a necklace on her the first day we came. After that I didn't see her wearing any necklace," he said.

"That's right," said Father. "She was probably hiding it from us. The important thing is that she keeps that necklace at all. It was my marriage gift to her. Later I tried to have it made part of a marriage exchange that I began but never finished for a woman of Pinesinger's lineage. That's the secret!" said Father.

Walking steadily, with long, even strides, he thought again. "We were feeding Bala's good will," he at last called back to us over his shoulder. "The marriage was difficult. The woman was married to someone else and had to get divorced from him before she could marry me. Just when people were starting to undo the marriage exchange for that first husband, the woman died. Some people said she hadn't truly been divorced and kept their gifts. So some of the gifts never went back where they belonged.

"Aal should have given up the necklace. She should have given it to the man being divorced. Since she didn't part with it then, she or someone should have given it to a man of my group when I married her kinswoman Pinesinger. But Aal wouldn't part with it. Aal doesn't know this, but she had made the necklace strong. Now it's a necklace without a rightful place. Whose is it? Someday, someone will figure out whose it is and demand it. Then Aal will lose the necklace, and the loss will be shaming. Bala won't spare her, though. When he sees who should own that necklace, he'll take it from Aal himself.

"But if someone of her lineage—someone such as you, Kori—married the right person in my group—someone such as Frogga or close to Frogga—then the men of my group should give Aal a very fine necklace. I think Bala could help Aal see how she could keep the very necklace she wears, but keep it with honor, as her right, not as she keeps it now, against reason and the wishes of many people. Kori, you will have Frogga."

Pinesinger turned to give me a teasing smile. *You'd rather have me,* her look said. But my mind was again forming an image of this Frogga who was to be my first wife, my own woman. Now, as well as long dark hair, I saw smooth skin and round dark eyes. No marriage gifts were in the image, and no other people, just my beautiful wife and me on a summer afternoon, alone on a plain. How quickly I forgot Father's Pinesinger after learning of my own Frogga!

That night was the last night we slept on the trail, on a moon-soaked grassy bank beside the water, where bats flew low over our heads and an owl's voice echoed from the ravine's walls. Mammoths had wallowed there. A wide mat of their shed winter hair had drifted against the riverbanks. Then dust had drifted over the mat, so it looked like solid ground. Mats of hair such as this had given the river its name, said Father. To warn Andriki and me, he told us that newcomers to the Hair very commonly mistook a mat for solid ground, stepped on it, and fell in. Pinesinger, who hadn't heard his warning, almost did this on her way to wash and drink. Andriki and I were watching, grinning, waiting for the splash. Too bad that she noticed the hair mat rippling.

After dark we ate sedge roots and a large fish we had found on a rock, as if an eagle had caught it and then been frightened away. The fish wasn't so sun-spoiled that cooking wouldn't help it. We roasted it in our fire as the bats flew in and out of the smoke.

Pinesinger talked gaily, telling stories about her kinswomen at the Hair, whom she hadn't seen since she was a child. Andriki talked with her cheerfully enough, but Father was in a strange, quiet mood. Pinesinger tossed a pebble at him to tease him. I thought that to be teased would make him happy, since in a way it was a promise of more play that night. But something was making him sad. After a long silence he said, "Kori!"

"Father?"

"Can you hear the bats?"

His question surprised me. "Yes," I said. "I hear them sometimes."

"Once I could hear them too," said Father. Again he fell silent. I waited. "Can you still see the star called the Mammoth Calf?" he asked after a while.

The moonlight had washed away most of the stars, but on another night I could have seen it—a tiny star beside a bigger star, the Mammoth Cow. "Yes, on a dark night," I answered.

"I see the calf and its mother as one star, very misty," said Father. "Can you see waterbears?"

Not for years had I looked for these tiny animals who live in the shallows of a river, but I thought I could still see one, though not at night. "I'll try to find one in the morning," I said, "if you like."

"No," said Father. "I was just wondering. I haven't seen one for so long I've almost forgotten about them."

I took a sharp stick and drew a huge waterbear for him on the sand—its fat body, its six legs, its claws, and its greedy mouth. Then I drew its food inside it, which no one believed that I had really seen. But I had: once I had held a waterbear on a grass stem in strong sunlight very close to my eyes. I had seen through its body, which was clear, almost like water, except for specks of dark food inside.

Father looked at my drawing but said nothing. His sadness puzzled me. What was the good, I wondered, of seeing the Mammoth Calf or waterbears, or of hearing bats? "Why does it matter?" I asked.

At first Father didn't want to answer. No one pressed him, but at last, after a long silence, he said, "People grow old."

Grow old? The tone of his voice gave me a strange feeling. I had spent all my life waiting to grow old like Father. If I did, I wanted to have the same things he had—a cave, women, hunting lands, in-laws. All this had won him Pinesinger, who each day seemed eager for night to come. Who cared about seeing a waterbear?

Certainly not Pinesinger. "You grew old," she said to Father. "But I can still see waterbears. Here's one!" She pointed at something on her palm.

Father laughed. "I'm not so old I can't make you eat whatever you have there," he said, reaching for her.

"Ah, no," she said, moving out of Father's way. "I help old men. I don't fight them."

Andriki laughed at Father, and Father laughed too. But I didn't. Father's sadness had given me a sadness, and I remembered all the things he had told me that day—

things of the past that he had done to help his people. He had won Pinesinger, it was true, but he didn't know certain things about her. He didn't seem to know that she still thought of me, although anyone else would have seen it right away. Andriki saw it, I knew. Surely the rest of the people would see it too. What would they think of him? Of me? In Father's place, I would have been angry. But he had let Pinesinger soften him. When he was young and could hear the bats, could see the tiniest stars or the waterbears, what had he thought that life might hold for him? What did he see ahead for me?

I looked into the fire, watching the flames against the dark, fast-moving river, sad because of Father's sadness, sad too that our long trip was over and that what had been between me and Father would now change, when we were with his people in his well-known cave.

Late the next afternoon, when I was hungry and tired and wanting to camp and find food, we smelled smoke and a strong stench of carrion. Soon we heard flies, someone chopping with an ax, and a sudden clamor of voices, one of which called out Father's name. We had reached the cave. Someone had seen us, and people came hurrying out of the ravine, up a path that led onto the plain.

The people crowded around us, all talking at once. A very beautiful woman embraced Pinesinger rather stiffly. She was Yoi, Father's senior wife, of Pinesinger's lineage. Soon this beautiful woman caught a little boy by the upper arm and dragged him forward to show him to Pinesinger. The child was also of their lineage.

At the edge of the ravine I took off my pack and sat beside it, looking among the many people for the girl who might be Frogga. I saw several men talking with Father—his in-laws and half-brothers, I knew. I saw a group of women, one with straight, pale hair and sky-colored eyes like Father and Andriki. She was older than Father—she would be my Aunt Rin. She caught my eye and started toward me, but stopped on the way to greet Father.

I looked around at the other people, hoping to see my

beautiful Frogga. I saw not one but two girls, one a little older than the other, both with glossy black hair. The two of them were in charge of several little children who were eyeing me unhappily, as children will when they notice a stranger. Not wanting to do anything wrong in front of my wife-to-be, I stared at my feet and sat still.

Near me a trail wide enough for mammoths led down the side of the ravine. Surely this was the trail Father had described, the trail used by mammoths to reach the water. From where I sat I couldn't see down it. I waited a long time for someone to greet me, if only my aunt, who was busily talking with Father, but at last I grew self-conscious at being ignored for so long. For something to do, I stood up and looked over the edge of the cliff.

Right below me was the egg-shaped back and bulging head of a mammoth half sitting, half lying, like a mammoth who has been asleep but is about to get up. Beside the mammoth stood a calf—a yearling. As I stared, amazed at the sight of a mammoth lying down so near where people live, the mammoth cow heaved herself once, heaved herself twice, as if to stand, and then, as if she couldn't stand up after all, rolled onto her side.

Then I saw that both her front legs were broken. Below her knees her leg bones showed like white spearheads in the holes they had pierced through her greatly swollen muscle and skin. The calf moved to stand behind her and began to twist the hair on her shoulder. She flung out her trunk at him.

Beyond, the shallow river ran through a floodplain strewn with the scattered bones and skulls of other mammoths. Some bones were bleached from years of weather. Others were in their carcasses, with hairy hide, dried hard like the carcass at Uske's Spring, clinging to them. So at last I saw what good summer hunting Father and his brothers had found, and I felt pride at belonging there. More food lay below me than I had ever seen in one place—enough for all the people of this cave and more besides. Rightly did Father call himself and his brothers feeders of foxes, men of meat.

I heard Father telling someone how I had come with him from Bala's camp at the Fire River. Then a huge man came to stand over me. Like Father, he had pale eyes and coarse, pale hair and red, raw patches on the bridge of his nose where the sun had peeled his skin. He was my Uncle Maral. I stood to greet him and saw beyond him that most of the rest of the people, with Pinesinger, Andriki, the two pretty girls, and all the little children, were going down the path to the cave in the side of the ravine. We followed. Uncle Maral took my pack and went ahead of me, carrying it for me into the cave.

When we began to move along the trail, the mammoth calf looked up at us, its trunk raised toward us, its ears spread. The mother, now propped on her left elbow, was also alert, her eyes open, her trunk searching. Soon she heaved again as if to stand, and when she couldn't, she rumbled. The calf trotted around to stand by her head.

Maral saw me watching. "Don't go down," he said. "The calf will chase you. And don't get into the big mammoth's reach."

"What plans do you have for them, Uncle?" I asked politely.

Maral laughed. "We'll eat them," he said.

But the mammoths couldn't be eaten yet, and I was hungry. I wondered what food the people ate while waiting for the meat. Smoke from the opening of the cave carried the smell of roasting onions. Just onions? I made up my mind that whatever the food, I would show no disappointment, although my mouth had started watering at the thought of the meat.

Hoping that the cooking would not take long, I followed Maral down the path into the cave, where most of the people were now gathered, listening to Father and Andriki tell of our trip. Many of the women wanted news of their kin on the Fire River, and forgot to pay attention to the roasting onions, which began to burn. I noticed the onions, though no one else did, but I was too shy to say anything. People might have thought me greedy. So I watched while the onions turned brown, then black, then flamed.

At last one of the pretty girls tried to beat out the flames with a stick, but she was much too late. She shoved the burned onions aside and in their place put five new onions. Soon a delicious smell came from them. My mind wandered back and forth between two questions: which of the pretty girls was Frogga, and how many people were the five little onions supposed to feed?

To take my mind off these questions, I tried to look around the cave. The walls were pale yellow sandstone and enclosed a huge, dim space, so high that a man could stand in it without touching the ceiling and so long that all of us, at night, would be able to lie down. Two fires were burning, but no one sat at one of them. All the people were crowded at the other, all talking at once to Father. Their voices echoed from the stone. Above the fires, black soot clung to the ceiling, and the handprints of children streaked the walls. In fact, the air in the cave smelled of soot and of children—of the urine and feces that little children cannot help but drop.

Although counting people is unlucky, I decided to do it anyway, although very privately, pressing a finger against my palm for each person I saw. In this way I counted five men besides Father and Andriki and ten women besides Pinesinger in the group in the cave. I could see which woman was Andriki's wife—she sat very close to him, pressing against him but not looking at him, and reaching now and then into a small skin bag to bring out fireberries, which she pushed into his hand. He tossed them one by one into his mouth as he went on talking. I already knew which woman was Yoi, Father's senior wife, and it pleased me that she had taken the place beside Father, crowding Pinesinger out of her way. Pinesinger looked sour and, perhaps for encouragement, kept glancing at me. But by now my mind was set for Frogga, so I ignored Pinesinger.

Suddenly the second group of onions turned black and burst into flames. Were we going to eat nothing? Now and then I could faintly hear one of the mammoths rumbling, still alive on the rocks below the cave. Again I thought of meat.

To pass the time before a third set of onions could be cooked, I counted the children. There were many of them, including babies hidden in their mother's shirts, and sooner or later I saw six. One was a little girl who had just learned to walk, which she did rather badly, as if she were about to fall forward with each wobbling step. A charm against diarrhea was tied around her belly on a string—her only clothing. She drooled, and her nose ran. When she saw me looking at her she stumbled toward me, then realized she didn't know me and stopped, unsure, to stare with wide eyes. Suddenly she glanced down between her feet. A puddle of urine was forming. This was more interesting than I was; she bent her head and her knees to watch the puddle grow. When it grew no more she turned herself around and tottered toward Maral, who caught her by the upper arm and pulled her into his lap. He kissed her. Then he noticed me watching the child, held her up, and said, "Frogga!"

That was how I met my wife-to-be. I had never before been so badly disappointed. I stared at her and she at me, neither of us liking what we saw. Worse, hearing her name, Father at once began to speak of the marriage, telling Maral how Bala could help him force Mother's agreement. Then, while Father and Maral spoke on and on about the gifts, some of the women pushed Frogga toward me, telling her she had a husband. Frogga resisted, then cried and hid behind her mother. The women forgot her and went back to their talk. I tried to forget her too, until another woman came up behind me and set her down in my lap. Her smooth, bare skin was cool and damp. She struggled to get away, and I didn't try to stop her. Pointing her anus at me, she left on all fours.

By now the idea of the marriage had caught people's imagination. They soon made so much of us that the baby herself must have begun to wonder about me. To my annoyance and surprise I felt something grasping my sleeve and found her pulling herself to her feet beside me. She had come to put a fistful of ashes, wet with something, into my mouth. Everyone praised her. This made her show off—when I pressed my lips tight against whatever disgusting thing her strong little fingers were trying to feed me, she gave a shout and smeared the ashes on my chin. The people cheered her for feeding her husband and said what a good wife she would be. Frogga grinned and danced from the attention. It embarrassed me.

I've had better nights than that first night in Father's cave. Never had I felt so much a stranger. If at first I might have thought I knew who some of the people were, I soon got confused in the crowd and shamed myself by mistaking one person for another. I even mixed up my Uncle Maral with another man. I caught Father watching me, his mouth pulled down in disappointment. I also caught Pinesinger eyeing me with a triumphant sneer after watching me with Frogga. Perhaps I should have been more helpful to Pinesinger. Late at night, when the corners of the cave were filled with darkness and all the new faces were lit with firelight, the few onions vanished down the throats of other people, and I knew I wouldn't even get a bite to eat.

At least, I thought, *I can drink from the river.* I stood up quietly in the shadows behind the circle of noisy people crowded around the fire, and taking my spear, I went to the mouth of the cave. No one saw me.

7

AT NIGHT THE VALLEY SEEMED DEEP AND VERY WIDE, FULL OF wind and moonlight. Far below I heard the river foaming over its rocks and over the white mammoth bones that lay in the water. Wondering what night hunters might be prowling there, I listened, but heard only the people chatting behind me. Except for the wind and water, the valley was silent. But silence doesn't mean much, not with lions. I slipped out of the cave, went very quietly partway down the trail, and listened again.

My right hand felt the balance of my spear. Light and dry, it felt good, very familiar. It was the same child's spear I had brought from the Fire River—Father had not yet kept his promise to show me how to work into a point the flint he had given me—but its easy weight gave me a good feeling. Much more sure of myself alone in the dark than embarrassed among strangers, I quietly followed the shadow of the ravine's wall until I was almost at the water. There I stopped again to learn what might be near me.

I smelled water, woodsmoke from the fire in the cave above, and the grassy smell of the two still-living mammoths, whom, after I stopped to listen, I heard breathing. I could also smell the raw meat of the cow mammoth's wounds. To learn more about her, I sat without moving, deep in the shadow of the rock wall, my spear ready. After a long time there came a deep, soft rumble, so low I could barely hear it, so low it seemed to come from everywhere, to shake inside me, pulsing my chest with the sound.

The cow mammoth had made it—she was calling. As if she were calling to me, I listened, while a plan took form in my mind. Then, taking a deep breath, I answered her.

Uncle Bala had often praised me for the animal calls I can make—they are as good as real, he told me. The rumble I made may have sounded far off to the cow mammoth, since my voice, compared to hers, was faint, but I must have sounded real enough to make her and her calf listen carefully. After I called, they suddenly fell silent. I heard nothing from either of them, not a rustle, not even their breathing, not a sound.

Suddenly the cow called again, louder, and I noticed the little calf against the sky. His head and ears were up, his trunk too. Alert and excited, he came hurrying toward me. Ha! Perhaps he thought another mammoth had come to help them! With all my strength, I threw my spear.

I hit him in the chest. He screamed. His mother started trumpeting and roaring, heaving herself around, flopping like a fish as she tried to get to her feet. I threw a stone hard at my spear to knock it out of the calf's chest, and when I heard the spear clatter on the rocks I threw stones at the calf's rump to chase him away from it. All this time the two mammoths were screaming, and when I felt gravel falling on me from the trail, I knew that men from the cave were hurrying down.

Before they reached me, I found my spear and shoved it between the ribs of the little mammoth, into his heart. He was as good as dead, in spite of his gasping and groaning, in spite of his mother's roars and screams. As the men from the cave crowded around me, I couldn't help but smile.

"Hi! What's this?" yelled my father.

"Father, I'm hungry," I said.

Then Father laughed aloud and put his arms around me, slapping my shoulders, rubbing my hair. "It's my son!" he shouted to the other men, crowded at the foot of the trail since no one dared go near the cow mammoth. "Was I right to bring him from the Fire River?"

But not everyone was happy. Although at first I didn't notice because the mammoth was making so much noise, many of the men were silent. Then one old man, whose name I didn't at the time remember, gave me an angry stare and said, "Look at the calf, where he's lying." I looked. The calf's last struggles had taken him within reach of his mother's trunk. "Now we'll have to kill his mother or we'll lose his meat. My son-in-law was supposed to kill this cow mammoth. Then he could have given ivory to me and my wife, as he still owes us for his marriage."

I might have known. At the Fire River, all the pieces of a carcass have owners, depending on who hunted and who killed the animal. What was true of meat would be more true of ivory. Now I saw that people hadn't left the female mammoth to die by chance, but had been waiting politely for her rightful killer to come.

Father tried to defend me. "We waited for your son-in-law," he said. "How long were we supposed to wait? If your in-law wants ivory, he should stay where it's found. What about the meat? Your in-law has been gone many days, and he can't expect us to starve while we wait for him."

But the old man didn't agree. "Kori is new here, and perhaps he didn't know he was interfering. But you knew. You might have warned him," he said sourly to Father.

"By the Bear! I would have warned him! If I'd thought he'd come into the ravine alone in the middle of the night to fight two mammoths with a child's spear, I'd have told him not to!" said Father.

Maral poised his spear. Sighting down its length, he said, "Enough talk. What happened can't be helped. Let's finish this." He threw the spear and hit the cow mammoth's side. She screamed. The other men threw also. Many of their spears struck deeply.

The mammoth grasped Maral's spear with her trunk, then pulled it out of her side. To my surprise she threw it at us. She didn't really aim, so the spear flew sideways and clattered harmlessly against the rocks. Even so, we stared in amazement. "My spear?" said Maral. "This cow doesn't want to give me ivory."

With great, loud groans the mammoth struck at the other spears in her body, then at her own front legs, where the broken, spearlike bones moved when she moved. She struck at her legs as if she thought her own legs were attacking her. I could smell her fresh blood, now flowing freely, and see it shining black in the moonlight. She was getting confused. From the streams of blood that ran out of her, I saw that she wouldn't live long.

At last she began to gasp and let her huge head roll. The men's voices grew excited and eager. At the happy sound of voices when a meal of meat is near, I knew the people weren't angry with me—or not most of them. Even so, I thought it best to apologize. "I didn't know you were saving this mammoth for some other hunter. I'm sorry, Uncles," I said respectfully.

"Never mind," said Maral. "After all, you killed meat for us. The women will thank you for that!"

The women! Already I heard them on the trail above, laughing and talking, making no effort to be quiet. "Wait," Maral told them, lest they rush up to the mammoths too soon. Impatiently the women crowded together near the foot of the trail while Maral threw stone after stone, hitting the cow mammoth in the eyes and ears to see if she flinched. She might have been living—I thought I heard her sigh—but her terrible strength was gone.

After a while Maral turned his back on her. Seeing that the mammoth was safe, the women hurried to the calf and lost no time in slashing chunks off him. Before the last women were at the carcass, the first were carrying meat back to the cave.

Their haste surprised me. Where were the manners of these women? I had been the hunter of the mammoth calf! At the Fire River, or at any other place I had ever heard of, people share the meat by how they are related to the hunter—the back legs for his in-laws, the front legs for his kin, the skin for his wife, and so on. Here, Maral was my uncle and also, I supposed, my in-law. Much of the meat should have been given to him. Instead the women were snatching whatever parts they could, without a thought for the owners.

"Father!" I whispered. "What's this? Why doesn't someone stop them?"

"Stop whom?" asked Father.

"Stop the women from grabbing! Don't they care for the hunter? Are they animals that they don't divide meat?"

Father laughed. "Do we divide water? No—we only divide what is scarce. Our women are always hungry for meat, and here, when there's plenty, they help themselves. Think about it! If we had a bison, we would divide it. But the meat of a bison is small beside the meat lying here. Lions and hyenas will eat their fill and still there will be more. Is one part of a mammoth so different from another that we should bother to divide mammoth meat?"

"What about the ivory?"

"Ah! The ivory! Ivory is different. The women won't help themselves to ivory."

"Who gets it?"

"Are you a child? How is it that you don't know?" he asked.

I couldn't answer. As far as I knew, all the men had thrown their spears into the mammoth. Perhaps they didn't know whose spear had killed her; perhaps that was why they all crouched at the carcass in the moonlight, poking the wounds to learn their depth, trying to decide. But whoever's spear had killed, it wasn't mine.

Father then answered his own question. "You don't know because your Uncle Bala's people won't hunt mammoths." This was true, of course. On the plain near the Fire River, where the riverbanks were low, the mammoths stayed together in large herds and drank fearlessly. Those mammoths chased people just as they chased lions. The lions stayed far away from the mammoths, and so did we. Father was right about us and mammoths.

He explained, "No one man can kill a mammoth. No one man can own the tusks. But the men whose spears made the big wounds and any man who risked his life in hunting her, they will have shares. Me, for instance—I'll have a share. I'll need it," he added, running his eyes over the moonlit backs of his two women as they bent to their work of butchering. Perhaps he was thinking of his tangled marriage exchange.

I looked at the cow's tusks, curved moonlit shapes against the sky. One man standing on another man's shoulders would not be as tall as one of these tusks. If someone else had speared the calf, my spear would have been in my hand when the time had come to kill the mother. I might have thrown it into her and earned a share of the ivory. With ivory of my own, I could give gifts in my own marriage exchange and could even have a say in the marriage. So after all, my hasty act had harmed me.

Yet very late that night, as I lay on my back in the cave, my stomach filled with mammoth meat and my ears filled with the praise of cheerful, meat-satisfied people, I knew my night's hunting had also done me good. In-laws may not want you if you can't get ivory, but their daughters won't want you if you can't get meat.

8

BEFORE THE MOON OF GRASS GREW ROUND AND ROSE AT sunset, we had eaten the legs and rump of the little mammoth, and by the time the moon grew thin and rose into the dawn, we had finished the upper haunch of the female and had cleaned her thighbone to the knee. When I remember that summer, I remember eating. I remember my stomach feeling tight with meat.

At night we slept with our ears open, listening for lions in the ravine, planning to drive them off our mammoths with fire and stones. But only one old lion came. Sometimes we met him near the carcass, but he didn't bother us and we didn't bother him. The other lions, a pride who used our part of the river, stayed in the east, where that year the grazing animals stayed.

During the Moon of Grass we set snares along the riverbank to catch the foxes, hyenas, and wolves who came for a share of the meat; we caught several, which kept the women busy scraping and softening the skins. Late one afternoon a bear came. Some of us took spears and went quietly into the ravine, letting ourselves down the steep sides, not using the trail. The bear was partly inside the carcass, eating. We crept around him and all together threw our spears into him. That was funny! On the far side of me was Andriki. Suddenly his spear flew past me. He had missed the bear and almost hit me! We laughed at him for that. We took the skin.

By day we cut and dried strips of mammoth meat, and strips of bear meat too. When the strips were ready, long and hard like sticks of wood, we stacked them in the back of the cave. But soon we had more than we needed. The summer is short; in autumn we walk back to our winter lodges. What use did we have for more meat than we could carry?

We were very happy during the Moon of Grass—we men were. After sunrise we would go to our lookout in a group of scattered boulders at the edge of the ravine. Here we would build a fire and spend the day. If the sun was hot the boulders gave cool shade, and if the wind was cold the boulders gave shelter and warmth as they threw back the heat of the fire. From that place we could see everything that happened up and down the river and out across the plain.

Every morning some of us would gather dry bones or dung or grass or sticks for fuel while others would visit the bear and the mammoths, swat off the great noisy swarms of flies, and cut strips of meat. All day among the boulders we cooked and ate while we worked stones or carved ivory. As we worked we talked of women, of hunting, and of strange things we had seen. Andriki told of Uske's Spring and how he and I had spent a night inside the mammoth carcass. Such talk was exciting, so we laughed a lot. Nothing disturbed us. Even when a man I didn't know came from the east and sat down among us, complaining that we should have waited for him before killing the mammoths so that he too could have earned some ivory for his marriage exchange, we felt no trouble, because he was Kida, half-brother to Maral, full brother to Father. Father said, "Think before speaking! You give ivory to your wife's parents, but now let your mind's eye follow that ivory. Your in-laws would give it for their son's wife, but here her only kin are my wives. So if you had gotten ivory, some would have come to me! This way I have my share already."

"Then you excuse the debt to your wife?" asked Kida.

We all laughed, even Father. "Ah? You want to trick me," he said.

* * *

So it was with the men—easy with each other, and sure that much good hunting was to come. On the plains to the east of us, Kida had been burning off the grass so that the grazing animals, especially the mammoths, would have to move west toward us, to where the walls of the ravine were high, where the animals would have to use steep trails to reach water, where we could hunt them. From listening to the men I felt sure that this year we would see more mammoth meat at the foot of the cliffs before we left for Father's winter lodge—more meat than we could ever eat, and plenty of ivory. So said the men, and I believed them. Such hunting in years before had left the piles of bleached bones on our side of the river.

Yet because of the women this good hunting was not to be. Matters with the women were not the same as with us. They spent their days working hides in the mouth of the cave, eating meat and drinking water just as we did. But unlike us, they weren't happy together. The trouble started not long after we had killed the mammoths. We began to hear from the cave the raised voices of Father's two wives, Yoi and Pinesinger. Almost every day Yoi found a way to make Pinesinger cry.

As we listened to their distant voices, Yoi's harsh and sure like an eagle's, Pinesinger's plaintive and wavering like a quail's, I would look at Father to see what he thought. At first the quarreling hardly seemed worth his notice, since it stopped when men were in the cave. "A man's wives sometimes fight when one of them is new," Father once said. "Then they get used to each other."

But day after day the irritating screams of Yoi and Pinesinger went on. At last Andriki told Father to take his belt to both of them. Bad advice, I thought. Beating Yoi could be risky, since she might be strong enough to get the belt away from Father, and beating Pinesinger would be pointless, since the quarreling wasn't her fault.

Father seemed annoyed by Andriki's plan—he didn't want to follow it, but neither did he want people to think he couldn't control his women. Under Andriki's accusing stare he set his teeth and scratched his beard and at last found a way out of the hard situation. "We don't know what's wrong," he said. "So I'll ask. Then I'll know what to do about my wives." And he sent me to bring him his half-sister, my Aunt Rin.

I did as he asked, feeling strange in visiting the dim cave with only women in it—women who, except for Pinesinger, I didn't know well. I heard them fall silent when I stepped inside. I caught the scent of them, their hair and skins. When my eyes got used to the gloom, I saw that like a herd of hinds all of them were alert, eyes open and chins up, watching me.

I looked around for Yoi and saw her, proud and serious, sitting with her back against the wall of the cave and her feet out, crossed at the ankles. From her ears hung shell earrings, in her braid was a strip of white ermine, and around her neck hung an ivory necklace. Yoi was at least as old as my mother, but so beautiful that my eyes wanted to cling to her. No wonder Father liked her. She was watching me with an annoyed expression. *What are you doing here?* her look seemed to say.

I dropped my eyes, then glanced around for Pine-singer. In the gloom I saw her apart from the others, her shoulders hunched, her hair escaping her braid, and her face swollen and streaked with dirt, as if she had been crying. Her prettiness was gone, like a wet bird's. She raised her large, sad eyes to me, her mouth sullen. *How pitiful,* I thought. *How lonely she must be.* I gave her an encouraging smile, which she did not return. My smile turned stiff, then faded. Embarrassed by the silence and feeling that whatever was wrong here had to do with me, I picked my way to Aunt Rin.

Aunt had been scraping bits of dry flesh from a red fox's skin, and she paused in her work to look at me. Quickly I sat down on my heels. It wouldn't have been right to stand above her while speaking. Far from it—I hugged my arms to bring in my shoulders, lowered my head, and waited for her to encourage me. When she nodded, I whispered respectfully, "Aunt."

"What is it?" said Rin.

"Will you come and see Father?" I whispered. "He'd like to talk to you."

"Now? Why?"

"I can't say, Aunt. He didn't tell me."

She gave me a look to learn whether matters were serious, and when she couldn't tell from my face, she rolled the fox's skin around her scraper and sighed. "I'll get water when I go out," she said, and called to Frogga to bring her a waterskin. From her parents' sleeping place little Frogga tugged a dry skin bag and dragged it to Rin obediently, daring to give me a pouting look as she passed by. I didn't like that. Another time I would have said something. But not that time, not in that hushed place, with all the women watching, waiting for me to leave before they would go on doing whatever they had been doing before I came. Gladly I followed Aunt Rin into the sunlight. What was wrong with these women?

Aunt Rin trudged up the steep trail to the rim of the ravine, one hand absently feeling her thin gray braid as if somewhere in her mind was the thought that her hair should be neat for the eyes of the waiting men. At the top of the trail she turned to me, handed me the waterskin, and told me to fill it. I would have liked to hear what she and Father said to each other, but what could I do? I went.

By the time I got back to the men's lookout, Aunt Rin and Father were sitting far from the others under a birch tree, and I could tell from the men's faces that something surprising or important had already been said. I looked at Andriki to learn what it had been. In the low voice that he saved for matters of great meaning, Andriki told me, "Your stepmothers are fighting. Yoi says Pinesinger must go back to her people."

"Why?" I asked.

"Jealousy," said Andriki.

That Yoi would be jealous surprised me, since in every way she seemed sure of Father and his fondness for her. I said so.

"True," agreed Andriki. "But she's childless. She may always be childless. And now Pinesinger is pregnant."

I must say, I seemed to have noticed that Pinesinger's belly was beginning to swell, so the news didn't come as a surprise. "Then Father will be happy and won't care what Yoi wants," I said.

"But the pregnancy is showing too soon," said Andriki. "Yoi says the baby's father is another man."

My long-ago adventures with Pinesinger in the willows by the Fire River, the image of her cold, bare skin with gooseflesh from the spring wind, seemed to have nothing to do with what was now happening, nothing to do with the angry women in the cave, with Andriki's serious tone, or with the distant figures of Father and Rin sitting on their heels in the birch grove, their heads together. Even so, the image of Pinesinger in the willow thicket stayed with me, and suddenly I felt my face burn. "By the Bear!" I cried. "How can this be? Who else could be the father?"

For a long time Andriki watched me steadily, and then, as if he saw the truth but didn't mind it, he smiled. As long as I live, I will remember him with thanks for that smile and for what he said after. "Who knows the hearts of women?" he asked, as if thinking aloud. "Anyone could be the father. I suppose he was a man at the Fire River."

9

WOMEN'S BUSINESS! HOW LIKE A WOMAN TO COME HERE AS Father's wife only to cause great trouble!

So I thought that night as I lay in my deerskins near the mouth of the cave, listening to the river and to the low voices of two of my uncles and their wives still cooking and eating by the women's fire. Those voices were peaceful enough; I tried to let their soft tones soothe me. But the thought of what Pinesinger and I had done wouldn't leave me. I told myself we weren't the only people to have made love secretly. I told myself that I ought to forget our misdoing, since no one, not even my mother, would have had much to say if we had been found out.

Even so, I saw that Father might feel differently. He had made much of getting a child from Pinesinger's lineage. If she was already pregnant he would have to wait for years before he could get his own child on her, and the thought of such waiting wouldn't please him. If he knew what I had done, what would he think of me? I saw that I would have to speak to Pinesinger.

At first the thought of doing this went against me. It would only remind her of something long ago, something best forgotten, something as good as forgotten but for her pale hips in my mind's eye like a dream.

Then I heard Father get up to join the people at the women's fire. Cupping his hand under his chin to shade his eyes from the light, he looked over the fire at me. Seeing me awake, he beckoned to me. "Come sit with us. We're cooking, Kori," he said.

So I got up and sat on my heels beside him. While I chewed the meat he handed me, I looked around the fire at the bearded faces of my uncles, at the quiet, peaceful faces of my aunts; I looked behind Father at his sleeping-skins, thrown back to show Pinesinger fast asleep inside them, and I knew I had been childish to hope that my misdeed with her would go away. I made up my mind to talk with her seriously in the morning.

Perhaps the women were as tired of the quarreling as the men. In the morning they went in two directions to gather berries on the plain. Pinesinger joined one group and Yoi joined another. I knew I had no hope of seeing Pinesinger until evening, so I waited in the men's lookout, planning what I would say.

That evening the men went to the river to wash and drink. I stayed in the lookout, hoping that when the women came by I could catch Pinesinger's attention without catching anyone else's. I remembered her tear-stained face, her cowering manner. By now I believed that if I could get her alone, I would soon have the truth out of her.

At the river the men had taken off their clothes and

were slowly washing themselves. I heard a woman's footsteps on the trail and shrank against a boulder so I would see this woman before she saw me. It was Rin who passed, carrying Frogga. Although Rin's eyes were on the trail, Frogga noticed me. Her round brown eyes grew bright, and her mouth opened, showing her even little teeth. "Kai!" she shouted. I thought she was trying to say "Kori." But no one pays attention to such calls from a baby. Rin never turned and soon disappeared around the bend of the trail. Frogga's shouts faded as Rin carried her away.

Just as I was about to give up and go to the cave myself, I heard the footsteps of a second woman. Again I waited, pressed against the boulder, and this time Pinesinger went by. I threw a pebble at her shoulders. She felt it and turned.

She too had been at the river. Her face was clean and her hair was combed. "You!" she said.

I stood up so that I would be looking down at her, not she at me. "I must talk with you," I said.

"Well, here I am," she said crossly. "What is it?"

"People say you're pregnant," I began. "Is this true?"

"What is my belly to you, Stepchild?" she asked.

This talk wasn't going quite as I had planned. Gone was the tear-stained girl I had expected, and in her place was a woman I seemed to have annoyed. And I didn't like her calling me Stepchild.

I said, "What I want to say is important, but I can't say it here. Father and my uncles will soon be back. I'm going to a more private place. Follow if you like." I turned and took the trail east, screened from the river and the bathing men by the blueberries and juniper that grew on the rim of the ravine. I thought it better to pretend to pay no attention to Pinesinger, but out of the corner of my eye I watched for her shadow. I noticed that it ran ahead of me as we went, and felt relief that she was coming.

Beyond the juniper the trail forked. One path was well traveled, the path we all took when we went to the plain; the other was so faint it could barely be seen. Andriki had once taken me along the faint path—it led to a grove of birch trees. Andriki had told me how spirits sometimes came there, and when people danced, they danced there. In the grove were the ashes of their dance fire and the circle worn by their feet. Also in the grove was the huge bleached skull of a mammoth. The tusks had been drawn and the lower jaw was missing; the skull rested on its molars, which were pressed into the leaf mold. The domed forehead had been rubbed with ocher and decorated with drawings of people and birds. This skull, Andriki had told me, belonged to my father, and in a way it stood for all the men who owned the cave.

Pinesinger didn't seem to know where the trail led. I felt her coming closer behind me, as if she had guessed that we were going somewhere strange. When we saw the skull, she drew in her breath sharply.

I led her up to it. He had been a bull mammoth, he whose skull owned the glade. Without tusks, from the side, his profile was flat, like a man's profile. From the front, the nostrils high on the forehead stared like a third eye, and the bone inside the eye sockets had been rubbed black with charcoal, so the eyes seemed to be watching. It stopped your tongue and made you think, this thing of Father's. I hoped that the sight of it would remind Pinesinger how far she was from home and how she now belonged to the men of Father's people. Here she might want to speak truthfully and seriously with me.

Feeling more confident, I sat on my heels and looked up at her. "Sit, Stepmother," I said.

Wide-eyed, she stared at the skull. As I had thought, she hadn't seen it before.

"The White Thing," I said, not liking to call the skull by name. "Do you know about it?"

Pinesinger shook her head. She didn't know. After all, people came here only for dancing, and this summer there had been no dancing.

"A strong place," I said. "Sit."

Folding her legs slowly, Pinesinger obeyed.

"We can't stay long," I said in my most manly voice. "People will wonder where we are. So let's be quick. People say you're pregnant. People say my father isn't the father of your baby. Have you told someone this thing?"

Pinesinger widened her eyes but didn't speak. I stared

hard at her, hoping to draw the truth from her with my expression.

"Am I the father?"

She blinked, as if surprised. Then wordlessly she shook her head: no.

"Another man at the Fire River?" I asked.

Again she shook her head.

"Then who?"

"Your father, of course," she whispered.

Strangely enough, I hadn't expected this answer. "Are you sure?" I asked.

"Why, yes," said Pinesinger, pretending surprise.

Now I knew she was lying, and I felt my anger coming because of the many troubles I saw her lies could bring. "Good," I said. "I'm glad you feel sure. Because I am going to my father and tell him what once happened between us. Then, if he doubts you, if he thinks your child is too large to be his, and if he brings you here later to get the truth out of you, you'll have no trouble answering his questions."

Pinesinger looked shocked. "Would you tell him what we did?"

"Yes," I said.

"But why would he bring me here?" she asked.

"Won't he want to question you alone, where no one will overhear what passes between you? Perhaps the voice of that," I said, pointing to the skull with my lips and chin, "will ask the questions."

"Does it speak?" whispered Pinesinger, looking at the skull. "Have you heard it?"

Although I had been told of the skull's voice, I had heard only what Pinesinger must also have heard, the voice that the wind pulled out of it. But, "Yes—he speaks," I said.

Pinesinger looked at me for a long time, then down at her belly, then up again at me. Our faces were close. Our eyes met. I saw her brown irises fringed with tiny yellow lines which pulsed around the pupils. Her eyes held mine. In a voice grown strangely calm she said, "Now that I think of it, you might be the father."

"Might?" I asked. "Don't you know?"

bad-mannered way of doing surprising, sudden things—
no man had ever made love to her easily. Even Father
had had trouble persuading her to lie with him. One
night when he had tried to take her with mild force she
had made such an outcry that she woke everybody,
which had badly shamed Father. That night had helped
to cause their divorce. "Maybe he's sorry now," said
Andriki. "Maybe your mother wasn't such a bad wife
after all. At least your father knew you were his son and
not some other man's—not from Aal! Being sure makes
him content, so he's nice to you."

Andriki's words gave me a strange feeling. Was that all
I meant to Father? That I was born to a woman who held
much against men?

One afternoon we stayed long after sunset in the men's
lookout, perhaps so that we didn't have to go into the
cave with the women. In the dim evening light a fox came
trotting down our trail, not even thinking of danger. I
threw a stone, hit the fox on the head, and killed him.

"What aim!" cried Father. "How did you learn to do
that?"

I had learned to aim as everyone learned—in my
childhood, throwing stones at birds. Father knew; he just
wanted to praise me. But his question reminded me of
Mother, and of the time before my guilt began, and
although the praise in his question would once have
made me proud, now it almost made me angry. I didn't
answer.

So Father grew sour even with me. Every day we sat in
silence in the lookout under the gray sky while the
women went gathering or worked hides in the cave.
Feeling the trouble, they too were quiet. If they spoke to
each other of Pinesinger's child, they didn't tell the men
what was said, and we didn't ask.

One day Andriki stood up in the lookout and faced the
rest of us. "Why are we sitting here helplessly?" he asked.
"Are we women, to be satisfied with carrion when out on
the plain is fresh meat?"

So at last we went hunting, or some of us did—we who
owned the hunting lands around the Hair. Father and
Andriki got the group together, asking only their broth-

ers, Kida and Maral, Maral's half-grown son, Ako, and me. The four other men who lived with Father at that time—White Fox (who was Kida's wife's brother), Raven (who was White Fox's father), Timu (who was Raven's cousin and the husband of Ethis of Father's lineage), and Marten (who was Maral's brother-in-law, Frogga's uncle, a man I didn't much like but was forced to respect)—might have liked to come with us, but they weren't wanted.

Each of us took several spears. Father by then had helped me shape the flint he had given me, so I had two spears. Besides our spears, we took only knives and firesticks. Maral's wives brought berries for him to carry with us, but he refused them. I could see from the mood of the hunters that our next meal would be meat or nothing at all.

So we left, following Father in single file as he strode west over the rolling grassland by the Hair. We crossed a wide plain of tough yellow grass and another of soft red grass, and then a huge burned stretch where soot blackened our moccasins. The fire had passed recently—the stumps of the juniper bushes were still smoldering. On the far side of that place, follows-fire grass was growing. Here a fire had burned long ago. With the old tough grass gone, tender green grass had sprung up, and the grazing animals knew it. We found the fresh dung of bison and horses, and to the southwest, on grass too short for us to cross without being noticed, we saw a herd of bison lying down.

I could see from the way Father looked around for the wind that he was thinking of stalking these bison. Andriki made the hunter's handsign for cow bison, and Maral made the handsign for circle. Then the four men spread out and walked west in an easy, strolling way that would take them at an angle near the bison but not straight to them. I didn't know this kind of hunting, but that didn't matter—it was enough that the four men knew one another's minds. Ako and I followed them.

The bison noticed us, of course. Some stood up. But we walked so calmly, so casually, our spears held very low, that we soothed the watching bison, who bent their heads to graze. The yellow wagtails, who hunt the insects stirred up by the sharp hooves, went on hunting insects. Except for our regular strides and our steady, plodding travel, everything stayed the same until, very slowly, Father and Maral moved up beside Andriki and Kida. To the watching bison, each pair of men must have looked like one person. For a little while the two pairs walked in step. Then quickly and carefully Father and Maral dropped down on their bellies on the short grass. Without breaking stride, the rest of us kept walking.

On we went, leaving Father and Maral behind. Andriki led us around the bison in a wide half-circle that never brought us near them but never took us far away. To keep us in view, the standing bison turned as we went by. This watchfulness of theirs is what makes stalking them so difficult.

After we had walked a while, we heard a great burst of noise from the bison—snorts, grunts, and bellows and the thundering feet of a full stampede. Off went the herd, almost hidden in its own dust, right out from under the wagtails, who screamed in flight. For a moment I was afraid that the bison meant to run toward us. If they did, they would trample us into paste. But they ran away to the north, and left behind themselves in the slowly clearing dust the figures of Father and Maral standing over the huge brown corpse of a young cow bison who lay, stuck with spears, on her side.

By the time we reached Father and Maral, they had gathered grass and bison dung to make a fire and had cut open the skin on the cow bison's thighs. The rest of us took our knives to the front legs and belly. By sunset we had loosened the skin and rocked the great, stiff corpse free of it. By dusk the shine had dried from the meat and we were scraping dried blood from our hands and sleeves.

A stiff east wind rose, but there was no shelter out on the plain. We gathered more bison dung and heather for our fire, then sat around it in the open near the carcass, letting the wind slap at us and whirl the stink of raw meat and rumen in every direction. At dark we heard lions, but they didn't worry us—we were six men with fourteen spears. We would worry the lions, if they came.

Then Father and his brothers did something I hadn't seen before—they chopped the upper front leg and ribs from the body, and as the opened chest filled with black, clotting blood, they dipped it out and drank it from their cupped hands. "Hona!" said each man after drinking. When my turn came, a rush of strength and heat from the fresh blood filled my body. No one needed to tell me that this was a man's thing, taught by the Bear. "Hona!" I said, hoarse from the rough, hot feeling. After each of us had drunk, we cut out the liver and set it to cook. As we did, the moon rose into the smoke on the horizon—a full moon, the Dust Moon, blood red.

Then we sat on our heels around the fire, my father, my uncles, my brother-in-law Ako, and me. The four men watched the meat. I watched the four men. They looked like each other, our fathers and uncles. As the wind blew smoke and their own loosening hair into their eyes, they squinted, and I saw that their eyelids, their foreheads, and the lines creasing their foreheads were the same. In their flapping shirts, the men kept their arms quietly folded, their elbows on their knees. And I noticed that a good feeling seemed to have grown among them. I saw ease in the way their shoulders touched; I felt comfort in the slow way they moved. At last the four brothers began to talk about Pinesinger. Then I saw that to have that talk was the reason we were there.

"You don't like to feel doubt, it's true," said Andriki. "But what can you do? Divorce her? After all, Pinesinger is young and strong. If she's carrying a child that isn't yours, she'll have yours later."

"And before you divorce her," said Kida, "remember how hard you tried to get a woman of her lineage. Remember your betrothal to Meri."

Meri? A girl named Meri lived in Father's cave. She was married to White Fox, Kida's wife's brother. "What Meri?" I asked.

"The Meri married to White Fox," Andriki answered. "What other?"

I knew of no other. Still, the news surprised me. White Fox's Meri was still young. She must have been a baby, almost like Frogga, when she was betrothed to Father. I saw how badly Father must have wanted someone of her lineage, if he, a grown man with children of his own, a headman, had been willing to wait for a baby.

"Ever since Meri," Maral said to Father, "you've had trouble with those women. Her sister spoiled your betrothal to Meri—her sister, Yanan! And then? Yanan talked you into marriage with her mother's sister, Yoi. So thanks to women of this lineage you have a wife who has always been childless. Yanan surely knew her aunt couldn't have children. Her own aunt? Of course she knew."

Now Andriki took another turn at Father. "But you wouldn't learn from your mistakes," he said. "When you couldn't get Yoi pregnant, you tried to marry Yanan. You were going to divorce Yoi."

"I would have had to," said Father. "Could I marry an aunt and a niece at the same time?"

"No. That you thought to marry an aunt and a niece even at different times shows how badly you wanted one of those women," said Maral. "And you wanted Yanan even though she was married, pregnant, and telling everyone she hated you."

"She didn't want me, it's true," said Father.

"So it's a good thing you didn't divorce Yoi," said Andriki.

"I suppose," said Father.

"You suppose?" cried Andriki. "Think what would have happened! You would have divorced Yoi and married Yanan. But Yanan died. If she had been married to you when she died, do you think her lineage would then have given you Pinesinger?" To me he said, "These days, Pinesinger's people don't want to give us women. They say we divorce them or kill them. Those people would have refused to give us Pinesinger if Bala hadn't helped us. Without Bala we would have come home with no one but you." To Father he said, "Be thankful that Bala doesn't listen to the others. It was he who found Pinesinger."

"A good man, Bala," said Kida thoughtfully. "Always a good friend."

"Do you still want a woman from the lineage?" asked Maral.

"Yes," said Father.

"Then keep Pinesinger," said Maral. "Her lineage has six women, and no others. The first," he said, showing his thumb to Father, "is Pinesinger's mother—married and past childbearing. The second woman"—he held up his forefinger—"is Yoi. Yoi is childless. The third woman is Yanan. Yanan is dead. The fourth woman is Meri. Meri is married to one of our own people. Not one of us here could agree to your trying to take Meri away from one of our own men. The fifth woman"—Maral now showed Father his little finger—"is Pinesinger. So you see? You have what you want. You're married to the only woman possible—Pinesinger!"

Eider, Yoi, Yanan, Meri, and Pinesinger made five. "Who is the sixth?" I whispered to Maral.

"Teal," he answered. At the mention of her name, the four grown men laughed, their bearded faces wrinkling pleasantly.

"Who is Teal?" I asked, puzzled by the laughter.

"Watch out for Teal," said Andriki.

"She's an old woman," said Maral, "one of the wives of the headman of the Char River people. She left the Fire River before you were born."

"Teal is a shaman," said Father quietly. "Her mother was Sali Shaman. Now do you know her?"

Ah! Who had not heard of Sali and the wonderful things she had done? She had brought the Woman Ohun to some of our people when they were camping by the Fire River. Before everyone's eyes, the Woman had given birth to a baby who got up and walked away, then to a bear who got up and walked away, and last to a reindeer who got up and walked away. The Woman then had vanished in a whirlwind. Ever since my childhood I had heard this story. I had also heard that Sali was killed by her husband and then became a tigress who in turn killed him. Ever since, whenever a certain tigress came to hunt on the banks of the Fire River, people feared that she was Sali, back again.

"Yes," I said. "I know her."

"Sali was very strong," said Father. "And her daughter, Teal, is strong too. The shaman's power of those women makes my own seem weak. Because of their power I want a wife from their lineage. I want the shaman-child I will get on that wife. That's why my heart has turned against Pinesinger, for the harm I think she did me."

"But how much harm has she really done?" asked Maral. "Suppose she is pregnant? Aren't all children welcome? After she gives birth to this child, she'll be ready for your shaman-child. Just be sure you get to her first."

We all laughed at Maral's words, even me.

"It doesn't help to brood," Andriki said later, after we had eaten the liver and were roasting strips of the bison's flank. The wind had died. The moon was high and had turned from blood red to bone white, licked clean by the hunters of the sky.

We had felt very bold about lions when the night began, but we were not so bold now. When we thought we heard a roar, we silenced Andriki so we could listen carefully. Perhaps we hadn't heard a roar. The plain was quiet.

"Here's how to look at this," Andriki began again. "Think back a few years. Do the things that worried you then worry you now? Of course not. This too will be forgotten. We offered Bala too many things in the marriage exchange. We'll tell him to expect less when we see him. That's how to look at this, Brother. Not with anger, especially since you can't do anything."

Again we listened to the night. We heard the wind around us and a nightjar very far away, one of the last of the year, but still no lion.

Then Maral spoke. "Andriki is right about the marriage exchange. Pinesinger's parents don't deserve a large share, since they left her so long unmarried. They were careless or ignorant. Compare how they managed their family with how we manage ours! We married your son to my daughter. When Frogga is ready for a man, Kori will be there waiting for her. But Pinesinger had no husband to watch over her. Only thoughtless people would expect men and boys to keep away from a willing girl of that age."

"The willingness of a woman has much to do with her pregnancies," said Father dryly. "You make it sound as if Pinesinger's pregnancy were her parents' fault."

"It was their fault," said Maral.

"It's womankind's fault," said Andriki. "Do you remember the story of the First Woman and her sleeping-skins? Shall I tell it?"

It is good to hear stories often, since there is much to be learned in them. "Yes, tell it," Maral said.

So Andriki told the story. According to him, the First Man, Weevil, gave a gift of sleeping-skins to the First Woman, Mekka. She was his wife, and the sleeping-skins were the same as ours today, winter reindeer hides sewn together with the soft fur inside and the tough hide outside. But Mekka wasn't grateful. She had fallen in love with another man, Wolverine, and when summer came she made Weevil go alone to his summer hunting grounds so that she could open her sleeping-skins to Wolverine.

When Weevil came home in the fall, he was hungry for his wife. He hurried into her sleeping-skins and coupled with her. Afterward he noticed that her belly was swollen. "What's this?" he asked. "Are you pregnant?"

Mekka pretended to be very modest and shy. She whispered, "Yes."

"When did you conceive this child?" asked Weevil.

"Just now, with you," she said.

They went to sleep, but during the night Weevil was wakened by the grunting voices of the reindeer sleeping-skins, right in his ear. "What was that?" he asked. "Are reindeer passing?"

"It was nothing," said Mekka.

Weevil went back to sleep, but soon woke again. This

time he heard the sleeping-skins saying, "If she just became pregnant, it must be summertime."

"Let's get up," said Weevil. "I want to turn the bed inside out to find who is talking inside it." Mekka tried to stop him, but he took the sleeping-skins away from her, pulled them inside out, and found them covered with short brown hair. At his feet lay their long white winter hair. Thinking it was summer, the skins had shed.

"Now I see how you tricked me," shouted Weevil. Seizing his belt, he turned Mekka under his arm to punish her for faithlessness and lying, but she became a red cuckoo and flew away. Even today when you hear a she-cuckoo calling in the woods, you know it's Mekka, jeering at Weevil and at every woman's husband.

The story made us quiet. For a long time we thought our own thoughts while we watched the wind send the fire this way and that, as if an unseen foot were kicking it. At last Kida said, "Ah, the people long ago, and the things they did. . . . If Weevil hadn't left his wife alone in summer, Wolverine wouldn't have had the chance to make her pregnant. And wasn't Weevil a coward to want to beat her in revenge? I'd rather beat the man."

"Now you sound ignorant," said Andriki. "A man can't watch his wife all the time, any more than he can teach all men to keep away from her. He must teach his wife to keep away from other men."

"So should I have done with Pinesinger," said Father. "Only now it's too late."

"She was pregnant when you got her!" cried Andriki impatiently. "From that day it was too late!"

11

WITH THE WANING DUST MOON CAME COLD GUSTING WINDS that turned the birch leaves yellow and sent flocks of birds whirling through the night sky on their way to their far wintergrounds. It was time for us to go too, leaving the cave to the blowing snow and to some hyenas who, said Father, used it in winter. It was time for us to travel to Father's lodge.

One morning after we had killed the bison but before we had finished the meat, people began to make up their packs, ready to travel. I had very little to pack—my sleeping-skins, my mittens, my outer trousers and parka. Looking at these things reminded me that I needed new moccasins for winter, since my old ones were almost worn through, and that I had this summer taken only one fox.

I thought of the skin of the cow bison, perfect for moccasins. But among Father's people, as among Uncle Bala's, the hide of an animal belongs to the wives of the eldest hunter. Since Father and Maral were each the first-born son of their father's two wives, each of them was eldest, so the skin of their cow bison had been cut in four pieces. Father's wives and Maral's wives now owned these pieces, and none of the four women would have any reason to share with me. So that morning my mind was at the Fire River, where my mother would have had a skin to make my moccasins.

As we would soon be gone, no one bothered to feed the fires, and the cave grew cold. It smelled of dust instead of smoke and roasting meat. It also began to echo as it emptied, as people took their packs out to the trail. I was among the first to be ready, so I sat on the trail with my pack, waiting. My mind was very much on my mother and my little brother, who perhaps were also packing then, under the hazy sky above the Fire River, getting ready to travel to Uncle Bala's lodge. So I didn't really notice that the echoing voices in the cave behind me had grown loud. Suddenly I heard screaming and weeping, and I turned, surprised, to see that Pinesinger had dropped her pack on the floor and was pulling it apart.

The people on the trail stood up, not sure what to do. The people still in the cave seemed angry and were all noisily talking at once. Yoi's eyes were stretched wide, and her voice rose above the rest. "Now see what she's doing!" she screamed.

But Pinesinger seemed strangely calm. Although tears were rolling down her face, she slowly unrolled her sleeping-skins and took out all her things, then sat on her heels, rested her elbows on her knees, and stared stonily out of the cave's mouth. Her chin was high and her tear-streaked face wore no expression.

Father strode over to her. "Pack!" he demanded. Her tears began again. Father softened. "Pack, Wife," he said. "The lodge is far, and snow might find us on the way." But Pinesinger didn't move.

Father looked around at the other people helplessly, at a loss for what to do. Some people were impatient and stood, waiting; others bent their knees to set their haunches on the floor. For a long time no one said anything. Then Andriki picked up a few twigs and dry leaves, ready to rekindle a fire, as if he thought we might not be leaving after all.

Although Father stood over her, Pinesinger seemed not to know it; her eyes were fixed on something far away, and her tears were drying.

Rin said wearily, "It's late. If we don't start soon, we'll have to wait for another day. If we don't start soon, night will find us on the high plains. We don't want to sleep there. There are lions."

"My sister is right," said Father to Pinesinger. "Don't be stubborn." Pinesinger's tears began again, but she sat motionless. Father reached down and gave her shoulder a shake. "Must I beat you?" he asked quietly.

Pinesinger didn't seem to hear him. She stared at the horizon while her breath came shallow and fast. At last she answered, her voice low. "Yes," she said. "You must beat me! You must beat me to death! Only then will I spend the winter with my co-wife."

"What?" cried Father. Then, "Where else would you stay?"

"I'll stay here," said Pinesinger.

The people in the cave had been very quiet while Father tried to move Pinesinger, but now everyone began to shout. Some people thought Pinesinger should be punished. "She wants to be beaten! Oblige her!" screamed Yoi to Father.

"Beat her. She'll find she'd rather travel," said Andriki's wife, sounding more like Andriki than Andriki himself.

But other people took Pinesinger's side. "Yoi forced her to this!" cried Frogga's mother. "Of course she doesn't want to come with us. Her co-wife wants to fight with her."

Above the noise, Aunt Rin kept trying to speak.

"Listen to my sister!" shouted Father at last, rather desperately.

"It's so late that darkness will catch us in a place without shelter," said Rin. "For tonight, let's stay here. I want to talk quietly with my sister-in-law. We can find a way around this."

"Let Rin talk with her," agreed Andriki, relieved, as if he felt sure his stepsister could mend matters. Some people grumbled, but at last they began to untie their packs and unroll their bedding. Maral's two wives went down near the rotting mammoth corpses in the darkening ravine to fill waterskins and gather dry bones to burn. Rin sat next to Pinesinger, as if to start talking. But Pinesinger raised her chin higher and squeezed her lips and eyelids tight. She wouldn't say a word.

Pinesinger! From my sleeping place near the far end of the cave's mouth, I watched her small shape against the evening sky, sitting on her heels, not moving. I couldn't help but admire her, so recently nothing but a weak young woman, damp with tears, wrongly pregnant and dangerously close to serious trouble—I couldn't help but admire how with a few words she had managed to defy Father, to shame Yoi, and to bring the travel of a whole group of near-strangers, half of them men and most of them older than she, to a dead stop. Whether she had meant it so or not, her act had been neat, quick, and surprising, like an osprey seizing a fish. It was as fine a trick as our second misdeed, by which she had stopped me forever from talking about our first misdeed to Father.

We didn't have much fuel that night, and the adults had to crowd around a pile of coals where strips of the bison meat flamed in their own fat. At the cave's mouth, Pinesinger sat in the dark. She didn't move, so I suspected she was listening. She wouldn't get anything to eat there, I knew, but she was scorning food and fire and every comfort, and I admired her for that too. As I sat by the fire, squeezed between Father and Andriki, waiting for a share of the meat, however small, I wondered if some of the others might also feel a grudging respect for Pinesinger. Anyway, people now saw how unhappy she had been.

"Quarrels burn like grass," said Maral's elder wife.

"A quarrel between two becomes a quarrel among many," said Maral. "No one wants to spend the winter in a lodge with people fighting."

The rest of us were silent for a while, thinking of winter. Surely each of us could remember long stormy nights in a crowded lodge with anger eating at people's hearts—anger as terrible as sickness, felt but not seen. People have killed themselves because of fighting in winter. People have walked off into storms, to be found later naked and frozen to death in the snow. These people were so deeply angered and shamed by fighting that they finally chose to die rather than to fight more. That is why, when we first reach a lodge after being gone all summer, we burn fat for the Woman Ohun and pray that She will give us food and patience until spring.

"I didn't foresee such trouble," said Father, standing up. "Before I married Pinesinger, her uncle promised me that she was good-natured." To his brothers he said,

"Come with me. I want to speak privately." Taking his spear, he left the cave, followed by his brothers. From the trail he called, "Kori, Ako, you come too." So Ako and I stood up and, brushing past Pinesinger on the way, followed our fathers and our uncles to the men's lookout.

We had no fire in the lookout, and there was no moon. I sat down beside Andriki in the dark. No one spoke—the men were looking into the ravine. Below us, an animal was looking up. Its two eyes were shining faintly green in the starlight. It must have been big to have eyes large enough for us to see at such a distance on a starry night. We watched the eyes for a time as they shifted this way and that; the animal was trying to make out our outline against the sky. We didn't like its doing that. With both hands Andriki threw down a large stone. The stone missed the eyes and bounced off a rock, but the zoom and crash must have frightened the animal, because the eyes vanished suddenly.

"So what will I do with my younger wife?" asked Father.

"It's your elder wife who causes trouble," said Maral.

"Yes," said Father. "And I have an idea. I'll take Yoi to her kin on the Char River and leave Pinesinger behind with you. Yoi will be happy, Pinesinger will be happy, and I'll be happy, because I won't have to watch Pinesinger's belly grow while knowing the child isn't mine." To me Father said, "I spent three winters hunting reindeer with Graylag on the Char. He's the headman. We joined our groups, he and I. I married Yoi, from his second wife's lineage. His sons married women from my lineage." To Kida Father said, "You should come with us. Your wife would like to visit her old home. Her parents will want to come too. Her brother too. And his wife! Meri will want to go—Yoi's lineage is Meri's lineage. This is a good thought, this idea of mine. Let's see, there's me and Yoi, Meri and White Fox, his parents, and Junco. And Kida. That's many. And their son too. That's very many. Even so, Graylag's lodge is big enough."

"I'd like to go," I said.

"You can't," said Father. "We're already too many for Graylag."

"And our lodge will have too few," said Maral to me. "Graylag's lodge will have plenty of men for hunting. But we will have only you, Ako, Andriki, Marten, and me. Andriki's wife hunts, but not well. No woman really hunts well. And look at the women we must feed this winter: my wives, Marten's wife, Andriki's wife, and your little Frogga." Maral laughed. "And Rin and Pinesinger," he added. "No, Nephew. You can't go to the Char. You must come with me."

"So it's decided?" asked Andriki.

"My part is decided," said Father.

"Your way is far, though," said Maral. "If you had left when the moon was new, snow wouldn't find you traveling."

"Haven't we traveled to the Char before?" asked Father. "I'll follow the rivers instead of crossing the plain. The way will be longer, but we'll be in spruce woods, where we can set snares and find shelter and fuel." Father thought for a while, perhaps about the journey. At last he said, "Or maybe there's no need to take every step beside a river. Maybe I'll cross the plain as far as the Grass River. I'll cross the plain to Graylag's summergrounds. Then I can follow the river."

"You'll get snow and strong winds on the plain," said Maral.

"A little snow is better than so much walking," said Father.

"You could ask what the others would like."

"They don't need to come if there's something they won't like," said Father.

So it was decided. In the dark cave Father told the others of his new plan. Most people seemed pleased with it, especially Yoi and her niece Meri, who were eager to visit their kin on the Char. Everyone seemed glad to have the fighting stopped. Only Pinesinger seemed unhappy. She had been outwitted and also punished, since her co-wife had been favored while she herself had been given no choice but to travel to a strange lodge without any people of her own, there to wait for Father, perhaps for a long time. She had been sitting so that when we came into the cave we would notice her high chin and her straight back, but when Father told his plan she turned aside. Her will didn't weaken, though. She lay down at last, but made no sound all night.

12

ALMOST AS SOON AS WE LEFT THE CAVE OUR TWO GROUPS LOST sight of each other, since the people with Father went east and we went west. In single file, getting more into our stride with each step, we followed the lanky form of Andriki along an unused game trail that traced the ravine's rim, walking into winter.

I was last in line. What would the winter bring us? I wondered. Which of us would be alive by spring to eat the fern fronds uncurling under the melting snow? Whose spirit would have left for the Camps of the Dead, to eat the sun with members of his lineage? Whose corpse would be stored in a tree, waiting for the thaw, for burial?

I remembered how Uncle Bala at the Fire River used to call his people "the hands of the lodge." "We need two strong hands to live through a winter," he would tell us.

With Father and Kida and all the others, we had been very strong. Twice two hands and more, we had been. Were we still strong? Were those who followed Andriki enough? Counting me and Maral's son, my brother-in-law, Ako, who was still young, the men were five—a right hand, as Bala would have seen it. But were we a strong hand? Maral and Andriki were the thumb and forefinger, strong enough for any group, and Maral's tall, thin brother-in-law, Marten, was the long finger, also strong.

But because I was new, and wouldn't know where I was in Father's hunting lands without someone with me to show me the way, I saw myself as the third finger, the stiff finger that can't move far unless it takes another finger with it, a finger that is strong but sometimes helpless. And since Ako was small, I saw him as the little finger, never helpless but not strong. Uncle Bala wouldn't have reckoned Ako as a man at all, but would have counted him with the children. Yet if Ako wasn't a man, our group wasn't a hand, so I counted him as a man.

There was also the left hand, the women's hand, with Rin as the thumb—Rin, whose brothers and stepbrothers were the owners of the lodge. Next to her was her daughter, Waxwing, who was Marten's wife. The other fingers were the wives of the owners: two women for Maral—his dark-haired Truht and his pale-haired Lilan, tall like her brother, Marten; and one woman for Andriki—his bold wife, Hind. There was Pinesinger, too—Father's wife. Yet she wasn't joined to the group, and I didn't think of her as one of the fingers. Even so, she belonged with us, as we were the right and left hands of the lodge, we who feed our group, clothe our group, and keep our lodge warm in winter.

Then, of course, there were also the children, they whom the two hands cradled. Our lodge had only two small children: Hind's daughter, Pirit, who walked at Hind's heels unless Andriki carried her, and my wife, Frogga, who rode on Lilan's pack. Last among the children were three babies still unborn but also traveling with us—winter children, to be born in the lodge, to honor the Bear with their animal names someday if they should live. One lay in Truht's belly, one in Waxwing's, one in Pinesinger's.

Never before had I thought so much about a winter, or found the future worrisome, or wondered who would live and who would die before spring. I looked ahead at Frogga's brother, Ako. Still young, he seemed carefree, as I had once been carefree. I wondered what Andriki was thinking as his long legs carried him westward. What did Maral think? Or Father?

At the trail's first bend I turned to look for Father, but he and most of the people with him were already hidden by blueberry bushes. I saw Kida's trouser legs under his huge pack, on top of which, holding tight to one of his braids, his little son was riding. Not for this child were fears of winter—just as the blueberry bushes seemed to swallow Kida, the little boy shouted with joy, and suddenly I remembered being very young, and the excitement of starting a journey.

Because the plain fell slowly, we walked downhill all morning. By afternoon our trail was almost as low as the river. We came to a place called Bison's Ford, where the hooves of scrambling bison had cut great notches in the sandy banks. We crossed the river there, taking off our moccasins and trousers to wade through the fast water on a bed of smooth round stones.

On the north side of the Hair the plain became a rolling heath where cloudberries grew in their red-brown leaves as far as the eye could see. We threw down our packs and began to pick and eat. Just before dark I looked around for the others but couldn't see them. I stood up. At last I made out the faraway form of one person, then another, then another, all scattered widely, all crouched low and busy eating, almost lost in the brown landscape under the wide yellow sky.

After that our way turned due north and we walked for six days, following Maral's easy strides over a brushy plain. We looked for sheltered places to camp at night, places beside rocks or in heavy thickets; we burned what we could—grass or heather, bones, dung, or wood, if we found these things. We watched for ravens in the sky, who might show us the way to carcasses, but on that trip we found no carcasses. Every evening we set snares for small animals and birds. All in all, the trip was easy. Cloudberries and black crowberries were in season, and we carried with us strips of dry meat.

One night Andriki said we would see the Breasts of Ohun by noon the next day. Beyond those hills was Father's lodge. I thought of Father as we walked, and how our journey was almost over while his journey, because of the great distance between the Hair River and the Char River, had hardly begun.

The Breasts of Ohun! My mind's eye saw two pointed hills, and I looked for them as we traveled. By noon we saw a few low, rounded hills that ran east and west with ridges between them, and I thought that among them we would see two peaks that would mark Father's lodge. The country rose toward the hills, and up we went, through a mossy wood of spruce and birch, out onto a sunny, red-brown heath of blueberry and crowberry shrubs. But from the heath we saw no hills like breasts, only mounds with a thick, red, rolling scrub of low-growing bushes on their sides. Among the bushes I saw sedges, and here and there a lonely black spruce, wind-shaped so that its north side grew no branches. The heath was sunny and warm and very quiet. Far away in the stillness a willow-tit sang its pure, sweet song: *Di! Di! Chibidi!*

Most of the people dropped their packs and made for some crowberry patches, where they squatted on their heels to pick and eat. Andriki pointed with his lips. "At the end of this trail, beyond the ridge, is the lodge," he said.

"Will we see it from the ridge?" I asked him.

"We could, but we won't," said Andriki.

His answer puzzled me. Was he going to shut his eyes on the ridge? "Don't we climb there?" I asked. "Is it so high?"

Andriki pointed with his lips again, and I saw how our trail would run west to go around the hills, tracing the edge of the heavy scrub. "Why would we climb the ridge?" he asked. "Were there no berry heaths where you lived on Woman Lake? The bush is thick and heavy. Some of the leaves are poisonous. Nothing eats them. Except for bears, who eat berries in the fall, there's nothing there to hunt. Birds and mice go there. Foxes go there for the mice. Women go there to pick berries and set snares. So that's all it is—woman's country."

I could see that Andriki was right. There were no trails, just birdsongs. Anything that walked was close to the ground. But the sunny, silent landscape looked so different from what my mind's eye had seen that I felt confused. "Where are the hills?" I asked.

Now Andriki looked puzzled, and pointed with his lips at the range. "Those are the hills," he said.

"Then which are the breasts?" I asked him, laughing.

He also laughed. "All of them. Aren't all hills like breasts? How can I know which hills are breasts? No one told me."

Ready to have a joke with Andriki, I looked around to see which hills were most like breasts. I saw only four bare summits, all much the same except that two were larger than the others. A pair of hawks flew high above them, one far behind the other, going south. Suddenly my skin prickled. Perhaps the hills were breasts, but if they were Ohun's breasts, Ohun wasn't a person. She was a very large animal asleep on Her back—a tigress, a lioness, a hyena!

I knew I should think a long time about the name of these hills and its meaning. Surely there was a story, with much to be learned from it. Hadn't Sali, the great woman-shaman from the Fire River, become a tigress after her husband killed her? Did Sali have something to do with Ohun? With these hills?

The thought was disturbing. I opened my mouth to ask Andriki, but when I looked around I saw him far away, squatting with the others, tossing crowberries into his mouth. I stood alone on the trail, strangely upset, feeling very much an outsider in this quiet, sunny land of Father's. I didn't even know the way to the lodge, and I didn't want to go without the others. So I too pushed through the scrub to a sprawled bush that still held some black crowberries, and I too sat on my heels to eat.

All afternoon, alone in the sunshine, I picked and ate crowberries while the light wind whispered through the hard little leaves, bringing the smell of juniper from the sun-warmed heath. Late in the day, as I was looking around for more crowberries, I happened to notice all the people far down the trail, already wearing their packs. Some had started! Would they have left me behind? I hurried to catch up, and once again I was the last person in line.

Horses, I saw, had used the trail before us, although our footprints had covered their footprints and flattened their balls of dung. The trail and the horse tracks took the quickest, shortest way out of the brushy growth into a valley and across a quiet, west-flowing stream where now, in the dry season, the water lay still. Dust and yellow birch leaves floated on it. In the low water grew little islands of grass. When I stepped on them to cross, water soaked into my moccasins.

On the far side the woods were open and sunny, welcoming to a hunter—man's country once again. Beyond the trees I saw a narrow meadow. The tracks of the horses led there. I soon began to look around. A fire had been through years before; now young larch and stone-pines grew, winterberries and bilberries, lichen, grass, and many good mushrooms. The shallow river would flood in spring, making the ground a bit soft for horses, but spotted deer and red deer wouldn't mind it, roe deer and moose would prefer it, and reindeer would visit it in winter for the reindeer moss that grew everywhere. In fact, the browsing of many kinds of deer had kept the birch trees low and dense, making good cover for deaf-grouse and ptarmigan. We would probably find a bear or two asleep in the hillsides, and since no bear could hope to wake up alive after a winter's sleep near Father, the bear we would find would probably be a young newcomer drawn by the berries on Ohun's Breasts. I saw how Father had chosen his place well.

Or chosen the hunting well. As for the rest, I also saw that the slowly moving water would freeze solid with the first heavy cold, so people and animals would have to work hard to drink; I saw that all the dry wood and low branches had been used, so we would have to work hard with our axes or else travel far for fuel; and although the woods seemed too thick for lions, I saw how a tiger might like them, so we would have to watch where we went. It was a hunter's place. But what had I expected? It was Father's.

Walking east, I found where the stream drained a narrow lake, and thinking that the lodge would be in sight of the lake, I followed the bank. In no time I noticed a dark mound half hidden in a haze of yellow grass and the thin green needles of sapling pines, the summer's growth which no feet had trampled. Like Uncle Bala's lodge, Father's was domed, but Father's was bigger— half again as long and also higher. The tallest men of Father's family would almost be able to stand inside. Grass grew on the arching roof among the stones that weighed down the sod. Some of the grass stood tall, waving gently in the wind, but in places the grass on the roof lay flat. Trails ran through it. Wolves had climbed there, using it for a resting place or a lookout.

I had not been inside a lodge since the winter before, when I had lived with my mother and stepfather in the lodge belonging to Bala. For as long as I could remember, my place had been with Mother at the fire by the door, in the cold end of the lodge, the bad end, the end used by in-laws or kinswomen of the owners. As I crawled down Father's coldtrap I realized I didn't know just where I was going, where in this lodge I should take my pack, or where I would sleep. I kept moving, though, because everyone but Maral was already inside.

At the end of the passageway I stood up. If the lodge had seemed big from the outside, it seemed small from the inside, small and dark and already filled with the smell of smoke, of the bodies and hair of all the people who, still bulky in their outer clothes, turned to look at me, some of them shading their eyes from a sudden blaze of birchbark they were using to start the fires. With its thick walls, the lodge was much colder than the outdoors, as if it still held the cold of last winter. And from the heavy smell, it seemed that wolves had used the inside as well as the roof.

Behind me, Maral squeezed against me as he stood up and, taking my pack from me, carried it past his stepsister, Rin, and her daughter, Waxwing, who, heads low, were blowing on their fire by the door. Moving carefully to avoid his brother and their wives, who were crowded together in the middle of the lodge, waiting for more light before they found their sleeping places, Maral led me to the rear of the lodge and put my pack by his.

I looked around. Piles of large stones had been used to brace the poles that made the walls of this lodge, heavy walls bent with the weight of crosspoles and with covering sod. In the middle of the lodge a line of four forked lodgepoles braced a rafter running the length of the domed roof, a heavy load, and although these poles were dug into the earth, they were also braced deeply with boulders.

In Uncle Bala's lodge, in a wide spruce wood that was the winterground of mammoths, the stacked bones of many young winter-killed mammoths had made the walls of the lodge—lower jawbones resting on their condyles with their chins up. Compared to rocks and poles, these arched bones were very strong but not very heavy. No bracing was needed, as the jaws interlocked. But no mammoths, dead or living, would be found in an open wood like Father's winterground; the men who had built the lodge would have found no huge bones and would have had no choice but to cut poles and carry rocks. Also, a lodge made with rocks and poles could be strong only if it was narrow. The people who would have to fit themselves into the rear of the lodge would be squeezed very close together.

I had never much liked crowding. I had never liked to inhale the breath of others. I had never much liked babies, with their sharp knees and their cold, smooth bodies, crawling over me, as Frogga might do here, to get from one place to another. I did not want to test myself by lying for a long time beside Pinesinger. But even so, even though the lodge was cold and dark and crowded, even though I was already coughing from the smoke and my eyes were already stinging, I felt a strange happiness to belong, for the first time I could remember, at the owners' fire.

13

Long after dark in Father's lodge, when people had settled into their places, Andriki tightened his drum. Then he with his drum and Maral with his deep voice led us in singing "Honor to the Spirit of the Lodge," to the one who would keep us safe in winter. Maral sang:

> Honored Spirit!
> We are burning fat.
> Fat is in the smoke!
> Come for it! Eat it!
> Remember who gave it!
> We who are singing,
> We gave it!
> Hona!

"We who are singing, we gave it!" sang the rest of us. When our voices and clapping joined with Andriki's drum the song grew huge, filled the lodge, and carried our prayer up the smokeholes into the wide, dark sky. "We who are singing! We who are singing! We who are singing! We gave it!"

So we prayed, but in truth we had no fat. All we could give the spirit was the name of fat, the word. That the spirit got over and over, although never from me—when the time came to sing "Fat is in the smoke" and "We gave it," I kept quiet. At Uncle Bala's lodge we didn't treat spirits so freely. I hoped the spirit here was of an easy nature. Since we had nothing but words to offer the spirit and only a little food and a little wood for ourselves, we didn't sing for long, but only until the fires burned low, and then we rolled ourselves into our sleeping-skins.

THE ANIMAL WIFE

On my right, almost touching me, Uncle Maral and one of his wives began to move rhythmically in their deerskins, softly grunting and huffing as they worked toward a climax. But which wife? Whoever she was, she was quieter than Maral; perhaps she was holding her breath. My mind sorted over the women of the lodge. Maral couldn't be prodding his short, round, dark-haired wife—Aunt Truht was too far pregnant. So surely he was working on his long, tall, pale-haired wife, Frogga's mother, Aunt Lilan. Yes! Toward the end, a woman's muffled voice said "Waugh!" The voice was Lilan's.

On my left lay Pinesinger in the deepest shadow. She was so close that I felt her breath on the skin of my face, a faint, soft tingle, like an insect's footsteps, which tells us when something alive is very near. And I could smell her breath, her hair. She too was listening to Maral and Lilan. My mind's eye saw Pinesinger's smooth skin, her pale brown eyes with yellow lines in them, her white teeth, her dry lips, and the tip of her tongue, moist, pink, wetting her lips. Then I saw her as if from above, as if I were standing behind her and she were crouching; I saw the back of her head, her shiny hair, her glossy braid. My mind's eye followed her braid down the midline of her shirt to the hem, then down the row of knuckles of her bare spine to where her body split in two, to where her wide, bare haunches rested on her heels. Two rows of raised scars, her Scars of Ohun, curved away from the damp cleft of her buttocks. As if I were an eagle I saw her from high above; her haunches were two bare hills, and the lines of scars were lines of geese flying close to the hills far below me. I thought of an eagle dropping out of the sky, and I thought how large, how strong, how alive a goose would seem to the plunging eagle when at last his body struck hers, as his claws dug through her feathers. Then I tried to think of something else. In those days every memory of my time with Pinesinger hurt me.

Before long I heard feet scrabbling on the roof. The wolves! I heard snuffling at the smokeholes, then the scratch of nails as a wolf slid from the roof to the ground. What boldness! I waited, ready to find my spear, to rush outside and punish the wolves, but no one else moved to chase them off. Wolves seemed to mean nothing to Father's people. At least there was no food they could steal from us. At last I dozed.

Suddenly I was wakened by the short, sharp bark of a wolf nearby. I opened my eyes. The quarter-moon shone dimly through the clouds, faintly lighting the smokeholes. I could just make out the shapes of some of the people in the dark lodge. All were tense, and some were sitting up. I made out Andriki, not in his bed but sitting on his heels, leaning forward. I made out the long, straight line of his spear against his shoulder. Sure from the way in which people were acting that something was very wrong, I threw back my deerskin and would have reached for my spear, but I felt Andriki's hand on my arm. Through the shadows I peered at him. Putting his hand between the smokehole and my eyes so I wouldn't miss his meaning, he made the handsign for tiger.

So! A tiger was outside! I listened hard, but heard nothing. I sniffed the air. At first I smelled nothing, but suddenly my head filled with a burning stench of tiger musk and urine, a stench that stung my eyes and closed my throat. The tiger must have sprayed our doorway!

What tigers spray is fear. In the cold lodge I began sweating, and to my shame, even though it was dark, my chin began to shake. I held my jaws apart so my teeth couldn't chatter, and I held my breath, waiting for the roar that would leave me deaf and melt the marrow in my bones. Everyone waited.

But no roar came. Instead the lodge creaked suddenly, and a shower of dirt from the ceiling rained down on our heads. In silence, the tiger had leaped to the roof. For a terrible moment, during which I saw the roof caving to drop the tiger among us, the lodge seemed to tremble, then the poles groaned in their braces and the dirt showered down again as the tiger leaped off the roof. He mustn't have liked the wobbling. Then he roared.

How much breath can a tiger hold? While the roar went on, fear took us like strong hands, shaking us. Near the end, as we heard the tiger half gasping to force the last of his voice through his terrible mouth, we also heard Frogga crying, her little voice drowned out by the great voice. Lilan tried to stuff her breast into Frogga's mouth to hush her, but Frogga wasn't hungry, she was terrified, and she wouldn't take the breast. Worst of all, when the tiger ran out of breath, Frogga was still crying and suddenly could be heard plainly! As suddenly, the tiger became very quiet. He was listening to Frogga.

In time Lilan managed to hush her daughter, and then everyone listened. At last the tiger gave a short roar, nothing like his earlier awesome bellow, then another short roar a bit farther away. He was moving.

A wolf barked again. With a short, impatient roar, the tiger answered. He was still moving. Quiet as corpses, we in the lodge sat motionless, listening, for what seemed like half the night. After a very long time, we heard another bark from deep in the woods, then another, then a third—not a wolf this time, but a hind. She too had seen the tiger.

"So," whispered Maral, breaking the silence in the lodge. "He's gone. He came to learn who was here."

I would have liked to ask what Maral meant, but I didn't want to seem unsure, unmanly. So I was glad to hear Pinesinger's voice in the darkness. "What do you mean?" she asked. "Were you expecting him?"

"This is a good place," said Maral, "this land of your husband's. We have red deer and roe deer, moose and reindeer. With so much to eat, does it surprise you that other hunters come?"

"I was surprised to hear one on the roof."

"He lives in the forest," said Rin. "And he roams very widely. Sometimes in the middle of winter, in the Moon of Roaring, his wife lives with him. They both roar. It's good to be very careful on the trails and to be in the lodge by dark."

"Why did he jump on the lodge?"

"When we come, he visits us. Not always the first night, but usually within a few nights."

"Why?"

"How do I know why? Am I his kin?"

"Aren't you afraid?" asked Pinesinger.

"When he's here, we're afraid."

"How do you know when he's here?"

"The wolves tell us."

"Do they keep watch for you?"

"When they're here, they watch. When they're away, we watch for ourselves. Tonight they were here."

"We have no firewood. How will we get firewood now?"

"Does nothing prowl your father's wintergrounds to make you take care?" asked Rin. "How do your people get firewood?"

"Never before have I heard of a big animal jumping to the roof of a lodge," said Pinesinger. "If I had known this place was dangerous, I would have stayed home!"

"Take it up with your husband," said Rin.

In the morning we found wolf tracks scattering in all directions and tiger tracks the size of a man's head. We saw that the tiger had come from the west, following the river upstream, walking rather slowly, standing this way and that way, as if he were wondering about us. After his visit he had gone back to the west, downstream, taking great, even strides that left the prints of his hind feet only, as if he had walked on two legs like a man.

We all looked, but no one wanted to speak of him. When I crouched down to look at the tracks so I would know them if I saw them again, Maral said, "We know this one. He visits every fall. Right now he's traveling. He knows we come every winter, and he doesn't want to live where we spoil his hunting. He knows he can hurt us, but he also knows we can hurt him. See his big steps? See his rear tracks covering his front tracks? See how straight he travels, like a fox? He has a far place in mind."

Maral seemed right about the tiger. Even so, I feared this animal. I had seen the width of his front footprints and how high his claws had reached where he had scraped a tree. He would be longer than a horse and as high at the shoulder. He would be heavier. His face would be as wide as our coldtrap, and his teeth would be longer than my fingers. Knowing his size made me fear him.

"We'll hunt today," said Maral. "If we can, we'll set snares. Wives! Take string with you. Set as many snares as you can find places to set them, or until you use all the string."

I had thought I would go hunting with my two uncles and Marten; I had thought these men would want to teach me how to find my way around the country. But Maral said, "Someone must gather wood, and we can't send the children. You, Kori, you gather wood."

Aunt Lilan said, "We're going to pick redberries, unless birds have eaten them. Kori should come with us, since he's new to this country."

"Thank you, Aunt," I said, "but if my uncles want me to gather wood, I'll go where we were yesterday. In that direction I know where to find wood."

"Watch carefully," said Lilan.

"I will, Aunt."

"We call him the Lily."

I knew at once what she meant. My mind's eye saw a soft yellow lily striped with black and white, a lily that grows in woods in high places. Such plants are few, but the bulbs can be eaten. "The Lily," I repeated.

"We see he went west," Aunt Lilan went on, as if her husband had not already told me. "But no one has followed to see how far. Perhaps he's traveling, as my husband believes, or perhaps he changed his mind and is still near. Sometimes he stays near us a long time. Sometimes he moves on. Anyway, don't forget him."

"Who could forget him?" I asked.

As I walked south toward the four hills, I kept watch carefully at every bend of the trail. I sniffed the air for the tiger's musky odor and listened for any sound, although I knew those huge soft feet of his would make no sound. Even the weather made me uneasy. At that time of year it should have been clear and cool, but the air was wet, uncomfortably heavy, almost cold and also almost hot. Across the sky stretched a band of clouds like a belt on the sky's belly. I thought I heard thunder. That was something so late in the year—thunder during the Moon of Fires.

In the berry scrub at the foot of the hills, the bushes seemed alive with willow-tits busily eating. Surely bad weather was coming to make them so greedy. I turned off the trail into the rolling woods below the hills, and watching carefully, trying to stay far away from thickets that could hide a tiger, I began to gather wood. When a pile was ready, I carried it to the lodge.

There I looked at the tracks of the other men, all together, off on a hunt in single file, with Ako behind them. Did my uncles see me as the wood carrier of the lodge, doing woman's work, child's work, just because there was a tiger? Well, I had gathered wood, a big pile of it. Did it make me a man of meat, a feeder of foxes? I put my ax beside the coldtrap so that all who came would see it. Then I got my spear, the spear with the flint that Father had given me, and then, head high, facing the wind, I took the trail by the lake again. Perhaps I didn't know the country to the north, where my uncles had gone, but I knew enough about the country to the south and east to keep from getting lost. I could follow the stream. I could follow the trail around the hills. I could hunt in the woods between the lake and the hills, using both as landmarks. Feeling very sure of myself, I ran at the stream and crossed with one wide leap.

The Lily had gone west on the north bank. I turned east, followed the south bank around the lake, and soon found myself at the edge of the open heath. Over the hills the south wind poured, shaking the tiny poisonous leaves. Reindeer might be lying in the open places, letting the wind blow away the last of the biting flies.

This thought seemed promising. I made my way through the thicket to the low edges of the open slopes. On a large, flat rock surrounded by red-leafed crowberry bushes and blue-needled juniper, I sat on my heels to scan the countryside. From there I could see far. I looked for the red plovers that sometimes follow reindeer to hunt the ticks in their hair or the insects chased up by their feet. Red plovers like a heath near water, but it was late in the year for plovers, and I saw none. I looked for the ravens that might guide me to reindeer. Even wolves reward ravens who guide them—that's why ravens help hunters—but I saw no ravens.

Instead I heard excited voices overhead, and looking

up I saw a long string of geese flying low, as if thinking of landing. Rather than circling back over the lake to land into the wind, though, they went straight on, making for the tops of the Breasts of Ohun. There they landed.

From the southwest, with the gusting southwest wind, a cloudbank crept toward us, pushing ahead of itself the queer warm weather. As I strained my eyes, looking to see where the geese had gone, I noticed against the gray cloudbank a pure white plume of smoke. The plume came and went quickly, like the flash of a bird in a thicket, like the flash of sunlight from a polished spear, giving me just enough time to know I had seen it. Smoke? I stared, not quite believing my eyes. Up in the hills was a fire. A brushfire? A campfire? Who had made a fire?

My first thought was a pleasing thought: the smoke was Father's. But why would Father make camp instead of coming to his lodge? The smoke couldn't be Father's. Nor would it be that of our kinsmen or other visitors, since they too would come to the lodge. No one would camp in the Hills of Ohun.

So surely I was making a mistake of some kind. Perhaps my uncles had gone into the hills without my knowing, perhaps to burn the berry bushes and make way for spring grass, perhaps to cook and eat something they had found. These reasons made the best sense, yet in my heart I knew they were not the reasons. My uncles had gone north. I had seen their tracks. The women had gone west, downriver. There was no reason for any of our people to cross the river, let alone to double back and go secretly up among the hills. So perhaps I hadn't seen smoke after all. The mind's eye sees what pleases it, or so said Uncle Bala.

But suddenly there it was again, a white plume of smoke. I was certain of it. Then I heard on the wind a slow, faint *ng, ng, ng*—the even strokes of someone with a hand ax, chopping.

Now I knew someone was there. I almost stood up, to go back to the lodge to tell the others. Then I wondered if I should climb the hills and see for myself who was camped there. Perhaps the people were visitors, sick or hurt. Perhaps they couldn't find us and had camped up high to watch for our smoke. If so, they would be waiting for us to find them.

While I looked up, squinting, I became aware that something was behind me. Something was watching me. Softly, the berry bushes crackled. Very quietly, something was creeping toward me. I carefully let my right arm slide down my thigh to my spear, which lay on the rock beside me. As I did, I slowly turned around.

Behind me was a reindeer! In fact, I could see four reindeer, but one was nearer, its head forward, its eyes and nostrils wide and searching curiously. It was a young male with thin, plain antlers. The others, all females, stood far back in the willow thicket, each side-on as if poised to run but watching me warily with one eye.

When I turned, the young male reindeer's head went up, and he jerked one of his hind feet sideways, a warning. One of the females gave a whistling snort. I raised my spear. When I moved, the young male turned, showing his side. Leading him a little, I threw hard. His leap brought him onto the spear. With a loud thump, it struck through the skin under his outstretched leg. He gave a coughing cry and ran bucking into the willows. Forgetting all about the smoke, cursing myself for not bringing two spears, I snatched my knife from the top of my moccasin and ran after him. By his footprints were great splashes of foaming red blood. My spear had pierced his lung!

Filled with joy, I crept into the willow thicket and suddenly found myself standing almost above him, where he had fallen to his knees. His eyes rolled as he tried to stand, moaning out a froth of red bubbles. I threw myself astride him, hooked my elbow under his chin, and lifted up, stretching his throat and burying my face in his long, soft hair. As I drew my knife across his throat I smelled him, like a sleeping-skin. He twisted and called, blood gurgling in his voice, but he was strong, very strong—under me I felt his hindquarters lift suddenly. He was standing! Then I was riding him, trying to hold his chin up with my elbow, trying to get my knife into his throat. He staggered a few steps and plunged forward, before I had decently cut him. Between my knees I felt him moving, trying to get to his feet again, but suddenly he collapsed sideways onto my right leg and lay still.

I freed myself and stood up. The wind had died. The day was ending, and into the depth of the quiet thicket cold air was creeping from the lake. My reindeer lay at my feet with his head on the ground, mouth open, tongue out, and a pool of blood forming. I could smell it. He lived a little longer, watching me, knowing at last who was the stronger of us.

Ah well. Our eyes met, and I held his gaze until his pupils widened in an empty stare. Then I was alone, with meat. But was I? I heard ravens, then saw three large black forms soar over the tops of the willows. The ravens had seen me hunting after all. Circling, they called, then set themselves down on the large, flat rock where I had been sitting, up in the red sunlight on the hillside, on the open heath. Restless, they shrugged their wings, all three of them facing me. I wasn't glad to see them.

I thought of my spear. My reindeer had ruined it entirely, I saw, since the shaft had broken off underneath him. As the rest of it was now inside his body, I would have trouble getting it out. I set my heel on his ribs and tried to grasp the tip of the blade with my fingers, but it was slippery with blood and wedged tightly. I had no hope of getting it. I tried my knife on his ribs, but the blade was not sharp, and it took a long time just to make a small white slit in the skin. Meanwhile evening was coming quickly. I should be doing something to protect the meat.

On the flat rock up the hill, the ravens called. They too saw the low sun, and saw that if I didn't hurry they would lose a meal. Who were they calling? Someone to help them? To hurry me? My mind's eye saw the wide striped face, the round yellow eyes of the Lily watching from the trees.

Although I tried to stop it, worry crept unwanted into my mind. I felt something watching me, and turned. Nothing. I looked at my knife with disappointment, remembering all the evenings we had spent on the trail, evenings of firelight and talking, when I could have been working the edge but had chosen instead to play Water Kills Fire or Stones in the Holes with Andriki or even with the little children. If Father could see me in a thicket at sunset with a big carcass and a useless knife, what might he say to me?

But then, I had killed! Perhaps the reindeer was young, but he wasn't small. Even the broken spear looked good, since it almost seemed as if I had thrown my spear right through him. Besides, the other men had taken Ako hunting but not me. I hoped they had also gathered wood. As for me, I had killed meat!

Where would I hide it? I looked around for a tree. No tree was tall enough, of course. I thought of the water. Perhaps I should sink the carcass in the lake, to come back for it later with my uncles. And so I should have done, but by then I wanted to walk out of the dark woods, with everyone watching, with meat.

Liking more and more the idea of walking into the lodge clearing with a carcass on my shoulders, with Pinesinger's eyes and all the other women's eyes on me, with my uncles watching me, just a little ashamed that they hadn't decided to take me hunting, I grasped the reindeer's hairy ankle and gave his corpse a tug that pulled him straight. He was very heavy. Would I have to drag him? Dragging him would get him there, of course, but not without spoiling the skin. My mind's eye didn't see me dragging him.

I shook his leg. It was still loose, but soon would stiffen. Getting down on one knee, I took his foreleg in one hand and his hind leg in the other and pushed my shoulder into his belly. Pulling his legs tightly across my chest, I stood up unsteadily. For a moment I waited with my feet braced, getting used to the weight. I saw that I might be able to carry him after all, at least for a way. When I got tired, if I couldn't put him down, I could lean against a tree.

Off I went, taking smaller steps than I was used to taking. From the corner of my eye I saw the three ravens launch themselves from the rock to the air, and soon heard them shouting above me. For a long time I staggered forward. My bending legs and straining shoulders ached, a place in my back became sore where my spear dug into it, and sweat stung my eyes. I went from the willow thicket to the pine woods, and keeping the shining water to my right, I made for the end of the lake. The ravens kept pace with me, flying from tree to tree and waiting. Round and red and far away, the sun went down.

Not long before dark I heard something close behind me. I also heard the ravens' excited screams. Sure that I would see the tiger, I turned my whole body, planning to drop the carcass and back away from it, leaving it to the tiger. Yet it was not the tiger who followed me but the wolves, six of them spread out among the trees, ears up, eyes wide, their minds on how they would soon be eating reindeer. If I could have bent down, I would have stoned them.

But how was I to turn my back to them? The wolves seemed to have asked themselves the same question. Their tongues rolled cheerfully as they stood waiting for me to try. Yet if I didn't keep walking, I'd be standing there forever. Unsure of what might happen, I started to turn around. The wolves moved forward. I turned to face them. They stopped in their tracks but now seemed almost poised to rush me. I saw how I would soon lose meat to these wolves, or even the whole carcass, and my mind's eye saw me arriving at the lodge with nothing at all, then explaining to my uncles how I came to lose my spear and a reindeer.

"Be gone!" I said.

The wolves stopped at the sound of my voice but didn't do as I asked. I thought to put the carcass in the water. Off I went toward the shore, the wolves following. Expecting to feel at any moment a tug at the tail or a tug at the antlers, I shouted again, hurrying. The next thing I knew I was stumbling backward into the water, glad that the carcass was saved. Down I threw it with a splash, and snatching up the biggest rocks I could find, I aimed one, then another at the nearest wolves, throwing with such force that the rocks moaned in the air. One hit a wolf on the side with a loud thump. The wolf cried, and all the wolves vanished.

"Lulululululululu iyo!" I shouted across the water.

"Iyo!" answered a woman's voice. "Kori? Is it you?"

On the far shore I saw Andriki's wife, Hind, standing still among the trees. She was carrying something, a waterskin. She had been on her way to the lake.

"Aunt!" I called. "Send people with spears to me!"

"What's wrong?" called Hind.

"I've killed a reindeer. The wolves want it. My spear is broken. Send someone here."

"Are you safe?" she called.

"Yes, Aunt. Please just send someone with a spear!"

"Wait there," I heard her say.

So I waited. What else did she think I would do? The daylight faded and the woods filled with faint moonlight as the first quarter of the Fire Moon shone behind the clouds. Strangely warm, the wet wind stirred the surface of the lake. The wolves came back and sat down to wait. I wished that Father or Andriki was with me, there by the lake in the windy night.

Suddenly a terrible new fear seized me. What if my uncles weren't back? What if my aunt came to rescue me? I prayed to the Bear. "Send my uncles, not my aunt," I begged. "I'll burn fat for you!"

The Bear agreed—just then I heard my uncles Andriki and Maral calling, "Kori! Kori!"

"Uncles," I answered, "I'm here."

14

ON THAT STRANGE, WARM NIGHT THERE WAS DISTANT LIGHT-
ning. Wind was in the cloudy sky, so the moonlight
flickered like flames. Outside the lodge we built a fire,
and by firelight and moonlight we butchered my reindeer
and cooked the meat. The Bear was near, waiting for the
fat I saved for Him. I could feel Him. He likes the wind to
carry the smell of smoke and meat.

People spoke of Kori's reindeer. For a while the only
sound we made was chewing, chewing. Hind noticed
something and stood up, then sat down again. I looked.
At the edge of the trees were six pairs of round green
eyes—the wolves sat on their heels, watching us eat.

I was very happy. Best of all, in a way, was that my
uncles had killed nothing, although they had found dung
and footprints in a wide thicket where the horses seemed
to shelter. The weather was so strangely warm that the
horses weren't taking shelter, though. My uncles had
come home with nothing but the smell of horse dung on
their hands and moccasins. I had brought a reindeer!

When I could eat no more, I rubbed the grease into my
hands and face. Andriki said, "You make us happy, Kori.
We will sing now. And you must choose a song."

I remembered songs to the Bear and the Woman Ohun,
but these were prayers. Not for fun would people sing
these songs. I also remembered my mother's "Frog
Woman's Song," but it was for women, and against men
at that. I was sorry I had even remembered it. "What
song, Uncle?" I asked. "I never learned any."

"You didn't learn songs?" cried Andriki. "It's a good
thing we took you from your Uncle Bala's people. Here
we teach young people how to sing. Since my brother and

I hunted horses, I will sing about horses." Clearing his throat, he did.

> You with round hooves,
> We will hunt you.
> You with woman's hair,
> We will kill you.
> You with a woman's voice,
> We will cook you.
> You with a woman's rump,
> We will crack your bones.
> Your husband won't avenge you.
> The first time he saw us,
> He ran.
> The last time he saw us,
> He also ran.

"That song is called 'The Mare,'" said Rin above the voices of the others, all by then singing. The style of singing was called wolfsinging: not all the voices sang the same notes, but men's and women's voices sang different notes, some high, some low, always weaving. It was a style used by Mother's people. So I sang too, noticing that the wolves had moved closer together and deeper into the trees.

"You did well, Kori," said my Uncle Maral when we had finished the song. "Hear how happy you made us. Last night we had no fat to give the spirit. Tonight we have plenty." Across Maral's palm drooped a long, lumpy strip of fat from the skin of the reindeer's belly. Carefully Maral placed the strip on the fire. "Honored Spirit," he said, looking up at the moon as the fat began to crackle and flame, "take this from my brother's son, your kinsman, Kori. Like us, he is an owner of this lodge. Like us, he feeds you. Hona."

"Hona," said we all.

"We must bring the meat into the coldtrap," said Hind. "Look at the wolves there, waiting to rob us."

Maral looked over people's heads to the wolves. In the dark woods their eyes no longer shone, but their shadows sometimes moved among the shadows of the trees. "Be gone," said Maral to the wolves. But of course they didn't obey.

Not until the rest of my reindeer was safe in the coldtrap and we were taking off our clothes and spreading out our sleeping-skins did I think to mention that I had seen smoke and heard chopping. At first no one wanted to listen.

"There's a warm pond in those hills," said Hind. "Mist comes from it. When my husband first brought me here, I took the mist that comes off that pond for smoke."

"Chopping?" asked Maral.

"Yes, Uncle, and smoke too."

"That was me. I was chopping," he said, easing his naked body into his sleeping-skins.

"In the four hills? Up in the Breasts of Ohun?"

"Not in the hills! Out there." With his lips he pointed north.

"Uncle, I think there are people in the hills," I said. "I saw their smoke. I heard them chopping."

At last my words seemed to find him. Across the low fire that burned in the owners' end of the lodge, Maral's eyes met mine. "Smoke and chopping in the hills?" he asked.

"Yes."

"Again, Kori. Tell us again what you think you saw and heard."

So I did, beginning with the line of geese, ending with the sound of chopping. The people in the lodge fell silent and looked at each other. At last Maral said, "I don't like it. We should go to see what made these sounds. We should go now, but there's the Lily. We'll go in the morning."

But by morning Maral and the others had convinced themselves that I had been mistaken about the sounds. No one was in the hills, they said, nor could there be. Who would know about the pond there? Nothing important was there except the stream that ran from it into Narrow Lake. Who would camp by swampy Leech Pond and not by its fresh-running stream? And who could find the little, hidden pond except by following the stream? If people had been following the stream, they would have come to Narrow Lake. We would have seen them. If they had passed before we came, we would have found their tracks.

Andriki still seemed doubtful, though. Leech Pond was unimportant, it was true, but a warm spring fed it, he said. He reminded Maral that he and I had found a long-abandoned camp of strangers near another spring, Uske's Spring. Perhaps there were strangers who favored springs. As for their finding it, by watching the geese anyone could see that water was there. With the geese as guides, all anyone would have to do to find the water was to climb the hills.

"That may be true," said Maral. "You should at least go to see. Go carefully. Just look. Come back and tell us what you find. Together we'll decide what to do. Until then the rest of us should hunt the horses before the Lily gets to them. Listen." We listened. Outside, ravens were calling as if they knew we had food. "Go out and stone those birds," said Maral to Ako. To Andriki he said, "We need wood. On your way back, bring wood. And you women," said Maral to the women, "you also bring wood."

So Andriki and I set out for the place where I had heard the chopping. By now it was full daylight of a cloudy morning. Under the clouds the pink light of the newly risen sun spread through the woods. Side by side we walked through the grass toward the steaming lake, each of us making his own trail in the dew.

Where I had stopped to listen the night before, we stopped again, and this time we heard faraway voices. I thought for a moment they were human voices, but no—we saw a flight of geese dropping out of the clouds to a place between the left Breasts of Ohun. Andriki and I looked at each other. "The pond," he said, and pointed with his lips and chin to the hillside. We would go to the water where the geese had dropped.

Up the slope we went, following for a time a trail made by hares and foxes, a trail as faint and thin as a spider's web. It was much too narrow for us and didn't go where we wanted to go. Leaving it, we forced ourselves through the juniper and the harsh, thigh-high berry scrub, Andriki leading. The summits were farther than they seemed, but we crashed forward, breaking twigs with every step, leaving a rough new trail behind us. Every now and then a grouse rose up, startling us with the noise of its wings. In the warm, damp air we began to sweat, so we took off our parkas and opened our shirts. Soon our skins were stuck with berry leaves. Our sweat drew little black wasps to bother us. When the sun was high, we stopped to eat berries, because it seemed a shame to leave them for the ptarmigans, and besides, the summit seemed almost as far as when we had started. We ate until the afternoon, when we looked at each other and began walking again.

It was midafternoon when we reached the summit. There the harsh berry growth gave way to patches of juniper among moss and lichen or to dense ground-willows growing from the cracks between bare, dark stones. Before us shone the pond, with snowball sedge along its banks. In the dazzle of light sparkling on the water I saw a dark thing moving. One of the geese? I poised my spear.

But like a muskrat the thing turned suddenly toward us. It was a human head, with hair floating behind it—a person! Just like an otter or a muskrat, the person was swimming! I had never seen a person doing that before. Quickly Andriki pulled me to a crouch, down so the juniper hid us, where we could watch unseen. But the person swam with his chin high, his eyes squinting against the sun and water—he didn't see us.

We could see him, though. We saw that he wasn't one of our people. He seemed young. His wet head was small, his face was round and flat, and down the middle of his forehead was a long blue mark. I knew what the mark was—a row of small scars rubbed with ashes, like the Scars of Ohun which our women put on their buttocks. I didn't know what to think of this muskrat person swimming toward us with such a private mark on his forehead! Afraid and excited by the sight of him, I was ready to laugh aloud.

On he came into the reeds, straight for us, squinting at

the sun's dazzle, as serious as a muskrat, the corners of his mouth drawn down. At the water's edge he suddenly arched his pink back and pushed his rump into the air, on his hands and feet in the water as if getting ready to stand up. His black hair, which stuck to his back, parted over his ears.

Then he stood straight, and to my great surprise, he was not a man at all but a small young woman with little pink breasts, a rounded belly red from the cold, and a crotch thick with curly hair that streamed with water. And I all but knew her! She was the woman with the horses, the naked woman at the pool by Uske's Spring!

Stripping water from her arms, she slowly lifted her long, rounded thighs, one after the other, as she waded right to us. She then took her hair in both hands to squeeze water out of it, turning her head sideways as she did. Thus she faced me. Our eyes met.

She froze. I saw her eyes growing wide and her mouth opening as she drew in her breath to scream. I saw her start to turn, and before I knew what I was doing, I leaped forward, dove at her, caught her wrists in my left hand, and ducking under her arms, forced my right shoulder into her belly. Her breath left her in a great cough. Burning with strength as if from drinking blood, I stood up straight. The woman rode my shoulder like the carcass of a deer.

I heard her gasping. Tighter than I have ever held anything, I held her wrists against my left side, her legs against my belly. Then, amazed at myself and what I was doing, I turned and ran. The woman's weight and my great speed astonished me. My eyes found the trail even as I leaped over the juniper, while a thought seemed to come from nowhere into my mind that I was leaving behind both my spear and my parka. I realized I didn't want them.

At my back I heard Andriki. He didn't dare to shout, but his hoarse whisper seemed as loud as a shout. "What are you doing? What are you doing? Stop, Kori! Stop!"

I didn't answer Andriki. I was saving my breath for running and my attention for the trail. I wasn't sure myself what I was doing. I only knew that whatever it was, I was doing it very well. Downhill I hurried, half running, half staggering, holding tight to the heavy, naked woman who jounced on my shoulder, whose bare skin was heating the side of my face and throwing sunlight into my eyes, making me giddy. I tried not to grunt or let my breath seem labored—I wanted her to know my strength. It didn't occur to me to wonder why she wasn't crying.

On I ran, Andriki behind me, until it came to me that the woman was choking. I stopped, bent, and set her feet on the ground, still holding her wrists tightly. It shocked me to see that her face was red and twisted; she was crying and choking at the same time. Suddenly anxious, I let go of one of her hands and waited while she gasped.

I was also surprised by the sight of Andriki. I had often seen him angry, but I had never seen him enraged. His face too seemed twisted as he looked wildly from me to the woman to the summits of the hills now far above us, the hills from which, I suddenly realized, this woman's people would soon come running. Andriki had thought to bring my spear and parka, which he threw down. "Her people will kill us!" was all he could say. "Let her go. We'll run while we can!"

I drew a deep breath while my eyes took in this gasping woman, at last getting air, at last not so red in the face. She was a stranger, it was true. She was crying and angry—I was sorry about that. And possibly her people wouldn't want me to have her.

Yet there she stood in front of me, the pulse of her wrist like a bird in my hand, the bare flesh of her body calling mine. I saw how Andriki could run if he wanted. I saw how this woman's people could chase us if they liked. And I saw that if they did, I would surely fight them, since this woman was theirs no longer. She was mine.

I turned to Andriki. "Run," I said. "I'll follow. Leave me my spear."

"There's your spear," said Andriki, pointing his lips at the spear on the ground, then looking over his shoulder at the brushy slope down which a band of armed and angry men should soon be charging. "Will you carry her and fight too?"

"I'll do my best, Uncle. I'll die before I let her go."

Andriki gave me a long look. Then, picking up my spear and parka, he pointed his lips at the trail. "Try leading her, then," he said. "But hurry! Let's not die if we don't have to."

By now the woman's breath was coming fast but naturally. Her eyes had opened very wide, and were looking from Andriki's face to mine. I pulled her arm. "Come on," I told her. She didn't move but instead, like an animal about to leap, stared at my eyes. What did she find there? I saw that her lids were swollen and her lashes very short, that her irises were the darkest I'd ever seen. On each shining surface I could see the brushy hills behind me and the tiny outline of my head and shoulders against the sky. Her pupils were shrunken, small, pointed at me. I saw danger.

"Move," said Andriki suddenly, poking her bare back with his spear. He shouldn't have done it. If he had seen her eyes, he wouldn't have done it. She kicked at my groin with a force that would have dropped me if I hadn't quickly turned to take most of the blow on my hip, twisting her arm behind her as I did.

Snatching my spear by its middle, I jabbed the blade at this woman. She stiffened, but stood still. "Walk," I said, poking her again. As the skin of a horse will shrink from a fly, her skin shrank from the blade, but she didn't obey. "Do you hear?" I asked. Her jaw began to shudder, but she gave no other sign.

Andriki put his face close to hers. "Walk!" he shouted. Now she looked terrified, and her eyes darted from me to Andriki, as if she were trying to learn what we meant. "She hears, all right," said Andriki. "Tie her hands. Hurry!" So although she suddenly began to struggle violently, I tied her hands, wrapping my belt around her wrists and Andriki's belt around her neck to make a lead between her and me.

Again Andriki started down the hill. I gestured with my lips and chin for the woman to follow. When she seemed slow to start, I poked her again with my spear. At this, out of her mouth came a flood of speech, a tumble of sounds without meaning. Her voice was high, nervous, and her eyes almost popped. Then suddenly she gestured with her lips and chin to something behind me. Startled, I turned to see, which was all she needed to aim another mighty kick. This caught me in the groin and doubled me over. Then Andriki clubbed her head with both his fists together, a blow that sat her down in the bushes with her legs spread.

Although the terrible pain had robbed me of speech, although my eyes could hardly focus, I clenched my jaws and forced the words "Get up!" between my teeth. She stared at me but didn't move.

"She doesn't know real speech," said Andriki. "Get up!" he said, jerking upward on the belt that tied her hands. She struggled to her knees, stood, then slowly followed Andriki as I limped behind her, the lead in one hand, my spear in the other. I saw that our tussles had raised a cloud of dust as conspicuous as a campfire, so I kept watch over my shoulder, sure that at any moment her people would come.

We reached the trail. My pain was leaving. To my surprise Andriki crossed the trail, led us into the woods, and started toward the lodge through the forest. A small doubt rose in my mind as I saw how he was taking us. "The tiger, Uncle," I reminded him. "The Lily."

"You think him dangerous?" asked Andriki. "What if this woman's people have set an ambush for us? Armed men are more dangerous."

Even in the forest, where our footsteps didn't raise dust easily, I tried to look for every sign of her people, and gripped my spear, ready to fight. But I couldn't keep my mind off the woman in front of me—my dreams for her had begun. I watched her scratched rump, untouched by Scars of Ohun. Our women would scarify her, and I would get her pregnant. I watched the callused palms of her upturned hands. She would make clothing for me with those hands. I watched the wind lifting her black hair, now getting dry and tangled. I would show her the ways of our people, how to speak, how to braid her hair. I almost forgot the pain from her kick as I watched her, as the sight of her filled my eyes and plans for her filled my mind.

Then, as my eyes roamed up and down the fine powder of dust on her skin, I noticed that the insides of her thighs were clean. The air had dried her after her swim, then dust had powdered her, then something had wet her between her legs. As I watched her there, interested, a drop of blood slowly crept toward her ankle. Menstruation!

The sight shocked me. The woman seemed unaware. Quickly I looked at my shirt, where I had carried her, to see if she had stained me. Blood there too—a smear on my chest! "Uncle! She's menstruating," I said.

His sudden stop surprised the woman. Both then faced me, Andriki anxious, the woman afraid. "Your shirt," said Andriki uneasily.

"I'll take it off. Watch her while I do." I threw him the end of his belt, so he could hold her. Andriki took it, and also prodded her with his spear so she would know we hadn't forgotten her. I pulled the shirt over my head, careful not to let the stain touch my face. Then I dropped the shirt on the ground as Andriki and I looked at each other, dismayed.

But the woman looked bewildered. Was she stupid? She didn't seem to understand what was wrong. She didn't even seem to care that she was menstruating. Didn't she know? Had she put menstrual blood into the pond? She must have! Why? Were her people animals that they didn't know better than to foul water?

Worried by this new thing, I put on my parka and used my spear to poke the shirt away. It was useless to me. The woman looked at it. Lifting it on the point of my spear, I thrust it at her. Of course, with tied hands she couldn't take it. Again she stared, first at the shirt, then at me, with dangerous eyes.

"Free her hands," said Andriki.

"You do," I said, my eyes on hers. "You're behind her."

So he did. She took my shirt and put it on. It hung partway down her thighs. Reaching into the neck, I pulled out Andriki's belt, and reaching up inside the sleeves, I found her wrists, which I again tied together. Then I poked her to follow Andriki. She obeyed, glancing in every direction for people who might save her. Now and then, as if from an animal, a drop of blood would crawl down her leg and onto the path, like a snare for my foot. But then and later no sickness came to me, so I know that I sidestepped the drops.

Perhaps I should have been angry with the woman for her reckless menstruation. Perhaps I should have been afraid of her people, of the revenge they might take for her capture. Certainly I should have worried about facing my Uncle Maral, whose anger I knew would be hot and very great. Yet the nearer we came to the stream, then to the lodge, the less these things worried me. Instead my heart beat so joyfully I could almost hear it, filling me with pride, with strength. All by myself I had taken this woman whose bare feet stepped neatly in the tracks left by Andriki. As in the very best of hunting, I had seen at once what should be done and I had acted quickly and bravely. By Ohun's will, the woman wasn't even pregnant. I would change that. This woman was young. She was strong. She had many children in her. This woman would start my lodge and my family. She and those children would be mine.

15

BECAUSE SHE SWAM I NAMED MY WOMAN MUSKRAT. LATER, after I could make some sense out of her speech—the jabber she had shouted while we brought her to the lodge—I learned she had another name in her own tongue, Dabe Nore. But almost from the start she answered to Muskrat. Anyway, we called her that.

So began a time of great excitement, for me and for us all, starting with Maral's rage when Andriki and I came home with a captive. As we waded across the stream,

Maral happened to crawl through the coldtrap and stand up. I almost laughed aloud to see how he looked at us three times—first the quick glance that noticed us, next the puzzled, scowling gaze that found three of us instead of two, and finally the open-mouthed stare of disbelief that took in Muskrat's bare legs and tattooed forehead. His anger came. "By Ohun's name!" he shouted. "What have you here?"

The shout brought people tumbling out of the lodge, gaping at what they saw. They all began shouting.

"Andriki has a stranger!"

"Is it a child?"

"It's a woman!"

"We'll be attacked!"

"The children—where are they?"

"Find them!"

"Death is searching for us! Get your spears!"

The excitement seemed to frighten my woman. Wide-eyed, she braced her legs and wouldn't move. With my spear I prodded her between the shoulders, and with my foot I gave her a shove in the rump. In spite of herself, she stumbled forward.

"Madmen!" shouted Maral. "Turn her loose! She'll get us killed!"

Strangely calm, Andriki shrugged to show his half-brother that he was helpless to change things. I, in contrast, was blazing with pride, shivering with strength and excitement. Nothing my Uncle Maral could have said or done would have made any difference to me. Far from it! I laughed because I felt so happy. And hot, but pretending to be cool, I answered him. "She's my captive, Uncle. You needn't fear her."

"Is this your doing, Kori?" cried Maral, turning toward me. "How will you fight her people?"

"There were no other people."

"But they're somewhere! You saw their smoke! You went to scout them! Are you insane, to say there was just this one woman alone?"

"We saw no others," I said.

"Do you say there are none?"

Andriki's show of calmness was fading. Seeing that I

was dodging Maral's questions, he answered instead. "Of course there must be others," he said.

To me Maral shouted, "Did you remember we have only five men here when you got us into a battle with strangers?"

But I had made up my mind that nothing would part me from this woman, so I was ready to fight Maral if need be. "I'll fight whom I must—even you, Uncle," I said loudly.

These words made him very angry. He strode toward me. So I stepped in front of my woman, ready to meet him. But Andriki stepped in front of me. "Save your fighting for the strangers," he said. "Are we women, to fear them? Let them come for us! They'll save us the trouble of searching for them. Or if they fear to visit us, I'll scout them, to learn how many they are and what weapons they carry. Perhaps we can easily fight them. Who knows? Perhaps we can capture more women!"

But Maral wasn't listening to Andriki. "So you would fight me, Kori? You, my son-in-law! My brother's child! You would fight me?"

"If he fights you, Elder Brother, he fights me too," said Andriki. "But he doesn't mean what he says. He's excited. We're all excited. Instead of thinking about fighting each other, we should be thinking about this woman's people and what they want in our hunting lands."

"Make her tell us what they want!" said Maral.

"How?" asked Andriki. "She doesn't know our speech." To me he said, "Aren't Maral and I your father's brothers? If you fight us, don't you fight him? Does the thumb fight the fingers? You shame us and you spoil your own lodge. You should apologize."

Andriki was right, of course. So I apologized to Maral. Like Father, he was quick to anger but quicker to forget. Putting an arm around my shoulder, he said, "You found a woman. Yet women don't roam the country alone, like roe deer. If you're sorry you made me angry, just remember that you've made some strangers really angry. They're not far away. Let all of us think about that!"

"I'm already thinking," said Andriki. "I think some of

us should stay here. We don't want to come back only to find our own women stolen by strangers. Three of us should stay while two scout. We'll go tonight." He looked at the western sky, where, low like a fire among the black trees, the round red sun burned on the horizon. Listening, we looked in all directions. The woods were shadowy, and wind was moving the trees. Andriki's breath steamed when he said, "We'll look for the strangers. If we find them, what then?" He paused, searching my face with his pale eyes. "You, youngster! You started this," he said. "Will you be as brave by night as you were when you captured a lonely woman in the daytime? Some big, grown man with a full beard and a strong arm owns this woman. Will you be as brave when you meet this man?"

"Come with me and see, Uncle," I said.

"If you set her free, I'll leave here forever and go to my Uncle Bala's lodge on Woman Lake," I said to Maral and the others who sat outside beside a large fire that threw light around the clearing to help us see whatever might be lurking at the edge of the trees. In the growing dusk the moon stood in the sky, casting the light Andriki and I would need for scouting. "Or die on the way," I added, remembering the enormous distance across the open plain.

"Set her free? Are we women, to oblige trespassing strangers?" asked Maral.

All the women were inside except Andriki's wife, Hind—she who sometimes hunted, she who owned a spear. Squinting into the dark woods, Hind sat on her heels next to Marten, her spear ready. When Maral asked if we were women, she glanced up at him.

The mood of the people of our lodge had changed greatly, from their first surprise at the sight of my woman and their anger at me for surprising them to a strong but quiet excitement, as if an important hunt were starting —as if we were after a bear or mammoths or large cow bison. As for me, I now saw Muskrat's people as my enemies, as hated intruders. I couldn't wait to find them.

So when the moon was high above the trees, Andriki and I went quietly back up into the Hills of Ohun. We were so ready to attack the strangers that we were almost disappointed to find, by the pond, the remains of a camp that had been abandoned in a hurry. The people had left by day, before dew fell, and had trampled their way across the brittle groundcover. The tracks belonged to a rather small man and two small women whose wide heel marks showed the weight of their packs. One of the women had also carried a burden on her right hip, probably a baby. The man was old and lame—he walked with a staff. These people had been followed by a young child, whose trotting footprints were the last in line. We followed these tracks straight east, down through the wide, moonlit sweep of brush and juniper, until the tracks left the hills. In all that distance no other people had joined the group. So we knew that my woman's people had been few, in a hurry to escape us. We had nothing to fear from them.

We went back to their old camp to learn what food they had been eating. In someone's stool in their latrine we noticed specks that were probably redberry seeds, and by the ashes of their fire we found some tiny fishbones— pike, maybe—and grouse feathers. These people hadn't been eating very well. Of course, with three women, two children, and a lame old man, that wasn't surprising. Also in the moonlit ashes we found the broken shaft of what seemed to be a tiny spear with a blade like the one we had found near Uske's Spring. Then we believed that these were the same people who had visited the spring, or at least the same kind of people, with their little bird-spears. We laughed, glad to have such good news for Maral. No wonder the strangers feared us! No wonder they had hurried away!

On our way home, down the western slope of Ohun's Breast, I happened to look back and noticed against the moon something dangling from the branch of a tree—a large wasps' nest, I thought at first. Round and black, it swung gently. But it wasn't a nest. Andriki and I took it down and found that it was a carrying bag. We opened it.

In it were some bits of shiny black rock, not found anywhere known to Andriki; some tinder; a bone needle; some twine; seven pieces of clothing, and a necklace. The necklace was very simple—part of an eyetooth with a hole bored in it and a string through the hole. The only thing was, Andriki and I couldn't tell what animal the tooth had been taken from. The tooth was thick, round, and as long as my thumb. It seemed to curve, but where the curve began the tooth was broken. What good does it do to wonder over things for which there is no answer? We set the necklace aside and spread out the clothes in the moonlight.

They were worn, shabby, and very strange. Although the leather had been worked like the leather of our clothes, it wasn't deerskin. The strange clothes were thinner and softer than ours, with much stitching in them, as many small skins had been sewn together. The ragged leather felt soft, as if it had once been soaked a long time in urine, and was black, as if it had once been rubbed with charcoal and fat. The clothes smelled strong, like foxes. And they were trimmed with balding fox fur.

When we separated them we found a long fur-trimmed shirt which pulled over the head, two ankle-high moccasins, a loincloth, a belt, and two long things that we finally figured out were pantlegs that tied around the waist, each worn separately. We laughed! How could people dress so strangely? They were my woman's clothes, we reasoned, left by her people in case she would follow them.

My woman would rather wear our people's clothes than her people's clothes, I thought. Anyone would. Even so, lest the sight of her things made her think of her people, I stuffed the bundle into a crack in the rocks. Foxes would take the leather clothing. From that time on, as I foresaw, my woman wouldn't walk in the Hills of Ohun unless she went with me.

The wind rose. We went back to the lodge, walking quietly and carefully and looking before and behind us on the trail, now dark with cloud shadows. More dangerous than my woman's people was the hunter who used trails at night, or watched beside them, crouched and hungry, with big green eyes.

* * *

At first my muskrat-woman seemed stupid. I began to think she knew nothing, as Rin was the only one of us she seemed to recognize. Every time she saw me she seemed bewildered, as if she had never seen me before. But if Rin left the lodge, my woman would watch the door until she came through it again. Of course, it was mostly Rin who fed her. Rin also gave her reindeer moss to soak up her menstrual blood and in time helped her make clothing.

Muskrat hadn't been with us long before Rin took one of my sleeping-skins to make proper trousers for her. I then had to sleep on my parka and other outer clothes. For moccasins Rin took part of the skin of the reindeer I had killed. The skin belonged to Frogga by way of her mother, Lilan, but as Rin pointed out, on bare feet Muskrat couldn't help with any of the work in winter, and someday I could give Lilan another skin, to replace the skin Muskrat owed.

For a bed we gave Muskrat two bald old skins that had once belonged to Father and had been stored behind the poles that braced the roof. The wolves had worried the skins and torn them trying to pull them free, but hadn't succeeded. Much hair fell out when we opened the skins. But they were better than nothing. Until her menstruation stopped, the woman couldn't sleep with me.

For a parka, Rin used the skin of the bear we had found robbing our mammoth carcass by the cave on the Hair River. Since Maral's and Father's spears had been the first into this bear, the skin belonged to Lilan, Truht, and Pinesinger. It had been carried from our summerground in three pieces. Before these women would part with their pieces of bearskin, I had to promise them the next three skins of reindeer hunted by me. And because any large skin gotten by my hunting would rightfully belong to Frogga, I had to promise Lilan my next three shares of meat to replace the reindeer skins.

I could see I would own nothing for a long time, not even the meat I killed or the new clothes I myself needed, because of my woman. I would have to borrow clothes and beg others to feed me. Yet not for a moment did I regret what I had done.

On the first night we were all too excited to think of

bedding, so my woman slept on the bare floor. I didn't notice, since that night I lay with my spear in the coldtrap, sometimes dozing but never really sleeping, to be sure she didn't escape. I kept looking up to check on her, and each time saw her sitting by the fire. She seemed lonely, staring at the flames, thinking her own thoughts and sometimes crying. The sight made me want to take her into my bed—to comfort her and keep her warm, I told myself—but I was afraid of her menstruation, so I waited. The other people of the lodge kept waking too, lifting their heads uneasily to see what she was doing. Perhaps they were afraid she might take a knife to us all.

During the night we heard thunder. The wind grew strong, and just before dawn wet snowflakes began whirling down the smokeholes. We had gathered very little wood the day before and were saving what we had to cook the reindeer meat, so to keep warm we stayed in our sleeping-skins, listening to the thunder and the wind over the lodge and watching the snowflakes turn to water on the still-warm ashes of our dying fires. Only Muskrat sat up. With her arms and legs tightly folded to her chest, she had pulled her whole body inside my shirt. The empty sleeves dangled; her tangled hair stuck out of the neck; the flattened edge of her bare buttocks and the soles of her feet showed under the hem. Meanwhile snow was covering all traces of her people—their trail, their night's camp, the guiding signs they might have left for Muskrat. Even with moccasins, my woman couldn't follow. I slept at last, content.

Catching Muskrat was very exciting; so were the anger and the stir she caused, and so was the hunt for her people. We were excited to think of a stranger in our lodge, and to think of her people returning to find her. In case they came, we took care each day to circle widely through the woods several times, looking for the tracks of strangers. They didn't come, nor did we really expect them—but the thought of them excited us so much we talked of nothing else.

And the woman herself was exciting, certainly to me! Not even in my dreams had I ever thought of owning a full-grown woman. But I did, and not because my relatives and her relatives had come to an agreement, not because gifts had changed hands. No—I owned her because I had seized her! So she was exciting in the same way that a large animal close by is exciting, filling a place with its unusual bulk, its strange look, and its special odor. Such an animal will always bring surprises, since no one can say what it will do. And it doesn't know speech!

But not until my woman finished her menstruation did the biggest excitement of all begin for me, which of course was the excitement of lying with her—a story in itself. I could hardly wait to do it, since day and night my mind's eye saw her red, wet, naked body standing up from the reeds in Leech Pond. My shoulder remembered the weight of her body, my face remembered the heat burning from her hip, my eyes remembered the light cast into them by her bare skin, and my nose remembered the pond water that had clung to her, and her musk, her woman's smell. From then on, I never seemed to notice the smells of the other people. Perhaps I knew their smells too well. It seemed that each time my nostrils caught an odor it was Muskrat's—her crotch, her feet, her sweat, her hair.

One night I smelled the faint, bitter odor of yellowroot slime, and I knew that Rin had given that slime to Muskrat to rub between her thighs, to clean herself of menstruation. Yellowroot was a plant of open grassland. How had Rin gotten its slime? Rin's yellowroot was a woman's secret that pulled my mind between my woman's legs.

That night, when people were asleep or lying still, I crawled quietly out of my bed in the coldtrap, saw Muskrat curled tight under one deerskin by the wall, and tossed a bit of burned wood at her. She raised her head fearfully. Our eyes met. I beckoned to her. She gave me her blank stare, as if she didn't understand what I wanted. I stood up and beckoned. She stared ignorantly. I walked over to her, stood above her, and beckoned again. She shrank from me, so I took her arm and pulled her gently. Fearfully she stood up.

Rin had not finished sewing Muskrat's trousers; all Muskrat wore was my shirt. Her hair was partly combed, though, and twisted into a short, ugly braid. I thought of loosening the braid, then decided I didn't care about it, and let it be. At the door of the coldtrap I forced Muskrat to her heels and pulled the shirt over her head, although she tried to stop me. Turning her around, I folded her into my sleeping-skin beside me, her shoulder blades against my chest. She lay still and felt cold, and didn't seem to know to press her rump against me. Even so, my penis found its place inside her; I pulled her to me and began to thrust. Her vagina was dry. She gasped. I put a hand over her mouth so no one would hear. Her bent body seemed to straighten and her vagina became short; she wasn't helping. But she wasn't fighting. Her breath was quiet, shallow. I knew she was waiting for me to finish so she could leave. Still, just holding a woman was exciting. My breath felt strangled, so that I almost had to gasp aloud. My climax came very suddenly, and with it, to my great surprise, a rush of tears drenched my face and would have dropped on Muskrat if I hadn't lifted my hands to wipe my eyes. Muskrat felt me let her go, and slipped away. I didn't try to stop her.

Ah, well. To lie with her at all was better than lying with no one, better than remembering Pinesinger, better than imagining how it would be someday to lie with Frogga, with her running nose and her cold, damp, too-smooth skin.

As I listened to Muskrat's clumsy footsteps going to her sleeping place and watched her rumpled shadow sweep the ceiling of the lodge, I wondered who else was listening and watching. Poor Marten, who slept at Rin's fire near the door, had surely heard me taking Muskrat. He surely envied me. At that time, if Marten ever climaxed, he did it in his dreams, since his pregnant wife, Rin's daughter, Waxwing, was not supposed to lie with him until after their baby was born.

Rin had surely heard me too. Rin would have been listening for the sounds of her daughter and her son-in-law together, for the sounds of their breathing, since their having coitus could frighten or bruise her unborn grandchild. Everyone knows that even a very pregnant woman can't always refuse her husband, since he can (like my Uncle Bala) usually command her, or, after she falls asleep, he can (like my stepfather) play with her softly until she wakes up lusting. So in a way it was Rin's duty as a mother-in-law to make sure no harm came to her unborn lineage; it was her duty to be listening for Marten, so she could say a few words that would help him chill his need.

Maral could have heard me. Andriki too, that light sleeper. In the morning he would tease me. Their wives would have heard me. Pinesinger would have heard and realized that Muskrat had no interest in me, or worse, that I had given her pain but no pleasure. This thought made me angry. The women would think little of me. Behind my back, they would laugh. I made up my mind to wait for a chance to show my woman how to do this thing. Then, if she and I made sounds at night, the sounds would show our happiness, not her fear and my need.

Because of the snow, my chance came soon. Muskrat couldn't leave the lodge until she had clothes. Instead, while everyone else was out, Muskrat waited by the fire, trying her best to keep warm. All I had to do to be with her was to wait until all but she were elsewhere, then come with my load of wood. The very next time I brought wood I knew she was inside alone. I scrambled down the coldtrap, found her sitting by the embers, pulled her to her feet, and took off her clothes.

Would I have acted so if she had been a woman of our people? Just the thought is funny. Our women can't be treated lightly—it makes them angry. Often it makes their kin angry. And always it makes the other women angry. Then all women turn against you, even the little girls. If I had tried to pull the clothes off one of our women, she would have boxed my ears and laughed in my face.

But my woman didn't know this. While I took off my own clothes and shook out my sleeping-skin to make a bed for us, she stood watching me, her bare, bent legs pressed tight together, her arms hugging her goose-pimpled body, her chin shuddering with cold, and her tattooed forehead scowling with puzzlement.

What did I think I could teach about coitus? I had known only Pinesinger, yet I fancied I had much to teach! In truth, of course, I knew very little, and Muskrat had a big surprise waiting for me, something that has stayed with me all the rest of my life, but something that I have seldom spoken of, not even to Andriki. Thinking of it now makes me smile, since the memory still pleases and shames me. To come out with it, what happened next, what happened when I pulled Muskrat down on her knees, bent her forward, and raised her hips so I could enter her, was that she rolled on her back like a beetle and opened her legs!

I had never seen a woman's vulva, yet there it was. Red! Like a ferret's den, like a small skull's eye, the hole stared up at me. Around it I saw damp, wavy ridges like the edges of a snail. And it was wide! As wide as my palm, or so it seemed. Something like a mouth, it had lips and gums, without true skin. All around it was her hair, and below it was her anus. I knew I shouldn't stare, but I couldn't stop.

Muskrat said one word to me in her twisted language. I didn't understand her, and don't remember the word. But her voice helped me tear my eyes from her vulva and set them on her face, where her own eyes, round and angry, seemed very impatient. She raised her head and said the word again louder, pointing her thumbs at her gaping red vulva. She wanted me to hurry!

So I did. I dropped my body onto hers and entered. She clasped me with her hard, cold arms and legs. The feeling shocked me, as if a hunting animal had seized me, or as if an enormous beetle had fastened itself to my hips and chest. I tried to thrust, but I was slowed by her clinging, and the position was so strange that I had trouble starting. Even so, it was very exciting. I heard her panting—her breath stirred in my ear! Her thighs gripping my waist, her two breasts squeezing tight between us, made me dizzy. I would have liked to get used to this new thing, to think how best to do the man's part, but she began to growl, then moan, then cry aloud. She frightened me! I thrust as quickly as I could and climaxed suddenly, then felt a sense almost of panic. I had wanted to teach my woman something. Instead, to my great surprise, she had taught me something, and I had no idea what she might do next to me, or what I should do with her!

I didn't have long to wonder. Almost at once she set her feet firmly on the floor, heaved her hips to get rid of me, slid out from under me, and hurried to the fire, where she sat on her heels almost in the flames and quickly pulled her shirt on, her teeth chattering and her lips blue. I stared at her, stunned by the suddenness of everything. We had gone against nature!

I was not a little frightened by this slave of mine and by what she had showed me. Desperately fighting animals, cornered animals, also insects, beetles, sometimes roll onto their backs with their legs up. Babies lie on their backs with their legs open before they understand decency, and so do women in difficult childbirth, if exhaustion overcomes them. But not even the animals turn wrong side up for coitus! Coitus is done by the will of the Woman, who shows us, Her children, how it must be. When we see the rainbow, we know it is She, head down and back bent, taking Cloud Woman's Son as Her lover. Rain is Her sweat, thunder and lightning are Her climax, and the rainbow is the arch of Her spine. Huge mammoths, lions, deer, birds, frogs, and everything else too, even flies, all do as She does, even though some get only eggs from doing it. Who were this slave-woman and I to do differently?

Suddenly ashamed, I swept away all traces we had left on the floor of the lodge, especially the places scuffed by Muskrat's shoulder blades and buttocks. I pulled up Muskrat's shirt and wiped the dust from her back, and took my sleeping-skin outside and shook it. Then I took my spear and ax and hurried away to gather more wood, before anyone came back to the lodge to make fun of me.

After that, though, I made one bed for both of us every night, and when Muskrat was in it, I, with a show of yawning, would lie down. Then, when I hoped the others were asleep or at least too tactful to be listening, I would roll over to face her as she had showed me. In truth, I liked her way of coitus. I liked to feel the grip of her thighs around my hips and the solid, fat pads of her breasts between her ribs and mine. I liked her breath in my ear and her arms around me. And I liked that she liked to be taken this way.

Not when others could overhear us did she growl or shout. And not in the dark, with my sleeping-skin over us, could anyone see that she faced me. So every night we made love in the way of her people. Then, with our arms around each other, we slept like children, while our spirits flew where they would in dreams.

16

WITH THE PINE NUT MOON CAME CRISP, COLD WEATHER, AND with the Reindeer Moon came deep, fine snow. We ate a horse killed by Maral; we hunted again, killed a roe deer, then a reindeer. My spear killed the reindeer, so I began to replace with meat the skins given to make clothes for my woman, Muskrat. The first person to get meat from me was my mother-in-law, Lilan.

By then Muskrat had a full set of clothes, so she could help the other women on their trips for pine nuts, winterberries, and firewood. She was also given the task of filling our waterskins, as she didn't need to know her way through the country to do it but needed only to walk from the coldtrap to the lake.

When the lake froze, Rin gave Muskrat a heavy pole to break a hole in the ice and showed her where on the lake she should make the waterhole. Although Muskrat couldn't understand her, Rin told her how one day in midwinter a few years before, she, Rin, had gone to get water and had seen a young wolf's face looking up at her from the waterhole. The wolf must have fallen in while trying to drink. By that time of winter the ice was thicker than the length of a man's leg, and the sides of the waterhole were steep and slippery. The wolf couldn't get out. Seeing Rin gave the wolf a new burst of strength, because it started to struggle, dancing its hind feet in the water, scraping its front feet at the steep sides of the waterhole. It might have escaped, but Andriki had come running and had speared it. Its fur soon lined Andriki's daughter's parka.

"If you fell in, you could slide under the ice," said Rin to Muskrat. "You couldn't climb out. Here the lake is deep. If no one saw you, no one could help you. You would drown. Anyway, the cold would quickly kill you."

"Io," said Muskrat, not having understood what Rin had said.

Because I sometimes heard her crying softly at night, and because by day she kept to herself, quiet and alone, I knew she was unhappy with us. It made me sad, but I didn't know what to do to help her except to try to be kind. From one of the reindeer's antlers I carved a pin for her hair. She took it, but it wasn't much help. She was homesick. But what could I do about that? Even if I had wanted to take her back to her people, I didn't know how to find them.

Still, I was always afraid she might run away. After the snow she had no hope of tracking her people, but just to be sure she didn't try to leave us anyway I took her to the tree that the tiger had scratched, to show her how recently he had visited us and how big he was. Her eyes grew wide at the sight of his scratches. Lest she mistake his sign for that of another animal, I drew a tiger's track in the snow, and also the stripes of a tiger's forehead. But I needn't have bothered. She knew what she was seeing. She made a soft tiger's moan and whispered "edde," which I later came to know meant both "eater" and "tiger" in her people's language.

Pinesinger tried to teach Muskrat our speech. Muskrat learned to say, "Eye sah-eeh," which meant "I'm sorry";

as these were almost the only words she knew, she said them often. No one expected Pinesinger to learn Muskrat's speech, yet that is what happened, and before long she and Muskrat could chatter together. Perhaps this should not have surprised me. Pinesinger had always been better than the rest of us at making animal sounds. She could cluck and rattle like a raven; she could call a fox to her in the voice of a vole; she could mutter like an owl and even rumble in the low voice of a mammoth, although not as loud.

By the time of the full Reindeer Moon, Muskrat and Pinesinger would talk long and, as far as the rest of us were concerned, secretly. Muskrat seemed somewhat happier after that, although the secrecy made the rest of us angry. Yet no one could really command the two women to do differently. My father wasn't present to command Pinesinger, and in what language could I command Muskrat? Speaking to her through Pinesinger came hard to me. Nor did Pinesinger help. Whenever I asked Pinesinger to use our language, not Muskrat's, she would ignore me and gabble for as long as she pleased while I waited to hear something understandable.

My anger, and the anger of the others, didn't bother either Muskrat or Pinesinger, since Muskrat hardly sensed it and Pinesinger ignored our feelings, knowing that most people hadn't forgiven her for dividing our lodge. On top of a wrong as large as that, how could a little strange speech be important?

Some nights I brought Muskrat to sit near me by the owners' fire in the back of the lodge, so she could watch me carve things for her. After the pin, I made her a needle and an awl. As I worked I would try, with the help of Pinesinger, to talk with her, since I wanted to learn who her people were and why they had come to our country. But Pinesinger's knowledge of Muskrat's speech wasn't up to the question. All she could say was that Muskrat called her people the Ilasi, that her people were few, that they had been forced to leave their old place in the south and had been looking for a new place. So they had come north.

Since we soon learned that "ilasi" meant "people" in Muskrat's language, we didn't feel we had learned much about her. Where did these people of Muskrat's come from? Through Pinesinger, Muskrat said the place was far.

Yet women often say a place is far. To some women, all places are far. That is because women and children travel slowly, as do men who travel with them. Men alone travel quickly, so men are more likely to know the truth about distance. Even so, Muskrat's home was probably really very far, or so we thought, for two reasons. First, not even Maral had ever seen people who swam, or who wore buttocks marks on their faces, or who spoke Muskrat's speech, or who wore clothes as strange as the clothes in the bundle Andriki and I had found at her people's abandoned camp. Second, in time Muskrat told us that in her homeland lived a kind of animal none of us had ever seen. Even Maral didn't know it.

This animal ate plants but also ate meat. It had a stomach like a wolf's stomach, but its feet were split into hooves like deer's feet. Its young were born in litters like wolves' litters, but the babies could stand up and walk like newborn fawns. The adult animal was plain gray-brown, like a reindeer, but the babies were striped.

Strangest of all, this animal was something like a person. Its hair was straight and coarse like human hair, with no soft undercoat beneath, and it called out with a human voice. Also, its feces were like human feces. And it could build a shelter from grass like a person's summer shelter. It would make a pile of grass, trample on the pile to mat it, then, like a child playing under a sleeping-skin, it would kneel, crawl under the mat, and stand up, making a dome!

The name of this animal was tai tibi. Two of them were tai tibidi, and many of them were tai tibisi. Tai Tibi was also the name that Muskrat's people used for Ohun. Think of it!

At first no one believed there was such a thing as a tai tibi. Some of us thought that Muskrat was describing an animal we knew but was using the wrong words. When she drew the tracks of a tai tibi in the ashes of our fire, Maral thought it was the badly drawn likeness of a roe deer's track in mud.

Then at last I remembered the strange eyetooth in Muskrat's necklace. Never since I was a small child had I seen a tooth or a track I couldn't recognize. Also, people wear the teeth of animals they respect, and what could deserve more respect than an animal named for Ohun? So the tooth on the necklace could have been the tooth of a tai tibi. I wanted to ask, but then Muskrat would have known about the bundle of clothes, and these might have held some sort of signal from her people, so I said nothing.

At the beginning of Muskrat's stay with us, the other people didn't like her. The men ignored her, and the women complained about her careless ways. If Rin hadn't stopped her, Muskrat would have fouled our lodge with her menstrual blood. But Rin had gathered moss for her to put between her legs. We asked each other what the women of her people might do when they menstruated, suspecting that the answer might be something we didn't want to hear.

Also, although the body of my woman was very fine, very beautiful, her face was flat and had been made ugly by the long blue buttocks scar. The skin of her buttocks, though, was plain as a child's. Rin and the others soon learned what Andriki and I had noticed right away: that the buttocks of my captive had no scars, although she was old enough to have them. We saw that Muskrat would have to take her chances in childbirth, since without the scars she wouldn't have Ohun's protection.

But then, in many ways Muskrat surely offended Ohun. She pointed rudely with her forefingers, sometimes with both at once, not only at things but also at people, and once she even counted the people of the lodge, as if they were beads in a marriage exchange! Her habits weren't clean, and when she tried to use our speech her words were thick and ugly, as if she carried a stone on her tongue. I overheard the women saying that she would urinate while standing. She would lower her trousers, spread her legs, bend forward a little, and turn her feet out.

She also didn't know what to do with her clothes. Sometimes she wore her trousers backward. Until Rin showed her how to braid her hair, she pulled it all back and wound a string around and around it, so that it looked like a child's foot in a moccasin. After she learned how to braid, her hair looked loose and messy, since she didn't braid well. Sometimes at night Rin would comb and braid her hair for her, talking angrily as she did, yanking the comb. Rin always talked angrily when she combed someone's hair—she was angry at the tangles, not at the person. But Muskrat didn't know this, because she couldn't understand our speech. She would try to hold her hair above the comb, but Rin would slap her hands away. Then Muskrat would fold her hands in her lap while her eyes shone with tears, although her face wore no expression.

One day I felt itching in my groin, and when I visited the latrine I looked at my crotch closely. I was very disappointed to see crotch lice. Because I had been free of lice since I had bathed in the Hair River with Father on our way to his cave, I knew these new lice came from Muskrat. I made up my mind to say nothing but to try to pick them off myself privately. Yet lice cannot be kept secret very long in a lodge in winter. They creep about. Soon everyone was scratching.

Early one morning when the air was so cold our breath froze in our nostrils, we made big fires in the lodge, then put our clothes and sleeping-skins outdoors in the shadow of the lodge to freeze any lice hiding in them. Inside we sat naked, searching our pubic hairs, throwing the lice and nits we found into the fires. We killed many, but not all. Some lice escaped notice, and soon we were itching again.

It wasn't hard for people to guess how the lice had come. Then the feeling against Muskrat grew large indeed. When she crawled through the coldtrap with her full waterskin or with a bundle of wood, or when at night I went to her bed near the door, all talking would stop, as if people had been speaking of her. They hadn't, of course. They fell silent because she had caught their attention and they didn't want to go on with their talk in her presence. But the silence was worse than words, and I couldn't help but feel that people were against me for bringing her.

But what could I do? I couldn't turn her loose. She was ours, at least for the winter. Besides, I loved her.

Perhaps because winter was just starting and no one wants to go through a winter with people ill at ease, Rin kept telling the others that having Muskrat could be good as well as bad. It was bad that we, with too few hunters, had to feed another woman in winter. But it was good that I could get children for the lodge on Muskrat while giving the wife's share of my hunting to Frogga's family, since a slave and a stranger could never be a wife.

The truth of that I had seen at once. With whom would my kin exchange marriage gifts? I laughed to think of it—running after Muskrat's queer little group, offering them ivory. It would be like trying to give presents to animals! And what gifts could they give to us? Even if we knew where they were, they had nothing we wanted.

So in time, perhaps because people saw Muskrat's value, or else because they feared a winter of bad feelings more than they disliked Muskrat's strange looks and manners, the men as well as the women began to show some kindness to her and to me. For a while they made sure that she got enough to eat, which meant they gave food from their own shares. If not, she would have gotten nothing, or I would have had to feed her always from my share, since she was not related by kin or marriage in any way to any of us and had no rights to anyone's hunting.

At first, besides me, only the women shared with Muskrat. Later Maral and Andriki did the same. I thought nothing about it. It seemed to me that my uncles were showing the same thoughts for Muskrat as the women showed, nothing more. But after a while I came to think my uncles had another reason.

One day I was with my uncles hunting to the north of the river. We were following a reindeer trail made the night before, and when we came to a ridge where the country sloped away from us into a basin, Andriki asked me to climb a tree to see if I could spot a shortcut to the reindeer in the countryside below. Trying to catch sight of the herd, I stayed a long time in the tree, while Andriki and Maral sat on their heels, waiting. Soon they began to whisper something about a woman. I didn't pay much attention until I overheard Andriki say my name. Then I strained my ears, and heard Maral whisper, "Face you," and later, "Clasped legs." Shocked, I climbed down and looked at my uncles. As if nothing had happened, they both stared blandly back at me. "Well? Are there reindeer?" asked Maral. But I felt too shaken to answer. I had seen why these men gave meat to Muskrat. As Wolverine had lain with Mekka, the First Man's woman, my uncles had lain with mine.

It was often our practice not to talk while hunting, so my uncles hardly noticed my silence on the way home. Yet my thoughts were like a storm. My mind's eye saw Muskrat like a beetle on her back, bending her legs, holding them open to show Maral and Andriki the secrets of her vulva, that private place that is for men to feel but not to stare at. I saw her smiling up at them shamelessly, sweetly. Why wouldn't she? Weren't they the senior owners of the lodge? The best hunters? And why wouldn't they want to try her? What rule, in their eyes, left her to me?

Sometimes it was Andriki and sometimes it was Maral whom my mind's eye saw kneeling between her legs, lowering his chest to her breasts, his belly to her belly. I saw her clasp his back with her arms and hips with her thighs. I saw her pull herself up to him like a beetle. In the cold air, my face burned. My uncles had looked on my woman as if they had watched her in childbirth, something not for the eyes of any man. Yet she had shown herself! Perhaps she had asked them to look on her. Surely she had asked them! How else could such a thing come to be?

That evening in the lodge, after Muskrat as usual took a waterskin and crawled out through the coldtrap, I waited a short while, then followed. In front of the lodge I found myself alone. The woods were growing blue with evening, and in the silent, bitter air I heard, like the rasping wingbeats of a red she-cuckoo, the soft, even crunch of Muskrat's footsteps in the snow. I hurried after her and caught her arm. Surprised, she turned to face me.

"Woman!" I said. "You lay with Andriki, I know!"

"Andriki," she repeated stupidly, open-mouthed, nodding.

"You lay with him!"

"Yas? Andriki?" Her eyes were squinting, and her speech was dull and slow.

"You lay with him! Lay with him! You!" I jabbed my finger at her chest and made the handsign for coitus.

Muskrat didn't know our handsigns, but this was clear enough. Her eyes flew wide as she stared at my fingers.

"Maral! Andriki!" I said.

"Maral? Andriki?" she repeated, troubled.

It was all the answer I needed. I slapped her with the full strength of my arm. She fell. Bending, I slapped her again, once, twice, as she struggled away from me. I saw blood on the snow. Her nose was bleeding. I picked up the waterskin and threw it at her. "Finish your work," I said, and turning on my heel, I went back to the lodge.

Long after dark, long after I had begun to worry that she had run away or that the tiger had found her, Muskrat came back with the waterskin. In the very dim light of the lodge I saw that she had washed her face, which was red with cold, and although a greenish bruise was starting on her eye and cheekbone, she showed no sign of blood or crying. She didn't look at me but took her place by the door of the lodge, unfolded her ragged sleeping-skins, and lay down. A feeling of great relief came over me to see her; I would have liked to lie beside her, bringing my own sleeping-skin to cover us both, but like the walls of a lodge my anger stood around me. I lay in its center, my eyes open but not seeing, my thoughts dark.

17

As the days passed my silence and anger brought questions from everyone. Everyone noticed that I slept alone. At last Maral asked what was bothering me. I didn't dare tell Maral. But later, as I was following Andriki home on a reindeer trail after an unlucky day of hunting, he called the question over his shoulder. By then my trouble had grown so large I couldn't refuse to answer, so I did. Andriki turned his head to look at me, and through the frost on his beard he laughed aloud. "Hi, Kori!" he said. "You think we lie with your woman? Don't we have wives?"

"Then how is it you know so much about her?" I asked quietly, sure he wouldn't be able to laugh at that.

"What is it we know?" asked Andriki, puzzled.

So I reminded him of his whispered talk with Maral the day I had scouted for reindeer from the tree.

"Haven't we seen you?" cried Andriki. "Do we have to do as you do to know what our eyes see?"

This shamed me very much. I hadn't thought of people watching us. Yet I could see how they might—our outline in the sleeping-skins, the way our heads showed, could cause wonder.

"Many of her ways are different from our ways," I said stiffly.

"True!" cried Andriki. "She doesn't know the ways of Ohun. She has the ways of animals. Just that would stop me. You can remember what I'm telling you the next time you suspect me." He thought for a moment, perhaps about the hidden insults his words carried. "But if I'd found her, I'd lie with her," he added with an uncle's loyalty. "She's young and beautiful. Any man would want her. But she's yours. You found her. You took her! No man would lie with her after that, to risk starting bad trouble in a lodge in winter. No woman is worth fighting for, not in a lodge in winter! Anyway, who has the courage to fight a man like you?"

That he was trying to joke away my doubts made me happier than I had been since my suspicions began. In the quiet woods I followed Andriki in grateful silence.

The wind rose, carrying snow, and soon the snow came heavily. Andriki's feet disturbed a ptarmigan, who burst up, startling us. We both threw our spears and both missed it. Away it flew on white wings. We looked at our spears to make sure they were not broken.

"My wife and I were like you and Frogga," said Andriki as we walked on. "When we were married, she was very young. I had two other women while I was waiting for her. Both of them I still remember. You'll remember this muskrat-woman long after she's gone."

"Gone?" I asked. "Where will she go?"

"Why, I don't know," said Andriki, as if he himself were surprised by the idea. "I just said it, that's all. One of mine died. The other was a widow whose second husband came from the Black River. Now, I suppose, she lives there. But yours could stay with you. You could have many children by her. And more with Frogga." Andriki walked in silence for a while, a gray shape ahead of me in the falling snow. "I might marry again," I heard him saying. "I think about it. I think next summer I may take Hind to the Grass River to see if her parents will give me her sister. Hind would like her sister as a co-wife. You've never been to the Grass River. You and your Muskrat could come with me. Well? Will you?"

"Gladly," I said into the cloud of snow.

"Then maybe we'll do it. But first we must get through the winter," said Andriki.

Before long I could see that the snow would be heavy. All signs of the trail had vanished, and the air was thick with snowflakes slanting among the trees. Soon I couldn't see where we were and would have been lost if not for

Andriki. But he strode on as if he were following a mammoth trail in summer. The Bear was guiding him, as He guides all men and animals in their home country, as He would have guided me at Woman Lake where I had grown up, as He would someday guide me through the Narrow Lake country after I came to know it. But that day I couldn't even see how far we had come. All landmarks, even the lake, had vanished in the whirling snow. Suddenly Andriki went down on one knee in front of me and ducked through the door of the coldtrap. I had hardly seen the lodge before I was inside it. We were home.

Sitting close around the owners' fire, all the other people were waiting for us. Seeing from our faces that we had killed nothing, no one asked about our hunting.

The fire by the door had burned to ashes, but on the rear fire people had laid strips of frozen meat. I was glad to see it. At Uncle Bala's lodge the women became uneasy at the start of heavy storms, especially if the food supply was low. They would want everyone to eat little in order to save food. At Bala's lodge during snowstorms the men and women had arguments over eating, since the men needed strength to hunt after the storm. I saw that at Father's lodge the women were ready to cook and eat with the men. Only firewood would be a problem. We had very little, hardly enough for the night—not enough for two fires, not enough to last through a storm. I saw that someone, probably me, would be sent out for more in the morning.

But not until then. As the meat cooked, filling the lodge with its delicious smell, my eyes searched for Muskrat, for whom I now had the softest feeling. She had not after all lain with my uncles. My anger had been wrong. Now I wanted her to be happy, and when I saw her in the shadows behind the circle of people, looking past Pinesinger's shoulder at the roasting meat, I smiled a coaxing half-smile and watched her, ready for her to look up at me.

But she didn't take her eyes off the meat. When the meat began to burn and Lilan knocked it from the fire, beat out the flames, and passed pieces of it to each of us,

Muskrat's eyes followed each piece. Only the people around the fire got a share—Lilan must have forgotten Muskrat. As food grew scarce, forgetting Muskrat had grown easy. Only when I was given my piece—I was the last except the children to get any of the meat—did Muskrat's anxious eyes meet mine. What could I do? Keeping only a small part for myself, I handed the rest to her. She ate it as if she were starving. Had she been fed nothing?

That night I went to Muskrat's sleeping place beside the door, crawled under her sleeping-skins behind her, and slept with the warmth of her naked back against my chest and the smell of her hair in my nostrils. Muskrat seemed not to know I was there and gave no sign that she was either sorry or glad to have me in her bed. She was acting as if nothing had happened between us. Her body felt so good and I dreamed about her so much that I slept lightly, waking to think about each dream and listen to Muskrat breathing, then falling asleep to dream again.

I dreamed at last of a night thick with blowing snow and moonlight. I was on a plain I hadn't seen before, yet it didn't seem strange. Far away I saw a mare and got my spear ready. But the mare turned and saw me, then walked straight toward me. Her eyes were brown, and the windswept hair on her neck and tail was black and straight. I knew at once who she was: the mare I had killed at Uske's Spring, whose spirit had once before come to me in a dream. Since at that time she had come as a woman, I wasn't surprised when she spoke to me. I wasn't surprised that she called me by name or told me her name, which was Dabe Nore. By the name I knew she was really Muskrat, and had always been Muskrat, all that time. She turned her rump and stood waiting, looking back at me over her shoulder. I knew she wanted me to make her pregnant. So I tried, because I knew she was a person and not a mare. I woke from that dream wanting Muskrat. But dawn was coming. People would soon get up.

I crawled outside to relieve myself and found the cold air whirling with snow. No matter what the weather, the men of Father's family didn't get dressed just to relieve themselves. If they were naked when they felt the need, they went outside, as if weather meant nothing. It was almost a matter of pride with them to stand naked passing urine in a storm. So of course I did the same. After all, I wasn't a woman. Yet that morning I thought I would freeze before I finished. I thought my urine would freeze inside my body. Never had I felt such cold.

As best as I could I forced my urine, making the veins stand out on my forehead. Then I scrambled back to my place in Muskrat's deerskins, to be warmed by Muskrat's body. In the dim half-light that came through the snow cover on the smokeholes I saw through the cloud of my breath the long, motionless bedrolls of all the other people, and knew that no one else had any thought of getting up. No animals would move in this weather—we would not hunt. I knew I would have to go for firewood, but I also knew that time would have to pass before I could leave the bed to face the storm again. So I made up my mind to go for firewood later, when the wind died. When I was warm enough, I dozed.

But the wind blew harder as the day wore on. Snow made a drift along one wall of the coldtrap. The fire by the door was out, and its dead ashes were wet with snow from the smokehole. The owners' fire was cold. If a few banked coals still lived to make the smoke that hung below the ceiling, they gave no heat. Nearly naked, Frogga and Pirit crawled out of their parents' beds and, as if they didn't feel the cold, made a tiny lodge with nutshells, bone splinters, cinders from the fire, and bits of bark and twigs from the walls. The adults slept.

In the middle of the day I opened my eyes to see Lilan standing over our bed. She poked Muskrat with her foot and handed her a waterskin. Muskrat had to get up, get dressed, borrow Lilan's ax and digging stick, and go to the lake in the blinding snow to chop open the hole in the ice and fill the waterskin. She was gone a long time. Images of Rin's drowning wolf filled my mind. At last Muskrat came back, her hair and clothing plastered with snow. In silence she gave Lilan the full waterskin and crept into our bed, so cold that the touch of her icy body hurt me.

It shames me to remember that my first thought was to push her away. Instead I folded my arms around her and pulled her close, my legs around hers, my belly against her back. For a long time I held her so, while slowly she grew warmer. She fitted her shoulders against my chest so that as much of herself as possible touched me. My warmth relaxed her. In time I knew from her breathing that she had fallen asleep.

And so we lay there, she sleeping, I soothed by Rin's low voice talking to Frogga and Pirit, telling them how a man called Salmon stole food and fire from the First Man, Weevil. As Rin talked, the cold lodge groaned in the wind. No wonder Rin was thinking of food and fire.

In the coldtrap, still in hairy skin, lay all that was left of our meat—the head and feet of a reindeer, her staring eyes dusty, her upturned hooves showing the cracks and wear of much walking. But with the head and feet were pine nuts, four bags full, almost the weight of a person. The head and the pine nuts would feed us for several days. The pine nuts could be eaten without cooking, so for a while there was no need for us to worry about hunger, and there was really no need for fire.

So I told myself, unwilling to go into the storm for firewood. But by late afternoon people were bored and easily annoyed, and the lodge was so cold that not even the children would get up. The frost of our breath was coating the walls. I saw that I would have to try to get at least enough fuel to last through the night.

There was no reason that Muskrat should come with me, so I tried to slide out of bed quietly, not to wake her. But she woke and turned over, and when she saw me putting on my clothes she sat up, looked at me, and put the palm of her hand against my face. Her palm was as hard and rough as the sole of a foot, but her touch was gentle and her hand was warm. She looked at me very sweetly. Then she dressed herself and followed me into the storm.

Outside, the light was fading and the biting wind was dangerous—in this weather, hands, feet, and faces freeze. The windblown snow had drifted deep; the trails were buried. Wishing I had gone earlier, I looked around for Muskrat. She was right behind me, her eyes half shut against the wind, waiting for me to go on.

So I forced myself through the drifts, choosing the thickest parts of the woods, where some of the snow had been caught by the trees and the snow on the ground was not as deep as it was in the open. Of course most dead wood had long since been gathered, but we found some dry branches on the tree trunks. We also found cones, and at last, after we had walked almost in a circle, we found a small dead tree bare of needles, a tree we had overlooked. Try as we would, we couldn't push it over, and we were too cold to take the time to chop it. So we broke its branches, tied them together, and dragged the bundle home, breaking a new, short trail back to the lodge.

On the way, like ptarmigans bursting out of the snow, three wolves jumped up in front of us. They had dug dens for themselves in the snow to escape the storm, as wolves will. We had almost stepped on them. Very big they were, with yellow eyes in their gray, snowy faces. I had no spear, as they saw when they looked at us carefully before turning to leave. Of course they couldn't leave quickly but had to leap, breasting the deep snow like animals trying to run through deep water. What could we do but watch them escape us? When they were gone we pushed on through the storm to the large white mound that was the lodge, with a plume of snow blowing off the top but no smoke blowing from the smokeholes.

All this happened without a word between us. Before we took off our clothes and got back under Muskrat's sleeping-skins, I divided my small share of pine nuts and meat with her. She ate some of each gratefully and gave the rest back to me. We had no need of words.

The storm blew for three days. One night we heard the voice of a wolf, not far away, howling above the voice of the storm. Later we heard the feet of three wolves scrabbling on our roof. Surely they knew of the food in our coldtrap. The next day when I visited the latrine I found that three wolves had left there just before I came and had been eating our frozen feces. I warned the other people so they wouldn't let Pirit or Frogga go to the latrine alone. These wolves might run from adults, but they could hunt children.

Three times Muskrat went for water, and three times she and I together went for wood. On the third night the wind died and the dawn sent clear, bright light down the smokeholes. By then all animals would need to eat and would at last be moving, slowly leaving deep trails behind themselves in the snow. There could be no better time for hunting. We got dressed quickly, planning to follow any trails we crossed. Although walking in deep snow would be cold and tiring, we knew the deer would be colder and more tired. Our hunting could not fail.

To my surprise, while I was putting on my outer clothes Muskrat turned to me and pressed her palm flat, upright, against the midline of my chest. "Tashe," she said. The warmth of her hand crept slowly through my shirt. "Tashe," she said again, gently placing her palm on her own chest. What did she mean by it?

Half out of her sleeping-skins in the owners' end of the lodge, Pinesinger was cracking pine nuts with a stone. "Stepmother!" I called.

"Hi!" she answered, chewing.

"My woman told me something. Did you hear?"

"No," said Pinesinger.

"Will you ask what it was?"

Cracking another pine nut, Pinesinger called out a question in Muskrat's language. Muskrat answered, "Tashe."

"I don't know that word," said Pinesinger, eating.

Although it hurt me to humble myself before Pinesinger, I took Muskrat by the arm, led her through the icy lodge to Pinesinger, and pulled her down beside me so that we sat on our heels at Pinesinger's side. Perhaps afraid that we had come for a share, Pinesinger ate for a while longer, ignoring us.

"Stepmother," I began again, "will you please help me talk with this woman?"

Over her shoulder Pinesinger jabbered away for a while in Muskrat's language, getting a word from Muskrat every now and then.

"The word means 'chest,'" said Pinesinger at last. "That word 'tashe,' that's your chest."

"What about it?"

More jabbering. "Now she says it's 'fire,'" said Pinesinger. "'Heat,' maybe." But by then Muskrat was speaking and the other people of the lodge had stopped their own talk to listen.

"She's cold," said Rin. "She wants you to bring more firewood."

"She loves you," said Andriki. "She touches you, then herself. The word means 'fire.' She wants to say she loves you."

Pinesinger repeated Andriki's words to Muskrat, who looked down at her hands, displeased and ashamed. She didn't seem to love me. I felt sure she meant something else.

"Talk with her privately," I asked Pinesinger. "Try to find out what she really meant. Do this for me, this one thing, Stepmother. Please!"

Pinesinger gave me a look of impatience. "You captured her. Why don't you learn her speech? Then you could ask her yourself."

"Please?"

"I'll try," said Pinesinger, "but don't sit there staring. I'll ask later. Go away."

So I did. I left them together, hoping that Pinesinger would share food with Muskrat. I had already eaten mine and had none to give.

18

MUCH SNOW HAD FALLEN. THE COLD HAD BEEN SO GREAT THAT it wouldn't pack. Nothing larger than a hare could walk on it. Instead the snow stayed fine and soft, making animals and people force their way through it. Not even the strongest of us could walk far in the thigh-deep drifts without getting very tired, since we had to lift each foot high with every step. Even then we couldn't lift our feet above the snow, but had to drag them through it.

This kind of snow was both bad and good for hunting —bad because travel was hard for us, good because travel was also hard for the deer. Our plan was to make a big half-circle north of the river, looking for the fresh trails of animals. Because the Lodge Moon had come, with long dawns and long evenings and the sun over the horizon for just a short time each day, we planned to hunt until we killed something, no matter how long that would take.

We headed for a swamp north of the lodge, on a stream like our stream that fed the Hair River. Reindeer and moose stayed near the swamp, taking shelter in the growth of low spruce that ringed its edges and eating the tips of swamp willows that stood above the snow. Maral kept a hunting camp there, a high hollow cone of overlapping hemlock branches which made a space big enough for four men to sleep in, if they lay side by side. Covered with snow and with men inside, this shelter could be almost too warm. In it Maral kept firesticks, a hafted ax, some spearpoints, and a store of firewood.

By dusk, when we saw the tip of the shelter against the red evening sky, we had found only the tracks of a pack of wolves who were also going to the swamp, one behind the other, taking turns breaking trail just as people do. We couldn't help but feel disappointed, to find no tracks but wolves' tracks. But thanks to the trail the wolves had broken, we reached Maral's shelter before night.

The night was long and moonlit—the round Lodge Moon was balancing the sun. For our meal we had only the scraps of dried meat we had brought with us and some frozen strips of inner bark peeled off a young larch tree. The bark is said to take away hunger. Perhaps it does for some; it didn't for me.

In the morning we sang, praying to the Bear to give us food. Then, with Maral leading us, we circled the swamp. Here the snow was very light but almost waist deep, so that Maral was sweating after a very short time of pushing through it. Soon Andriki took Maral's place in the lead and Maral took my place at the end of the line. In this way we took turns breaking trail and walking last in the path made by the others. We stopped to rest many times, being hungry and not at full strength. Often in winter one must work hard on an empty stomach, yet one never gets used to it.

Because we were hunting and also saving our strength, we didn't talk as we walked, but when we stopped to rest we talked a little, softly. We had been following a ridge where no trees grew, where the wind had blown away most of the snow, and where we could see far in all directions—white snow, gray sky, and black spruce trees. We looked for plumes of snow, which like dust can be caused by the movements of animals. But against the vast white landscape and gray sky a plume of snow would have been hard to see.

As we rested we spoke of the snow, of how it was much deeper than usual, deeper than I had ever seen. Since it had come in the early part of winter, it would stay. Also we spoke of the trail we were making with such effort. The wind would soon blow snow to fill it in, unless we used it often. We planned to use it. Other animals would also use it, Maral pointed out. This would be good and bad for us—good because we could hunt the animals with hooves, bad because our open trail would be helping the wolves and even the tiger, who also hunted animals with hooves. Marten reminded us that a single well-worn trail would bring hunting animals straight to our lodge.

"Wolves already know our lodge," said Andriki. "How can we show them what they already know?"

"I wasn't thinking of wolves," said Marten.

"Perhaps you were thinking of the Lily," said Andriki.

"That one," said Maral. "He makes his own trails." To me he said, "If enough snow falls that we must make trails, we find that he has also made trails. Like us, he keeps his open. And although it is true that he uses ours, we use his. They lead where ours would lead. He thinks like a man, the Lily."

"He eats like a man too," said Andriki. "He eats like many men. All of us here could fill our bellies on just one of his meals."

"Since we respect him," said Marten, "let's not speak of his meals."

"If I had food, I would share with him," said Andriki.

Struck by the thought, I guessed that Andriki was saying something that would please the Lily if he should happen to be nearby, listening to us. "Hona," I added. "I too."

"There are four of us here, hunting for many hungry women," said Maral. "Are we going to rest all day?"

We got to our feet, brushed the snow from our clothing, and, choosing a place we could see from the ridge, a distant, low-growing thicket where roe deer or reindeer might have sheltered from the storm, we went on.

As we moved down the slope, a raven called. Soon two ravens flew above us, both calling. They who follow hunters, they were calling their kinsmen, but what good would that do them if they frightened our prey? Marten and Maral kept walking, ignoring them while they soared above us through the sky. But I looked up at them. Why, I wondered, were they excited? High up, they could see things we knew nothing about. They knew something.

Sure enough, in the thicket we found a long trail left by reindeer. They had used the thicket to shelter from the storm, and when the snow had stopped they had gone into the swamp in single file. Breasting the snow, following in each other's footsteps, they had packed their trail so hard we could easily walk on it. So we did, not minding the ravens or worrying too much about being quiet. The herd hadn't made this trail easily, and since we were behind the deer, they couldn't use their trail to escape. In fact we wanted to chase them forward, to founder them in the snow. Heads up, eyes open, we hurried on, first Maral, then Andriki, then Marten, then me. Now and then we passed a place where the deer had dug for moss. At last we found dung that wasn't even frozen. We were so near we could almost taste the meat.

Suddenly Maral stopped. We all stopped, even the two ravens, who landed behind us in silence on the very tops of two trees. We looked. There in the open woods ahead we saw the rumps and antlers of many reindeer. They were kneeling, using their faces and brow tines to dig the snow. They seemed hungry, and so they should be, kept from food for three days by the storm. Yet it cost them their lives, that hunger, since all were eating. None were watching for danger, and none saw us.

Motioning us to wait, Maral moved quietly toward a large doe. Quiet as he was, she heard him, raised her head, and whistled an alarm. Maral's spear struck high in her groin, making her kick upward. The ravens screamed. The other deer tried to run, but the snow was too deep. Instead they plunged helplessly in different directions.

I had time to choose the fattest of them. Another doe, she was. I ran up behind her in the trail she had packed for me, trying to step on her footprints, and when she turned to face me, perhaps to aim a kick at me, I threw my spear. I was so close that it hit her very hard, the point sinking deep behind her collarbone. Her knees buckled and she went down, blood pouring from her wound, bright red on the snow. All around me deer were crying. Mine fell dead, but Maral's gut-wounded doe was still moaning as he tried to cut her throat. So too were the deer speared by Andriki and Marten. Hearing something behind me, I turned and saw a doe plunging toward the trail. As hard as I could, I threw my second spear. Ng! I hit, but in the belly. More kicking. I should have led her more, but I hadn't guessed her speed. Jerking my first spear free from the dead reindeer's side, I chased the struggling doe, leaping through the snow until I overtook her, then pushed the spear hard into her rib cage. Speared twice, she was as good as dead. She fell.

Six deer, all females, lay in the snow. One was Maral's, two were Andriki's, one was Marten's, and two were mine. Even though the wind stirred their soft hair, they seemed very still—six heavy bodies on their sides in the long shadows of the trees. What would we do with so much meat?

First we would eat. While Maral and Marten rolled a fire, I opened the belly of my first deer and took out her liver. I did this with bare hands, and my fingers almost froze. While the meat cooked, the ravens flew down to eat the scraps and the quickly freezing clots and even the bloody snow. Somehow other ravens heard them or saw them, and soon many ravens were eating.

When the meat was ready, we ate too. Hot meat! Strength from it went all through me. My happiness came. My pride came, since I had killed so much of it.

"Well, Brother," said Andriki to Maral, "how will we get this home?"

"We can't cover it," said Maral. "It's too much for us to carry, and I see no tall trees. Marten should go get the women. That's the only way. The trail is packed solid for him. He'll travel very quickly on it. He'll reach the lodge by night and bring the women back in the morning. So, Marten. You'll reach the lodge by dark if you go now."

"I agree," said Marten. "I'm going."

"Take meat with you," said Maral. "The women will be angry if you don't take them meat."

But Marten was already skinning the deer he had killed. "I will," he said. "I'm afraid of those women."

We helped him skin the deer and cut enough meat to make a large load. He left. I didn't envy him, setting off alone with the smell of fresh meat making a cloud around him.

"Look at the sun," said Maral later. We did. It was round and red, like a fire in the trees. "Feel the cold coming. We must work fast before these deer freeze.

Skins off, meat into strips. Kori, you get wood while the daylight lasts. We may fight for our meat before morning."

Andriki looked around at all the carcasses. "There's much work here," he said.

"Let's begin," said Maral.

So we began. Since no one had gathered wood in this place before, or not for a long time, there was lots of it, easily found. Before the sun reached its resting place I had made a large pile of it—enough, I thought, for the night. "More, Kori," said Maral. "We may want firelight tonight." So in the dusk, as the woods grew dim and blue, I gathered more, the same amount again. Then I helped Maral and Andriki, and among us we skinned all the deer except for the feet and heads, scraping the hides quickly and roughly and rolling them up so they could be carried after they froze.

Two hides, it came to me, were mine. I wanted to give them to Muskrat, because I knew how happy they would make her. In fact, though, they were my wife's share of the hunting. I would have to give them to Frogga. Since Frogga was too young to need them, her mother was sure to take them instead. Then, since the hide of Maral's deer would belong to his first wife, his second wife might give him one of Frogga's hides so that he would have a deerskin like the rest of his family. As for my deer, the best meat from the hind legs would go to Frogga's family. Meat from the front legs and neck would go to Rin and Waxwing. Through Waxwing I would be giving to Marten, he with a large reindeer of his own. Much of the rest of the meat was already promised in return for clothing that had been given to Muskrat when she first came. I would have liked to take Muskrat something of her own, but I didn't see what it would be. We hunt for our in-laws, truly.

The long blue twilight began to fade, and in the east the moon rose, yellow-white with faint, dark markings on it, for all the world like a skinned carcass. The ravens had gone long ago. I wondered if they were roosting in the trees—I hadn't seen them leaving.

On the bloodstained moonlit snow the naked carcasses

lay freezing. "They'll soon be solid," said Maral. "We don't have time to make strips of all the meat. For the rest, just cut the joints. Kori, start with her." Maral pointed with his lips at the first deer I had killed. "Cut the hind legs at the hip and knee. Cut the ribs at two places. Cut the neck separately. Do the legs first. Leave the guts to the last. There's still heat in the guts." So I did as he told me, spreading out the joints and pieces so they wouldn't freeze together, squeezing the feces from the gut, leaving the gall and rumen behind on the snow.

At last we were finished. The firelight showed Andriki and Maral dark with blood stuck in their beards and smeared on their clothes and their hands and faces. I looked at my hands as I warmed them over the fire and saw that I was filthy too.

"Hi," said Maral, stretching and looking around. "We should bring everything near and cover it with firewood. Look there."

We looked. A black shadow moved stealthily among some of the guts. Maral threw some snow. As the shadow turned, its eyes flashed red. It was a marten. It ran.

So our long night began. We had no thought of sleeping, because we had to keep watch. What would we have told the women if we had slept while animals ate our meat?

Our fire was sheltered by a growth of low spruce trees, but to give us more warmth Maral and Andriki made a long lean-to of branches, which I packed tight with snow on the outside and piles of our frozen meat on the inside. When the wall was finished, it broke the freezing night wind and reflected the heat of the fire. Between us and the wall, our meat was safe even from small robbers like sables, who, low to the ground and hidden in shadow, might otherwise be filling their bellies where we couldn't see.

Comfortable in the shelter, we cooked and ate and then cooked more, eating slowly, sighing as we grew full. The deer were still fat from their summer feeding. We did not forget to cut some fat for the Bear, who had made our hunting possible. This offering we laid on the fire; then we sat quietly, watching it burn. In the lodge we would have sung to praise the Bear, to wake Him so that He could get His gift, but out here in the dark woods, with the Lily waiting somewhere, crouching, listening, we thought to let the smell of the fat wake the Bear. There would be time later to give a song.

The heat of the fire was very good; the meat was even better. Andriki and Maral told hunting stories and stories about themselves when they were boys. The stories carried my thoughts far away to a time gone by, to a wide, dark wood of spruce and birch on a west-flowing stream that fed the Hair. Father, his three brothers, and Rin grew up there. The four boys did daring things when they were young! Rin was good, but the boys took risks and didn't mind punishment.

Warmed by the fire and full of meat, with my uncles' laughter in my ears and my mind's eye filled with the doings of long ago, I laughed too. As soon as one of my uncles finished a story, I asked for more. "Who but Kori would want to hear these old tales of ours?" asked Maral.

"Tell him how you made Uncle Hooked Gandre throw his spear into a wasps' nest," said Andriki.

So he did. Yet as we laughed, we saw a pair of huge green eyes shining beyond the firelight, and we stopped laughing and stood up. The eyes watched. We cupped our hands under our chins so we could see over the firelight into the dark woods beyond. There some large animals were gathered—great black shadows in the shadows of the trees. One of them watched us steadily, but now and then several would look at us together, and their eyes too would flame green. "Wolves," said Andriki.

I raised my spear, but Andriki caught the shaft. "Wait," he said. "They're eating rumen. We don't mind that."

"Next they'll try to get the meat," I said.

"Then we'll spear them," said Andriki.

"While they're here," said Maral, "they watch the woods. Better than we, they know what walks there."

I knew Maral was speaking of the Lily, and I quietly lowered my spear. We sat down again, with our hands cupped under our chins, and watched the wolves move from place to place where the six dead deer had lain. The wolves were finding things to eat—the rumens, the gallbladders, and the bloody snow.

In time they sat in a half-circle, facing us. The moon cast their shadows on the snow. We could just make out their gray faces, and see how their green eyes roamed over the meat behind us. I thought of Father and Andriki together at the Fire River, and how they with their pale eyes had sat across the fire from its owner, Uncle Bala, as visiting hunters will. If the wolves had been nearer the fire, they would have been like visiting hunters. Like visitors, they knew us, since these were the wolves who stayed near the lodge. No wonder they had found us, on our well-packed trail. When crossing the trail, they could have learned of Marten on his way home with meat, and then they could have backtracked him to find the carcass.

They hadn't watched us very long before their headman raised his chin slightly and sang a high, clear call that lifted quickly, broke, and fell slowly. As it ended, all the other wolves joined, and all together their voices rose and fell. They sang a long time, some voices high, others low, some steady, some trembling, some breaking. Up to the moon they threw their song, so that the sky filled with it and the woods filled with it—a song so loud, so pure, so perfect that tears stung my eyes from its beauty. These wolves had eaten only shit and rumen, yet they sang. Think of it!

As suddenly as they began, they stopped. Then they were standing on their long legs, on their big feet, they were giving their rough coats a little shake, they were sneezing lightly, they were nosing each other's faces, and they were gone. They were gone, leaving nothing behind but moonlight and the shadows of trees on the trampled snow at the far side of the fire, nothing but the empty feeling that came behind their singing, nothing but the three of us to watch for the Lily.

"Maybe we should have given them something. They might have stayed," I said. "The lungs, maybe."

From the tone of Andriki's voice when he answered, I saw that he too had been much taken with the song. "You thought of that too late," he said. "They're gone. But why did they stop here? They'll have no trouble finding the reindeer that escaped us. They have the trail to lead them, and they'll drive the deer into deep snow. Why would they want lungs? They'll soon have a whole reindeer. Maybe more."

But I hardly heard Andriki. I was wishing we had given the feet to the wolves. There were more than enough feet, and most likely we would be leaving them behind anyway. The feet would be the last things we would put on our loads. "They might have stayed if we had given the hooves," I said. "As it is, they'll probably get them after we leave. Just the chewing would take a long time."

"You must have been talking with your father," said Maral. "He's the one who likes to give the wolves something to eat."

"Perhaps they'll come back," said Andriki. "I would give them the hooves, at least of my deer."

"I too," I said. So we dug through the pile of frozen meat until we found the hooves belonging to me and Andriki. We tossed them into a pile, sure of most of them. But two hooves were in doubt. Both were the right rear, but which was mine and which was Marten's? We added both, ready to throw all to the wolves when they came back.

But they didn't come back. The moon sank low. All night we waited, feeding the fire, cooking and eating, thinking of the Lily but not speaking of him, and when the sky began to turn gray before morning we heard the wolves sing again, but far away.

As the sun came, we sang too, praising the Bear for letting us kill six reindeer and not lose any of the meat.

> You whose fire burns in the sunrise,
> You whose fire burns in the sunset,
> You whose fire burns all day across the sky,
> As You love hunters,
> Know we are hunters.
> As we gave You fat,
> Now make us fat.
> Give us life!
> Do not kill us!
> Hona!

With the sun came the ravens, who seemed disappointed to find nothing to eat within their reach. Even the bloody snow had been eaten. Soon they flew off, searching in the direction from which we had heard the wolves. Perhaps they saw the wolves on a carcass.

Late in the morning Marten came back with all the women except Waxwing, Truht, and Pinesinger—they who would soon give birth. Much as the women must have eaten the night before, they sat down to cook again right away. Muskrat held back, looking at me. From the belly meat of one of my deer, the hunter's own portion, I cut many strips for her and put them on the fire. Even before they were cooked she took some and began to eat hungrily. Afraid she might choke, I frowned at her and tried to take the strips back, to feed them to her slowly. She thought I was refusing her, and looked at me almost with terror. Her fear shamed me. I wondered if she had eaten the day before, if people had shared with her. I suppose there was no real reason anyone should have shared. I would have liked to ask her quietly, inconspicuously, but without Pinesinger's help I couldn't, since I would have to use loud, simple words and big gestures.

When the women had finished eating, they brushed the fat and ashes from their hands and faces and stood up. We helped one another make large packs of the meat, and then helped one another lift the packs into place on our backs. With so many of us, we didn't have to leave meat behind, not even the hooves. Maral's son, Ako, carried almost a man's load, and even Andriki's little daughter, Pirit, carried a small pack with one round reindeer hoof sticking out of it. In single file, over the well-trampled trail, we went home.

That night, with the mounds of meat stored safely in the coldtrap but with only a small supply of wood, which Ako, Muskrat, and I had had to gather as best we could at the end of the day, we cooked meat again, using only one fire. As the fire was in the owners' end of the lodge, I felt comfortable sitting close beside it.

"Woman!" I called to Muskrat at the far end of the lodge. She stood up and came to see what I wanted. I told her to cut belly meat from my share so I could cook.

"Knife," she said. So I gave her my knife. She was gone a long time. At last I saw her standing behind everyone, trying to catch my eye, and when she did, she gave me a handful of frozen strips over the heads of all the people. I put them on the fire, and when they were cooked I called her again. "Woman! Come and eat." Again she stood behind the people. I passed her the cooked strips on the end of a forked stick. "For you," I said, smiling at her.

Before taking the meat, Muskrat made a fist and hit herself on the breastbone. Then she hit herself between the eyes. Then she bent a knee, lowering her whole body. "Sank," she said.

It reminded me of her word "tashe." "Stepmother," I said to Pinesinger, who was sitting right beside me, "do you remember Muskrat's word 'tashe'? Did you find what it means?"

"Yes," said Pinesinger. "It has no meaning."

"No meaning? Then why did she use it?"

"Perhaps it has meaning to her, but not to us. Her people call a place on their bodies 'tashe.' There's no such place. They think there is, though, here in the middle, on the chest and belly. If her people feel warmth there, 'tashe' is what they call the warmth. A woman says 'tashe' when she holds a baby. The warm feeling of the baby is 'tashe.' It makes people happy. When your woman said 'tashe' to you, she meant you felt 'tashe' while you slept in her bed. The 'tashe' came from her body. She's glad you became happy from that, because she's pregnant. You frightened her when you became angry, when you hit her. She told me how you hit her. She thought because we had so little food, you would drive her away. She wants to go, but if you forced her out now she would die in the snow."

Later, as I lay in bed with my arms around Muskrat, under her breasts, with my belly against her back, as I listened to her quiet, even breathing, I was too joyful to sleep. The woman in my arms was pregnant! And by me. A child gotten in the fall is born the next summer—she would bear this child on Father's summergrounds. I remembered the sound of children's voices echoing in Father's shadowy cave. Soon my child might be among the others. That pleased me.

Yet Muskrat wanted to leave. That worried me. I told myself I wouldn't let her, I'd stop her. But I didn't want to have to stop her. I wanted her to stay willingly. If she learned our speech, I told myself, if she saw how well I treated her, if she learned how to live as we live, with people's ways, not animals' ways, she would stay willingly. My woman. My child. I was happy!

19

THE LODGE MOON PASSED SLOWLY, WITH MUCH COLD AND snow. The meat of the six reindeer, piled frozen in the coldtrap, helped us live, but we kept hunting. We worked to keep the trails open, only to find wolves using them to reach the deer before we could. When wolves find deer, they choose one to kill and eat to the last scrap of offal but scatter the others widely and make them wary and shy. Thinking to make warm clothes for Muskrat, she and I set snares for the wolves. Then we learned that people had been trying for years to snare them. Maral said that in the past people had snared wolves, and the year before a snare of his had caught a young wolf, but the older wolves seemed to have learned about snares. We wouldn't succeed, he told us.

He was right. Instead of getting caught, as all other animals seemed to, these wolves sprang our triggers, ate our baits, and often ate our sinew nooses as well. If they didn't eat the nooses, they bit through them, ruining them, since a noose with knots doesn't work. Muskrat knew much about snaring, but these wolves stopped her. If she set out a line of snares, the wolves tracked her to get the baits or the animals caught in the snares. Then they took to tracking her anyway, just in case she was snaring. Where she would urinate, they would urinate. Why?

The wolves didn't seem to care that they were angering us. They camped near our lodge as always, digging deep holes in the snow and letting more snow bury them, so that they slept within hearing distance but sheltered from the wind and hidden from our sight. At night we sometimes heard their claws scratching on the roof, then heard them at the smokeholes, sniffing, digging, whining. But by the time we could get through the coldtrap with our spears, they would be gone. We had to watch Frogga and Pirit carefully, especially at the latrine. Small children crouching down put themselves in danger.

Yet we weren't completely sorry that the wolves chose to live where we lived. When they were near, they gave warnings. To be sure, their warnings were meant not for us but for each other, yet when we heard the warnings we took care.

In the Hunger Moon, the Lily came back to Narrow Lake to hunt the deer. At first we didn't know it, and we were more than surprised to find his footprints on our trails. After that we began to hear him roaring at night, frightening us and keeping us awake. He then took to squirting urine on the snow, as if he were trying to tell us something. He left enormous hairy scats beside his terrifying footprints on our trails. We were so frightened of him that we used our own trails with great care.

The ravens loved him. Whenever they found him, they showed their happiness in the sound of their calls and in the way they flew, as if they were playing. They even flew upside down. Often we could tell where he was because of ravens—if we saw two or three circling, or waiting in trees, or following something, we stayed away from that place.

Like the ravens, the wolves also seemed to keep track of him. If he came near the lodge when they were camping there, one of them might bark just once. The bark had a sound of its own to it—"Hi! Look there!" it seemed to say. We understood the meaning of that bark as well as the other wolves did. If we heard it, we guessed that the Lily was near.

When the Hunger Moon was new, Maral, Andriki, Marten, and I saw two reindeer crossing the ice on Narrow Lake, which the wind had cleared of snow. They were making for a trail on the north bank. We hurried to meet them, reached the trail before they did, waited in the snowdrifts, and speared them both. That night we ate heavily. When we could eat no more, we burned fat for the spirit of the lodge and sang to praise the Bear.

Because Andriki and I had together speared one of the reindeer, and because we couldn't be sure which spear had killed, we divided the hunter's portions. This meant we had to cut the hide. Thus Muskrat got some reindeer skin after all, since Lilan and Frogga already had skins to scrape and soften and didn't at the time want part of a cut skin. Muskrat surprised us by making strips of the hide.

As the Hunger Moon grew round, the sky became hazy without growing warm, and we saw that more heavy snow was coming. The full moon wore a hood of fox fur, and the next day we looked up to see two suns. Rin said they were the Woman Ohun and Her stillborn child, come to warn us that the Bear was no longer helping us but hunting us and that we should pay close attention to the food in our coldtrap, eating it sparingly lest we starve.

That night, in cold silence, snow began to fall. By morning the trees and the lodge were covered. By night of the next day we could hardly find the trails. The deer left. Perhaps they had known the snow was coming. The wolves and the tiger must have followed them. Where the animals went we didn't know, because the falling snow covered their footprints.

After that we heard no voices at night but the *hruhu* of an owl. Then we began to see a large gray owl hunting in the daytime, even though he was afraid of the ravens, who hated him. The women asked each other what it meant, this daytime hunting. They said the owl could be waiting for the death of one of us, searching for one of our spirits, as if he wanted to guide a spirit to its lineage in the Camps of the Dead. That the women should have such thoughts showed they were frightened.

Should we all have been frightened? I didn't know. The country, the snow, and the ways of the deer were all new to me. I had never seen so much snow before. By Woman Lake, where Uncle Bala spent the winter, snow was seldom more than dust, and not in my memory had the deer left Uncle Bala's winterground. But Narrow Lake was Father's country. The men who knew it didn't seem afraid of anything, not of the deep snow, not even of the Lily. My uncles spoke of our going on a long winter hunt, walking until we found the deer, staying until we killed something. I liked that. The women's fears seemed pointless, childish, making the rest of us think of death when we should be thinking of hunting. The women's reasoning reminded me of my mother.

"I say the owl hunts in the daytime because he can't hunt now," I dared to say at last to Aunt Rin and the other women one night as we sat in the lodge. "Think of his pellets. They have the hair and teeth and bones of voles and weasels—night animals. Yet now these animals are under the snow, where he can't find them. His death, not ours, is worrying him. He has to hunt squirrels. Maybe he doesn't know how to do it."

"Listen to Knows Everything," said Rin scornfully, "here for his first winter. Even the owl isn't used to this much snow. And do you think the rest of us have nothing to do but pick apart owl pellets?"

Of all the women, only Muskrat seemed unworried. Of course, she couldn't tell us if she was worried. But she didn't seem worried. She went on with her usual work in her usual way, as if nothing had changed.

One day when I was gathering wood I saw Muskrat crossing the lake, not by the trail but by a new way, walking spread-legged on top of the snow. In one hand she carried a dead ptarmigan. I then saw two strange things tied to the bottoms of her feet. When she came near, I stopped her and made her show me. The things were frames made of sticks, with strips of reindeer hide like nets inside the frames. To make them she had cut the hide I had given her. The things were for walking on snow. With them on her feet, she had walked on the surface like a lynx or a ptarmigan, and hadn't sunk with each step like deer or a person. I was impressed. Had my woman thought of something so clever?

That night I held up one of the things and boasted about Muskrat to the other people in the lodge. Maral and Andriki laughed at me. "Your woman is good, I don't doubt," said Maral. "Perhaps she will gather more wood for the lodge, now that she can walk on the snow."

His mocking tone annoyed me. "Let me show you what she brought," I said, looking around for the ptarmigan. But all I saw was a pile of feathers and, burning in the fire, a few small bones. In the dark shadows by the door sat Muskrat with greasy lips. She had eaten the ptarmigan!

My uncles saw this too. "Where is the thing she brought, Kori?" asked Maral. "Show us."

"She ate it," said Rin scornfully. To Muskrat she said, "Are you an animal, that you eat alone?" To me she said, "Aren't you going to teach her that food is shared? You brought her here. Yet all of us must live with her. We are people, Kori. We won't live with animals. What kind of children will you get on this Muskrat? Will they also eat as she eats, offering nothing to anyone?"

Dismayed, I looked at Muskrat. She too looked dismayed. Perhaps she had heard her name. Anyway, she knew we were speaking of her and the ptarmigan. As she wiped the traces of eating from her mouth, her eyes searched mine, as if she were asking, "Now what have I done?"

I couldn't blame her. For one thing, we already knew that she didn't understand how people should act. Until she learned speech, we couldn't teach her how to act better. For another thing, although each and every one of our people, even the smallest children, always shared everything, some people didn't always share with Muskrat. Too often she was left out of the sharing. This was natural enough; Muskrat was different. Also she was shy. If she was left out, she wouldn't remind us, as anyone else surely would. But if other people didn't share with her, she might wonder why she should share with them. What was more—as the women should have remembered—Muskrat was pregnant, so perhaps she was unusually hungry, especially since she wasn't always fed.

I almost spoke these thoughts to Maral. But he had turned away, angry with me because of Muskrat. So I saw how she had shamed me, and I said nothing.

Before going on a long trip to hunt deer, we thought we should first try asking the Bear to bring the deer back. One night we rubbed ourselves with ocher and sang. If any of us could have tranced, we would have done it, so that the trancer's spirit could have asked help from the Bear. But none of us knew how to trance—Father was the shaman. Without him we could only pray. "The Lily is hunting where we hunt. Do not help him," we begged. "Favor us. Give us the deer. Kill one and let us find the corpse. Hear how we respect You, Great Brown Leader, Owner of Hunting, Voice of the Storm."

The Bear heard us. By the time we were sucking the bones and picking the hooves and skulls of the two reindeer, storm winds had packed the snow so hard that animals with wide feet could walk on the surface. A few small herds of reindeer came into our woods again, on their large round hooves. The deer couldn't paw down through the snow for the lichen, but the snow was so deep that when it was packed they could stand on it, which put them nearer the branches of the trees. These they browsed down to the underbark. One day we killed three of them, so we suddenly had plenty to eat.

That same day, while we were hunting, Waxwing had her baby. Back from our hunting, we went into the lodge one behind the other as we always did, waiting for the women to notice that we were dragging a great deal of meat. Yet that day it was we who noticed that something had changed. I happened to be first to crawl down the coldtrap, and as I stood up, I felt the difference. Wondering, I looked around the dark lodge at the shadowy faces of all the women and saw their dark eyes watching me. No one spoke, yet as if lightning had struck nearby, the air seemed changed. Behind me came Maral, then

Andriki, then Marten, each in turn pausing as he too sensed something new.

But none of the women spoke, so we sat down as if everything were the same and we had sensed nothing. Presently we heard Rin and her son-in-law, Marten, murmuring together, so we guessed what it was that was new. The baby was a girl. As I think back about this child, I can't say that I remember ever having seen her. She died in her first year, killed by Ohun, but before that Waxwing kept her in her shirt. Now and then we heard her tiny voice. We also heard Waxwing talking to her. But she stayed among us so short a time, she returned so quickly to the people of her lineage in the Camps of the Dead, that I for one never knew the shape of her face or the color of her hair. And she was of Father's lineage.

Soon after the birth of this tiny kinswoman of Father's, a baby was born to Truht and Maral. This baby too was a girl and was my wife Frogga's half-sister, yet unlike Waxwing's baby, this one seemed almost a stranger. She and Truht were the only members of their lineage I ever met or knew. But so it always was with women and lineages, and so it will always be. Truht's child was not her first—the Woman Ohun had killed the others—but from bearing the others Truht had learned how birthing was done. Although she gave birth at night, she managed so quietly that I woke only enough to know that something was happening in the lodge, something quiet— women's business, a dreaming child perhaps, but nothing worrisome. Beside me, Muskrat was awake and listening to something, that much I knew. During the night someone went outside—Lilan, it was. Later she came back. Some people put wood on the fire and sat talking in low voices, and that was all.

The next day Truht slept a long time, rolled in her deerskins. When I happened to sit near her, I thought I might have heard faint suckling. Otherwise this little girl, like Waxwing's, was almost perfectly quiet. Days passed before I saw her. Unlike Waxwing's baby, though, this girl lived a long time, and because she was born in the depth of winter she was years later given the animal name of Deaf-Grouse, in honor of the Bear.

Meanwhile, almost every night during the length of the Hunger Moon Pinesinger kept saying that her baby was coming. More times than I can really remember, those of us at the owners' fire were shaken out of our sleep and told to move to the fire by the door. Rin scolded me for rudeness when I once asked no one in particular why Pinesinger couldn't do as other women did and not bother the rest of us so often. But I suppose she couldn't help it. If she thought her baby was coming, she thought it was coming. She lacked experience, and since the baby was her first and could take a long time, there could be no real question of her trying to birth it privately. Anyway, Pinesinger was not one to try birthing outside in winter. Instead, when Pinesinger's real pains started—a fact we all quickly learned, since she seemed to want to be as childish as possible about her discomfort—the men almost by habit got up to leave the owners' fire and crowd together by the door. Pinesinger had asked this of us so often we were used to it.

Learning at last the true meaning of birthing, Pinesinger complained and cried. Rin and Truht sat with her and gave her a stick to bite. Pinesinger threw the stick into the fire. Later I overheard her tearfully asking Rin to make the rest of us leave the lodge! "Be calm," said Rin soothingly. "In time this will end." Soon Lilan and Waxwing joined them, taking Frogga. Hind must have felt left out, because she got up and joined them too, followed by little Pirit, leaving only Muskrat at the men's fire.

I at least was glad to be far away from Pinesinger. Hunched at the crowded fire by the door, with Andriki's big shoulders pressing against one side of me, making me press down on Ako, I used the time to sharpen my spear. With Andriki's antler chisel I slowly took off one tiny piece of flint after another, making the blade very, very sharp, trying not to think of fathering that baby nor to hear Pinesinger's moans.

Instead I tried to think of something very exciting, to take my mind off Pinesinger. Lovemaking was always exciting, but as Pinesinger's cries grew from moans to shrieks, thoughts of lovemaking didn't seem sensible. I tried to think of hunting. Yet when Pinesinger began to scream, "Ohun! Kill me!" I shut my eyes and blocked my ears and could think only of birth.

For I had seen birth. I wished I had not. What I had seen made me fear it just as the women feared the deep snow. I had been with my mother when she gave birth to my sister. That sister didn't stay among the living very long. In fact, as Waxwing's baby would one day die young, this little sister of mine had died before she was named. But when she was born and while she lived, we were on Uncle Bala's summergrounds at the Fire River.

In those days I was still too young to stay with other children, so Mother took me with her wherever she went. One day she left the other women to dig sedge roots out of sight of anyone else, by herself, far away. I didn't understand why. Of course I stayed near her, hunting beetles while she worked.

Suddenly, without a word of warning, she seized me by the arm and dragged me into a fireberry thicket, where she shocked me by taking off her trousers. Mother always seemed to have her mind on her own affairs and never explained anything, so I was used to sudden, unexpected things, but this time I felt bewildered, because she seemed almost frantic. For one thing, she was passing huge amounts of urine, as if she didn't even know. The ground and her feet were soaked with it, and still she passed more. Meanwhile she was gasping, panting, and aimlessly brushing her face as if her hair were in her eyes.

I was frightened and wanted to run, but in a tight, angry voice she told me I would have to sit down and wait. For a while I obeyed. Squatting, she crossed her arms on her knees and leaned her forehead on her arms, her jaw trembling, her eyes shut, her body shuddering as if she were terribly cold. She then began to grunt as if she were together with my stepfather or were trying to move her bowels. I stood up to go. But snatching my arm, she jerked me down hard and held me with a grasp so tight her nails sank in my flesh. My hand went numb. I cried, but she didn't hear. Angrily I tried to pry open her fingers, but she was too strong for me. In the end there was nothing I could do. I tried not to look at her, but I couldn't help myself. At last I stared openly at her parted, naked thighs, at the thatch of wet pubic hair between them, and at the crawling skin of her huge bare belly, which had begun to ripple like a lake.

For a very long time Mother crouched without moving or speaking, one hand over her eyes and the other clutching my arm. When I tried to tell her she was hurting me, she just squeezed harder. Later she began to drool, then moan.

"Mother! Let me go!" I cried.

"Then stay still," she said between her teeth.

"I will," I promised.

"If you don't, I'll whip you," she said. So I obeyed.

Time passed. For a while she lay down. I tried stroking her arm, but she didn't seem to feel my touch. Later I found and picked a few ripe fireberries for her. She didn't see them, so I tried to put them in her mouth. She knocked them to the ground. I ate them. Then I tried singing to her, although I wasn't sure she could hear. At last she sat up again, her elbows on her knees, her hands clasped, her forehead resting on them, and in this way we waited together, she with her eyes shut, moaning and snarling to herself, I singing and looking around.

This happened during the Grass Moon, when the days were long. We went into the thicket in the late morning, but we stayed so long I began to worry that night and lions would find us. I was very thirsty. The sun moved down until its red light shone through the long grass, until the air turned cool. I saw swifts far above us in the yellow sky, and heard a partridge calling in the thicket: *kriik, kriik,* its summer song. Then I felt something wet on my foot, and looking down, I saw blood on the ground. "Mother! There's blood!" I whispered. "I want to go home."

"Keep still," she gasped. "Not long now." Suddenly she changed position, so that she squatted on her hands and feet, leaning her great belly between her knees with her back arched and her head up, like a frog about to leap, and I saw a baby's head bulging out of her, a baby's head with wet, black hair, with its mouth open and its eyes shut. Terribly frightened and excited too, I stared.

Mother reached one hand between her legs and cupped the little head, then the whole slimy body slid past her wrist and bumped on the ground.

It was a baby girl. To her belly clung a great, thick, twisting cord, like a dark intestine, like a vine, that came from inside Mother. Taking up her digging stick, which all this time had been lying beside her, Mother chopped the cord until she cut it in two. Then she picked up the baby and put it in her shirt. All I could see was the sole of a tiny foot, pink, with the toes stretching. I had never seen anyone so small.

Meanwhile, the dark, twisting cord, dripping blood from the severed end, hung out of Mother's vulva. It was terrible to see, and it smelled, too. Bending over, pressing her belly hard with her hand, Mother grunted a few times, straining, and soon a great, dark, bloody thing like meat flopped between her heels.

Mother sat back with her legs stretched far apart and sighed deeply. Then, reaching for grass, she wiped herself clean. From her carrying bag she brought out a handful of moss, which she packed into her oozing vulva, and using her digging stick to brace herself, she stood up. She shook out her trousers, put them on, dug a deep hole with her digging stick, and buried the dark bloody thing, and then, without a word, she turned her back and started for camp, knowing that I would follow.

So I followed. As we walked, I saw her bend her head and heard her murmur tenderly to the baby. Realizing that it was up to me to guard against anything that might try to surprise us or overtake us, I kept watch behind, but saw only the red sun very far away on the edge of the plain. I remember how the sight of it, going fast, gave me a strange, lonesome feeling. For just a moment I stood still, looking west to watch the sun sink, looking east to watch Mother striding across the plain, she and the sun both moving quickly, both going farther and farther away. Neither one thought anything about me.

After the sun set a cold west wind began to blow, bending the long grass in waves as if spirits were running. I tried to see the thicket where we had spent the day, but it had vanished among all the other thickets. In the sky on the horizon, though, I saw a river of flame. Then I knew that in the Camps of the Dead my mother's people were kindling their evening fires, because the child they had sent to us was now with Mother and their work was done.

Pinesinger's baby came in the dead of night. The fires had burned very low, down to embers. At the fire by the door where most of us were dozing, we were awakened by a high, thin cry. At once I came wide awake, listening. A baby! Although I had not expected to have any feelings, certainly not good feelings, I suddenly felt joy. Why? I didn't know why. I just felt like singing! Of course I didn't even speak—that was no time to be indiscreet. Yet I wanted to know if it was a girl or a boy. Birth and babies are women's business—it wasn't my place to ask. Men find out when someone thinks to tell them. Not wanting to wait, though, I stood up and stretched, to see if I could glimpse the baby.

There it lay on the cold floor, naked and crying: a baby boy, waving his fists and feet. What was in the minds of these women, to leave him there? I almost cried out for one of them to take him, when Rin's strong hands snatched him up and handed him to Pinesinger, who slid him inside her shirt. The crying stopped short. All the women were talking and laughing, most of all Pinesinger, who so recently had been begging for death. Lilan motioned to Muskrat to build up the fire and clean the floor. Slowly Muskrat obeyed. When she started to put the placenta on the fire, Lilan quickly showed her that she must take all the mess outside. Again Muskrat obeyed.

Then all of us but Muskrat gathered at the owners' fire, bringing the last of the reindeer meat in strips, which we laid on the coals. Perhaps because Pinesinger had made such a fuss about this baby, people seemed to want to forget that it wasn't Father's. Rather, the women praised Pinesinger and told her that the next birth would be easier. She laughed, cooked, and ate, as if the praise excited her.

I too felt excited, although I tried to be calm. Even so,

Andriki watched me carefully. "So, Kori," he said at last in his bland way. "You must be glad to have a brother, since you smile so much."

What was he doing, saying such a thing? Long ago he had guessed our secret. Whatever he meant, I was already wary—he couldn't upset me into saying something I'd regret. "Am I a woman, to talk of babies?" I asked. "What pleases my father and stepmother also pleases me."

Pinesinger ate and smiled, smiled and ate. I didn't remember ever seeing her so happy. Was it that people at last were praising her? I tried not to look at her, but couldn't help it, and caught her looking at me. Our eyes met. Then, in front of everyone, she took the baby from her shirt and held him up so we could see him. She pretended to be showing him to everyone, but I knew she was showing him to me.

20

AFTER THE STORM MOON CAME THE MOON THAT AT UNCLE Bala's we had called the Moon of Cast Antlers but that Father's people called the Carcass Moon. I learned why when I heard people praying to the Bear to lead us to a carcass. But that would not be easy, even for Him, since with the new moon came more and more new snow. In spite of the fears of the women, this time the deer didn't leave our Narrow Lake country. Instead more deer came, as if they had found other places the same or worse. The wolves came back, and the Lily too. Hunting in the snow was easy for us, since deer were at the end of every fresh trail. We found them struggling in snowdrifts or sliding on the crust. Whatever way, they moved slowly. After the new moon Maral and Andriki together killed two reindeer.

At the quarter moon Muskrat chased a hind onto a snowfield, where one of the deer's thin front legs pierced through the crusted snow. She fell forward, snapping her bone. When Muskrat brought me there, the hind was heaving herself, trying to stand and run. After spearing her, I praised Muskrat very much and promised that this time nothing would keep me from giving her the hide. "San kew," said Muskrat. She was learning more of our speech. I would have rolled a fire and cooked the liver for Muskrat then and there, but there were only willows, no wood, and also I wanted to take the meat to safety. I was afraid of the Lily.

Only the scarceness of firewood kept us from eating day and night, since by now we had more meat in the lodge than we needed. By the end of the Storm Moon at Uncle Bala's lodge we were always traveling far for firewood, since we would have picked up all the dead wood nearby. But in the deep snow that year at Narrow Lake, wood was especially hard to gather.

So getting wood fell mostly to Muskrat. Her work began almost as soon as she had enough clothing to leave the lodge, and it went on all winter. At first Rin or Lilan would simply hand her an ax, show her some sticks, and push her toward the door, sure that she would know what was wanted of her. And she did. Every night she came back to the lodge with wood. In time she went without being told. When she got the reindeer hide and made her little snow-walkers, it was easy for her to walk on the deep snow, so although the rest of us brought back a few sticks each time we went out, most of the wood we burned was gathered by Muskrat.

Behind her back the other women made fun of her. One day when Muskrat was getting wood I entered the lodge to find Pinesinger imitating the strange, spraddling steps Muskrat took when she wore her snow-walkers. The other women were already laughing, and when Pinesinger finished they laughed until they cried. "You looked just like her," said Hind.

That they would make fun of my woman angered me. I wanted to ask why they were in the lodge burning wood while Muskrat was out getting more for them. But Hind was my aunt and Pinesinger was my stepmother; it wasn't for me to criticize them. I said nothing.

That night I took one of Muskrat's snow-walkers and held it up, pretending to look at it in the firelight. "I think I could make some of these," I said. To my surprise the women began to laugh again, and this time the men joined them. I saw there was a secret joke that I didn't understand. Taken aback, I glanced at Muskrat. She seemed startled. "Why do you laugh, Aunt Hind?" I asked.

"Ah, Kori, never mind," said Andriki, trying to seem serious. "It's just these women. They're not sensible. Don't pay any attention to them. Your aunt is worst of all." He looked at Hind affectionately. Their eyes met, and both snorted with laughter.

So I saw that no one would answer me and that I as well as my woman was the butt of a joke. We were to be left out, pushed aside. Angry at the others for mocking me, angry at Muskrat for shaming me, I put away the snow-walker, and lifting my chin I stared at the fire, making up my mind to leave the lodge and all the people and go back to the Fire River.

Only Pinesinger didn't want to drop the subject. "Would you wear those?" she asked, grinning and pointing her lips at the snow-walkers as if she would burst with the laughter she was holding.

I didn't answer, but instead gave Pinesinger a look that made her eyes widen and her laughter fade. Andriki noticed. My face must have bothered him, as any threat to the peace of a lodge must bother everyone, because Andriki said, "We're not laughing at you, Kori. These lewd women have a joke of their own, and they won't tell you because you're a man and their nephew and stepson. It's just a woman's joke, not seemly and not funny. Let it go."

"I'm not interested, Uncle," I said stiffly. "I don't want to know."

People began to talk about other things, but the talk

was forced, unnatural. As soon as I could move without drawing too much attention, I unrolled my sleeping-skins and lay down in them, leaving Muskrat to make her own bed alone. Whatever the joke, it had shamed us both, and the shame of each had shamed the other. After that, everything went on as before, but I had nothing more to do with Muskrat's snow-walkers.

At the end of the Carcass Moon came a spell of mild weather. The snow sank and hardened, and animals and people could walk anywhere. Now hunting became more difficult, but because of the bad winter the carcasses were so many that we ate meat without hunting. The days grew long again, and we began to think of spring. More time would pass before we could think of traveling, though. The ice on the rivers would melt and break and the rivers would flood. After that, and after green things began to grow in the woods so we could eat, then we would travel.

But as a journey is hardest just before it ends, as a night is coldest just before morning, so winter is hardest to bear just before the time to travel comes, since the cold seems deepest, the firewood is gone, no green food is growing, and the animals are leaving for their summergrounds. Also people are angry with each other after being so long in the lodge, after all the bad feelings and grudges of winter. The lodge smells from stale smoke, spoiled meat, children's feces, and the unwashed bodies of us all. Just then the flies come. First come blackflies, then mosquitoes, so thick that they make even the deer crazy. Sometimes we see an animal running, running, bucking and kicking, and we know it has been made crazy by flies.

The moon is named for them. What Uncle Bala called the Moon of Flies at Father's lodge was called the Blackfly Moon. At Father's lodge the blackflies were thicker than I had ever seen. Perhaps because of the sheltering woods or perhaps because of the water by then lying on the ice of the lake and flowing in the streams, there were so many biting flies that we became gray with them each time we left the smoke. The children cried terribly; their eyes were swollen shut from bites. For a while Frogga cried all the time. She scratched herself until she bled and fell asleep still crying. We all grew impatient and ground our teeth to keep from shouting at her. Privately, I began to wonder what kind of a wife she would be if she complained so freely. Of course, older people didn't complain. But older people were more used to the biting. Maral, for instance, hardly noticed. I still felt bites, but I pretended not to notice. Would Frogga someday do the same? I hoped so, or she would find much trouble from her husband.

Then there were the lice, thanks to Muskrat. One day Maral said he was tired of itching. We would bathe. All of us took axes and cut spruce branches, and then, on the slippery, packed snow beside the lake, we wove them into a domed shelter. The shelter had to be heavy, since we had no way to give it thickness except with layers of spruce twigs, and it had to stand on its own, since we couldn't dig holes for its lodgepoles. Cutting the branches and making the shelter took a day. The next day we covered it with our sleeping-skins, built a fire inside, and heated stones. By late afternoon the bath was ready. Many of us went in naked, shut the door, and poured water on the stones. The great heat and the burning steam made me feel so good I almost wept. All the bad things of winter came out of my body through my skin, and when I walked over the wet ice to the waterhole and in a cloud of my own steam let myself down through the ice into the lake, I became new, as it must be to die or to be born.

There wasn't room in the bath shelter for everyone, and we didn't have enough wood to keep the bath going. Rin's daughter, Waxwing, and her husband, Marten, because they didn't belong to the families of the owners of the lodge but instead were a sister's kin and in-law, held back politely until some of us had finished. Because of her new baby, Pinesinger came in only for a little while, hardly enough to get hot, and Frogga came in with her parents but went straight out again because she didn't like the steam. Ako was kept out until others had finished, because the bath was too crowded and no one felt the need to be polite to someone so young. Among those invited inside while the bath was at its best, I was last.

Muskrat wasn't invited. When everyone was finished, I showed her how to go inside, but by then the fire was smoking and the bath was cold and wet like a cave. Muskrat looked in and shook her head. "She doesn't know what it is," said Rin, watching. But Muskrat's face showed that she knew the bath would not be good, so she must have known what it was. She probably hadn't hoped to bathe with the rest of us anyway, since she knew she wasn't treated the same. Even the children could choose ahead of her.

The waning Blackfly Moon brought a warm spell that lowered the snow. The new moon—the Goose Moon, as Father's people called it—brought more melting, so that the stream from Narrow Lake became a torrent. At night we heard it roaring. We also heard the ice moving on Narrow Lake. The air was fresh and wet with vapor from the snow—the air of spring. The new moon, the spring wind, and the long evenings opened my mind, so I no longer thought of the lodge and the people in it but of far places, different people, and other times. Strange to say, I often found myself thinking of my mother's son, my little half-brother. By then, if he was still living, he would probably have a name.

Rin too thought of people and places far away. One evening when we had built our cooking fire outside the lodge to let a strong, fresh wind blow away the biting flies, she looked up at the yellow sky. It made her think, she said, of a place far down the Hair where long ago her widowed mother, Akima, who was also Father's and Kida's mother, had married Father's father, my grandfather. Although Rin was just a little girl at the time, she remembered meeting her stepfather, my grandfather, and the wife he had already. Rin's mother and the other wife became the mothers of Father, Maral, Kida, and Andriki, and of other children who died. Rin remembered the birth of every one. She also remembered things her half-brothers were too young to remember, or things that had happened before they were born. "I used to lie in the grass and watch the nesting geese," said Rin. "I wanted to steal the eggs. But the geese were so fierce they drove me away."

"I remember the geese!" said Andriki.

Rin shook her head. "You're thinking of other geese," she said. "We left that place where the geese nested before you could walk."

"We did?" asked Andriki.

"Yes. And when we left, your mother was so sick she made me carry you. She died on the way. I was sorry. She was a good woman. She was my stepmother, but she was good to me."

"It's strange," said Andriki. "I remember the place and I remember you, but I don't remember my mother."

"You couldn't remember the place. You were too young," said Rin.

That evening the south wind brought us the sound of geese talking far away. We all fell silent, listening. The geese seemed to be flying into the Hills of Ohun, to the open water of the warm spring in Leech Pond. I turned to look at Muskrat, sitting on her heels alone behind our circle around the fire, since her people had been camping by Leech Pond when we had found her. I caught her looking eagerly toward the sound. Did the time of year make her too think of far places? I remembered the strange animal Muskrat had tried to describe to us, the animal like a wolf but also like a deer and like a person—the tai tibi. How far would someone have to travel to find such an animal? Only the geese, who travel so far in winter that no one has ever seen even one of them—only they could imagine how far.

"Would you like to fly with the geese, to see where they go?" I asked Andriki.

My question made people laugh. "Yes," he answered. "If I got hungry, I'd reach out and catch one."

I shouldn't have asked. I knew better. But Pinesinger looked at me and said, "I'd like to travel with the geese. I'd visit my parents."

"I too," said Hind.

"I too," said a voice behind us.

We turned and stared. It was Muskrat. Had she been listening? Had she understood what we said? She smiled and nodded, her flat face with its blue buttocks mark all wrinkled up as she tried to seem agreeable. Still we scowled, puzzled by her speaking. So again she smiled and nodded, then softly called *kakakar* like a goose and pointed at the sky.

By the time the snow had melted enough to show patches of dead yellow grass, the reindeer had gone. The wolves had long gone. Now and then we might see one of them, or find the tracks of one of them, but never all together as we had in winter. Somewhere, they were probably trying to raise a litter of pups in a den. The tiger was still around, though. Sometimes we found his tracks in the fresh mud by the water. Sometimes at night we thought we heard his voice deep in the woods. He stayed away from us, for which we were grateful. One night when we were speaking of him, very respectfully and not very loudly, we reasoned that he alone ate as much as we ate, perhaps more. By then we were not finding much to hunt but were eating whatever our snares caught, even foxes. We were also eating winter-killed carcasses and any dead fish we found floating near the shore of the lake. What was the tiger eating?

Another night we heard something breathing at the door of the coldtrap. When the sky grew light in the morning, we found the tiger's footprints in the soft earth. From then on we were even more careful, knowing that the tiger was nearby and thinking of us.

One evening we noticed a brown thing in the open water on the far side of the lake: the back of a moose browsing for plants on the bottom. We reached for our spears, ready to circle the lake and hunt the moose. The moose raised her head to draw breath. We stood motionless, waiting. Peacefully she breathed for a time, her ears dripping, then she put her head under water again. We started to run. But just then, on the far side of the lake, the red, striped, flamelike tiger suddenly burst from a thicket and in two great leaps fell with a huge splash on the moose. A fearful struggle followed, with much flying water, roaring growls from the tiger, and one loud bellow from the moose. Quickly the struggle grew less frantic. For a moment we saw nothing but the rippling surface of the lake, and then we saw the sleek head and folded ears of the tiger swimming for shore.

Out onto the stones he climbed, then shook so that a great cloud of water stood out all around him. He finished with a whiplike shaking of his tail. Then he turned to the lake and noticed us watching. For a moment he stared, then he gave a great, booming roar that filled the basin of the lake, echoed from the trees, and seemed to shake the ground under our feet. Even at that distance I felt the roar inside me. My chest felt full of the sound. Strangely, though, I wasn't as frightened as I might have been. This was partly because the tiger was far away. But partly it was because he suddenly seemed small. There he was, soaking wet, looking much thinner and smaller, yet as if he didn't know he no longer seemed frightening, he was trying to scare us just the same. I could have laughed at him.

Then, from all parts of the forest, ravens called. Whether their god was wet or dry, when he spoke they answered. "By the Bear," said Maral. "What now?"

"Look there," said Andriki. We looked. Something brown and hairy had broken the surface of the lake. Around it floated something dark and thick that stained the water. It was the she-moose, with blood. With his ears raised and his forehead wrinkled, the tiger also looked at her. Quickly, as if he had forgotten all about us, he plunged again into the icy lake and swam to her carcass, sank his terrible teeth into her, and gave her a good tug. Suddenly he vanished. He had pulled himself under.

He must have let go, since he quickly bobbed up. In low voices we told each other that he now would swim ashore again and perhaps come to try to hunt us, but instead we saw his wet face and raised chin, like the face of a beaver, as he swam around the carcass of his moose.

On the far side of her, his ears showed as he tried to pull her from another direction.

By now the ravens were sitting in the trees on the far side of the lake, cheering for the tiger as people will cheer for wrestling men. As if their calls encouraged him, he began to move the carcass. Soon he and his moose were in shallow water, and soon after that he was dragging her ashore. While she lay half in, half out of the water, the tiger shook himself again and looked up at the ravens flying excitedly above him. Then, biting the moose through her spine just before her shoulders, he raised his head as high as he could, and half straddling her forequarters, so that most of her body dragged beside him, he hauled her into the woods.

"By the Bear!" said a deep, strange voice behind us. "We'd need three men to move that carcass!"

Astonished, we turned. There stood a big, bearded, light-haired man, wearing a pack, carrying two spears, and dressed in a fur-lined parka. It was Father.

21

"MY YOUNGER WIFE," HE EXPLAINED CALMLY, "WAS MUCH ON my mind. I saw her in a dream. Then I knew I should visit her. So I traveled two days for each of my fingers. Now I'm here."

"You'll find her well," said Andriki. "The child too."

"A girl?"

"A boy."

"Ah," said Father.

"Your journey," said Andriki. "Did you travel easily?"

"I left as the ice was breaking on the river," Father answered. "And I came northwest, through the spruce forests east of here. If you must travel through a spruce wood, spring is the time to do it. I ate ptarmigan, mostly. And winterkills. I found the deer weak after such a bad winter. They're still dying because of the snow."

"So," said Andriki. "Welcome."

"Why are we standing here?" asked Father. "Have you no food to offer me after my journey? Have you let the tiger eat everything?"

We laughed at that, of course, but it was not lack of food that made us hesitate. We were thinking instead of the sights that would greet Father—the baby that was not his, and the strange woman.

"Come then, Brother," said Andriki at last. "There is much for you to see."

I must say, Father surprised me. I had thought the birth of Pinesinger's baby might anger him. Instead, in the dark lodge he gravely opened Pinesinger's parka and looked into the baby's small face. I had thought he wouldn't want to touch it. Instead he held out his arms. Pinesinger too was surprised by Father. She hesitated at first, looking to see if he meant what she thought he meant. When it seemed he did, she hurried to give him the baby. He took it carefully, but the baby noticed his strange face, pulled down its lips, trembled, and began crying. As if Pinesinger feared that this would anger Father, she hurried to take the baby back. But Father rocked him and spoke to him in his rumbling voice. "Yes," he said gently. "Be easy. Don't be afraid." The baby fell silent and stared up at Father as if he had realized his mistake.

Father turned to Pinesinger. "Well then, Wife," he said. "I've come." She looked from the baby to Father anxiously. Smiling faintly, he slowly handed her the baby. The rest of us had been watching in silence. When Pinesinger took the baby, many of us let go our breath.

All this time none of us had thought of Muskrat. Just then she came back from the forest where she had been gathering wood and began to crawl into the lodge, her bundle of sticks scratching the sides of the coldtrap. A puzzled expression crossed Father's face. If all of us were in the lodge, what was scratching? He gave a start when he saw her, with her pregnant belly and the blue buttocks mark on her face. "Waugh!" he said softly.

Muskrat's head snapped up and her eyes flew wide. She stared for a moment, taking in his beard, his size, his age, and his parka. Then her eyes found mine. She gave me a long look and sat down, leaving me to explain her to Father.

So I tried. As I began telling how I had noticed the sound of chopping in the hills, I heard my own voice echo, and soon realized that Father was not the only person listening. The others must have been holding their breath, so quiet the lodge became. With all ears straining to hear each word I said, I knew better than to try to hide the truth or to lessen my part in Muskrat's capture, a part that Father might take to be a large one. For a time I thought someone might help me—Andriki perhaps—but no one did, so I struggled on, trying but not always managing to keep my eyes on Father's. Meanwhile his hard, pale gaze made me think of the tiger. Trying to finish my story with encouraging thoughts, trying to put the best face on the matter, I reminded Father that the winter had passed without Muskrat's people trying to find her. To my way of thinking, I told him, her people were afraid of us, and we were safe from their revenge.

I stopped talking then and waited for Father's answer. Time passed. The lodge stayed very quiet. Father shifted his weight but didn't speak. At last he cleared his throat. The sound reminded me of a tiger growling. I tried to tell myself that I was grown, not a child but a man, or nearly so, and that I shouldn't wait anxiously for a word from Father. I tried to hold up my head and look him in the eye. But I couldn't. I knew what he thought.

So did everyone else. In time the other people began to talk quietly. Father said nothing to me, and I said nothing at all. I pretended to search in the ashes for pine nuts. Rin and Pinesinger talked together of a piece of meat they planned to cook for Father. Meanwhile Father began to tell his brothers of his long walk. Late at night, we who were still awake heard a number of sudden booming roars from the Lily on the far side of the lake. Perhaps the wolves had come upon him on his carcass.

"How can I speak freely when I don't know what the woman understands?" asked Father the next day, speaking of Muskrat. We were sitting on our heels at the foot of one of the round hills, where Father had brought the men of his lodge to dig out a wolf den. In fact it was the den of the wolves we knew. Father had found it on his way from the Char. Long, sparse grassblades marked it, as they seem to mark most wolf dens. Behind a screen of low-growing juniper bushes high on the hill, one of the wolves watched.

We had chopped away the earth to the depth of my forearm. Peering into the hole, I could see from the length of the tunnel that our work had hardly begun. Inside the earth was perfect silence, although each blow of my pick sent little stones hopping downhill.

"You ask how we can speak freely in front of Kori's woman," said Andriki. "And I ask how we can speak freely in front of the other women. Kori's Muskrat doesn't understand us. The other women do." Maral and Andriki laughed noisily. I smiled, encouraging Father to laugh too.

But he didn't. "I can't see why my son would snatch a woman from strangers thinking that no one would avenge her," he said. "What has happened here? Aren't my brothers two grown men? Isn't the good of the lodge important to them? How could they let such things happen?" Father spoke these words to the lake and the woods and to any person who might happen to hear him.

"Be easy, Brother," said Maral. "Will we quarrel?"

"I understand your anger," said Andriki, "but why turn it toward us? Is he our son? Did one of us divorce his mother? Did we bring him here? Did we choose to go away, leaving him with people who hardly knew him?"

"I'm thinking of her people's revenge," said Father. "I was far away when he caught her. How could I stop him? Why didn't you stop him when you knew her men could come to get her back? Is Kori's woman worth the death of some of our people?"

"What makes you think men will come?" said Andriki. "Why haven't they come already? We watched for them. We were ready. Where were they?"

"Isn't she someone's daughter?" asked Father. "Couldn't she be someone's wife as well? Shouldn't we expect revenge? Could her people come here and drag off our women and children?"

Andriki pointed with his lips at the bushes on the hillside where the wolf watched. "Look there," he said to Father. Father looked. "When we take their pups," asked Andriki, "will you worry about their revenge? I, for one, don't fear Muskrat's people or their birdspears. Let Kori enjoy her. After all, he's a young man, with a young man's thoughts and a young man's ways. Yet his wife is an infant. If he has his muskrat-woman, he keeps away from other women, and we have peace in the lodge."

"Do you need a slave to keep peace in the lodge?" asked Father.

"Shouldn't every man have a woman?" asked Andriki. "Now that Pinesinger's child is born, even you, the man of many wives, can also have a woman." He laughed. I liked how the talk was turning.

But just as I began to feel easier, Father turned to me. "So tell me, Kori," he said. "What are your plans? I see she's pregnant. Is it yours?"

"Yes, Father," I said.

"Are you sure?" he asked.

What could I say? I was quite sure! If I had said so, though, I might have sounded brash. "I think the child is mine, Father," I said.

Then Andriki spoke for me, and bluntly, too. "His woman was menstruating when we caught her," he said. "Even Kori knows they can't menstruate while they're pregnant. After that, only he had her. He thought we were having her as well, but in truth I didn't want the crotch lice. Neither did Maral, here. No—the rest of us let her be. If any man can know he's truly a father, Kori is that man."

"Crotch lice?" asked Father.

"Yes, but by now they've crept all over the lodge. Everyone is scratching. You'll believe me soon! But yes, the crotch lice kept us off her." Andriki laughed aloud. Father sighed.

"Her crotch lice and her strange way of coitus," added Maral.

Now Father stared at Maral. "How so?" he asked.

"She's different," said Andriki. "Tell him, Kori."

"Uncle!"

"Tell me!" said Father.

I put down my antler pick and turned so that I didn't have to look at Father. "You're shaming me," I said.

The three men were suddenly quiet and I felt them watching me. I looked at the ground, my face hot. I wouldn't speak of coitus.

Andriki cleared his throat. "Must we shame him?" he asked. "After all, what was done was done long ago. If you didn't know about it, Brother, how is that Kori's fault?"

"By the Bear!" said Father. "You hint at strange things, then won't explain yourself. Why do you anger me?"

"I don't hint, Brother," said Maral very seriously. "I speak my mind openly or I keep silent, just as you do. About this woman, though, I only meant that there's a right way and a wrong way for everything. There's a right way to throw a spear and a right way to roll a fire. If you throw your spear wrong, your spear will fall. If you roll your fire wrong, your tinder won't burn. The same is true of coitus. She who gave life to all the animals and all the people, She showed us how to do this thing. We do what She taught. But not Kori's woman. Kori's woman . . ." Maral hesitated.

"Is she like Bobcat Woman?" asked Father, truly alarmed. I had to join my uncles in promising that Muskrat was nothing like Bobcat Woman, who in the earliest times had been one of Weevil's wives, until she tricked him into having coitus while she was menstruating. This had made his penis like a bobcat's penis, bright red and very small. When he learned how his wife had tricked him, he divorced her, and his penis became normal again.

"Not like Bobcat Woman," said Maral. "Kori's woman just faces him. It's her way, that's all."

Father seemed interested, as if he was trying to imagine Muskrat and me together. "It's not the boy's fault," said Andriki. "Which of us could say he wouldn't do the same? Surely any of us would do exactly the same if the woman didn't know how to do differently and wouldn't learn."

Still Father seemed to have trouble taking it in. "Hi!" he said at last. "Crotch lice and this too! No wonder her people don't want her."

On the hillside the watching wolf ran nervously to the far side of the bush that hid her. We rested, listening. Still no sound came from the den in the earth. "Are we digging for nothing?" asked Maral.

To answer Maral, Father pointed his lips at the wolf, now watching from a new thicket, as if she had hoped to see a change. "Do you see her?" he asked.

"Yes," said Maral.

"You who think that Kori's woman has no people who want her, how do you explain that wolf?" Father asked.

"If you want an answer from a wolf, watch what happens now," said Maral, and lying on his belly, he reached his arm deep into the hole, felt around for a moment, and sat back on his heels, holding in his large hand a soft brown pup. At the sight the wolf on the hillside stopped still. "Will she fight us?" asked Maral scornfully. Handing the pup to me, he again stretched himself on his belly and reached down the hole.

I looked at the little animal. It was a male, I saw when I turned it on its back. The long hairs at the end of his penis were wet with urine. I held him in both hands, noticing that his brown eyes stared into mine, noticing that he held his body rigid, his neck arched, his front legs stiffly bending at the wrist and elbow, his hind legs stretched so long and straight that he pointed his toes. Between his hind legs curled his tail, its tip trembling. Under my thumbs I felt his ribs, as delicate as a baby's, and under his ribs I felt his beating heart.

Never before had I held a living wolf pup. The fur

surprised me, soft and brown, although an adult's was coarse and gray. How would he change his fur when he grew up? I turned him over to look at his back, and suddenly, with strength that surprised me, he twisted out of my hands and ran. "Hi!" I shouted.

"Hi!" cried Andriki, grasping his spear behind the blade and bringing down the shaft like a club. The spear moaned through the air, so fast Andriki moved it, and it caught the cub a great thump that laid him flat, with his teeth through his tongue and his legs spread like a pegged-out pelt.

"Hi!" cried Father. "Be careful! I want it alive!"

Andriki and I stood over the pup. His ribs heaved slowly, and blood ran out of his mouth. "It's still alive," said Andriki, poking the pup with his foot. Without knowing why, I glanced up the hillside to see what the watching wolf thought of this. But the watching wolf was gone.

Behind us Maral said, "You've killed it, and he wanted it alive."

"It could still live," said Andriki as the pup gave a shuddering sigh. "Anyway, if I hadn't hit it, it would have run away. He still would have lost it. Kori! You let go of it. Why?"

"I didn't think it would move so fast," I answered.

"You were daydreaming," said Father.

For some reason I couldn't take my eyes from the pup, as brown as the brown dust, his eyes filming. I heard Maral scratching at the dirt. "Here," he said behind me. "Pay attention this time." And he put a second pup into my hands.

"I will," I promised. I took off my belt and wound it tight around the new pup's feet and neck and jaws. Another little male, perhaps not as large as the first one, this pup couldn't have moved if he had tried to. But he wasn't trying. Perhaps he had seen what had happened to his brother. Perhaps he was too frightened by us. As I tied him he trembled violently but otherwise lay perfectly still.

"There might be more," said Father, and for a third time Maral groped in the depths of the den.

"If there are, I can't feel them."

"Shall we dig deeper?"

"Hi! Aren't two enough?" asked Andriki. "Are we going to spend the day here? Won't we hunt? You've come so far, and we have little to eat here. Aren't you hungry?"

"If we leave pups here, the adults will move them. We won't find them again easily," said Father.

"You have two," said Andriki. "How many do you need?"

"Are you impatient, Little Brother?" asked Father. "Very well, let's see what we can see from the ridge of the hills. We don't want to hunt near here. Remember the Lily?"

"Will we take this hunting?" asked Maral, touching the second wolf pup with his moccasin.

"We'll take him to the lodge. One of the women can keep him for us," said Father. He pulled his beard, looking down at the two pups. "They must eat," he said. He thought again, a long time. "Years ago," he said, "I lived on the Char, just like I lived this winter. One of my wife's kinswomen kept a wolf pup. It came and went of its own free will, and of its own will it helped us in hunting. I saw this. It even made a reindeer stand still and wait for me until I could spear it. As that wolf helped the people on the Char, so this wolf will help us. And what my wife's kinswoman did for their wolf, my wife will do for mine. She won't refuse. Come. We'll tell her now that she must feed it." He took a few long strides in the direction of the lodge, Maral and Andriki following.

Just then we heard a loud, pure voice behind us. It was the wolf who had been watching. Her call rose high, held steady, and flew far. After the call came a deep silence, as if even the trees were listening. Father and his brothers stopped and waited, as if rooted to the earth by the sound. How could a cry cause so much silence? We held our breath, listening. At last, from the east, behind the Hills of Ohun, a wolf's voice answered. Then, from the south, two others answered, and from the north a fourth answered, almost too far to be heard.

"So," said Father softly. "Now they'll come."

"Then what?" I asked him.

He gave me a long look, as if he couldn't decide whether or not to answer me. At last he said, "They'll come and they'll sing. Then they'll leave, and years will pass before they use this place again. Well, Brothers. What of us? Are we going to stay here?" He turned on his heel and strode off, with Maral and Andriki behind him. I picked up the second pup and followed. I would have brought the first one too, but it was dead.

22

NO ONE WAS IN THE LODGE, SO WE LEFT THE PUP TIED TO THE door of the coldtrap. Father thought if we didn't tie the pup's jaws shut he would bite through the sinew string, so we wound it very tightly around his muzzle and looped it around his neck. Then we tied his legs together, because we didn't want him pawing off the string. When we finished, he looked like a hafted ax with eyes. I couldn't help but laugh.

Then we went hunting, Father and Maral going west downstream, Andriki and I going east upstream. On the eastern shore of the lake we found the tracks of the she-moose the tiger had killed, oval dents in the wet earth, partly filled with brown water. She had looked at the landscape for a long time. Since we had never seen her or her tracks before, we knew she had come here as a stranger and had tried to learn about the lake before hiding her eyes and ears in it. There was no use to follow or learn more about her, of course, so we set off to the northeast, bending our trail to keep far away from the tiger.

All day we hunted. Our way led over the great, low-lying plain of sedge and willow, all red with spring.

At midday we saw a large brown bear making his way toward the horizon. At a distance, a fox followed him. Two of us were no match for that bear. We kept still until he was gone. By late afternoon we had seen no more than two pairs of ptarmigan and a small herd of reindeer, who saw us as soon as we saw them. Then the shadows of the willows grew long and the cold evening wind began to blow. We knew darkness would soon come, and not wanting to meet the Lily without daylight, we turned to go home.

When we reached a pine woods, Andriki stopped to cut branches, explaining that Father would need them. He didn't say why, but I helped. The branches were fresh and green, with new growth showing. Andriki had brought a string with him. We used the string to tie a large bundle, which we dragged into the lodge as the sun went down under the cloud-streaked sky. In the embers of the fire I saw the palms of two hands and the soles of two feet shaped like a person's but darker and smaller— Father and the others were cooking one of two marmots that some of the women had killed with stones. It was skin and bones, poor food after its long sleep, and like any bit of women's food a disappointment after the animals Andriki and I had seen.

When we had eaten, Father left the lodge and was gone a long time. We sat waiting while the sky above the smokeholes grew black and the wind grew strong. After dark Father came in and we sat a while longer. "Build the fire," said Father at last. "I will show you that the Bear is not far."

So we gathered up dry wood and the fresh pine branches and brought them to the Bear's place, which is the owners' fire, where the Bear would sleep if the lodge were His den, if the braces of the ceiling were the roots of His pine tree, which is the lodgepole of the world. Maral's two wives knelt to brush the floor, smoothing out the footprints, gathering the chips of bark, the scraps of marmot bone and marmot hair, the bits of pine cones and seed hulls, making the sacred spot ready for its fire. We scooped up the last embers from the cooking fire, and shaking them gently so they didn't burn our hands, we put them on a fresh pile of twigs. A little blaze started. When it flamed, the people sat around it. I squeezed myself in between Pinesinger and Andriki.

Then Father stood up and brought from his pack a little drum like Andriki's drum, made of a bird's skin stretched on a branch bent in a circle. He gave the drum to Maral, who tapped his fingertips on the skin, making a flat, dry sound, a steady rhythm, which the rest of us kept by clapping our hands. We sang:

You whose fire makes the stars
You whose song splits the black ice
You whose breath makes the snow
You whose dancefire is the moon
We call You with the voices of geese: hariak! hariak!
We call You with the voices of lapwings: wiri! wiri!
We call You with the voices of eagles: kiriar kee!
We are burning fat.
Fat is in the smoke.
Come for it, host of the springtime,
Come from Your long sleep.
In Your own voice we call You,
Hona! Hona! Hona!

Then from the darkness by the coldtrap came a roar, which rose very loud, then fell, then rose again as Father whirled something on a string around his head. At the frightening sound, Muskrat forced herself into the circle beside me. Pinesinger turned to look into my face. Even in the dark her eyes showed white. "What is it?" she whispered. It looked like the shoulder blade of a large animal, carved and scraped to look like the blade of a spear. But I didn't know what to call it. When Pinesinger saw that I couldn't answer her, she leaned across me to ask Andriki.

"A voice," he said. "The Bear's."

"Can this be so?" whispered Pinesinger, listening.

But as suddenly as it began, the great voice stopped, and Father stood over the fire. Naked to the waist and thin from winter, his big, gaunt body looked for all the world like a skinned bear. In one hand he held the blade, now silent. From the other, which he raised high and opened, he dropped a withered string of yellow-brown fat on the fire. Before bursting into flame, the fat sang in the voice of a mosquito. "Fat is burning. Fat is in the smoke," sang the rest of us. "Come for it! Come!"

I sang too, yet even as I called out to the Bear, I couldn't help but ask myself where Father might have found a strip of fat. We had none. Had he brought it from the Char River? He had no other meat in his hunting bag. Then a thought struck me that made me blink my eyes: in a willow thicket across the lake lay a carcass, the tiger's moose. Had Father robbed the tiger?

I had no time to think this over, because just then Father threw the pine branches on the fire. The singing grew stronger, the drumming and clapping grew faster, and the voice of the Bear, booming from the blade now whirled by Maral, grew so loud it hurt. Almost hidden by the cloud of smoke and steam that billowed from the pine branches, Father calmly washed his hands with coals. Then, lifting coals to his head by handfuls, he set his hair on fire. Tossing his head so that the sparks flew, he poured coals over his arms, over his shoulders, until we smelled his burning skin and hair. When we heard his skin sizzle like meat, my aunts screamed like falcons. Then suddenly, in the cloud of smoke, Father vanished. He had been there in front of us, but he was gone.

The singing died, and silence filled the lodge so that we heard each other breathing and the snapping of pine pitch in the fire. In the smoky dark, we looked around. I saw Pinesinger's eyes, with the whites showing, on one side of me and Muskrat's eyes, also with the whites showing, on the other side. "Hona!" said Maral.

"Hona," said we all.

"Sing," said Maral to the women. So, their voices pulsing like hornets' voices, the women again took up the song.

Some of the men made their way under the cloud of smoke to the coldtrap, where they crawled outside. I followed. Under the black sky the wind sang with the Bear's voice in the little spruce trees around the lodge. I smelled rain and the lake—water smells. I smelled the pine smoke from the smokeholes when the wind whirled it to the ground. I smelled burning hair; Father had been here.

Near the door to the coldtrap, we sat on our heels, waiting for Father. Inside the lodge the hornet voices died and the women were silent. We heard the wind in the trees and the broken ice on the lake. A fox called twice, its spring song. Very far away, over the Hills of Ohun, surely at the little lake where I had captured Muskrat, we heard the voices of geese as a long string of them flew down in the dark. Then, over the black rim of the hills, under the low clouds, rose the moon. It was the old moon, the waning moon, with the ghost of the new moon tight against it. Up it came below the clouds like an otter swimming to the surface of a lake, an otter with a kit in her arms.

For a moment the old moon flooded the windy clearing with light. Then it rose higher, behind the clouds, and the gloomy darkness closed in around us again—but not before I noticed, on the path of white ice on the way to the lake, the pale form of a person stretched out on his back. We hurried to him. It was Father. He was unconscious. His body was rigid, his teeth were clenched, and his eyelids were squeezed shut. His harsh breath, which was labored and rasping, echoed the wind in the trees. None of us touched him, and none of us spoke. I looked at his skin to see the burns. Perhaps it was the dim light, but I saw none. I looked at the sky, at the clouds that hurried past the moon, I listened to the wind flying through the spruce forest, strong and near, weak and far, strong and near again, and I thought of Father's spirit flying through the night sky, wind-tossed like a raven, hunting with the Bear. We sat on our heels to guard his body.

We waited a long time. When at last his spirit came back to him, Father sat up with his face in his hands. Then he wiped his eyes; then, looking almost like himself again, he shifted his weight to sit on his heels with the rest of us. Only when he spoke could we hear from his voice that his trance still clung to him.

"I have seen the Bear," he said. "He gave a message. It

206

is this: the next time we hunt a bear, we must leave its head where we kill it, with fat between its teeth. And we must not break its bones for marrow. When we finish eating, we must scatter the bones. That is what He told me. If we do as He asks, He will show us where to find food in winter and where to find women and ivory in summer. He will help us. Hona."

"Hona," we answered. I thought for a time about what Father had told us, then said "Hona" again.

Slowly Father rubbed his face. His trance didn't want to leave him. Patiently we waited in silence while the wind forced itself through the trees. We felt raindrops. Time passed. "Hi," said Father at last, without raising his eyes. "The Lily is coming."

Startled, we looked up. At first we saw nothing, so we looked very carefully for the huge, dark shape, perhaps hiding under the low, spreading branches of a tree. But there was only the flickering moonlight and the wind moving the branches. Yet my skin prickled—my hair rose slowly on my arms and neck. Father was right about the Lily. I knew he was on his way.

We all knew it and we waited, our heads raised, listening. We heard the wind in the pines, the ice moving on the lake, Father's wolf pup crying by the lodge where we had tied him, and the sound of Father's heavy breath. I wanted to feel fear, but I couldn't feel anything; instead my mind seemed flat, like the surface of a pool. Fish or eels might be under the surface, but none broke it. In my head, secret, shadowy thoughts must have been lurking, thoughts I didn't want to think. So I thought of the animals in the woods—of the wolves with two of their children missing, the wolves on their way to a new den; of the reindeer, who kept trying to escape us; of the she-moose who had picked her way to Narrow Lake only to be killed by the Lily; and at last of the Lily himself, eating more meat than three men could carry and resting beside the bones. Suddenly my mind's eye saw him crouched under the lowest branches of a hemlock, watching, waiting, then leaping as he had leaped at the moose, with his ears turned back, his tail stiff, and his strong arms and fingers stretched out, reaching.

"Hi," said Father a second time. "The Lily is here."

And he was. Behind Father the clouds grew thin and moonlight shone through, very pale and dim, but not so dim we did not see the huge black form on the white ice of the path, and two huge, round, pale eyes. The tiger was standing not a spear's throw from us.

It must have come to all of us together that our spears were still inside. I reached for a piece of firewood. Of course I didn't throw it. Rather, I grasped it so tightly my fingers turned numb.

Slowly Father straightened his legs and stood up. With his trance still on him and the tiger watching, he turned around. "What now?" asked Father in a soft voice, facing the tiger. "Have you come for your fat? The Bear has it. He helps us. He might help you if you gave Him something. But you eat everything greedily and by yourself. You think only of your stomach. Be high-minded as we are high-minded and forget your piece of fat."

The Lily listened, watching Father with round eyes. When Father finished speaking, the Lily let his jaw open so that the tips of his two lower eyeteeth showed white like the ice in the moonlight. Then his gaze faltered. He dropped his head slightly and turned his ears so that the white spots on the backs showed. All of us could see that Father had shamed him. Soon his pale eyes blinked, then vanished. As secretly as he had come, he was gone.

Later, after the lodge was quiet, after we were rolled in our deerskins trying to use what was left of the night, we heard something crying. It was Father's wolf pup again, still tied outside the lodge. He must have been asleep for a while, or else afraid of the tiger, because for a long time he had been quiet. We had forgotten him. Not wanting to leave my sleeping-skins or the warmth of Muskrat's naked body, I tried to ignore the muffled sound. For a while I did, and I had almost fallen asleep when suddenly, in the middle of a cry, the wolf's voice stopped. His silence made me more wakeful than his crying had. What had happened? Listening carefully, I sat up. The pup began to make many joyous squeaks, as if something was exciting him. Seizing my spear, I hurried through the coldtrap. Muskrat followed.

Now high, the otter moon swam behind the clouds. By its light we saw a large gray wolf with green eyes standing over the pup, her head lowered, looking at us. At the knees of the large wolf, the pup's green eyes, smaller and much closer together, also looked at us. I threw my spear. As it flew over the large wolf, the green eyes blinked and the gray shape vanished. The large wolf had leaped away, quiet as smoke. The pup cowered. When I picked him up to bring him inside, I saw that the sinew string that had tied him was bitten through. I held up the string in the moonlight so that Muskrat could see how close Father had come to losing his wolf pup.

But Muskrat was looking east, toward the Hills of Ohun, her bony legs and winter-shrunken buttocks dark in shadow, her two round breasts and her great round belly softly shining in the pale light. She gave me a chill, my naked woman. She reminded me of the little figures shamans sometimes carve in bone, the figures of Ohun that are placed in the graves of women who die in childbirth to remind those women why they were sent to stay among us, and why after a short rest in the Camps of the Dead they must come back to try again.

Then I thought of Father's trancing spirit and of the bath of red coals that had made his spirit fly out on the wind. I thought of large animals, and meat, and hunting, and burning fat, and the sun. All of those are men's things, strong things, fire things, with life and death in them. Yet there beside me was my woman, a moon thing, cold, perhaps, naked and poor and still very thin from winter, but alive like the moon with a fresh moon inside, with a fresh life coming from the Camps of the Spirits. There beside me, paying no attention, stood my naked moon-washed Muskrat, leaning back to balance the weight of the baby in her belly and the thin white milk in her breasts.

23

LATER THAT NIGHT, AFTER OUR SINGING ENDED AND WE HAD gone in the lodge to sleep, rain began. The walls of the lodge were thick; the storm didn't wake me. Not until I crawled out of the coldtrap after dawn did I hear the last of it—the wet wind in the spruce trees, the rainwater dripping from the branches, the waves against the shore.

Getting water was Muskrat's work, but she had been so frightened by the tiger that she refused to go. Instead of trying to make her go, I went in her place. I didn't want to draw attention to her, not from Father. As I went, gusts of cold wind wet my face. The path to the lake, pressed to ice by the many passing feet, now stood alone and white in the woods. The rain had made it very slippery. Surely, I thought, in spite of what Andriki had told me, Father would not want to go far from the lodge that day. But when I hurried into the lodge with the dripping waterskin, I saw that Father was ready to travel and that the other people were rolling up their packs. "What's wrong?" I whispered to Rin.

"Can't you see what's wrong?" she asked crossly. "It's cold and dark here because your woman didn't bring enough fuel. We want to cook and eat the other marmot before we travel, but we have no fire."

Hurt by Rin's anger, I said, "My woman brought fuel. How was she to know we would be singing? Was it her fault that we burned it all?"

"Whose fault if not hers?" asked Rin.

I said no more. After all, Rin's anger was pointed not at me but at Muskrat. I left the waterskin by the dead ashes and in a dark corner quietly spread my sleeping-skins, getting them ready to roll into a pack. But when I had the skins smoothed out, Muskrat lay down on them. "Get up. You pack. We go," I whispered. Slowly Muskrat shook her head. "I think she's afraid of the Lily," I said, turning to Father. "Must I force her?"

"The tiger, the tiger," said Father, no longer bothering to call him the Lily. "Are you women, that he worries you so? Unlike us, he is lazy. He wants to sleep in the bushes with his carcass, eating his fill each time he wakes. What of you, Kori? Has he also frightened you so badly that you can't get wood?"

I didn't know what to say to this and from habit turned to Andriki. But I could see from the way he stopped tying his pack that he was as surprised as I was. "Hi, Brother," he said to Father. "What now?" But Father was getting his spear and his ax. Seeing that he might go for wood just to shame me and Muskrat, I took my ax and hurried outside.

I had not gone far among the dripping spruce trees when I heard soft footsteps behind me. Half expecting the Lily, I turned. It was Father. "Wait, Kori," he said. "I'll go with you."

I looked at him. Taller than I may ever be, Father seemed as big as a bear in his heavy parka. With his mist-bright beard the color of a larch in winter and his pale tiger's eyes, he belonged to these woods as their herds of deer belonged to him, a hunter in a hunter's country. He carried an ax and a spear. "We'll talk," he went on, "while we get wood, so we can cook and eat before we leave. Where are the trees you ringed this winter?"

We had ringed no trees that I knew of. At Bala's lodge we didn't do this thing, killing trees in the fall to use as the winter grows older. But Bala's lodge was in a vast, low-lying fir forest where dry branches gave us all the wood we needed without our bothering to ring the trees. I saw now that Father might find fault with me. Because I was the newcomer and couldn't hunt alone, getting wood had been mostly my responsibility. I didn't answer.

"Well then," he said at last. "I'll show you some." Without waiting to see if I was following, he strode off along the little game trail that led west.

Quite soon I noticed the Lily's footprints under Father's footprints. This was the path the Lily had taken the night before! I had meant to let Father do all the talking, but the sight of those huge wet prints loosened my tongue. "Father! Look there," I whispered.

He looked down. "Yes," he said, "we'll see his tracks turn back soon. He's already far from here. We won't meet him."

As if giving no further thought to the big footprints, Father walked west beside the river for a time, and at a place where the tiger had leaped over the stream and gone south, perhaps to turn back to his moose carcass, Father left the bank and headed north into a clearing surrounded by many ringed trees. The branches were bare. The trees had died, and wind had long since blown away the needles. Here was all the dead wood we would need for a long time. Yet no one had told me about it! Perhaps only Father knew. He went to one of the trees and began to rock it. I helped, and soon, with much breaking of branches, it came crashing down. We began to chop.

At last Father turned to face me. "This is the thing as I see it, Kori," he said. "This place is not good. There's danger here for us. For one thing, your woman's people should be here soon, looking for her. And although I didn't want to say so before, the Lily is getting very bold. Now spring food is waiting on the Hair River. It's time to go. But if your woman wants to stay, you must let her."

"Why?" I asked.

"She wants to wait here so her people can find her."

"Father! Where are they?"

"They'll come."

"But she has no one."

"Women don't live alone like musk deer," he said.

"Her people ran when we caught her. Uncle and I, we found their camp. We found the tracks of the people with her—two women, a child, and an old lame man. They ran like hares. They won't come back for Muskrat. And if they do . . . well, two were women. If this lodge were mine, I'd keep those other women too."

"But the lodge is mine," said Father in the quiet voice

of a headman. "Just as your Muskrat is another man's woman. Somewhere that man is sharpening his spear, warming his anger, calling his brothers and his brothers-in-law, and planning how to kill us. And he knows where we live. Must we risk our lives to fight him over this strange woman? Last night I saw the Bear. He spoke to me. He told me how to hunt bears, who are His creatures. But I saw that He meant more than that. The scattered bones He spoke of are strangers who would harm us. Yet He told us not to break them. He told us to let them be. We must not hunt for trouble. We will leave these strangers alone."

"Why hasn't my woman already gone to them?"

"How would she find them? She leaves them signs, and she waits."

"She leaves them signs?"

"She does. On my way here I found twists of grass, piles of stones, scratches on the trees and the rocks, and also the tracks of those snow-walkers of hers on a trail in the woods where the snow still lasted, as if the other signs weren't enough. I thought them very strange, too. In fact, they worried me. I didn't know what to expect when I reached the lodge. But when I saw your woman, I understood."

I must say, his words shocked me. I too had seen these things and had known that Muskrat made them. I had even seen her make them. But were they signs for her people? How could Father be sure?

"If so," I asked, "why haven't her people come?" Yet even as I spoke, I knew that Father had seen in a day what I had tried never to see. Muskrat didn't want to be here.

"Wasn't it winter?" answered Father.

Father led the way back along the stream. At a place where the stream fed a pool of still water, he stopped and looked down, motioning with his chin for me to look too. I did. In the shining pool I saw two shadowy faces, Father's and one like it, which of course was mine. Father's face was very serious. "You see?" he said. "We're much the same. Your face is like mine, not like someone else's. That's good. My first wife's children looked like other men. My fourth wife—well, she was pregnant when I got her." He smiled slightly, watching me.

"Do you know what Andriki thinks about that?" he asked a moment later. "He thinks I'd welcome this child of hers if I knew who the father was. Andriki seems very sure, so I believe him. Where does he learn these women's secrets? Anyway, here is my plan. This summer, after we eat summer foods for a while, after the fireberries on the plain ripen so we can eat as we travel, I will send my fourth wife back to her parents for a time. If after all she wants to be my wife, then she can come to me when she's older. If not, her parents should give back my marriage gifts and not ask for more. Your mother won't like that, since any change will make it hard for her to keep her favorite necklace. That's Aal, though. Who can please her?"

But I couldn't think of Mother—not then. I was too surprised by Father. Since I had first learned of Pinesinger's pregnancy, I had been afraid of Father's anger. Yet now that he knew I had fathered his wife's child, he seemed not to care. I was also surprised by his plans for Pinesinger. In fact, my thoughts were swarming so thickly I couldn't follow all of them. In the dark pool Father's face watched my face carefully, as if waiting for my thoughts to grow still. "Does my stepmother agree?" I asked, wanting to say something.

"I haven't told her. And I mean to tell her myself, so don't let me come to her only to find that she knows. Don't tell her or any of the women."

"I, Father?" I asked. He gave me a sideways look that said, *Don't play with me.* "I wouldn't tell your thoughts to women," I hurried to add.

We walked on, reaching the clearing and the lodge just as a cloud of mist swallowed all but the tips of the longest branches of the trees. I wondered how Pinesinger would feel about being sent back to her parents. I knew that Bala's people would take it as some kind of disgrace. My mother had turned all the blame for divorce onto Father; according to her, the divorce was his fault. But Father must have learned from his experience with Mother. He might not want to let his name be spoiled again. Next

214

time the fault would be his wife's, I felt sure. Also Pinesinger was younger and softer than my mother. She wouldn't know how to turn the blame onto anyone, or not in time to do any good. Instead Bala's people would blame her for spoiling the marriage and losing the gifts of the marriage exchange.

And the boy—what of him? What if Pinesinger didn't come back to Father? Was this boy, if he lived, to stay with his mother's kin as I had done, as a guest of his lineage, instead of staying with me and Father as a man in the man's place, where he belonged? It seemed wrong. Also, how would the rest of Father's people feel about Father's doings? Would the people be glad? On Pinesinger's account, we had divided our lodge. Wouldn't it be better to wait, to see how things went before sending her away? I searched for a way to ask Father these questions, but we were almost at the lodge.

"Is your pack made?" he asked. "We'll eat now. Then we'll go. The day is growing old, and we must travel fast because of water."

"Water?"

"Yes. Didn't you eat milkroots when you came?"

Of course. On our way in the fall, we had gotten water from eating milkroots. But these are fall foods that wither in spring, when their vines sprout. In fact, after the melting snow soaks into the earth there is nothing to drink on the plains. But because with Bala we had always reached our summergrounds by following the river, I wasn't used to thinking about water.

Father's habit was to eat before starting a long journey. In the cold lodge he put wood on the owners' fire, and when the flames grew bright he sat on his heels to cook a piece of marmot meat. "Wife!" he said to Pinesinger. "Ask Kori's woman where her people are."

So Pinesinger left Father's sleeping-skins, which she had been rolling into a pack, and came, her shirt open and the baby nursing, to sit on her heels beside him. When the meat was ready, he gave her a strip of it. Muskrat watched. In the darkest shadow of the lodge, almost hidden by a heavy lodgepole, Father's wolf pup also watched, his feet and jaws tied. Under these eyes, Pinesinger ate the meat, then spoke in Muskrat's language. Muskrat answered with one word. Pinesinger said, "She hasn't seen them."

"Now ask her name," said Father.

But before Pinesinger could do it, Muskrat and I spoke at the same time. "Muskrat," said I. "Dabe Nore," said Muskrat.

"Hi!" said Father. "She understood."

"She understands some but not much," I said.

"I understand," said Muskrat.

This surprised me but not Father. When he saw that she understood him, he spoke to her directly. "Leech Pond," he began. "How did you find it?"

But Muskrat just looked at him. Perhaps she couldn't find the words. So I answered. "They came here by chance," I said. "Her people were here only for a short time. They were on the move, just as they were when they passed Uske's Spring. Do you remember that camp? Before that, they came from the south."

"Why did they leave their homeland?" asked Father.

I had already heard the story, so I answered for Muskrat. "Long ago something bad happened to them," I said. "Perhaps an illness. Her people went in all directions. None stayed behind. All left."

"Where in the south?" asked Father. "Has the place something by which it's known? A river, perhaps?"

"No river," said Muskrat.

"It has a strange animal," I said, and I told Father about the animals who were halfway between wolves and deer, who built summer shelters as people do, who cried out with human voices, and who shared their name with Ohun.

"Io. Tai tibisi," said Muskrat, who seemed to have understood this too.

"Hi!" said Father, wondering. "Can that be true?"

"It's what she once told us, unless she was lying," I answered. Muskrat nodded.

"Ask if her people will come for her," said Father.

"No," said Muskrat without waiting for Pinesinger. "They not come. They far. I not see where," she said.

Suddenly she pointed at me with her thumbs. "He come," she said. "Hiyiyiyi! He catch me. Snow come." She gestured with her hands to show snow falling. "I look." Scowling, she pretended to search the ground. "Ah. I see nothing. Then I wait. I wait. Much snow. Much, much snow. I still here. My people, they far. Very far. Where? I not know. They not come. They forget me. They forget me." She fell silent, then suddenly began to cry. With her left hand she wiped her eyes. With her right hand she twice cupped her left breast, leaving space for the nipple between her third and fourth fingers. Like our handsigns, her gesture meant something. But her tears and the lift of her shoulders showing that she didn't know how to find her people were the only signs we could understand.

"Why must you sit here talking?" asked Rin. "Is there something to say that won't wait for night? If we mean to travel today, we should go now, with Kori's woman or without her. We will travel very slowly, and water to drink is far."

But Father wouldn't be hurried by his sister. "Truly," he said thoughtfully, becoming serious, "this is what I think of Kori's woman. We don't want to fight strangers for her. We have women of our own, women who can be our wives. When we need more, we'll visit Bala or any of the people on the Grass River or the Black River or the Char or the Hair, and we'll marry. Marriage is the way to get women. That way we get in-laws, not enemies. We see marriage gifts, not spears. My son is young. He has had no one to teach him except his mother. That's why he acted rashly and did what he should not have done. We won't risk death and wounds to help him do it, and we won't be forced into fighting to make up for his mistake."

Andriki, who had been listening closely, frowned and pushed back his yellow hair. "Will her people use our hunting lands without asking us?" he said. "Will they come here freely? Perhaps Kori seized the woman, but I helped him bring her here. We taught her people to fear us. That was right."

"You taught an old man and a few women to fear us," said Father. "But the men, do they fear us?"

"I don't like your way of thinking," said Andriki. "We aren't cowards. Why do you talk as if we were?"

"Be easy, Brother," said Father. "No one is calling you a coward. No. I am just saying that we must save our fighting for something big, not for Kori's mistake. Do you want to risk your life for his woman? Would you, just for strangers who know nothing about us, who can't speak with us, who eat fish and hunt birds—just so they will think us brave? No. That's why I say she should go free."

I looked at Muskrat to see what she thought of this. But she was leaning against the wall with her eyes shut and didn't seem to be listening. Perhaps Father's speech held too many words for her.

"I think my half-brother is right," said Maral. "From the start I've been against keeping this woman. I was angry with Kori for bringing her here. It's best if she doesn't come to our summergrounds. Let her stay where her people can find her. She sets snares, and soon she'll have frogs and swans' eggs from the shore of the lake. There's summer food here, not like some lodges. She can go into the hills where she was camped when Kori found her. There are frogs and birds in Leech Pond. Well, then." Maral looked around the firelit lodge, warm at last thanks to Father. "Come, wives," he said. "If we're going, we should start."

"We'll go together," said Father. "So, Kori. Are you content?"

"I am," I said. But of course I wasn't. Whatever Father and the Bear might have said to each other, I had no thought of leaving Muskrat.

Dragging our packs into the blowing mist, we gathered in front of the lodge, where the adults helped each other lift packs and children. By habit we moved quietly. The fog and the damp earth kept us even quieter. Mist beaded the spruce needles and the pine needles and rose from the gray water of the lake. Because we wouldn't drink for the rest of the day, I went to the rocky shore and dipped my cupped hands into the water. Just then the mist cleared, and looking across the lake I saw the tiger.

Scanning the woods, he too was drinking. When our eyes met, he raised his chin. Drops of water clung to his whiskers and ran from his mouth. He stared at me a moment; then, without taking his eyes off me, he carefully lowered his chin and drank some more. Slowly, meaningfully, his great red tongue slapped the water. I didn't move. In time the tiger finished his drink, sighed, and giving me a last long look, strode into the forest, his tail out stiffly, as if he knew I was watching him. I waited for his roar, but none came.

"The Lily is there, going east," I said to the others when I went back for my pack and my spears.

"He mustn't follow us," said Hind. "We must let a little time pass before we cross his back trail."

"Better to go quickly before he comes around the lake," said Rin.

"Give me that," said Father to me, pointing with his lips at his wolf pup, who, with a thong around his neck and another around his jaws, was pressing himself against the outer wall of the lodge, trying to hide. I picked him up, noticing how soft his fur was, and how tender his body, and handed him to Father, who then tied his feet together and stuffed him in his pack. "We are many," said Father, "so no animal need worry us. We'll keep together until we're off the Lily's hunting lands. Don't fear him."

"Perhaps we're just foolish people who can't help fearing him," said Rin.

Maral and his wives fell into step behind Father. Rin lifted her pack and strode after Lilan. The rest of the people struggled into their packs and hurried to catch up. I put my pack on my back and lifted a full, wet waterskin to my shoulder—my share of the extra load. But I didn't follow the others. Instead I waited to see what Muskrat would do when she saw the rest of us leaving.

Curious, Pinesinger waited too. "So, Kori. Your wife goes ahead of you," she said, speaking of little Frogga, who rode astride her father's neck. "Is your woman also coming?"

But Muskrat sat on her heels behind her big belly, resting her head and her back against the lodge.

Lifting her pack to my shoulder, I stood as tall as I could. "Muskrat!" I said firmly. She looked up. "Come!" I said. She stared. Her eyes seemed wet. Was she crying? "Come!" I said louder, taking her small pack and settling it on top of mine. She shook her head. I had expected this, but even so I began to feel angry. "Come!" I said a third time. "Your pack is leaving, even if you stay." Muskrat stared, not moving.

This seemed funny to Pinesinger, who laughed and said, "She's not coming! Even she would rather live alone than live with you, Kori."

But that was not to be. Turning my back on anyone who might have been watching, so that no one could see what I did, I stood in front of Muskrat. "Look here," I said, stretching my lips and pointing to my upper eye-teeth with my first two fingers. "Tiger," I whispered, staring at her. Muskrat blinked. She took my meaning. I turned on my heel and walked away, and in no time heard her panting behind me as she struggled to keep up.

"What did you tell her?" asked Pinesinger at last, after we had caught up with the others.

"Not much, Stepmother," I said, out of breath myself by this time. "I told her that I was going to our summergrounds and that if she didn't come with me, she wouldn't find me, since I wasn't coming back."

"Did she understand all that?" asked Pinesinger doubtfully.

"Most of it," I answered.

24

Up we went through the blowing mist, over the mossy shoulders of the Hills of Ohun, our group very quiet because of the tiger. Even the children made no sound. When I heard Muskrat panting at my heels, I stood aside to let her follow Rin, who was just ahead of me. Then if Muskrat fell behind, I'd know it. As we walked a gap appeared between Muskrat and Rin, and soon all I could see was Rin's outline, a shadow in the mist. Then I couldn't even hear footsteps, just the faint creaking of my own clothing and Muskrat's heavy breath.

On the far slopes of the hills the wind had made the mist thin and I could see the rest of our people, the many brown forms moving south in single file. Their line wound through the berry heath, red with new leaves, white with tiny flowers. To think how long the heath would lie quietly waiting for the berries to grow reminded me of how long it might be before I would eat again. I almost felt sad to see flowers just starting, without even the buds of berries, as if the heath were keeping food from me. Just then a fresh north wind cleared the mist around us. I looked up and for a moment saw the four dark breasts of sleeping Ohun. Then the wind turned and blew mist from the south, hiding the heath we were leaving behind but carrying the fragrance of the land ahead of us—the sweet, grassy breath of the plain.

At dusk the people stopped suddenly. Far ahead of me and Muskrat, their long open line closed and shortened, and they stood side by side, shading their eyes and looking west at something I couldn't see. Yet I knew it was an animal when Father and the other men put down their packs, bent low, and crept over the short grass. "Stay still," I whispered to Muskrat. She stopped in her tracks, and I hurried to catch up.

Just then Father's arm whipped and his spear flew. All the men ran forward. Chasing what? I saw a yellow animal running, dodging, with all the men scrambling to cut off its escape. It was a colt. Young and alone, it must have been lying down when the men first noticed it. The chase ended suddenly when the colt burst between Andriki and Marten, who threw their spears. Both missed. A plume of dust rose behind it as it ran away. Soon it stopped and turned to face the hunters, but by then they had no hope of getting it, and they didn't try. Instead they picked up their things and began looking for a place to camp. I went back to Muskrat. Disappointed and hungry, we at last caught up.

We camped in a thicket of blooming fireberry bushes, where we found a few dry branches to burn. The thicket also gave us shelter from the wind. In place of wood we gathered balls of dung left by grazing bison and horses, and in place of food we drank water.

Father opened his pack and took out the little wolf pup. After looking him over, Father untied his feet and jaws and set him down. The pup stood on wobbling legs, his head bent. Then his trembling hind legs suddenly folded, and he fell. The night before he would have run away, but that night he seemed too ill to notice us. Father hadn't had him long. Although it seemed longer, we had dug him out of the earth only the day before. He had lost his good condition surprisingly soon. With a long moccasin lace, Father tied the pup to the fireberry bush and watched him a while. When the rest of us drank more of the precious water, Father tried to squirt some into his mouth, but the pup struggled, wasting it. Father sighed, then turned from him, as if he had lost interest.

It came to me that I could spit water into the pup's mouth and I offered to do this, expecting Father to thank me. Instead he seemed not to hear. So I began to worry about what Father thought of me. I remembered how easily I had ignored his wishes. In fact I had ignored almost everyone's wishes, even the Bear's. That Father might not have liked this came to me slowly as I sat, ashamed, under everyone's eyes. When I could, I got up and went to sit behind Andriki. From Andriki's shadow I tried to listen to the men's talk, but I couldn't take my thoughts from Muskrat's swaying, heavy form, which still struggled along the trail ahead of me in my mind's eye. Even she had not wanted to come with us. I saw that I had pleased only myself.

But to have left her behind? I couldn't have done it. My big, heavy woman, round and pregnant? I couldn't! I made plans to take her to the Fire River, where, as I saw it, we could live with Uncle Bala. He wouldn't refuse me. He would understand. Best of all, Muskrat's people wouldn't find us there.

In no time I was lost in a daydream of the Fire River. When the evening star rose to hang above the horizon, glowing like an ember but giving no light, I remembered the same star rising out of the grass on Uncle Bala's plains. When a herd of scattered clouds ran past the stars, I remembered how people would say that the Bear was chasing bison. When the wind brought the voice of a short-eared owl—*hu ah ha hu*—I remembered a child's story of a little night hunter who killed small deer. Then I remembered how hungry I was, and other times of being hungry, and found myself thinking of the colt alone in the dark and how lucky we were to have found it, since we would probably be eating it soon. Was I a child, to let Father's anger worry me?

Most of the women were sleeping. At the far edge of camp, where I had left my pack, Muskrat had unrolled our bedding. She would be asleep in no time, I knew, because she was so tired. But the men were not sleeping. They sat on their heels around the fire, waiting for the clouds to clear, so the stars would give more light. Until we were ready to hunt the colt, though, I made sure to sit on the far side of Andriki from Father. Until I could see how things were, I kept out of his sight.

But not out of hearing. Hidden by Andriki, I listened carefully as Father told us once again of the wolf pup a woman had kept at Graylag's lodge and how this wolf had helped with hunting. One winter day when Father had been hunting in a wood, he told us, he had surprised a male reindeer in a thicket. The reindeer had run up a hill when out of nowhere Graylag's wolf had appeared and chased the reindeer, who was forced to stop and lower his antlers to keep the wolf from biting his legs. When the reindeer had shown his side, Father had thrown his spear and killed him.

So Father had hopes for the pup. "If the pup were old enough," he said, "he could find that colt tonight and make it stand still for us until we caught up. A wolf can run as fast as a horse. A person can't."

"Is that true?" asked Andriki.

Ignoring Andriki, Father began to tell the story of a second hunt with Graylag's wolf, a hunt Father had heard about but hadn't seen, when suddenly he was interrupted by a cry from Pinesinger. We all turned, and Father seized his spear.

"Get him away!" cried her voice in the dark. Her baby also started crying.

"What now?" asked Rin, her voice tired.

"The wolf!" cried Pinesinger.

"Speak softly, woman," said Father. "You'll drive the colt farther. Don't you want to eat?"

"What's wrong?" I asked.

"His wolf came touching me! I was sleeping. I thought it was the baby. Hi! Filth! Get him away!"

"Came touching you, Wife?" asked Father.

"Yes," said Pinesinger. "He came to my breast."

It was almost as if Father had planned it. Of course the wolf was hungry, being so young. Of course Pinesinger's milk-filled breast had lured him. Of course he had helped himself to a little taste. At first I thought it funny, and looked at Andriki, waiting to laugh. Then I felt annoyed that an animal would take food belonging to Pinesinger's child, and I opened my mouth to object. But at last I saw that I should keep quiet, since both the pup and the woman were Father's and I had already given him much reason to complain. So I hid in Andriki's shadow to see what came next.

Father got up and went to speak with Pinesinger. But

instead of standing over her and speaking in his matter-of-fact headman's way, he sat on his heels, very politely crouching beside her bed. He spoke so quietly, his tone so kind, his voice so low, that none of us could overhear him. He wanted something.

Soon we stopped straining our ears to hear him, because Pinesinger began calling out her answers. "If my mother could hear that, she'd weep," she said. Then, "They'll want their gifts back." Next, "My father will fight you." And last and loudest, "We aren't animals!" No one had to tell us that Father was asking her to feed his pup.

"Does this mean she'll do it?" Andriki asked the men around the fire. We couldn't help but laugh.

After a while Father came back to the fire, looking neither disappointed nor triumphant but satisfied, as if he had finished something. With his foot he lifted his spear to where his hand could grasp it. We looked at him with curiosity. "Well? What is it?" he asked, as if he couldn't imagine why we were watching him.

"It's we who want an answer," said Andriki. "Will she?"

"Will she what?"

"Don't tease us, Brother. Will she feed your wolf?"

"Yes," said Father.

"She will?"

"Yes."

"But that's not what she said!"

"What?" cried Father, playful at last. "She was speaking privately."

"How could we not hear?"

"She'll feed it, and someday we'll have a hunting helper, just as Graylag once had. Unlike Graylag, we'll keep ours with us and won't let it run away into the woods. For now, though, we must get meat for ourselves. Are you coming with me, or must I hunt alone?" To Rin, still awake, he added, "Build the fire, Sister. We'll cook soon."

The wind had risen and the clouds had gone; the bushes on the plain showed faintly in the starlight.

Spears ready, we spread out and walked very quietly toward the place we had last seen the colt. Because he was so young and without parents, he had nowhere to go, so we knew where to find him. Our thought was that lacking a protector, he might stay still as we got near; he might try to hide instead of moving to stay beyond us, as a grown horse would. With luck he was sick, or had been orphaned or separated from his mother for so long that, like Father's wolf, he was weak from hunger and thirst. With luck he might be lying down.

Since the yellow-brown colt would be hard to see we went slowly, keeping watch for lions, as must everyone who hunts at night. When lions hunt on such short grass, they like dark nights. Even so, we weren't much afraid of meeting them. And I, for one, did not expect our hunt to take long.

I was right, although we almost lost the colt. As I was carefully walking, setting my feet in the hunter's manner, little toe first, no scuffing, a nightjar burst up shouting in front of me, its voice so loud my heart stopped. I had been thinking of lions. The next thing I knew the men were running, chasing the colt, who at first dodged among us, his little hooves pounding. Then he screamed, and I knew he had been speared. For one so small he struggled greatly. Maral and Marten held him down while Andriki cut his throat.

As we finished butchering, which we did very quickly because he was so small, we sent Ako to camp with meat, and soon the delicious smell of cooking floated in the air. Wiping the blood from ourselves with grass, we picked up the hide and the rest of the meat and went into camp all together. Most trouble fades with the smell of good food. On the way to camp I felt Father's hand fall lightly on my shoulder. He meant that he wasn't going to hold Muskrat against me. That made me happy. In the starlight, I smiled to thank him. He seemed not to notice, which was his way.

The colt was delicious, tender and sweet, his flesh filled with juice if not fat. Without waiting for my first piece to cook through, I lifted it with a stick from the burning dung and began to eat it anyway. The women got up and came to eat with us. Pirit and Frogga came too, stunned with sleep, rubbing their eyes as they waited for their shares. Pinesinger arrived with the wolf behind her, not just following her but pressing against her as it shrank from the rest of us. She had been suckling it. I wondered what Father had said to her, what threat he had made or what reward he had promised, to get her to do that.

I looked around for Muskrat. She wasn't there. I was surprised, since when food was cooking she was always watching, never failing to let her face show that she wanted a share. Not liking to think of her being so tired that she missed a chance to eat, I got up and went to wake her. I found my sleeping-skins unrolled but no one in them. "Muskrat!" I called, but no one answered.

I walked all through the camp then, looking at everyone's place and in everyone's bedding. I looked at the people around the fire, and I looked at the black shadows on the starlit plain. I saw everyone else, by now glancing around doubtfully to learn what was the matter, but I didn't see Muskrat. Muskrat wasn't there.

25

WE WAITED, THINKING SHE HAD GONE TO RELIEVE HERSELF. When she didn't come back, we looked in the shadows of all the bushes. She wasn't anywhere. In fact, while we peered into the night for anything moving, the plain grew so still it was almost frightening—no animal called, not even the nightjar, who had kept up his ugly shouting long after I had frightened him. Yet a woman doesn't vanish like an animal. Was this Father's doing?

After a time the air began to move again, very slowly, faintly chilling our skins as it went by. Again the cloud shadows crept over the stars, and again the nightjar began his loud, tiresome call. "She was here—I saw her on the plain just before dark," said Rin. "I thought she was looking for fuel."

"I saw her sitting in the bushes," said Pinesinger. "She was too tired to gather fuel. She left that work to the rest of us, although we were tired too."

"Staring at the dark does no good," said Father. "If she wants to hide, you won't see her. Remember that she didn't want to come with us."

"But she was tired," I said, although I knew the other people had no plans to help me look for her. "Why wouldn't she rest now?"

"What better time to escape you?" asked Father. "She has to cross a short-grass plain. By daylight you'd see her."

Of course he was right. By daylight I would see her, and I'd bring her back, too. I said nothing, but made up my mind to look for her when the sun rose. My mind's eye saw her trail in the dew. Then one last thought came to me—the Lily. "Uncle," I said to Andriki, the only person still on his feet, still looking out over the moonlit plain. "What of the Lily? Would he follow us? Could he have taken Muskrat?"

Andriki looked down at me thoughtfully while rolling my question through his mind. "No," he said at last. "He's too big. Where would he hide? Anyway, his habits wouldn't let him come here. He stays in the trees, and after snow melts he doesn't go far from the lake. He likes his drinking water. And he was still eating his moose. Why would he walk so far to hunt so small a thing as a woman when if he rested in his thicket he could get another moose?"

In time most of the women built their own little fires and lay down by them to sleep. The men slept too. I had no fire—Muskrat hadn't gathered fuel for me—and I couldn't sleep, so I sat alone by Father's fire. The air was moving faster by then, chasing sparks from the ashes, whispering in the grass and in the bushes. Overhead the clouds had gathered, but stars showed above the horizon, and once again I felt the size of the space around me, as if the plain went over the edge of the world to the stars. I was as small as a waterbear in that space. If I got lost, no one would find me.

So it was with Muskrat. Unless she called out or built a fire, we wouldn't find her. Maybe her homeland was open, huge, so that when she saw the space she felt free. When I was a boy, I once threw a stone at a wheatear and stunned it. I took it in my hands. Then I felt it moving, and put it on the ground to see what it would do. For a moment it squatted with its rump down and legs flat, swaying a little and looking at the sky. Then suddenly it flew. I remember its bobbing, hurrying flight, its rear getting smaller and smaller, with its little gray feet curled in fists under its tail. Was it the same with Muskrat? Did she leave when she saw the big sky?

Late at night I heard someone beside me. The fire was no more than embers; I added fuel. The flames showed Pinesinger warming herself, sitting on her heels with her shirt open. I saw her baby asleep in his sling, his dark head far back, his eyes shut, and his small mouth open. In the shadows behind Pinesinger shone the green eyes of Father's wolf. Strange that a wolf should have stayed while a woman ran away, but so it was to be. I nodded a greeting to my stepmother. I thought she was sitting a little too close to me, but I had nothing to say.

The same was not true of Pinesinger. Under her breath at first, louder as she forgot herself, she leaned forward and with her face next to mine began to denounce Father. Calling him selfish and cruel, calling him an animal, she said so much so fast that I couldn't quite understand her. Her dark eyes blazed with tears, and her face grew red in the firelight. I could feel the heat of her breath. The matter was that Father had made her suckle his wolf pup, but a little time passed before I knew that.

Perhaps it was wrong of her to lose control, to speak in such a way about Father, and perhaps I should have tried to stop her, but in truth I was amazed by what she was saying and was afraid Father might be listening. "Stepmother," I whispered, pointing with my lips at Father's long, dark shape stretched out in his deerskins just beyond the firelight, "he'll hear you."

"He won't. He's sleeping," said Pinesinger furiously, turning to look for the wolf. "Your father can sleep. I cannot, with that nose nuzzling me." Seeing the two green eyes, she flung a handful of dirt at them. The pup cried out and the eyes vanished.

"But didn't you agree?" I asked Pinesinger.

"Of course I agreed. Don't you know your father?"

I did, of course. If he asked something of me, I wouldn't refuse him. He was too strong a person, and the headman too. People didn't refuse him.

"That's why you must tell him," Pinesinger went on. "Tell him I won't do it. Tell him the animal is taking milk that belongs to a child. You must do it, Kori."

Again I looked at Father's long, still form. Black in the shadows, he lay motionless. I felt sure he was listening to us. Too old to sleep soundly and too much of a hunter by day not to think of those who hunt the plains by night, he would have an ear up and open, listening for everything, even in his sleep. Knowing he might hear me, I said nothing.

But my silence wasn't enough for Pinesinger. "I'm afraid of him," she insisted. "I don't want to anger him, yet I can't please him. I don't know what he wants me to do or where he wants me to go." She thought for a moment and then, perhaps in case Father after all was listening, she added, "I think he's angry because of this child of mine. He thinks I lay with other men, and for revenge he makes me suckle an animal."

Now that wasn't true, not as I saw it. Nor was it true that Pinesinger couldn't please Father. He was pleased when she did as he asked. Although I could have told this stepmother of mine what lay ahead for her, at least as far as Father's plans went, I kept silent, as I had promised. "Who can know his thoughts?" I asked.

At last Pinesinger seemed to see my discomfort. She leaned close to my ear and whispered, "For the sake of your child—and he is yours, Kori—make your father free me from this animal. If he won't free me, kill it. I'd kill it, but he'd know if I did."

She made a person think—I'll say that for Pinesinger. She wasn't an animal to be feeding a pup with the milk of her body, milk that belonged to her baby and mine. The thing was, though, I couldn't quite see how it was right for me to spoil Father's plans for a hunting helper. He had a plan in mind when he dug out the pup—he had been making his plan for a year or longer. What the plan was, I didn't know, but did I want to spoil it before I understood it? I thought not. Besides, would feeding the pup really harm the baby? Again, I thought not. A she-wolf is no larger than a woman, yet a she-wolf has milk for many pups. How could just one hurt my stepmother's milk?

The fire had become a red glow in the smoldering dung, a mound of embers that the wind flamed now and again. Lit by the fire, Pinesinger's angry eyes searched mine for an answer. I couldn't help remembering how, in a haze of green leaves, the same face had watched me just a year ago, just before we made love by the Fire River. Then I would gladly have killed an animal if she had asked me. In fact, I would have done anything at all for that carefree and beautiful woman. Anyone would. But things were different now. The child might be mine, it was true, but the woman didn't seem the same. Also, she and the animal were Father's.

When a faint yellow glow in the east showed that at last the old moon was coming, I lay down and fell asleep, then woke to feel air passing over my face. When I opened my eyes I saw, almost at ground level, that the haze of moonlight had grown very bright. I had hardly slept a moment. Something had wakened me. The hair on my skin lifted. Something was moving. I heard a footstep, then another. Something was slowly creeping upwind toward my back. On short grass, where a tiger can't hide, he must finish his hunting by the time the moon rises. Before my eyes, the first bright spot of the moon came over the horizon. I reached for my spear and turned over.

There stood Muskrat. Her head, her tangled hair, were dark against the stars in the dome of the sky, but her legs in her sagging trousers showed against the pale band of light that was growing on the eastern rim of the plain.

Without a word and very slowly, as if she were in pain, she bent down and untied her moccasins. If she saw me turn, she gave no sign. Instead she drew her feet out of her moccasins, first one, then the other. Then, so slowly that she seemed exhausted, she untied her belt and let her trousers fall.

The day before she would have had to tug them down, but now with a soft noise they dropped around her feet. She stepped out of them and knelt beside me, and I saw from her loose belly, a belly that sagged from her ribs and hipbones, that her baby had been born.

Of all the things that might have taken Muskrat away from us, her baby had not occurred to anyone. Shocked speechless, I watched her. Shrugging one shoulder, she drew her arm out of its sleeve. In the same way she freed her other arm, so that the shirt hung around her like a bag, the sleeves empty. Leaving it like that, she sat on the ground beside my deerskins, and using her feet to kick them open, she put her legs in next to mine, chilling me with her icy touch. Then she eased herself onto the skin beside me and lay down. As she did, I noticed a large wad of moss wedged into her crotch. It was a pad to stop the blood that flows from women when they menstruate or after they give birth. No such moss grows on the plains— Muskrat had brought it with her. She had no pack—she must have carried it in her clothing. So she hadn't run away, but instead had given birth, and for at least two days, ever since the day before we left the lodge, she had known she was going to do it.

Where Muskrat had been standing, the pale light grew. It was almost morning. In the dark camp beyond us, people were walking around, adding the last twigs and balls of dung to the ash-covered embers of the fire. I heard Father telling Pinesinger to make up his pack. Would he expect Muskrat to travel? She lay on her side, her back to me, her legs in the sleeping-skins, her arms hidden in her shirt. Unless Muskrat had left the baby somewhere, it was also hidden in her shirt.

I looked down at her. Her eyes were shut and her lips were parted; she was already fast in an exhausted sleep. What must have happened to her during the night, alone on the plain without even a fire? And where was the baby? Was it a boy? A girl? Was it early? Was it living? Healthy? Was it there at all? Inside her shirt, Muskrat's arms were folded. Her shoulder made the only lump I could see. Yet a new baby is very small.

Carefully, slowly, so as not to wake or frighten her, I lifted the hem of her shirt. There was her waist, her loose, empty belly sagging toward the ground. I raised the shirt higher. There were her ribs, each one showing, rising and falling with her even breath. Gently I raised the shirt higher still, pulling it so softly that she wouldn't feel it move. There was her bony elbow, crooked below her round breast. There was her nipple, almost black in the gray light, erect in its circle of skin, lumpy like a plucked bird's. Like our women, Muskrat had this "skin of Ohun"—like our women, she too was joined to the air, the place of spirits, birds, and shamans. At the end of the nipple clung a drop of milk.

I raised her shirt as high as it would easily go. There, lying pressed against her breast, lay a small, thin baby. Its knees were drawn to its chest, its tiny ankles were crossed, its face was dark and wrinkled, and its eyes were squeezed shut. Between its legs was a great hairy pad of moss, which I lifted. A penis. He was a little boy—a son. Perhaps he was tiny, but he was mine. I, who hadn't wept since I saw the last of Mother, I felt my eyes burn with tears, I felt a swelling grow inside my throat so tight that I couldn't swallow, for this child was mine as surely as he was Muskrat's. I had gotten him on my woman. He was the child of my body, and the pulse that beat at the top of his skull, the pulse that made his black hair gently flutter, was the pulse of my life.

The cold air on her bare skin partly wakened Muskrat. She scowled and clenched her teeth, and grasped her shirt to pull it down again. Her hand meeting mine woke her fully, and she looked up at me over her shoulder. For a moment she stared, then took in the fact that I was crying. My voice was hoarse, but I whispered "Muskrat" and touched her forehead, brushing her straggling hair as gently as possible from the blue tattoo on her face.

"Ah. You see," she answered, pulling up the deerskin

to cover herself but turning on her back and lifting her cold hand to my cheek. Her face was relaxed, and her eyes were tired but contented. At last she smiled.

For a long time we looked at each other, then at the baby, now lying rump up under the deerskin on her chest. "He's small!" I said at last.

"Io. Small," she whispered.

I was still weeping. "He's ugly!" I said through my tears.

Now Muskrat smiled a little smile in the gathering light of the sunrise. "Hi!" she said. "Not ugly."

Very happy, I stroked my thumb over her eyelids, closing her eyes, letting my touch tell her to sleep. Cupping the baby in one hand, she held him against her chest while she turned toward me, so she lay on her side with him between us. Before I knew it she was asleep again, now smiling faintly. I pulled the upper deerskin over her head so she wouldn't see the day.

There was no question of our traveling until the following morning, or not in my mind. Although the people were surprised at themselves for not having guessed why Muskrat had left us, most of them grumbled when I said that if they didn't wait for her, if they didn't let her rest before traveling, they would travel without me. Perhaps they could have gone without Muskrat, but it went against them to go without me. This was especially true of Father, who as headman would have to arrive at the Hair River, perhaps to meet Graylag's people, and tell them that he hadn't kept his group together, that he had left his own son and newborn grandson behind.

Yet if even for one day we failed to go as far as possible, we would run out of water before we reached the Hair. Crossing the plain took six days, or the time it would take us, drinking sparingly, to empty both of our waterskins. But we had been using water thoughtlessly, and by night we would have all but emptied one of them. We solved the problem by emptying the skin I had carried, drinking it dry, even waking Muskrat so she could drink a full share, then giving it to Maral and Andriki, who set out at

a fast stride for Narrow Lake. They would fill the skin
there and come back to us, traveling twice the distance
that they had traveled when forced to be slow by women,
children, and the weight of their packs.

Everyone grumbled at the change of plans, but what
could be done? The sun was bright and the day was
growing warm—it was too bright and warm for hunting,
especially on a short-grass plain with no way to hide. And
there were no ripe berries. Sorting through the bones of
the colt, seeing how little meat was left on them, we
decided to look for more food while we searched for the
dung and bushes we would need to keep our fire going
one more night. Too far from the lodge to know well, the
plain was strange to us, except that we had traveled
through it. Not even Rin could walk straight up to
something worth eating, so we spread out and went
slowly, searching for bitter-root sedge and birds' eggs.
The roots of this sedge pucker the mouth and the eggs
were tiny, but we found enough of these foods to bring to
camp.

There the breeze brought us the smell of grass and the
drone of bees trying to drink from our waterskin. Bored,
most people slept, but I was too happy and too excited.
Instead I begged some string from Father, found three
stones, and made a throwing snare. When I tested it, it
flew like an eagle, so I went out to find its prey. It was too
small for the bison that grazed in the distance; a bison
would have kicked it aside. It was too big for the larks
that flew up under my feet; the larks would have flown
between the strings or would have been crushed by the
stones. Yet my throwing snare was just right for a bustard
I saw picking his way across the grass, his head tipped
back so he could keep his eye on me, his long whiskers
swaying.

As I walked slowly toward the bustard he walked
slowly away, keeping a certain distance, never thinking
that I had something to throw at him. As I whirled the
throwing snare around my head, though, he grew frightened, spread his wings, and began trotting, and when he
took to the air I let go. The snare wrapped itself around

the bird and brought him down. He was too badly hurt to fly anymore, but I wasn't taking chances—I ran to him and stamped on his neck. I had to give the legs to my in-laws and the muscles of one wing to my kin, but since I was the only person of my lineage north of the Fire River, the muscle of the other wing was mine. So I killed meat for my woman. "It will be good for her milk," I said to Father as I cooked it.

Dressed again, with her hair combed and quite well braided, Muskrat came to sit on her heels between Rin and me. Father nodded a greeting. Muskrat nodded to Father, then opened the neck of her shirt to show him the baby. Moving very slowly and carefully, Father looked down at the little face, at the shapeless nose, the swollen eyes, the fine black hair.

"He boy," said Muskrat. "Kiu Ngarr."

Father looked at me for an explanation. "What does she mean by 'kiu ngarr'?" he asked.

"He name," said Muskrat. "What I call him. Kiu Ngarr."

"A name?" asked Father.

"What's she doing, naming an infant?" asked Rin.

That had been my thought too. It wasn't right. In fact, it's very dangerous to name a child before its legs are strong enough to run. In the Camps of the Dead, people hear the name and believe the child is grown. Then they set tasks the child can't manage. It's almost sure death to name a child too young. But after all, because Muskrat knew so little of the way of things, perhaps we were expecting too much of her to know better.

"That's not to be his name," I told Rin.

"You must tell her," said Rin. "Get your stepmother."

Although her eyes were still swollen from the crying she had done the night before, Pinesinger sat obligingly on her heels between me and Muskrat, listening carefully to Muskrat's stream of words. At last she said, "This is quite bad, what she's telling me. She knows what you want, but she refuses."

"Tell us what she says."

THE ANIMAL WIFE

As Pinesinger began to do it, Muskrat broke in. "He must have name," she insisted. "How we know him, no name? All child have name. He name Kiu Ngarr." Muskrat thought a moment, started to speak to us again, then changed her mind and, turning to Pinesinger, began to talk in short bursts of her own language.

"She says a child must be named," said Pinesinger. "How else can people know him? All children have names, she says. Our children have names too, she says. We wait to call our children by name, but her people don't wait. She says it is useless to wait. She asks why we wait. Are we trying to hide who our children are? Is something wrong with the names? Do they shame us? As for her, she isn't ashamed of the name of this child: Kiu Ngarr. That is his name. So says your woman, Kori."

I hadn't expected so much force from Muskrat, and my anger came. Turning to Muskrat, I took her by the chin. "By the Bear," I said, "you won't name my son."

She jerked her face free of my grasp. "I name," she said. "Kiu Ngarr, Kiu Ngarr. He mine, and he name Kiu Ngarr. You want to talk him, Kiu Ngarr what you call him. Io!"

"Don't worry," said Father that night, after Muskrat and all the women had gone to sleep and after Maral and Andriki had come striding into the firelight, bringing water and a clutch of swans' eggs from the bank of the stream. "Don't worry. That word she calls your baby, that isn't a name. Let her say what she likes. Anyway, it's her lineage. Perhaps her lineage knows what it wants by way of names."

I didn't think so, but I saw no gain in arguing with Father. I planned to save my voice for Muskrat, whose show of strength had come as a surprise. I couldn't remember a time she had ever refused to do as I said, at least as far as she understood me.

Later I sat on my heels by her bed, and as best I could I explained the danger in talking too much or even in thinking too much about a new baby, let alone in giving it a name. I explained that in the Camps of the Dead, people hear the talk and take notice of the baby. If they like it, they want it. Then they send a sickness to kill it and a bird to find its soul.

When I finished, Muskrat looked at me impatiently. "True for you childs, may be," she said. "Not for mine."

26

IT ISN'T GOOD TO THINK TOO MUCH ABOUT A VERY YOUNG child, or to plan for him until he is named, yet when I was awake, unless I was doing something that needed all my thoughts, like hunting, I would find myself thinking about the child born to my woman, perhaps in the same way that I once thought about her. At night, if I sat looking at the fire, I would find my son in my thoughts without knowing how he came to be there, like waking from a dream.

In this way I planned what I would do with him as he grew. I saw myself teaching him snaring, then hunting. I saw myself making spears for him, at first a child's spear with a bone point, later an adult's spear with a point made of flint or some other good stone that I would find. I saw myself in the hills behind Woman Lake, the place where Uncle Bala and his people went for flints. In my mind's eye I went there, although the journey took more time than I liked to think. That daydream made me wonder if perhaps Father knew of flint somewhere close by. Then I saw that I still had much to learn from Father. I would start soon, with the flint.

I saw myself taking my boy to far places, so he would know the world. I saw myself teaching him the hunting lands at Woman Lake and the Fire River, the lands I knew, the lands where I could hunt alone and not get lost. I also saw myself teaching him Father's hunting lands—

Father's, my son's, and mine—the heaths and forests that I had just begun to learn but that Father and my uncles would teach me by the time my boy was old enough to hunt.

I saw myself taking him to Uske's Spring and showing him where Andriki and I had spent the night inside a mammoth carcass. I saw him at the Fire River, learning how to catch whitefish with his hands and how to move the old lion away from meat, if the old lion still lived there.

My mind's eye saw danger too. I remembered a place on Woman Lake where an underwater spring weakens the ice. I had always been drawn to that place, because unknown to the adults, the other boys and I had played a game there: with hands joined, we would run at the weak ice, then stop suddenly, so that the boys at the end of the line slid over it. This made the ice groan. It once had seemed very exciting, but I wouldn't let my boy do it! In fact, just thinking of that place began to frighten me. My son was too dear to me—I couldn't let him play dangerous games.

I would find him a wife. Young as he was, named or not, it was not too early to think of a wife. People planned marriages for children as yet unborn. With this in mind, I tried to remember the many little girls. At first when I thought of girls I thought of lineages, until I saw that as Muskrat's child my son had no lineage. So lineage didn't matter. That was good, because any girl could marry him. It was also bad, because the girl's parents might not want to give their daughter to a boy who had no lineage, to a captive woman's child. I saw that I might make up for this lack with ivory. We might have to offer twice the wedding gifts, enough for the mother's side as well as the father's, but if the wedding gifts we offered were very good and very many, the girl's parents might be willing. Her relatives might also like the fact that they would be asked to give only half as many gifts.

I saw how I should find a girl soon, before some other family found her, as Father had found Frogga for me. In this way I began thinking of ivory and hunting and how the next time we killed mammoths I should take care to get my spear into one of them, to earn a share of the ivory.

I also began to think of other fine things, beautiful things, such as the breast feathers and wing feathers of Woman teals. As far as I knew, these small birds nested only in the reeds of Woman Lake. I couldn't remember ever having thought about their feathers before, since I myself had no use for them, yet I knew people loved the shining rainbow colors. People tied the feathers in necklaces or hung them from their ears or braided them into their hair. People accepted them as gifts in marriage exchanges. Then I wished I was back at Woman Lake, where I could set snares, since I knew just where the nests were. Ah well; as my Uncle Bala used to say, "To every good place, a trail leads." He meant that if you need something, a way to get it becomes clear. I guessed that sooner or later I would find a trail between me and those feathers.

I even thought of amber. Now amber would not be found easily—not even Uncle Bala would find too many trails leading to amber, and I knew of nowhere to get any. Even so, I had heard of it and even seen it—I seemed to remember that some kinswomen of my mother's had owned amber. Then I remembered the first time I had seen Father, and how he had given a necklace of lion's teeth to Uncle Bala. Although I had paid it little attention at the time, I remembered that an amber bead had hung from the necklace. Father had given an amber bead to Uncle Bala! Would he know where I might get such a bead? He would. I suddenly felt as sure of getting amber as I did of getting teals and ivory. Knowing that something such as an amber bead might make the difference between reluctant in-laws and willing in-laws, I began to feel hope for my son.

Small as he was, the baby knew me. Even when his eyes were shut, he knew my voice, I could tell. His mouth twisted into a smile when I spoke to him, and he took my finger when I touched his hand. He was very, very strong. There was no one I could talk to about how much all of this pleased me, since the other men seldom spoke of such things. So my joy was secret, unless his mother knew. Yet joy it was. As he lay between me and his mother in my deerskins at night, I sang in a very low voice the songs the people on the Fire River sang to their children. Or I whispered to him, telling of the things I would make for him and the things I would show him. But most of all I told him that the Bear Himself would see him and would not forget him, knowing he would be a hunter, a feeder of foxes, a man of meat.

It hurts me to remember that I let something happen —helped it happen, really—that could have harmed my little son. Yet on our third night on the trail, I was so new at being a father that when my father and Pinesinger came to me with the wolf pup, I didn't think clearly. I understood at once that they wanted me to make Muskrat give her breast for the use of this animal. I saw how Muskrat was the perfect answer to the question of feeding the pup, since Muskrat wasn't the same as Pinesinger and no one would be insulted if we used her. For a while it even seemed like a good idea. It never came to me that I should defy or disobey Father for the sake of a captive woman, and it never came to me to get rid of the wolf, as Pinesinger had asked of me, since the wolf was Father's. Instead I brought the pup to Muskrat and pointed to her breast.

At first she refused. She pushed the pup aside. When I told her, with Pinesinger's help, that I would make her an ivory necklace if she nursed it, her face grew bitter, and when I insisted that she help us, she snatched the pup away from me and threw it to the ground. Of course it cried very much, a high, wailing *yi yi yi* that brought all the people to their feet to see what was happening. Muskrat began to weep, and the baby began to scream. I hate to hear a young baby screaming—the breathless *kaa kaa kaa* sets my teeth on edge and makes me want to choke the mother. Nor did the other people like it; some of them came to stand over Muskrat, telling her to control herself and calm her baby, all in words she didn't understand. She got up and went to sit at the edge of camp, hushing the baby by putting her nipple in his mouth.

Meanwhile the people looked at me to see what I would do about my woman. Would she do as I asked, or would she not? Afraid to let her think she could defy me, I caught her by the arm and pulled her to her feet, then dragged her to the far side of the fireberry thicket, where the other people couldn't see. There I took off my belt and shook it at her. She stared as if she didn't understand. I lashed the belt through the air so that it made a frightening whistle, then cracked it noisily against the ground. Again I swung the belt and hit the ground, and again and again. A second time I shook the belt at Muskrat.

She was weeping silently, her eyes wide open, tears shining on her face. Giving me a long look, she sighed deeply, wiped her face with both hands, and opening her shirt, took out her breast. Then she turned her head to gaze at the horizon, at the sky, at the plain, at anything but me, but she left her breast bare. So in a way she consented. In the opening of her shirt I saw the tiny hips and thin, bent legs of my little newborn son, asleep again in the sling she used to carry him. I felt angry and very much ashamed.

We went back to camp, I leading, Muskrat following, and from that time on she nursed the pup for Father. It hurt me that in no time some of the other women and even Pinesinger made fun of her for nursing it.

All the next day I walked last in line, with Muskrat just ahead of me. To her fell the task of carrying the pup, whose mouth and feet were again tied with string. At first she carried him by the string like a bag, but later that same day she cradled him in the crook of her arm. By the end of the day she had untied him. The pup seemed to know not to struggle and even to realize that Muskrat's feelings toward him had changed. How did I know? I had all day to watch her walking ahead of me while I worried about what I had done.

Father had very little interest in the pup, but seemed to be satisfied that Muskrat had him in her care. In fact, her care of the pup surprised us. Very soon he began to fold his ears and lower his head when Muskrat looked at him.

But not in fear; he seemed to like her. He would even lie on his back for her, his tail trembling between his legs, his ears flat, his eyes watchful. Otherwise he sat near her, ready to get up when she got up. If she spoke to him, which she did only in her own language, he would listen, now and then tipping his head because he didn't understand her. Of course he didn't. Neither did we!

Of his own will the pup stayed with Muskrat even after we reached the cave, which was all cool and shadowy, smelling of dust and so quiet that even our whispers echoed from the dome of its ceiling, where in some of the deep cracks bats clung. Father, my uncles, and their wives settled themselves in the back of the cave but left the pup with Muskrat, whose place of course was near the front. We soon saw that she wouldn't need to tie him. By that time he followed where she went, pressed himself against the back of her legs when she stood, sat by her when she sat, and lay beside her when she slept. Sometimes at night I would open my eyes to see my little son's face right beside mine, his eyes squeezed shut, his lips open; then Muskrat's blue forehead, frowning even in sleep; then, like the edge of her hood, a crest of fur behind her head, which was the little wolf pressing against her, lying curled at the back of her neck. He stayed close to her long after she stopped feeding him from her breast.

One day Muskrat came home with a bundle of yew she had found growing upriver in crevices of the ravine's walls. We didn't like to see the yew, because of its poison. But using her teeth, though taking care to spit afterward, Muskrat peeled the bark in strips so thin they were like hair, then rolled the strips on her thighs and made twine, and with the twine made snares. With the snares she set a trapline.

Off she went one evening, looking as if she were alone but with my little son in his sling hidden under her shirt and the wolf pup behind her hidden by the grass. Watching, all I could see was one woman knee-deep in grass, with the red sun casting her shadow. Really, though, the three of them were there. Muskrat came back just before dark. At dawn she went out once more, again with our little son in her shirt and the pup at her heels, and this time with my small carrying bag, which she had borrowed, over her shoulder. When she came back the bag was bulging. She turned it upside down and shook it. Out fell mice and little birds.

Then we began to laugh. "Bobcat food. We don't eat it," we told her.

"Io? I eat it," said she.

At last I understood the cleverness of this woman. Her catch would not need to be shared. Yet she did share it—the wolf pup ate the heads, the feet, the feathers, and the little piles of guts.

The trouble with Father's cave, that second summer I spent in it, was that food and fuel were scarce. People had used the cave for many summers, and the women had picked the plain clean of food. When we tried to hunt the bison, they seemed to know what we wanted, and they moved downriver. Each time we went west along the river, we saw them.

Father told us of another cave of his, a cave in the south wall of the ravine, right under where the bison grazed much of the time. There the asparagus and onions would be plentiful; there would be frogs, sedge, and bulrushes by the river and cranes, bustards, and marmots on the plain, where they could be snared. True, if we went there we would leave behind the steep ravine with its dangerous trails that helped us hunt, but mammoths wouldn't drink from the river until the pools of meltwater on the plain went dry. Not until then would mammoths use the trail near the cave, and only then could we stampede them over the edge of the ravine. We could come from somewhere else to do this. We didn't need to live in that particular cave.

We ate frogs and fish, waiting for Graylag's people. At last some of them came, Graylag among them. The others had stopped to visit relatives on the Grass River summergrounds. Graylag also favored going to the new cave. The rest of his people would find us later, he said.

So again we set out. We followed the river for about half a day, keeping to the plain as the land fell away. In time we saw a line of blue hills to the southwest, and soon afterward Father showed us a faint trail leading down the side of the shallow ravine and disappearing under the bank. We had walked right by this trail on our way from the lodge to the old cave, never thinking that it was more than a simple trail for horses or other animals to reach the river, never thinking that a place to live lay right under our feet. Father had his secrets.

The new cave was very different from the old one, and not as good. The old cave had a comfortable feeling to it, because of its long use; the echoes were familiar, the smells too, the people all had places, the floor was clear, all sharp stones had been thrown out, and there were places for the fires. Even if the fires weren't burning, the ashes showed us where to sit. But the new cave was strange to most of us. We didn't know where the good places were—not that such a thing would matter to me, since I was too young to have a good place. Even so, I always felt uneasy if I didn't know where to put myself. I might sit somewhere only to have an old person scold me for sitting in his or her place. Such mistakes could be shaming.

For another thing, the new cave was shallower than the old cave, and its ceiling was lower. Also the new cave was not high above the river, since the river was very wide there, and the plain was low. There were no bats. Perhaps the cave was too damp for them. But where there are no bats, Ohun sends mosquitoes instead, and these swarmed on us as soon as we went in. The smoke from the fires would discourage them, but to choose between smoke and mosquitoes discouraged me, since to get away from these bad things was the reason I was always ready to leave a lodge in spring.

What made the women most dislike the cave was that lions had lived there. True, no lions seemed to be there at the time, but perhaps as recently as the past summer lions had filled the cave with scats, bones, and fleas. With the smell of lions in our nostrils, we sorted through the litter on the floor, stirring the piles of little dead willow leaves that the wind had brought in the fall. We were looking for bones, since they burned better than dung.

Hidden in the leaves we found plenty of bones left by lions after years of summer hunting—the hip sockets, skulls, and horns of bison, the gnawed skulls of deer and saiga, and the heavy leg bones of a young mammoth, perhaps the calf we had killed. Andriki even found the bones of lion cubs, three skulls about the same size and all close together, their milk teeth loose or missing. Something had killed them here.

Finally, in a corner, Andriki found a human skull. "Hi!" he cried, stepping back. Then, "Hona."

We all came to look. The skull lay half hidden in damp leaves, near enough to the opening that snow would have blown on it. The lower jaw was missing, the face was broken between the eyes, and the bone was not white and clean like some of the other bones, but brown and dirty. It was very strange to see. Whose was it?

Father and the others began to think. No one had been killed by a lion that they knew about, and they would know, since only Father's people lived on Father's hunting lands. No one had been lost or was missing. Either the lions had robbed a grave or they had found a passing stranger. At an earlier time, the idea of a stranger would have been laughable. But by then, of course, there was Muskrat.

We looked around for her, thinking to ask if she knew anything about this person. But she was gone. Snatching up my spear from the sleeping place Father had given me under a low overhang beside the opening—the worst place in the cave, without a doubt—I hurried to the plain. Not this time would Muskrat get away from me. Yet I needn't have worried—she and the pup were sitting with their heads above the grass, she nursing the baby, the pup looking on.

"The skull," I asked. "Did you see it?" She seemed puzzled. She didn't know "skull." "Head. Head bone." Of course she had seen it. "You know him?" I asked. It was a mistake to put it like that. Muskrat's eyes flashed, and she suddenly stood, turned her back, and walked away. When she felt she was far enough from me and my rudeness, she sat down. I saw that we needed Pinesinger.

This time Pinesinger came quickly to help us, glad to

get out of the cave. Behind her all the young women came out to wait, to sit on their heels in the afternoon sunlight until Father and the old people decided what to do about the skull. Soon Muskrat spoke to Pinesinger with much feeling.

"What does she say?" I asked.

"We are talking of the skull," said Pinesinger. "She thinks the cave is spoiled by it. I agree. She doesn't want to stay here. Neither do I."

"I want to ask her a question," I said.

"Later," said Pinesinger. "Not everything I say can be the words of another person. Some of the words have to be mine."

Ah well. It went against me to be angry at these women. I was learning patience, it seemed. "Then please, Stepmother, ask if her people passed here."

Again Muskrat spoke to Pinesinger a long time.

"What is she saying?" I interrupted finally.

Muskrat hardly stopped her conversation to let Pinesinger answer. I went to get Father.

With Father standing over them, the women took more notice. Father finally pried from Muskrat the fact that her people hadn't lost anyone to lions. Her people had been further east. Nor had anyone died near this river.

Then Muskrat looked boldly up at Father and spoke for a long time. I kept hearing the words "ila" and "ilasi," which meant "person" and "people." When she finished, Father looked at Pinesinger, waiting to learn what Muskrat had said.

"I'd rather not tell you," said Pinesinger. "When you hear her words, you might blame me."

"Speak," said Father.

"You asked to hear this," warned Pinesinger, as if she were about to enjoy herself with Muskrat's insults.

"Just say it," said Father. Pinesinger was boring him.

"Well then, she says if one of her people had died near a cave, that person would have been taken far away, since her people treat their dead with respect. That's what she says. She says her people wouldn't keep the corpse of someone they loved near where other people live. Such a thing would be out of the question for them. And she says she knows less about the skull than you do, Husband, since she didn't stay to look at it. She says her people dislike long-dead corpses, or buried bodies, or human bones."

"By the Bear!" said Father. "She thinks we keep corpses with us? She thinks we handle human bones?" He looked at me.

"I didn't understand her, Father," I said, not wanting to be blamed for Muskrat's words or to have to deal with her because of them.

Graylag and Maral came out of the cave, carrying the skull between them with sticks through the eye sockets. At that, they had only the upper part of the head—the lower jaw was missing. Where was it? Where, for that matter, were the rest of the bones? Calling to their wives to dig a hole, Graylag and Maral set the skull down near us. Muskrat got up and moved farther away. The wolf pup came to sniff at the skull, but people leaped to their feet, shouting and throwing stones. The pup ran.

While in the distance the women took their digging sticks to the thick sod of the plain, Graylag reminded us of a boy who had died here years before. This boy had come with Graylag's stepson the first time the stepson had brought his family from the Fire River to spend a summer at the Hair. Could the skull have belonged to the boy?

A boy who had come from the Fire River? Shocked, I realized that I knew him. He was an orphan named Kakim who, having no family, had slept at our fire for several years. I remembered the day he had left the Fire River, following his new foster father, who in turn was following some women visitors returning to the Hair. "Father," I asked. "Was he Kakim?"

After looking at me curiously, perhaps surprised that I should be the one to know whose skull we had found, Father thought for a time, then admitted that he hardly remembered Kakim. He turned to Graylag. But Graylag had known the boy only a few days and didn't remember his name. At last some of Graylag's people remembered a little about the boy and felt sure that the skull must have been his. Already sick when he arrived, the people remembered, Kakim had died of diarrhea in the Moon of Dust and had been buried in a shallow grave, where, the people admitted, animals might have found him. He had been an orphan without close relatives, so no one had bothered to dig deep. Was that how people had seen Kakim—worth no trouble? If so, he must have known it. How lonely he must have been!

Lost in thought about Kakim, I was watching the skull and its burial and didn't notice that on the plain above the cave Muskrat had cleared some grass and was making a small thornbush barrier of the kind that helps to keep animals from walking up to people who are sleeping on the ground. What now? As best I could with my few words of her language and her few words of mine, I asked her why, when a good cave waited for her, she was getting ready to sleep in the open.

Poor Kakim's skull had frightened her, it seemed. Muskrat made it clear that she would not even go into a cave where a human skull had been found, let alone sleep there. So I tried to explain how the skull came to be in the cave, but she didn't want to know about it, and once again I had to call Pinesinger. Pinesinger found that Muskrat also refused to sleep near people who handled the dead. By this she seemed to mean Father's people. They might reach out and touch her with their corpse-fouled hands. Or the cave might be a burial ground, she seemed to think. The rest of the body, or other bodies, might still be there.

I said the cave was Father's, not a burial ground. I said I thought I even knew whose skull it was, which should make it less frightening. Muskrat wasn't interested. Perhaps I was trying to trick her into going back inside. I could say what I liked, she said; it wouldn't matter. I could beat her or kill her, but I couldn't make her go in. If I dragged her in, she'd come back out again. And she would have—I saw that.

I also saw how I would have to stay outside with her. I couldn't leave her alone with a baby; something might happen to them. After all, the cave still smelled of lions, who hadn't been away long enough to starve the fleas.

Who could say that the lions were gone for good, or even gone for long? Much as I might have liked to let Muskrat do as she pleased without me, I couldn't. I left her nursing the baby and went to get dry bison dung.

So began the Grass Moon. I enjoyed sleeping under the sky, and I saw how it was that a man sometimes takes his wife and moves away from the rest of his group for a while in summer. It was almost as if we were alone. Father's and Graylag's people sometimes used our fire as a dayfire, but at night they went to sleep in the cave. Then the stars began their journeys and the moon rose out of the grass on the horizon. We would sit quietly, watching the fireflies. We would listen carefully to distant noises, straining our ears to hear the roaring that would tell us if lions were near. We didn't hear lions. They must have been far away, at the meltwater pools on the plain. But often we would hear other animals in the great distance —bison, mammoths, nightjars, owls, and wolves. The wolves' song, sung by many weaving voices, although very far off, always brought the pup to his feet, his ears stiff, his body trembling, straining to hear more. As the distant song faded the pup would give many little cries, and when the song stopped he would raise his chin and call. Several times he would do this, then wait, listening. Each time a wolf would answer. The pup would run back and forth in excitement or stand perfectly still, listening, trembling, waiting. But at night we tied him up, in case he thought of leaving. After all, he was Father's.

Although we lived apart, the people in the cave, especially Father, were much in our thoughts. But I'm not sure we were in theirs. This became clear on one of the first nights we spent apart from the others, the three of us. On that night I was already sleeping while Muskrat sat quietly by the fire, when suddenly I was wakened by loud singing, clapping, and screams. The people below were dancing, probably to clean the cave. I listened carefully. Father was trancing. I heard him calling in the voice of a deaf-grouse, then an eagle, then a woodcock, then a bee. Then I heard the other people calling to

Father, calling his trancing spirit home from wherever he had flown in the night sky.

They made me think, those voices, coming up out of the ground below us. They made us both think. Muskrat fell silent, listening and thinking. And the baby listened! I reached out to Muskrat, who handed him to me, and I watched his face as he listened to the voices below us. His mother seemed puzzled and almost frightened by the singing, so I thought the sound might upset the boy too. At least, I thought, his face would show wonder. But in fact he showed no sign at all that he heard anything unusual. What a child he was, that even a sound as strong as that would not frighten him! Instead, like an old person, he seemed to understand.

27

AS WE HAD HAD TOO MUCH SNOW THAT WINTER, SO WE had too much rain that summer. The meltwater pools, which should have dried, were filled again, over and over, and the animals went on drinking from them. To lure the animals to the river we burned the grass, but still they stayed away. The rain that filled the pools kept the grass on the plain as fresh and green as any new grass that might grow after our burning.

So we were forced to travel far for hunting. Almost every day we who owned the hunting lands of the Hair River went out with Graylag's men. That summer we seemed to be lucky with horses. It was almost as if every time we tried, we killed one. I think this was because horses run best on hard, dry ground, and the ground was soft that rainy summer. Running far on soft ground seems to tire horses. Often when we hunted them we found them already tired, because every animal that hunts was also running after them that summer. Anyway, we had plenty of horsemeat.

By the time the Grass Moon was full we had killed three horses. Each time I had been one of the hunters and had earned a hunter's share. Of course the best of the meat I killed, the good parts of the rear and flanks, were for in-laws and always went to Frogga's family, but I kept for myself some parts of the liver and neck, my rightful portion as hunter. I also got in-law shares from Maral. Perhaps these were small, as I was young and not yet living with Frogga, but they were meat. I got meat from Pinesinger too, who shared with me because I was her stepchild. Her shares came from Father but also from the people of her lineage, and so were almost always from the forequarters. This was no bad thing; the forequarters of a horse are thick with good meat. Whenever I got meat from Pinesinger I gave some to Muskrat, whose milk fed my son.

I especially remember all this sharing because that summer was the first I spent as one of the grown hunters, not as one of the children. It was the first time that my place in a large group in summer was as one of the men, with women to feed and in-laws to favor. Before that I had had just a boy's place, and my elders had been responsible for favoring and feeding me. When I was a child, each piece of meat that came into my hands was given to me to eat. Each piece of meat was simple food. But that summer, more than ever before, each piece of meat was far from simple food. It was heavy with meaning, to me or to someone else. When I gave meat, I had to think carefully not to make a mistake and anger someone. When someone gave meat to me, I couldn't help judging the size and cut of the piece and wondering what the giver meant by it. Sometimes I think that if I had to name that time, I might call it the time of pieces of meat.

Or the time of rain. Every few days it rained. Sometimes we would see little rainstorms in the distance as Ohun filled the pools on the plain. In the evenings we would see clouds rising over the western horizon, clouds with thunder and lightning in them, which by dawn would be over us with falling rain—sometimes the gentle rain of Ohun, more like a mist than like a downpour; sometimes the harsh, fierce rain of the Bear.

The people in the cave were dry, of course. But nothing would make Muskrat go inside, where, as she had told Pinesinger, a corpse could be hiding, and I wouldn't go in without her. So to keep us dry, Muskrat built a shelter. At the Fire River in summer, my mother and the other women built shelters for shade as well as for protection from the little showers that sometimes came. These shelters looked like bushes—little bristling domes made with branches thatched with grass. They shaded us from the sun and wind but weren't much protection from the rain. It rained so little, though, that we didn't need much protection. During rainstorms we would wait all crowded together, crouching inside these dripping domes. If we got wet, which we did, we waited for better weather.

But Muskrat made a different kind of shelter. Hers was like a fir tree, with piles of branches woven in rings that grew smaller and smaller, ending with a thicket of branches at the top. Over the rings she laid grass in lengthwise bundles. Unlike our shelters, hers was truly dry. I remember thinking two things the first time I slept with Muskrat and our little boy in her dry shelter during a rainstorm: that my woman must have lived in a place of much rain and snow if she could make such a shelter and snow-walkers too, and that I wished my mother could see me, to learn how this shelter-making should be done.

I must laugh when I remember wondering where I had seen such a shelter before. As Pinesinger and I stood staring at it after Muskrat had built it, I told Pinesinger that it looked like the shelter a real muskrat might build in a swamp. How well I had named my woman!

One day when the air was warm and hazy, when the new crescent of the Dust Moon hung in the afternoon sky, Muskrat noticed something coming. She stood up, watching. I stood too. Far away we saw a line of people swaying. We stared. They were too far to recognize. I called to Father, and up came the people from the cave. We all stared. After a very long time we saw that they were Graylag's people, and we sat down to wait. I couldn't help but notice Father and how young he suddenly seemed. Like a boy, he was joking, laughing, his face no longer still and set but moving and alive. When at last the people were among us, when we were greeting them, loudly exchanging the first bits of news, helping them to take off their packs, I saw Yoi and Father looking very happily and boldly at each other, as if they couldn't wait to lay hands on each other but were too proud, too old and dignified, to show it.

Pinesinger noticed it too, and her face grew stiff. As soon as she could, she crept into the cave, and that was the last I saw of her until night. Meanwhile we built a large fire near Muskrat's shelter and found strips of horsemeat to cook for the newcomers. For the rest of the day we cooked and ate, Father and Yoi sitting side by side, offering each other shares. Now and then Father, his face mock-serious, would say something very softly to Yoi, and she would laugh too much. As all of us could see, they were glad to be together.

I'm still not sure just what happened in the cave that night, because I was dozing in Muskrat's little shelter, but when I heard some loud voices and terrible screaming I looked out—Muskrat had built the bottom of the shelter so that we could see outside, to keep watch on what moved at night on the plain—and in a short time I saw Pinesinger, weeping, carrying her weeping baby and her deerskins and coming to our fire. Of course I got up and went to sit with her, feeling a flare of anger at Yoi and Father. Why should they treat her badly just because they wanted each other? Pinesinger had never asked to come here.

"You would have been better off to stay at the Fire River, Stepmother," I said, trying to be kind. "You might have married Kestrel," I added, naming one of my cousins. Then I saw that she was moving stiffly and that a blue bruise was starting to show on her face. "Oh?" I said. "What's this?"

But Pinesinger wouldn't speak. Still sobbing, she

opened her shirt and offered her nipple to her son, but he was crying too much to take it. I looked around for Muskrat, who was just getting out of our deerskins. Our eyes met: She went to Pinesinger, and taking the baby in her hands, she cradled him gently, sang a little, and put him at her own breast. After a while he took her nipple. But whatever had happened must have upset him greatly. He would nurse for a moment, then stop to cry some more. "Hi?" whispered Muskrat, wondering.

I wanted very much to ask what had happened. Up from the cave many people were coming—Graylag and his wives, Yoi and Father, my aunts and uncles, and many others, all talking at once. Taking over our fire, they made a thick circle around Pinesinger, crowding Muskrat and me to the side. Many people sat on their heels to talk to Pinesinger, while Father stood over her, looking down. Waiting to hear someone apologize to Pinesinger, I was surprised when some of her kinswomen began to scold her for starting trouble and insulting Yoi. "Of course you were beaten!" said her eldest kinswoman, Graylag's wife, Teal.

A sad story unfolded. Poor Pinesinger had been jealous of Yoi and Father. She had let herself speak angrily to Yoi but hadn't been ready for Yoi's answer, which, because Yoi was so clever and was standing so close, had caused Pinesinger to forget herself. Unwisely, she had pushed Yoi, who was taller and stronger. Yoi had snatched the baby out of Pinesinger's arms, thrust him, screaming, into Teal's arms, then seized a stick to hit Pinesinger. Rooted to their places in the circles around the fires, the other people had been caught by surprise and hadn't gotten the stick away from Yoi until she had forced Pinesinger through a fire. The peace had been spoiled, the fire too, and most people were angry with Pinesinger.

I must say, when the story was told, I felt like laughing. I had only felt angry when I thought that Father might have raised his hand to Pinesinger. Since the problem was with Yoi, it was less serious—or so it seemed to me. The people began to stand up, to look around, to think of going back to their beds and their fires. I saw no reason why the whole trouble should not be forgotten then and there.

But to my surprise, Pinesinger refused to stand up. She refused to go back to the cave. She would live with Yoi no longer. "Hear me, Aunt!" she said to Teal, her kinswoman. "I won't be treated so carelessly. Since my husband lets my co-wife attack me, I'll live with my stepson, Kori."

And she did. That is how Pinesinger and her baby came to live with Muskrat and me and our baby on the plain above the cave. There was barely enough room for Pinesinger's sleeping-skins in Muskrat's good shelter, but from that night on she made her bed there, squeezing Muskrat up against the poles. But nobody worried about that.

Just before the full moon, there came a soft south wind that trembled in the feathergrass. Then came heat. The faraway line of blue hills seemed to wobble when we looked there.

On the night of the full moon, as Muskrat was about to cook a frog for me on the embers of our fire, we heard women's voices on the trail leading down the bank of the low ravine. I thought I heard Pinesinger's voice among the rest. When I looked at the river, I saw her with many of the other women. They were starting to bathe. Into the shallow water they splashed, until the river seemed alive with naked bodies. The heat had caused the women to do this, the heat and the light of the full moon. Perhaps also the fleas in the cave had done their share—usually women sing and play in water, but that night the women weren't playful. Rather, they sat right down and began scrubbing purposefully with sand.

Beside me, Muskrat was looking too. Suddenly she opened her shirt, took out the baby in his sling, handed him to me, and hurried down the trail. Soon I saw her on the sandbank, stepping out of her clothes. Naked, she walked into the river, wading past the other women out into the fast water, until she was chest deep. There she lowered herself so that the river flowed through her hair. The pup ran back and forth on the bank like a gray shadow in the moonlight. He even waded belly deep into the river, to get as near as he could to Muskrat. But she had begun to scrub her hair and took no notice of him. He didn't dare swim and soon backed up to the dry ground. I saw him later, his legs still wet, half hidden in the grass. In fact, while I had been watching Muskrat, he had stolen the uncooked frog.

In the cave below the men were very quiet. Like me, no doubt, they were watching the women. How could they not? After a summer of good food, the women were round and smooth, and when they were wet they shone brightly in the moonlight. Their wet hair shone like mica. Naked and slowly washing, they were beautiful to see.

Later some of Graylag's women began to clap and sing. All the women stood up then, formed a line where the river was shallow and the bottom was sandy, and danced to their own singing, crooking their elbows, lifting their knees very high, double-stepping with stamps and splashes at certain beats of the song. They sang:

> Our legs are thin
> Our breasts are narrow
> Our eyes are small
> Our necks are long.
> When our husbands call
> We answer, "Kiak! Kiak!"
> When our children call
> We answer, "Goorgoorong!"

The song was called "The Crane." My mother once knew it. No wonder these women were singing it—it is a song for the water's edge, a song for bathing, and with their many Fire River lineages, these women would enjoy a Fire River song.

Behind me the moon shone down on the moving water, making it sparkle with points of light, and on the wet, dancing bodies of the women as they moved along the sand. One among them caught my eyes; she was Pinesinger. Ah, but she was very beautiful. She always had been, and until old age changed her she always would be. I watched how her wet hair lay still, stuck to the skin

257

of her back, how gracefully she moved her round arms and legs, how the moon shone on her milk-filled breasts, on her perfect hips, how the long, curved line of her throat showed against the moonlit sky. Ah! How was it that my father preferred Yoi?

As my eyes ran over Pinesinger's body, which my own body well remembered, I noticed her belly. It seemed round. Was she pregnant? I told myself she could not be. Her child wasn't able to stand unless someone held his hands for him. Even then, the most he could do was to stiffen his legs and bounce. But he certainly couldn't walk, and years would pass before he could live on hard food without his mother's milk. Again I told myself that Pinesinger could not be pregnant.

Even so, I couldn't help but compare her with the other women. I didn't know the women of Graylag's lodge—his two pretty daughters-in-law, for instance, who were Father's kinswomen—and it didn't seem right to be staring at them as if I were a woman curious about a woman's thing. Right or wrong, though, I saw that most of the other women had flat bellies. But wasn't Pinesinger more recently delivered? Wasn't her child younger than the other children? The only woman with a younger child was my woman.

I looked around for Muskrat. For a long time I didn't see her. I had almost decided she had finished washing and started back when I noticed a wet, dark head moving through the water far downstream on the other side of the river, making for the opposite bank. It was Muskrat, of course, swimming like an animal, with her face raised. But why was she on the far side of the river?

Alarmed, I watched her. Into my mind's eye came a frightening scene: Muskrat gone and me left with the baby, without milk to feed him and with no one to help. In my arms my boy was gazing at the sky, his large eyes bright with moonlight. I looked down at him, then back at his mother, whose dark form, like an otter's, had reached the far bank and was hauling out of the river onto a wide, flat rock. There she stood up, stripped some of the water from her skin, and leaped to the bank, where she strode along, a shadow in the moonlight, not stopping until she was as far upriver from the other women as she had been downriver before. I saw that she planned to swim back to us after all, and would allow for being carried by the current. Much relieved when at last she waded in, I watched the progress of her dark head in the moonlight, and when she waded out on our side I remembered to look at her belly. Muskrat's child was much younger than Pinesinger's, but Muskrat's belly was as flat as a man's. So it was hard not to think that Pinesinger was pregnant. Surely Father had made her so. The child would be my half-brother. As Andriki was to Father, so that child would be to me. By the Bear!

Yet what would a new child mean for the child in her arms? For my child? I didn't often give much thought to Pinesinger's child, since my thoughts were so much on Muskrat's, the child I had a right to think about. But right or wrong, both boys were mine. Now a new child of my father's would be pushing against my son, pushing him before he was strong, before he was named.

This could not be good. In the Camps of the Dead, the lineage hears about it. The elders of the lineage think the living are playing with them, disrespectfully calling for one of them to come and be born to a woman who already has a baby. No woman can feed two children at the same time, or not for long, so the spirits of those children know they have made the long trip from the Camps of the Dead for nothing. They must go right back again.

How could Pinesinger have gotten pregnant so soon? Didn't she care for my child, even if perhaps she should never have had him? Was that his fault?

As I watched the slow dancing of the women, I listened to the song, wondering about it. What did they mean with their strange words, those dancing women? When my mother used to sing the song I must have been very young, too young to know that a woman's secret lay behind the crane's answers to her husband, her children. If I had asked my mother to explain the song, she might have laughed at me, but she would never have explained. Women's secrets are about children but are not shared with children.

So I waited in the moonlight with my son in my arms, we who knew nothing, listening to the river, to the singing, to the wind in the long grass of the plain. The sky was huge that night, with moonlit clouds like mountains in it. Very, very far away I heard mammoths, and later lions. Below me in the cave a child began to cry. It was a baby—perhaps the baby who was mine with Pinesinger. Most likely, I thought, it was he, since the voice sounded very young. Soon I knew it was he; from the riverbank the women heard him too, and Pinesinger left the dancers, put on her clothes, and climbed the trail to the cave. In a moment the baby was silent.

Then, still smelling of the river, Muskrat stepped from the shadows, reached out her hands, and took our son from my arms. She spoke to him in her language, calling him Kiu Ngarr, as she did very often those days. I didn't like to hear it, but what could I do? After all, it wasn't a real name. The baby gave a little cry of joy when he saw Muskrat. I noticed the wolf too. He seemed to have followed Muskrat up from the river. As was his habit, he threw himself down at a distance from our fire, but not so far he couldn't make sure he was near Muskrat. Now and then the firelight made his eyes shine green as he watched her from the long grass.

Of the two bad things that mark that time for me, Pinesinger's pregnancy was the first, but Muskrat's hidden doings were the worst. These were accidentally discovered by Andriki and to my shame were made plain to all the men.

One day we men went hunting. All together we were many, and as we walked our line was very long. There were the four brothers who owned the hunting—Father, Maral, Kida, and Andriki; their sons who were old enough to hunt—me and Ako; and the husbands of Father's kinswomen—Marten, Timu, and Elho. Timu and Elho were the sons of Graylag, who also came with us, bringing his stepson, the Stick; his nephew, Raven; and Raven's son, White Fox. The old Dust Moon was still in the sky on the morning we started. We headed southeast to the short-grass plain where the summer before we had killed a cow bison, where Father said we could always find horses. The day was warm and windy, and the clouds, almost always overhead that year, made shadows as they slowly flew by.

With all of us carrying nothing but our spears, all walking fast without packs or women, away we went, one after the other behind Father, the long grass parting to let us by. In the evening we were very far from the cave but had not seen game. Just at dusk we saw horses a long way off, and we decided to stalk them in the morning.

We camped on the plain. Before dawn we set off for the horses, who had thought themselves safe from us since we hadn't at first hunted them, and before the sun had gone far on its way we had surrounded them. We were so many that the herd could not escape us. We killed a yellow mare. The spears that killed her belonged to Andriki and to Timu, Graylag's son, and the division of meat began as we sat down to take off her skin. Because we were so many, and because Andriki and Timu were in-laws in a way, the division of the mare was done with much talk and difficulty. We made the division fairly and kept our speech polite, but it strained us to do it, and the day passed before our work was done. So we camped a second night on the plain. Not until the next morning did we bring the meat back to the cave.

When we got there, we found the women gone. This was not surprising—they had gotten hungry while waiting so long and had set off to find their own food. But there was plenty of meat for all, and no need to wait for the women to eat it with us. Father and the other men sat down by the ashes of the dayfire near Muskrat's shelter and looked around for fuel. Against the shelter lay several piles of sticks and dung that Muskrat had gathered, and while I went for one of these piles, Andriki went for another. He bent to pick it up, then suddenly drew back as if he had seen a biting spider. But he would have stepped on a dangerous spider. Instead, in a strange, quiet voice he said, "Kori, look here."

I went to see. Stuffed into the thatch of the shelter was

a little bundle wound loosely around with the spotted bark of a redberry bush. Andriki poked at the bundle with a stick. It fell out from the thatch and lay on the dust in the sunlight. The bark dropped off. Not knowing what to say, I looked down at it. What was it?

Of course some of the other men noticed us, and some came to see too. Father came, and Graylag. When Andriki moved to make way for them, his shadow fell on the bundle. Father took Andriki's arm and pulled him so that his shadow fell clear. "Don't touch it," said Father.

"What is it?" I asked.

"This is your shelter," said Father. "So we must ask you."

But I didn't know. I looked at it carefully. Its main part seemed to be a peeled bent branch, with a sinew string somewhat shorter than the branch tying the two ends together. The branch in itself was harmless—perhaps a firestick of some kind, though not as good as ours. But from one end, by horsehairs strung through holes so small I wondered how they had been made, hung three of the flat front teeth of a horse. Here was no proper use of horse teeth—there seemed something unhealthy about them. To the other end, horsehairs tied three short sticks, each with the bark peeled off and one end sharpened by burning. With them was tied a white owl's feather such as the ravine's swallows use to line their nests. These sticks reminded me of something I had seen before, and showed me that the bundle was the work of Muskrat. I looked at Andriki and he looked at me. I saw we agreed. We had seen such things at Uske's Spring: her people's little bird-spears.

Yet what made the branch terrible, and what made us afraid of it, was that a short dead thing was bound to the middle with human hair, probably Muskrat's. The thing was like meat, black and dry, as long as my thumb, thinner than my little finger. We knew exactly what it was, but because it was a woman's thing we didn't like to speak of it. So it shamed me and at the same time frightened me. It was a dead, dry umbilical cord and had surely been my son's.

"Waugh," said Graylag.

"The place is fouled," said Father.

"We'll build another fire away from here," said Maral, and they did.

Far from Muskrat's shelter their many dark shapes crowded close together around the little fire that cooked their meat. Alone at my own fire, filled with shame, I watched and listened to them, thinking that they looked like ravens at a carcass. Smoke from their fire rose into the yellow sky, and the smell of cooking horsemeat spread like a cloud over the plain. I heard them talking, not of the thing we had found but of the teeth that hung from it. How was it that Muskrat had them? They were from one of the four skulls of horses taken that summer, yet none of the skulls had belonged to Muskrat. Whose were they?

Andriki's spear had killed the first horse, and the head had gone to his kinswoman, Waxwing. Had Waxwing given teeth to Muskrat? Her husband, Marten, said she had not. One day Waxwing had dug a pit, built a fire in it, and roasted the head, which she then had shared with most of us, including Frogga, who through Lilan had shared with me. The bones lay strewn near the pit, or in the cave, or on the riverbank where we had thrown them. The fire-split teeth had fallen out.

The spears of Graylag's son and stepson had killed the second horse, and the head had been given first to Yoi and later to Graylag's wife, Teal, who was Yoi's kinswoman. Both women had claim to it, but Teal was older and her claim was stronger. She then had shared its ownership with Yoi. The flesh had been scraped from that head and cooked in scraps. As Yoi's stepson I had been given an ear from her portion. The raw skull, teeth and all, had later been stolen from us by a hyena.

My spear and Graylag's had killed the third horse, a colt. The head had gone to Father. He had torn out the tongue and pried off the lower jaw but had taken his ax to the rest of the skull and cooked the brain and ears on the cave's rear fire. Some of the teeth of this horse might be scattered in the cave where the chopping had thrown them, but the rest would have been in the lower jaw, which, through Father's own carelessness, his wolf pup had stolen.

Because of the theft, ownership of the fourth horse's head was still in question. Father's spear had killed the fourth horse, and if the jaw of the third had not been stolen, the head of the fourth would probably have gone to one of Father's brother's wives. But shouldn't the jaw of the fourth horse replace the jaw of the third? The question was made hard by the fact that the third horse was owned by both groups of people, Graylag's and Father's. So the matter had not been decided. Meanwhile, flat on its chin and severed neck, the flyblown head of the fourth horse lay in the cave, its ears back, its eyes squinting, its eight long front teeth bared.

Thus the men around the dayfire remembered each horse and who had owned each of the six jaw parts from which horse teeth might be taken. They saw that no one had given teeth to Muskrat. They saw that she must have used them anyway. They wondered why. Now and then one of them would glance at me, sitting at a distance but listening carefully, and at last Andriki called me. "Don't sit alone, Nephew," he said. "Have you done wrong, that this should shame you? The food is ready. Come and eat."

So I went to sit with the others. Politely, the men spoke no more of Muskrat or her doings but of the meat that lay around us and how this horse would be shared. Even so, I felt a stiffness, a discomfort among the others, and I noticed that they were unwilling to look at me.

After we had eaten and were gathering up the rest of the meat to carry into the cave, Father took me aside. "This is no good thing, this work of your woman," he said. "We don't know what she means by it, or what the thing she made is for. We don't know what harm can come of it. She should bury it. Perhaps Graylag's wife will trance to clean the place, but then again, perhaps she won't. As for me, I won't. I'd feel foolish trancing over a bit of woman's filth, even if it could cause sickness. After all, who but your woman will suffer? But see that she does this no more."

28

THE SUN SET. THE SKY TURNED BRIGHT BLUE, THEN PALE gray, and the stars came out. I heard voices, and standing up, I saw the line of women coming through the dusk from the plain, each woman bristling with her load of branches for the night's fires. While the other women took the trail to the cave, Pinesinger broke from the group and came to my fire. From the very end of the line of women Muskrat came too.

Pinesinger dropped her firewood, looked around, and noticed the embers of the men's dayfire and the burned bones. "You killed today," she said. "What is my share?" But it must have been clear that whatever her share was, I didn't have it, so she went down the trail to ask for it from the people in the cave.

Muskrat dropped her load of branches at the side of the shelter. There she saw the thing lying untied, with the little bird-spears, the horse teeth, and the umbilical cord all spread out. In her quiet, matter-of-fact way, as if nothing much were wrong, she knelt to tie them up again.

I felt a terrible anger. How stupid she seemed there, kneeling in the dust, her hands busy with foul things! She had made a spell. How evil she seemed, misusing a part of a child to do it, since it is through the umbilical cord that the heart climbs from the placenta and finds its place in the body. As a bird flies home on the same path through the air and finds its old nest after the winter, the heart remembers the umbilical cord and the placenta, and that is why women must treat these things with respect, especially the stump of the cord after it falls off the baby. How could Muskrat treat a life so carelessly?

And how could she be so careless of my safety and the

safety of our men? What if we had touched the thing, made dangerous with birthmatter? Did she still not understand? That seemed impossible. She had learned about menstruation, or at least she didn't foul the lodge. Was that only because she had been pregnant? Was it possible she didn't understand the rest?

But most of all, what was she doing, making a spell? That this foul thing of Muskrat's was a spell I had no doubt. Shamans make spells, the spirit-snares they put on corpses. Yet here was Muskrat meddling dangerously with her bundle that perhaps had powers none of us could understand. The feathers in her bundle spoke of the air—the world of spirits, birds, and shamans. The teeth in her bundle spoke of the forests, the rivers, and the plains—the world of animals. And the wood spoke of fire, of camps and lodges—the world of people.

I could have killed Muskrat. I wanted to kill her. I saw myself standing over her, my foot on her neck, my spear raised. I saw myself, my fists filled with her hair, dragging her over the plain to beat her with a stone. I saw myself leaving her wounded on the plain, to be found by the hyenas. I would have spoken to her, but rage was choking me.

So I did nothing. I watched in silence as, in the starlight, she tied the redberry bark around the bundle and put it into the thatch again. When she finished, she happened to glance my way. My rage must have showed on my face. Her eyes flew wide in surprise. For a moment she watched me, as if trying to judge what was the matter. If she had smiled, I think I would have leaped at her. But her pained look seemed to accuse me. What was happening? My anger waited. In time, innocently, Muskrat got up and went quietly into the shelter.

Pinesinger came up the trail carrying the right front leg of the horse, from the hoof to the elbow. Absently I watched her, thinking that Father must have given her that meat. In fact the whole right foreleg was his, because the spear of his brother had killed. Who was now cooking the foreleg from the elbow to the shoulder? Probably Yoi.

"Will you share with me, Stepmother?" I asked, to say something.

Pinesinger put the foreleg on the ground and took her knife to it. "You have two stepmothers," she said. "My share is small, without much meat on it. I have kin to satisfy too, remember. You must also ask my co-wife for some of hers."

"Are you refusing me?"

"Listen to yourself, Kori," said Pinesinger. "You sound like an animal growling. What have I done to you that you speak harshly to me?"

I didn't know I had spoken harshly. "I'm sorry, Stepmother," I said. "I don't want meat from your share, because I'm not hungry. I won't eat."

"And your woman?" asked Pinesinger. "What of her?"

"What of her?" I asked. "All day on the plain did you find nothing to eat?"

Pinesinger had cut free the long, thin muscle that lifts the hoof. She put sticks on my fire, getting ready to cook. The hoof drooped sharply. Still holding the leg, she lowered her head to blow on the coals, leaning so far forward between her raised knees that her child-swollen belly pushed against the ground. As she did, the wolf came up behind her and seized the hoof. "Hi!" she shouted, jerking the hoof away from him and bringing it down on his head like a club. Crying, he vanished into the dark.

But I hardly heard him. Anger seemed to have overcome me. My thoughts were fixed on killing Muskrat. I saw how I would do it if my anger weren't calmed. I had to speak with Andriki. I stood up and took the trail to the cave.

At the cave's narrow mouth, in a cloud of smoke and scent from the cooking horsemeat, I waited for people to see me. Many firelit faces turned to look. My eyes found Andriki's, and seeing my trouble, he raised his chin to beckon me. Making my way to the men's fire, I sat on my heels behind him. "It's Kori," said one of Graylag's women at the women's fire.

"Child of Aal, tell me something," called Graylag's wife, Teal, from the dark, over the heads of the people. "What has your woman made?"

I stretched my neck, but I couldn't see Teal because of

the darkness and smoke. So I called my answer in the direction of her voice. "Aunt, I don't know."

"It's filth," said Father. "It's not important. That my son lets his woman play with birthmatter and take the teeth of horses that aren't hers to use, that's what's important."

But Andriki looked at me with great meaning in his eyes. Seeing that he had words to speak for my ears only, I lowered my head to wait until he was ready. "What are your plans?" he asked, when at last people began to talk of something else.

In a voice as low as his I answered, "I won't say."

"Come," he whispered, looking around at the other people, some of whom were watching us curiously. "There's no need to tease those who want to overhear us." Straightening his long legs, he stood up and led the way out of the cave, down to the river, and over some boulders to a large, flat, starlit rock in the middle of the current. I saw how well he had chosen the place—there we could talk without anyone hearing us yet be as safe as if in a cave. Andriki always knew what to do. "So are you troubled by your woman?" he asked.

It shames me to say so, but I began to weep. "I'm going to kill her," I said.

"Ai, Nephew," said Andriki calmly, as if he would have expected any man to weep. "I saw from the start that this matter was troubling you, perhaps more than it needs to. Yet what is so bad that it can't be fixed? Tell your woman to bury the thing. That's all you need to do. Getting Pinesinger to help will be your problem." He laughed.

I tried hard to control myself so I could answer him. When he saw I was having difficulty doing this, he went on. "The teeth your woman used, they're nothing much. Your father's wolf stole a jawbone from the cave, so perhaps your woman didn't take the teeth—perhaps the wolf brought them to her. The little spears, those are her people's things. What do they mean to us? Nothing. The hair? It's her hair. Her people can't be wise or clean. She hardly knows how to braid hair. What does it matter that she uses it? The feather? A bird stole that feather for its nest. She stole it from a bird. And the umbilical cord fell from her baby. Your father looked at the thing. He isn't worried. He sometimes talks about important things that were done by shamans—things that mattered. He doesn't talk of your woman's doings, because they aren't important and don't matter."

"It's that she plays with things she doesn't understand," I said. "It's that she named my child, never thinking that a name could be harmful. She doesn't understand our ways and doesn't want to. She doesn't understand anything. She's stupid and dangerous. I want to kill her. If I did, no one would avenge her. But who would feed my child if she were dead?"

"You want to kill her?"

"Yes."

"But why? Tell her to go."

"I don't want her to go."

"You're in a bad state of mind, Nephew," said Andriki.

"Yes.

"Yes," said Andriki thoughtfully. "This happens. A woman can put a man in a bad state of mind. It's in her power."

I drew a deep breath of damp river air and felt some of my anger and madness leaving. "It's my little boy," I explained.

"Yes," said Andriki. "Children are the power of women. Children make them strong."

I saw how this was true. "If you were me, what would you do?"

"I'd make her bury the thing."

"How?"

"Tell her that if she doesn't, you'll force her. Then you'll be sorry and she'll be sorry, but the thing will be buried, no matter who is sorry. Do it soon and then forget about it. That's the best way."

For most of that night I lay awake, and in the morning I found Muskrat and Pinesinger together, eating marrow from the shin of Pinesinger's share of the horse. Trembling, Father's wolf pup looked on, his ears folded, his eyes bright. He seemed very hungry. I sat on my heels near the women, waiting for Pinesinger to offer marrow to me, but she didn't. When the marrow was eaten, the women burned the bones. Then in her own language Muskrat took leave of Pinesinger, but not, I thought, of me. I watched her pick up her digging stick and walk out to the plain. The little wolf grew very anxious, torn between Muskrat and the fading hope of marrow. At last he followed Muskrat.

When she was far away, I drew a deep breath, and trying to keep my voice from shaking, I asked Pinesinger to help me speak with Muskrat. But Pinesinger just licked the last of the marrow from her fingers. "Why don't you learn her tongue?" she asked. "Why doesn't she learn your tongue? You're always asking me to do what you should do for yourself." It seemed that my stepmother wanted me to beg her. But my anger was too strong. I stood up to leave. Instead of letting me go without taking notice, though, Pinesinger looked up at me very directly. "You're angry with her because you don't trust her," she said. "But why should I help you punish her? What makes you think you know better than she how to treat your son?"

"By the Bear!" I said. "Now I see why my father doesn't want you. Now I see why he plans to send you home. You who are always smiling, always thinking you know more than others—do you know what your husband plans to do with you?"

I saw at once that she did not. Her mouth came open and her face grew red. "What's that?" she asked. "What do you mean about your father?"

I couldn't help myself—the confusion on her face gave me a wild, happy feeling. "Goodbye, Stepmother. You're going home," I said. I think she started crying. I'm not sure, because I was striding away as fast as I could without breaking into a run.

Across the plain I went, following Muskrat's distant figure. If she had been near me, I might have taken her by the hair. But she was far, and a strong, fast walker. It was all I could do to keep up, let alone overtake her. Perhaps it was the wolf who noticed me. I saw her look down at him, then back at me, over her shoulder. When she saw me following, she turned around to face me and stood still.

This and the walking took away some of my anger. By the time I reached her, my voice, at least, did not shake. "Come," I said. "I want you to do something."

"Hi?" she asked. "Is what?"

But I wouldn't try to tell her, not out on the plain. I took her arm. She looked at me, trying to learn from my expression what might be in my mind. Her eyes were wide and soft, her face questioning. She thought something was the matter, that I needed her help. I kept my face stiff and jerked my chin to show her where I wanted to take her. "Io. I come," she said.

Back at her little shelter, I made the handsign for sit. Muskrat knew it and sat down, opening her shirt and offering her nipple to the baby. In the shade of the shelter, the wolf pup threw himself down. I stood over them, making Muskrat glance up at me, as if to ask why I did not sit also. I looked around, wondering how to begin. Perhaps I should have been more patient with Pinesinger. Yet such thoughts came too late. Floating from the cave's mouth were the sounds of argument and weeping. Pinesinger had decided to confront Father, it seemed.

But I couldn't worry about Pinesinger, not then. With the point of my spear I probed in the thatch. Out dropped Muskrat's bundle. Her eyes flew wide, and she reached for it. But I blocked her hand with the shaft of my spear. She looked up. "That thing," I began. "You must bury it."

"Ho! Bury? I not bury!" said Muskrat, alarmed.

"You will bury," I said, staring straight into her eyes.

Muskrat stared back. "No," she said sharply. "I not bury. Bury is corpse. I not bury. This thing not for you, Dza Goie. This thing for him, Kiu Ngarr."

"Dza Goie?" I asked, wishing at once that I hadn't.

"Kiu Ngarr, he name. Dza Goie, you name," said Muskrat, looking down at our baby and very gently smoothing her hand over his belly, where his umbilical cord had clung. "He life there," she whispered. "He keep life. He grow tall, like you, he father. He eat. He grow strong. He keep this. I not bury."

Again Muskrat reached for the bundle, and this time I didn't stop her. Rather, I watched her unwind the bark that held it together and watched her separate the parts. Taking up the long branch, the peeled branch bent by its sinew string, she put one end in her mouth. Then she picked up one of the little bird-spears and gently tapped the string with it. The string played a song. The song was very soft—I had to bend low to hear it—but I knew it. It was the same song the women had been singing while they bathed in the river: the crane's song.

So I lost my fear of the bundle and my anger at Muskrat, all at the same time. I knew then that she had meant nothing harmful but had done no more than make a dirty thing because of her people's ignorant belief. I gave up all thought of forcing her to bury the thing. Forcing her would upset all of us—her, me, and the baby—and what would be gained? Rather, to please Father, I would bury the thing myself after dark.

But Muskrat didn't guess my thoughts. She smiled her wide white smile, put her bundle under the wall, and took her digging stick, ready to go back to the plain. Just before she stood up, she groped inside her carrying bag and took out a twig, a bit of yew, which she lay on the ground in front of me. "Is dza goie," she said.

"What? That's poison. You call me that?" I asked.

For just a moment she looked puzzled. "Io. Very strong. Most strong thing. Is good," she said. Then she touched my hand, stroking me. "And now is all right," she added gently. "Now you happy, Dza Goie."

Meanwhile the argument in the cave had grown much louder. As Father's voice flew from firm to dangerous, he was drowned out by Pinesinger's angry screams. "Animals," she called the women, and "women," she called the men. Perhaps I should have let Father choose his own time to tell her his plans, in his own way. Feeling that he might soon give her cause to regret her outburst but not wanting to hear him do it, I decided to take myself away for a while. So I took my spears and Muskrat's bundle and followed the river toward the old cave until I was far upstream.

As I walked along the plain at the edge of the ravine, I looked down at the river and noticed a few little holes freshly dug in the bank. Something had been digging sedge roots. A person, it was—I saw the marks of a digging stick. On I went, my eye on the riverbank. Soon I saw more holes. More sedge had been dug there. On I went, keeping watch on the river's sandy shore, and soon, even from quite far above, I saw the prints of strong, broad feet. As I had suspected, I was following Muskrat, who had been going from clump to clump of sedge grass, digging and eating like a bear.

I had nothing important to do that afternoon except to bury Muskrat's bundle. Not wanting to bury it near the cave, where anyone might see me, or where Muskrat could track me and find it, I had planned to bury the thing after dark, far away. But although I was a long way upriver, it was only early afternoon. For the rest of the day I had nothing to do. I could think of no better way to spend the time than by watching my woman, so, feeling strangely excited, as I might if starting to hunt, I set out along the ravine's rim to track her. Soon I noticed her dark shape below me, hip-deep in a spreading raspberry thicket, reaching carefully for the berries over the thorns.

Under the bush the pup waited, watching her. Often she would toss him a berry, which he would catch with a snap I could hear from afar. Sometimes she would drop a berry into her carrying bag—for me! Interested, I watched closely to see how many berries she meant for me, and saw that she was saving about half of what she was eating. Would our women save as few? I tried to remember what I might have learned from watching my mother, but found I didn't know. A long time passed while Muskrat picked and ate, picked and ate, her hands and mouth busy with berries as her eyes searched for more.

Quietly, close beside a juniper, I sat down on my heels in front of the sun. A raven soaring overhead noticed me and called. Muskrat glanced up into the sun and didn't see me. Back to the raspberry bush she turned, to pick and eat some more. When the berries became so few that her picking grew slow, she left suddenly, like a waxwing, and hurried on her way. The pup crept out of the shade of the raspberry bush to trot behind her. I stretched myself and followed, noting how the wind blew so the pup wouldn't catch my scent. I saw that he would make stalking my woman interesting, this animal.

At the water's edge Muskrat poised her digging stick like a spear. The pup grew tense at the sight of her. Setting her feet down slowly, quietly, she crept forward. With a hum, her stick flew. She and the pup ran to the place it had struck, where a small creature—a frog, I think—lay sprawling. The pup reached the frog first and bolted it down. Muskrat seemed to have expected this. On she went, stalking. Again her stick flew, and again the pup ate something.

On she went a third time, to a patch of sparse round spears of onion leaves with fading purple flowers. Squatting on her heels, she chopped the tiny onions out of the ground, catching them in her hand and throwing them into her mouth or into her bag with the same smooth motion. Far away as she was, I heard the onions between her teeth, a faint crunching.

When she finished the onions she noticed purslane and ate some. I don't much like purslane, so I don't eat it unless I'm truly hungry. I was interested to see that Muskrat didn't save me any. Had she noticed that I didn't eat it? Farther on she noticed an elderberry bush with berries still clinging to it, and ate there for a time. Still farther she found parsnips, which she dug up, saving some and chewing others. From the plain above her I could once again hear her eating her food; this time the sound was the watery noise of the wet parsnip cracking apart in her mouth.

That's what she did that afternoon beside the river. Once she had a drink; several times she offered food to the wolf, who refused nothing; and several times she offered her breast to the baby. But otherwise she found and picked small bits of food. In the later afternoon, her carrying bag bulging, she climbed the bank and turned back toward the cave, causing me to hide in a thicket until she had gone. I wouldn't have wanted her to know I had nothing better to do than to watch her gathering.

Down by the river I broke the foul things in her magic bundle and buried all the shattered pieces. Then I climbed back to the plain and started home. The sun set. Below me in the ravine I heard a rock turn over. Looking for what made the sound, I noticed, in the dusk, horses drinking from the river. One, the stallion, swept his head high, water dripping from his mouth. He must have seen me against the sky, because strange to say, he called out a challenge. His voice rang from the rocky banks of the river, and his mares looked up. All watched me for a time, then went back to their drinking, perhaps knowing that I couldn't reach them from so far. When they were ready, they turned and made their way over the stones, up the far bank to the plain, their hooves scraping. They had noticed me, had spoken to me in a language I didn't understand, and had gone on their way to a place I didn't know to do something I couldn't foresee. They reminded me of Muskrat.

I thought she might have found her bundle missing by the time I reached her little shelter. In the firelight I saw her looking at me anxiously, as if something worried her. I sat down slowly across the fire from her, watching her face to learn her thoughts. But she turned toward the cave and waited, her head low, listening. I listened too, but I heard only a strange silence, as if no one were there. Puzzled, I looked at Muskrat for an explanation. She sadly shook her head. Something was the matter. "What?" I asked. She shrugged and turned a hand palm up, to indicate that she wouldn't even try to tell me.

So I had no choice but to learn for myself. With some misgiving, yet knowing that whatever was wrong had saddened but not frightened Muskrat, I took the trail to the cave. The silence was very deep, but fires were burning. Before I reached the opening I saw their light.

At the two fires the people sat quietly. They looked up when they saw me but didn't speak. I thought that the women seemed sad and the men seemed worried, but I could see at once that whatever was wrong was not too terrible, and that no one had been killed. Then I saw that both Father and Pinesinger were missing. I looked at Andriki. He caught my eye and stood up.

This time he followed me to the plain, to Muskrat's fire. When the two of us sat down, Muskrat got up and left. I saw her going inside her shelter, perhaps to hide in the shadow. I didn't care. I looked at Andriki, waiting.

"Here's the thing," he began unwillingly. "Your younger stepmother left here. She said if your father wanted her to leave, she would leave. She started for the Fire River. We thought she'd come back when it got dark, but when she didn't, your father went to find her."

"They were fighting this afternoon," I said, as my own part in this trouble began to come to me.

"They were," said Andriki. "By evening your father's patience was gone and he used his belt on her. Not badly, but she left afterward."

"He beat her?" I asked, although I must say I had almost seen it coming and wasn't too surprised.

"So would many of us have done if our wives had spoken to us even once as she spoke to him."

"Hi!" I said.

"Yes. And your father is displeased with you. He said you began this."

I couldn't deny it. "He's right," I said. "He once asked me not to tell her something, but I babbled like a woman. No wonder he's displeased."

"Never mind," said Andriki. "Your father will forget. You should forget too."

That seemed to be good advice. Before long I had taken it. Andriki and I were playing Stones in the Holes with ten pebbles and five pits each, and I was winning, by the time Pinesinger walked up to the fire out of the night. I don't know what I had expected, or why it surprised me that her face was drawn and strangely quiet, without bruises or tears. All I could think was that this walking about at night was not good for a baby, and I had to stop myself from telling her so. Instead I looked up at her, questioning. Where was Father?

Andriki too was looking up at Pinesinger, saying nothing, taking her in. We sat, she stood. "Come then,

Kori. We'll see if my brother is here," said Andriki at last, and we did.

Father must have slipped past us in the dark. We found him in the cave by the men's fire, talking in a low, serious voice with two of Graylag's men. They were Pinesinger's kinsmen, I realized, yet they seemed very sympathetic to Father, nodding reasonably at whatever he said as if to assure him that they had no quarrel of any kind with him. He told them how he had followed Pinesinger's tracks and where he had found her, at a little fire she had kindled far out on the plain. She thought she was going to her parents, but she never would have found them, not the way she was heading, said Father. After all, she had made the trip only once and in the opposite direction.

Her kinsmen smiled and shook their heads in wonder. A woman going alone on a way she had never taken before—what folly! They thanked Father for finding her. As they themselves would be traveling to the Fire River very soon, they offered to take her there for Father if he liked.

When Father noticed me in the opening, he called me to his side and made me answer to him for telling Pinesinger of his plan to send her home. In front of all the people I had to explain how angry she had made me. She had made him angry too, said Father, loud enough for everyone to hear. Very angry. There were only so many times a wife of his could call him a liar and a woman before he would take his belt to her, and Pinesinger had gone beyond that number. So he was glad, he said, that I had explained myself, or he would have sent me to the Fire River with her. Hi! When he told me that, I saw how much I had upset him.

Yoi stood and over the heads of many people handed Father six long strips of meat. These he placed on the men's fire for himself, me, and Andriki. We were the only people there who had not eaten. As we listened to the meat sizzling and smelled the good smoke, I felt Father's hand on my shoulder. As both of us knew, all was well.

Or so it seemed until we heard a scream from my camp up on the plain—a scream that brought us to our feet and made Father and Andriki reach for their spears. Mine was in my camp. I caught up a burning stick and rushed up the trail, with Father and Andriki and most of the other men behind me. But the trouble was only that Muskrat had found her magic bundle gone. I took Father aside and explained in a low voice what had happened. After all, the matter of the bundle was more or less between me and Father, not something everyone needed to be told. Father listened seriously. Pinesinger sat with her child in her lap and her face stony, staring at nothing, wishing us gone, but Muskrat gaped at me, astonished. She might have been crying. I could see she had not expected such a thing. The other men watched her, looking puzzled. "Women's business!" explained Father in his easy way. The other men understood and turned back to the cave.

I suppose I should have stayed with Muskrat and Pinesinger, yet that night I didn't want to. I saw them heavy with anger, drawn silently together against me and all our men. I also saw that the men would be in the cave below, not worrying about the two women but enjoying themselves with laughter and meat and good feeling. We who are the men of Father's family are not afraid to show our anger, but when the trouble is over, we know how to forget. Not so our women. Rather than let two of them punish me, I left them to sulk, thinking that Muskrat at least would be happy by morning.

But by morning she was gone. She had run away without a word, taking Pinesinger, both children, and Father's wolf pup with her.

29

IF WE HAD KNOWN RIGHT THEN THAT THEY HAD GONE, WE would have caught them. But that morning I stayed inside the cave, planning with Father and Graylag to hunt for the horses I had seen. We had forgotten all about the quarreling.

In time I left the cave and climbed the little trail to the plain. There stood Muskrat's shelter, shining with dew. It seemed very quiet, so I went to look inside. No one was there. But that didn't surprise me—the digging sticks were missing, so I supposed that the two women were digging parsnips and onions as Muskrat had done the day before. I didn't think to look for the dark trails the women should have left in the dew if they had crossed the grass that morning. It simply didn't come to me to notice that there were no trails. If the women had taken their digging sticks, it seemed to me, where else but by the river could they be?

Just then Father and his brothers came up the path, followed by Graylag with his sons and stepsons, all with spears. I snatched my spears from Muskrat's shelter and caught up to walk behind Father as we set off to look for the trail of round hoofprints. After a while we found the tracks and followed them to the horses. But the horses were alert and wary. All the tricks that we tried did not put us within spearing distance of them. At last we had to give up and go to look for some other animal.

In the afternoon we surprised a roebuck in a thicket. He burst out, but I raced after him, threw my spear, and very luckily got him in the rump. He then ran on three legs, bucking and so slowed down that the other men overtook him. By late afternoon we were cooking his liver. My part in this hunt very much pleased Father.

When we returned to the cave, I took my share of meat to Muskrat and Pinesinger. Still they weren't there. Then I began to worry. This seemed a long time of gathering for late summer, when much could be gathered quickly. At first the other men refused to share my worry. By dusk they did, but then it was too late—the women were a day's travel ahead of us, and we couldn't track them until morning.

The waning moon rose right before the sun. By its light Andriki and I set out after the women. They hadn't tried to hide their trail, which led downstream and crossed the river where the plain was low, at the place we had forded on our way to and from Father's lodge. We guessed that the women were going to our wintergrounds, perhaps to the lodge. Muskrat was leading, carrying our child on her right hip. Father's wolf followed her.

The speed of the women surprised us. The prints were far apart and few; the women were all but flying. "Hi!" said Andriki when he saw how old the tracks were, even after a whole day of following. "Are we women, that we go no faster than they?"

How could I answer? That night we only got as far as their camp of the night before, and the next day we gained very little on them. They were running and resting, running and resting, as if their strength were failing, yet they were traveling at hunters' speed. During the days that followed we merely shortened the distance between us, but we didn't overtake them. And we had food with us—strips of meat from the roebuck. What they were eating we couldn't say.

Their speeding footprints led not to Father's lodge but to the stream from Narrow Lake, where the women had stopped to drink. Then they had doubled back and climbed up into the Hills of Ohun. Thinking we would find them at the little pond where I had found Muskrat, we followed. It seemed strange to be on Father's wintergrounds when the willows and birches in the woods were green and the berries were just ripening.

Even the stillness was strange—nothing broke it but cloud shadows slowly moving over the great heath, and now and then the faint, sharp voices of willow-tits singing. We found where the women had been eating berries. I found berries in a scat left by Father's wolf, and I also found some tiny mouse bones, some feathers, and some very fine, short, dark hair in the scat, which I showed to Andriki. Then we thought we knew how the women might be feeding themselves: by catching little things every night with Muskrat's yew-bark snares.

Following the women's trail on the heath took time, since their moccasins left few prints on the dry ground. But taking our direction from the footprints, we climbed the hill, sure that we would find a camp. We came at last to the long grass on the shore of the pond where Muskrat had been swimming when I had first seen her. There we found a camp with no one in it. That did not surprise us. We looked around, and then we saw why the women had come here and what we could expect when we tried to get them back again. In the camp were the tracks of six people—four strangers besides Pinesinger and Muskrat.

"Waugh," said Andriki, looking down. "Are these adults?" He put his foot beside one of the footprints to show that his foot was almost half again as long.

"Perhaps it's a child," I said.

"These are the same people who camped here last fall. I had forgotten how small they are. Who are they?"

Of course they were Muskrat's people, they who were called the Ilasi. They seemed to be back again for another season, as if our wintergrounds were their summergrounds, although why anyone would want to spend a summer eating birds and berries was more than we could understand. But because they were so few—the old man who walked with a stick, the two women, the child—I could see how the heath might seem good to them. Then a new thought came to me. Perhaps they had been waiting for Muskrat.

They feared us, we saw, and they had known we were coming. Perhaps they had seen or heard us. They had left quickly, hurrying out of the hills and into the forests to the east, just where they had gone after we had captured

Muskrat. The ashes of their fire still held embers. We might have followed, but evening was near. Instead we decided to hunt and eat, to give ourselves strength before following them. So we spent the rest of the afternoon picking and eating berries in the warm sunshine, and at sunset we went around the lake to Father's lodge.

Wolves had used it. On the floor lay their scats and shed winter hair. As we crawled into the lodge, we caught their heavy smell. But even the wolves were gone from that round, quiet space—only the evening sunlight lay on the bare floor, and only dust motes moved above it. We built a little fire in the owners' end of the lodge and planned our hunt, and then lay down to sleep in the dust. We had not burdened ourselves with sleeping-skins. After dark we heard wolves snuffling and whining at the coldtrap, and later we heard them singing. Later still we heard a tiger roaring far away. We looked at each other—the voice didn't sound like the Lily's.

Yet the Lily was the tiger I saw in my dreams that night—the Lily crouched under the low bough of a hemlock, his pale eyes green with starlight. I saw his huge, long shape, his spine just touching the branch, his head low. He was hiding, waiting for me. Then the dream changed. I saw the dark shapes of men crouching under the hemlock's branches, hiding, and I knew they were the men of Muskrat's family waiting for me. Waugh! I woke up in the perfect darkness of the lodge. Not a coal glowed in the ashes, not a star shone down through the smokeholes. We had used all our firewood. Frightened and unhappy, sure that by then the little men of Muskrat's family must be hunting for me, I sat up in the blackness, holding my spear.

When the light turned gray, Andriki opened his eyes and saw me sitting there. He could tell I had not slept. I tried not to show that my thoughts or dreams had bothered me, but he saw that too. "Hi, Kori," he said, sounding very cheerful, very easy. "What can we do? Can we leave your father's wife here? Even if your woman stays, we must try to reason with Eider's Daughter. What will her mother say to us if we manage to lose her? What will Bala say? He'll never give us another woman, you can be sure of that."

I smiled, trying to seem as carefree as Andriki. Encouraged, he went on. "Those people of your woman's," he said, "they make me think of Weevil in the days gone by. Weevil was small, you know. A little person. And his in-law was Wolverine, a big person. One day when Weevil and Wolverine were hunting, a snowstorm came. The two in-laws decided to wait out the storm in shelters made from pine branches. So they each made a shelter. Wolverine made his in a short time, but Weevil's took a long time. Wolverine went inside, but he was getting cold and snow was blowing into his clothes even before Weevil finished. Weevil didn't get inside until night. Then Wolverine looked over at Weevil and asked, 'Is your shelter warm?' Weevil said yes. Wolverine asked, 'Is it dry?' Weevil said yes. 'Good,' said Wolverine. 'I'm taking it.' And he did." Andriki looked at me sideways, laughing. "He could do it, you see. He was bigger."

We crawled out the coldtrap, urinated down the cold east wind that had begun blowing during the night, and then, since we had no food and didn't want to drink water, we very slowly and quietly walked off toward the east end of the lake, hunting. In our minds was the she-moose we had seen killed by the tiger. But the woods were empty. With wolves and a tiger hunting there, what chance had we? We turned north toward the grassland with willows. There we saw a group of hinds, far away. We stalked them. The wind changed and they smelled us. The leader's tail went up and she whistled a warning. Away the herd ran, all together in perfect order, the old leader first, the young hinds in the middle, the lookout last. While they went through a little valley, the lookout kept us in sight until the leader reached the high ground on the far side and could watch us. What could we do? They knew too much to let us scatter them. We watched them go.

When much of the day had passed, when both of us were trying hard not to show hunger or disappointment, Andriki saw a marmot sitting by his burrow. From a distance so great I could scarcely believe it, he threw his spear. On and on flew the spear, getting smaller and smaller, until suddenly it knocked the marmot over backward and pinned him, twitching, to the ground. We ran to him and broke his neck. Then we took him to the lodge, cooked him, and ate most of him, saving his legs and feet for later.

That night the wolves, who must have smelled the cooking, swarmed over the lodge. I even thought I heard one of them in the coldtrap. In the morning we climbed the Hills of Ohun and took up the cold trail of Muskrat and her people.

30

THE SPEED OF THEIR TRAVEL SURPRISED US. THE FOOTPRINTS we found when the sun set the first night had been made before noon. These were in damp earth, where Pinesinger and the Ilasi had made their way around one of the bogs that lie on Narrow River. The tracks were so clear, so plain, that I saw I knew the people—they were Pinesinger, Muskrat, and the people who had been with Muskrat when I caught her. These were two women, one young, one old; a little girl, as I learned when I found that her stream of urine had dug a hole behind her heels; and the man who led them, the old man with his stick. All this I saw, yet who these people were and how they came to be there meant very little to me. I fixed my eyes on Muskrat's footprints and followed them.

The group had traveled northeast across a wide plain where juniper, sage, and fireberry grew to shoulder height, as thick as a wood. The people surely were hiding from us, traveling where we couldn't hope to see them. On the far side of the plain they had chosen a valley where a river ran through a heavy spruce wood. I didn't know the river, although Andriki had followed it with Father and said it led to the Hair. On the far side of the valley the plain rose high, open, and rocky, with no cover at all but stones and heather. Still we couldn't catch sight of Muskrat and her people.

But they couldn't hide their tracks. Sometimes we lost their trail and had to search for it, but each time we did we needed only to follow their line of travel to find the trail again, straight ahead. It struck us that the old man wasn't trying to hide their tracks or to trick us or confuse us with a false trail—surely knowing that we were following him, he acted as if he thought his best chance was to reach a certain place quickly. We realized several things because of his way of travel. We realized that his people had not been near our lodge the winter before, or if they had been, Muskrat didn't know it, and we realized that we should be ready to fight when we found them; the old man acted as if he knew that help lay ahead and was running toward it. But a fight with the people didn't worry us too badly, as they were so clearly afraid of us.

When we found where they had spent the night, we saw that they had done without a fire, perhaps because they were afraid of showing us the light. The wolf had scraped a hollow for himself nearby. Perhaps Muskrat had relied on him to give warning if we caught up to them during the night. The people had done without water—the thicket where they had slept was in the middle of the plain—and they might also have done without food. We saw no scraps, no seeds, no teeth or bones, no rinds. Perhaps I should have been encouraged, but it gave me no satisfaction to think how tired and frightened they must be. The little girl and even the babies must have been hungry and exhausted. Muskrat and Pinesinger were probably having a very hard time.

We were tired too, even though Andriki's marmot had been good food for us. Yet when we ate berries with the marmot's legs, we felt almost as strong and as ready to travel by night of the second day as we had on the morning of the first. We were out of food, though, and we had to stop in the afternoon to hunt again. We got a partridge, small for two men. After that we ran our tongues over our teeth to get rid of our thirst, we chewed juniper needles to get rid of our hunger, and we kept walking. I followed Andriki or he followed me, our strides matching perfectly as we kept the long, swinging pace of hunters, a pace that carried us fast and far. We didn't speak. As we walked, I planned what I would say to Muskrat. I would be gentle. I wouldn't be angry. I would welcome her back.

On the morning of the third day we were trying hard to ignore our hunger, knowing that Muskrat's people were hungry too but no more than half a day's travel ahead of us. We thought we would soon be starting home with our women, free to hunt as often as we liked. And we were almost right. By the afternoon we had found a milkroot, which gave us food and water, and we were traveling as fast as ever. Muskrat's people, in contrast, were stopping on every high place where they could keep watch for us while they rested. Pinesinger no longer carried her baby; the task seemed to have fallen to the older of the two Ilasi women. Pinesinger no longer seemed sure-footed, but was using her digging stick as a cane. Perhaps her fatigue wasn't surprising; she was pregnant, and she had traveled a long way. The old man, though, was as strong and sure as ever, in spite of his cane. With his people at his heels, he was all but flying. Yet he wouldn't run ahead of the others. He stayed to lead them. So when we camped that night, as I rolled our fire in a wormwood thicket out on a lonely plain, I knew we would find them the next day.

I knew where we would find them, too. Their trail led straight for a ridge of hills that ran north and south, standing above the plain like the fin of a grayling might stand above the surface of a pond. Surely the Ilasi were camping in those hills. I was leading all the time now, as if my woman's footprints were pulling me forward. While the sky was still black, I felt that dawn was coming, so I woke Andriki and we started for the hills before it was light enough to see.

By midmorning we were above the plain on gently rising ground, in a sunny grove of pines that covered the southern slopes. The smell of the warm needles was sweet, and the woods were quiet. The old man had taken a well-worn trail, a clear, smooth path among the trees. I followed carefully. The woods were open so people couldn't hide, and I felt safe from an ambush. But we didn't much fear Muskrat's people, with their small bodies, their mouse-eating habits, and their little bird-spears. Instead we worried that we would frighten them into running farther. As if they were a herd of deer, we stalked them quietly. On we went, slowly moving up the slippery, needle-covered slope, stalking the Ilasi with all our skill. When I thought I saw the sky through the pine tops, I turned and looked at Andriki. "We might hear them," I whispered. "Listen." So we listened, straining our ears. But we heard nothing.

Very carefully we went on. The trail led to the base of a cliff and followed it. Above us the cliff was a scrambled fall of boulders, a tumble of rocks too thick and steep for trees to grow among them. Here and there grew tufts of juniper and red-leaved berry bushes. High above I saw an eagle soaring, following the ridge of the hills on his way south. We took a few steps, as silently as we could. I saw another eagle, a she-eagle, and not far behind her a pair of hawks. The range of hills would have to be a long one, to draw south-flying eagles and hawks. I guessed that Andriki knew the range and surely the cliff too, since a range of hills as large as these would not have escaped his notice. But he didn't seem to know the trail, because he kept looking down among the trees below us, as if we might be leaving by another way and he were fixing the place in his mind. Though neither of us knew the trail, both of us felt we were very near the people. Again we went forward slowly, almost creeping up among the boulders, taking care not to roll rocks with our feet.

I was thinking of fighting, of killing, of the Ilasi men who might be lying in wait, ready to try to keep me from my woman. I was thinking of the blade of my spear, its edge and its sharpness; I was thinking of the hafted ax thrust into my belt and of my knife in the top of my moccasin. I was waiting to hear a man shout, or the hum of a rock thrown at me, or the crashing of a boulder rolling down on me. My eyes were stretched wide and my ears were straining, but I wasn't ready for what I heard next. First I heard a wolf bark once, short and muffled, and while I was looking around to see where the sound had come from, I heard a child's voice. "Father," it said. The voice was my own little boy's. Again he spoke: "Father!" Only that wasn't how he said it—he couldn't talk that well. "Baba," said his little voice, or "Bada." The voice came from above. Astonished, I looked up. No one was there.

The voice had stopped Andriki in his tracks. At once he backed against the cliff, his body almost in a crouch, his spear ready. But I lay my spear down by my feet and started to clamber up the cliff toward my son.

Suddenly I heard a murmur of voices, among them someone saying the name that Muskrat called me, the name of the yew, Dza Goie. A group of strange faces appeared, looking down on me. Because they all wore blue buttocks scars on their foreheads, I thought at first that one of them was Muskrat. But they were men, six of them, with black hair and beards and hard, dark eyes.

Holding to the rocks with my hands and toes, pressing my body to the cliff for balance, I stared straight up at them. Beside their bearded faces bristled a number of their little bird-spears, weak and ridiculous. No wonder our long spears worried them. Still, who could say what other weapons they might have? I knew better than to feel too sure of myself. So I tried a smile, hoping that my smile was happy, confident, and not a grin of doubt. "Waugh," said one of them, the only one who was looking at me.

The others were looking at Andriki. He was of course below and behind me, and I suddenly wondered what he was doing, that five men were staring past me at him. But I had to trust his judgment, since I couldn't turn to see. Behind the row of bearded faces I heard a sudden burst of the Ilasi language, men's voices and women's too, so I knew we had found not just one of their hiding places but their den.

One of the men picked up a large rock and held it above me, showing me that he would throw it down on me if I came nearer. So that was how they meant to defend themselves—with rocks. Yet the rocks were very large, I saw, large and heavy. With them the Ilasi could break our bones. I didn't want to loose a hail of rocks down on us, so I kept still and tried to smile again.

"Ia waugh!" one of them cried, making gestures. Slowly I moved backward until I stood by the spear I had dropped, beside Andriki, who, with his eyes on the men above us, slowly lowered his body until he could lay his spear quietly beside mine.

Then, as if the men were lions, Andriki began to talk in an even, soothing tone. "We see you, Old Ones," he began. "We honor you. My brother, at home, has lost his wife. My nephew here has lost his woman. The child up there who spoke, that is his child. We have come for our women. We mean no harm."

"Waugh," answered one of them, while behind him the jabber of language began again.

At last I heard Pinesinger's voice, speaking to me from a place that echoed. "Kori? Is it you?" she asked.

"I'm here, Stepmother," I answered.

"I won't go back with you. I don't care what your father says."

"I came for my woman, Stepmother," I said. "I came for Muskrat. I want her and my boy to come back with me."

"You won't get them," she said, her voice floating. "Don't anger these men."

"Aren't these my father's hunting lands, Stepmother?" I asked.

"Ah, Kori," she answered, "I wouldn't want to say who owns these hunting lands."

"Come down and talk with us, Eider's Child," said Andriki beside me.

"I'll talk from here," she said. "I don't want you to snatch me, so I'm coming only far enough to see you."

"This isn't good," said Andriki. "My brother will weep if he learns you won't come back."

Above us, holding her blue-eyed child tightly against herself, pregnant Pinesinger sat on her heels among the six men, all in a line in the mouth of their cave. Her face was very dirty, but her hair was braided and around her neck hung a beautiful necklace of horse's teeth and teal feathers, a necklace never given her by Father or any of our people. Doubtfully she peered down, clutching her child as if she were pretending a confidence she did not feel, as if she too were wondering what might come of this meeting. Looking at the necklace, I wondered if she had chosen a man from Muskrat's people.

But the black-bearded men kept glancing at her with suspicion. They hadn't known her but a day, and they would have been foolish to trust her. They surely didn't trust us, as their faces showed, and they kept looking over our heads, as if they were expecting something to appear behind us. That made me uneasy, of course, and kept me glancing backward too, until it came to me that I also might seem to be expecting something.

"Kori and I are going to sit down," Andriki told Pinesinger. "Please tell the men there, so we won't frighten them."

In a questioning tone, Pinesinger spoke a word or two to the men, who scowled and twisted their heads as if they didn't quite understand her. To us Pinesinger added, "They are many. Be careful of them." Then, "You say he will weep. Where will he do his weeping? Isn't he with my co-wife?"

Andriki spread his hands wide, palms up, appealing to Pinesinger. "Sister-in-law," he began. "You must come back with us. We can't leave you here to eat mice among stone-throwing strangers. After dark tonight I'll get you away from here safely—by the Bear, I promise you."

"No, Brother-in-law," said Pinesinger in her high voice. "These people aren't keeping me against my will. I wanted to come here. I want to stay. These people came to your country from the south, but for now they live here. Sometimes they get flint from a place on the Fire River. It must be the same place my parents get flint. Anyway, it's on the river. When they go, I'll go with them. Until then I'll stay here. I will. I can't live with your brother."

"You can," said Andriki. "He's not a bad husband. You're young. You've only known your parents. A wife can't speak to her husband as you spoke to my brother, not even here among these people. I'm sure of it. You're better off with men you know than with strangers. Anyway, your husband has forgotten all the trouble. You'll see I'm right. You'll thank me," said Andriki.

I didn't like the way the talk was turning. Andriki was letting himself be drawn into an argument, as if he had forgotten where we were. I was getting worried, even if he wasn't. I kept my eyes on the men around Pinesinger, trying to learn from their strange faces what thoughts might be in their minds. I didn't have long to wonder. One of them stood up, and as if he were waving flies from meat, he rudely waved Andriki and me away. Afterward he turned to Pinesinger and jerked his chin at her, motioning her to go back inside the cave. "There," she said, wide-eyed. "You see he wants me to stop talking. And he's telling you to go. You'd better obey him."

"We don't obey strangers, Sister-in-law," said Andriki. "But you know that."

"This time is different," said Pinesinger.

"These hills are in our hunting lands," said Andriki blandly.

"Don't anger these people," said Pinesinger, starting to her feet to show the man that she at least was making ready to obey. "Don't start a fight. There are many of the Ilasi. More men are inside, I warn you."

"We don't obey strangers, and we don't fear them either," said Andriki.

Andriki's matter-of-fact tone was very encouraging, but I still felt worried by the Ilasi men. "We'll go," I said to Pinesinger. "Without you, if you like. But I won't go without my woman and my boy. Ask Muskrat to come out to me, please, Stepmother."

Pinesinger gave me a long, doubtful look, then went back inside the cave. We waited, looking up at the six black-haired men while they looked down at us. They reminded me of ravens, free to go, unafraid, watching. Behind the men came voices from the cave. For a time the men talked back and forth with the people inside. Then at last the oldest man stood up and pointed one of his fingers at me—a gesture my woman used to make, until I taught her not to. "Ah!" he said. "Weh!"

To my surprise, I understood him. He had said, "You come." I had learned these words from Muskrat. Perhaps she had told him what he could say to me that I would understand. "I come?" I asked him, touching my chest.

He glared down. "Ah," he said again, louder and more slowly. "Dza Goie weh!"

Andriki and I stood up together. The man in the cave scowled down at my uncle, and stooping suddenly, he snatched up a stone. This he shook at Andriki, threatening. He meant that Andriki should not take a step farther. "Ah!" he coughed impatiently, staring at me. "Ah! Ah!"

"They mean me," I said to Andriki. "That's what he said, and he's looking at me. I'll do it."

"No, you won't," said Andriki, slowly reaching for his spear. "They won't get you up there alone—not while I live."

When Andriki's hand touched his spear, all the watching men leaped to their feet.

"Io. Io," I said to them, trying to sound soothing. "We respect you. Mi weh, io. I'm coming." To Andriki I said, "Be easy, Uncle. I'll be careful." And to Pinesinger, out of sight, I said, "Well then, Stepmother, here I come. Can you speak the right words to tell these men I come without my spear?"

The mouth of the cave was very low and narrow, just a slit in the tumble of boulders. Pikas had used it—the opening was thick with dung. The six men moved aside as I climbed toward them, but they hardly seemed to see me as I got on my hands and knees to crawl inside the cave. They were watching Andriki so intently that I knew he was doing something that worried them, so instead of going inside, I turned to look at him too. He had moved closer to the cliff, as if ready to climb it, his spear and mine in his hands. His untroubled face was almost smiling, as if he had taken the measure of the Ilasi men and now was challenging them to touch me.

"Uncle," I said in a voice as quiet and soothing as I could make it, "I see a large pile of stones here. If you anger the people, they could stone us. I can hear from the voices that many people are inside. We can't fight all of them with two spears. You're below them, in the way of their stones, and I'll be trapped in here. Sit down. Don't scare these men."

In the same kind of soothing voice he asked, "Is your stepmother there? I want to see her."

"She's not in sight," I said.

"Call her."

He was making me uneasy, and the Ilasi men too. "Uncle, she's gone and we're troubling the people, talking so. Let me go in."

"Your stepmother," said Andriki softly, "must tell them that our people are many, and if harm comes to you, the people here will be hunted down like animals and killed."

"Before we talk of killing, let me see my woman," I said, also softly. "The people up here are watching you, not me."

"Good, then. Go on. Be very careful."

"I'm going in now."

"I'll be here."

"Be easy, Uncle," I said, and on hands and knees I went in.

31

A GREAT SMELL MET ME AND ALMOST CHOKED ME. IT WAS THE smell of many sweating bodies and much spoiling meat. Rolled up near the cave's mouth was a fresh bearskin. Had these people killed a bear? The skin was huge, that of a very big bear. And I had thought the Ilasi were simple mouse-eaters! If they had killed this bear, how had they done it? With rocks? Surely not. With their little bird-spears? Not possible. How then? I looked around the cave for larger weapons but saw none. Soon the great stench made me wonder if the people could have found a bear already dead. I would have liked to show the skin to Andriki.

Suddenly Pinesinger's voice spoke in the darkness ahead of me. "The people ask you to sit down, Kori. They want to talk with you," she said.

"Where is my woman?"

"Not here."

"But she is," I said. "I heard our child's voice. He spoke to me. My woman is here."

"Never mind her now. The men have something they want to say to you, Kori. Perhaps you should hear them."

"Yes, if it's about my woman," I said. I sat quietly, my arms resting on my knees so that everyone could see my empty, harmless hands.

While standing below the cave looking up at the Ilasi, I had also been looking into the bright sky. My eyes were taking a long time to get used to the darkness. Meanwhile I could only listen to the echoing talk, the booming jumble of men's voices that took turns speaking to me. "What do they say, Stepmother?" I asked.

But although Pinesinger could understand one person speaking slowly and clearly, as if to a child, she couldn't understand many excited men speaking quickly all together in the echoing cave. She had to ask questions. Impatiently they answered her as they repeated themselves to me, as if they thought I should be able to understand. I heard the same words over and over, getting slower and louder. Perhaps these men were as unused to strange tongues as I once had been. In the back of my mind it came to me that this had been the way we had spoken to Muskrat.

As I waited for Pinesinger, my eyes grew used to the dark, and I looked around, hoping to see my woman. But she wasn't there. I saw a ragged crowd of other people, men and women, young and old, almost as many as the people of Father's lodge. They looked like Muskrat—their faces were broad, like hers, and their hair was thick and black. They wore it as Muskrat would have worn hers if Rin hadn't braided it for her: pulled back and wound with string into a bent club that looked like a child's foot in a moccasin. All wore dull, dark clothes trimmed with balding fox fur, like the clothes that Andriki and I had once hidden from Muskrat. The adults had blue scars on their foreheads.

Nearby sat Pinesinger, her back very straight, her face alert, as if she were trying to please, to seem obedient. She had more respect for these dirty people than I did. When an old woman near her plucked her arm and asked her a question, Pinesinger shook her head, then gestured to me and with the same hand patted her breast. She seemed to be telling the old woman that she was my stepmother. I felt a twinge of irritation. What business was it of Pinesinger's to explain to these bobcats about me?

From a dark corner an old man watched me closely. His face was deeply wrinkled, and he braced himself with a long staff. Surely it was this man who had run from the Hills of Ohun on the day I captured Muskrat, the same man who had led Muskrat here. Who was he to her? Her father? I didn't know. Never before had I wondered about Muskrat's mother or father, or any of her family. His face bitter, scowling, the old man watched me until at last he noticed that I was also watching him. Scornfully he looked away.

"Tell me what they're saying," I said to Pinesinger. "Can't you hear?"

"Yes, I hear," she answered, "but I don't think I understand. They're trying to tell me your woman is dead."

"What? That's not what they're saying! Don't her tracks lead here? Didn't I just hear my son's voice?"

"I don't know what they mean. Wait a little," she said, and turning to the Ilasi men, she spoke some more. I could hear from her voice that she wanted to please them. For a time I listened as hard as I could, hoping to catch a word here or there. But Pinesinger's powers with this strange tongue were far beyond mine—I didn't understand much of what she said, let alone what the men told her. At last I stopped trying. Instead, in hopes of seeing something that I knew was Muskrat's, I let my eyes roam through the cave.

Because of the overhang, the narrow entrance, and the fact that the cave faced east, by this time of day no sunlight came into it. And although the cave was near a wood where there was plenty of fuel, the people didn't seem to have bothered with a fire. So it was very dark. Yet as I was looking around at the people's piles of sticks, I saw something that I had taken for firewood—a stick bent from being tied with sinew, just like the stick of Muskrat's foul magic bundle, the stick she had hung with a horse's teeth, an owl's feather, and my son's umbilical cord. As soon as I noticed one sinew-bent stick, I noticed several others stuck into cracks in the rock, lying on the floor, or propped against the wall of the cave. Some were hung with teeth, others were hung with feathers, and all were dark, as if rubbed with fat. So I saw that whatever they were, they were common things that came easily to hand, not things of the spirits but things of the people—tools like digging sticks, perhaps. Muskrat had played a song on hers. Perhaps all the Ilasi played music. The thought was soothing. For just a moment it seemed that people who would play music would not make trouble for my woman and my child and me.

But the next moment I began to worry. The talk was taking far too long. I knew Andriki would be anxious. Perhaps his concern would make him restless. I didn't want him to frighten the people or in any way to alarm them. For all I knew there was a back way out of the cave, where my woman could escape from me again. I could have taken Pinesinger by the throat and shaken her for jabbering away with Muskrat's people as if she were no wife of Father's. I also didn't like the squinting faces of the people watching me. Very slowly I started to stand up.

"Stop," said Pinesinger. "These people are angry. They want to tell you something."

"Then speak, Stepmother. What trick are they playing on me?"

"I don't know just what they mean, Kori," said Pinesinger, her voice barely above a whisper. "I don't know what they want you to think. They say your woman is dead, but I can tell you, she's not. But that is what they tell me to say to you—she's dead. I don't like it."

Neither did I. I looked around at all the dark, quiet faces, at the watching eyes, and although I didn't believe I was in real danger, I sat down again while Pinesinger tried to talk some more. "It's this," she began again, doubtfully. "Even if she isn't really dead, she's dead for you. You harmed her when you captured her, they say. You made her pregnant. Then you harmed your child when you took away his hunting power—the bundle your woman put into the thatch. Your child could starve because of what you took away from him, they say. So they won't let you see the child or the woman. She's not yours." Pinesinger listened to one of the men, whose voice was beginning to sound excited. "It's this," she said, her eyes wide. "He says that only if you and your uncle leave right now can you leave here alive. If you go now, the people will spare you, although some of them want to follow you a way to make sure you're gone. They'll spare you and your uncle because your woman has asked them to. They want you to touch your mouth, so they'll know I told you what they wanted and that you understood me. To them, touching your mouth is a sign."

I don't know what I had expected, that these words should astonish me so. I suppose I hadn't thought that the Ilasi, who were as simple as animals, and intruding on our hunting lands too, would say such things. I tried not to let my face show my astonishment. "But the woman is mine now. She belongs with me," I said. "And the child wants me. He's mine too."

Pinesinger gave me a long look, a look of warning, and thought for a while before she repeated my words for the silent, carefully listening Ilasi. One of the men answered her with a short, quick burst of speech. "He asks what child," said Pinesinger. "No child of yours is here."

"Hi!" I said, too loudly. "I heard my child. Didn't he call me? Where is he?"

"Your voice, Kori," said Pinesinger in alarm. "In the name of Ohun, keep your voice low."

But my anger had come. "Where is he?" I asked. "He's

here. He's in this cave somewhere, in these hills. Our hills. These are our wintergrounds, our hunting lands. Muskrat is my woman, and the child is my child. I took her before, while her people ran like hares. I'll take her again. Do these people think they can keep her? She comes now, or all our men come for her with spears. With spears!"

"Be quiet, Kori!" warned Pinesinger. "I don't dare tell them that. Go now, quickly. Get up and thank them. I'm going to tell them you thank them." And she began to speak soothing words in the Ilasi language.

But it was no use. On the cliff was a commotion. I hurried out. With his hafted ax between his teeth, Andriki was scrambling up the rocks to the cave. The Ilasi men began to shout in high, excited voices. Then, behind me in the dark cave, everyone began to move quickly, grabbing things, bumping each other. Over and over Pinesinger tried to speak, until her baby began crying. Then even he was drowned out by the echoing noise in the cave.

"Wait, Uncle!" I called. "Stop!" But I was too late.

Andriki's eyes flew wide and his mouth fell open, so that his ax clattered down over the rocks. His hands flew to his chest and throat; he fell backward to the ground with a dull thump. On the pine needles far below, he lay still. I leaped from the cave and landed on my feet beside him, then knelt, moved his hands aside, and yanked out the things that were sticking in him—two things, two bone-tipped things now red with his blood, one from his throat and one from his heart. Two weak, thin little bird-spears.

"They killed me," sighed Andriki.

"No, Uncle!" I cried. But he was right. They did.

"Uncle!" I shouted, and "Ohun help him!" But Andriki was watching the Camps of the Spirits—his pupils glazed and his eyelids relaxed in a look I had seen many times before, if not on a person. He was dead.

Then I felt a terrible anger, and a red light filled the corners of my eyes. How had this happened? The Ilasi had killed him with their tiny spears, which somehow they had gotten deep inside him, although the spears were light as grass and both of them together snapped in two as I held them. I dropped the pieces and snatched up my spear, shouting that I too would die that day while killing Ilasi. Looking up at the people on the ledge, although bird-spears seemed to be flying by like bees, I chose a man, balanced my spear, and reached backward to launch it.

Suddenly I was knocked flat on my back. On top of me, pressing me to the ground, soft and heavy in a cloud of hair and breath, her eyes huge, her face heating mine, lay Muskrat. Inside her eyes I saw her pupils widening; inside her mouth I saw her white, wet teeth and pink tongue. "Stop now," she said, in my language.

Above her people were gathering. Men began to take her by the arms and clothing and try to pull her to her feet. But she wrapped her arms and legs around me and buried her face in my neck, holding me so tightly that when the people tried to lift her, I felt myself rising. Meanwhile she was shouting past my ear a stream of her own language.

I tried to free myself. A baby was crying, I noticed as I struggled with Muskrat—our baby, who sat in his sling astride the hip of a little girl. She stood nearby, her eyes on Muskrat, her face filled with fear, and her arms around the baby as if she would protect him. Both Muskrat and I turned our heads to look at her. Then one of the Ilasi men said something that sounded strong and definite, and Muskrat let go of me and got up. The next moment she was sitting on her heels beside me, her shirt open, our child at her breast. "Ah! Weh!" she called to Pinesinger, beckoning with her thumb.

Badly frightened, Pinesinger came forward, unable to take her eyes from Andriki, who lay on his back, very still. Muskrat waited. When Pinesinger was near, Muskrat spoke to her briefly. I listened. Everyone listened. In the quiet, warm air of early fall, Muskrat's voice made the only sound except for the pulsing cry of locusts and the droning of the first few flies to learn about Andriki. Behind me in the woods the wind breathed in the pines, and high above the ridge of the hills, in the dazzle of sunlight, another hawk followed the path in the air that took him south.

"She says this," said Pinesinger, her voice trembling. "You may go. Your woman won't go with you. She wants to stay here. Do you see that girl?" Pinesinger pointed with her lips at the little girl who had been holding the baby, surely the girl whose footprints had so closely followed Muskrat's. "She's Muskrat's daughter. Do you see that man?" Pinesinger pointed with her lips at a broad-shouldered, bearded man, the man who had spoken so angrily to me in the cave and who seemed in the daylight to be almost the age of Father. "He's her husband. Do you see that woman?" Pinesinger pointed with her lips at an elderly woman from whose wrinkled face the blue buttocks mark had almost faded. "She's her mother. Do you see that elder?" Pinesinger pointed to the old man with the staff. "He's her father. Her people wouldn't let her go even if she agreed. But she says she doesn't know why you followed her, since she never wanted to stay with you."

What could I say? My thoughts wouldn't come. I waited. Muskrat spoke again, and sometimes one or another of her people added a quiet word or two. The people were very calm now. Their voices were low and reasoned, and their gestures and faces were serene. "Muskrat says you can go," said Pinesinger. "For the sake of your child here, Kiu Ngaar, her people agree not to kill you if you go now. I think you should do it. Just stand up and go."

"I can't leave my uncle. I must bury him."

Muskrat and some of the Ilasi men spoke together for a little while, and at last Pinesinger said, "They don't like it that we bury dead people. It isn't the right thing to do, they say. It's a bad practice, not safe, because of the corpse. If you want to bury your uncle's corpse, you must take it away."

"If I don't?"

This time Muskrat answered. "Is all right you leave him," she said to me gently. "He you uncle. We pull him in woods. Then we clean our hand, where we touch him. Soon he gone."

300

"I'll take him," I said. I got up then and stood over Andriki, looking down at his half-open eyes. "Forgive me," I said to his spirit, which might still have been near us, waiting in the air for a bird to guide it to the sun's place in the west. I hope he heard me. I won't see him in the Camps of the Spirits. He'll wait for Maral at their mother's fire, while I will go to Uncle Bala and my mother. The lineage claims us in the Camps of the Spirits, where women own all of us, living and dead.

I took Andriki's right wrist, already cold, the flesh stiffening. Pulling him up, I knelt so that my shoulder fitted to his belly. Then I stood, with him riding my shoulder; bringing his cooling arm around my back, I clasped it and his legs against me. Pinesinger handed me his spear, then mine, then his hunting bag, then mine. I looked around at Muskrat. She stood nearby, with our baby in his sling on her back, her hands on her daughter's shoulders, and her eyes on her husband's face, listening intently as he spoke to someone else. But my little boy was watching me. He raised his head from his mother's back and looked at me closely with his dark, knowing eyes. For a moment we watched each other. His face became suddenly anxious, as if he knew something wrong was happening. Very sad, I nodded to him. "May you have life," I said to him, and turning, I walked away.

Soon I heard someone hurrying behind me. I had to turn my whole body and Andriki's too to see who it was. Pinesinger caught up with me. All out of breath, she was carrying her blue-eyed baby and her pack too. I would have waited so that she could rest, but she motioned with her chin for me to go. So I did, she following.

When we had put some distance behind us, she began to talk. "I left as soon as I could gather my things," she panted. "I don't want to be their hostage. And I think they'll leave that cave now. I heard them speak of fast traveling. They want to escape our revenge."

For a time Pinesinger hurried after me in silence. Was it possible that I was going too fast for her, even with the weight of Andriki's body? When she spoke next, she was still out of breath. "It's bad about Andriki," she said.

"We will grieve now. Your father, he'll grieve. All of us will miss Andriki. You most of all. How he loved you. He used to speak of you as if you were his brother or his son."

I didn't answer, because I couldn't bring myself to speak. But Pinesinger didn't want to notice my silence. As if words would make things right, she chattered desperately. "Perhaps you should have offered gifts," she said. "I believe they like horse teeth. You had some—you could have brought some. Ah well, it's too late now, and I'm not sure that gifts would have made a difference. As long as the men of your family act thoughtlessly, these things will happen to us. Even so, this is too bad."

32

I HARDLY HEARD PINESINGER. INSTEAD OF LISTENING, I WAS planning to come back with Father and kill the Ilasi. If Andriki were carrying my body, he would have been planning revenge for me. Yet revenge could only happen if I lived to find Father, to tell who killed Andriki and to lead our men to the killers in their cave. Then it seemed to me that the thoughts of the Ilasi might be following the same paths. In that case, if they reasoned well, they would come after us to kill us too. So I decided to leave Andriki's body. I put him down where the trail followed the bottom of the tumbled boulders, taking time only to cover him with rocks. That's what he would have done for me, I was certain. Yet it hurt me, and as I carefully placed the rocks, I spoke to him—although by then, I knew, a bird was guiding his spirit to the west. But I told him what he needed to know—that his brothers and his in-laws and all the men of our people would be back to avenge and bury him.

Then we hurried away from the Ilasi, as they had twice hurried from us. I had to carry Pinesinger's pack for her. We didn't have much of a head start, so while Pinesinger went forward I laid false trails. We walked down a stream and broke our line of travel on wide spaces of bare rock so that our footprints seemed to vanish, as if we had flown into the air. All this took us away from the route we had used to find the Ilasi, so we spent six nights instead of five on the plain before we crossed the Hair. We had no food but berries, and at night we built no fires. We had nothing to say to each other, so we went most of the way in silence. Early on I had threatened to choke Pinesinger if her chatter didn't stop.

When the people learned of the death of Andriki, their grief and anger were very strong. Weeping, Hind took her knife to her face and breasts. Tears and blood soaked her hair and trousers. I couldn't look at her. If not for me and my wish to keep Muskrat, Andriki would still be living. The people didn't say this, but they thought it. I could feel their anger burn.

Their anger also burned at Pinesinger, who had helped to lead Andriki to his death by running away with the Ilasi, even if she had come home in the end. For a time after our return, people wouldn't answer her if she spoke. It wasn't that they scorned her, but that they didn't seem to hear her, as if they wanted to forget she was there. That, I thought, was how people felt about me too, and I all but hid myself in the shadows of the cave, so I didn't give them a chance to show me their anger.

A few days after Pinesinger and I returned, Father and the other men called me to join them at the dayfire, which they still kept at Muskrat's old camp. The men wanted to talk with me. Rather fearfully, not knowing what was in their minds, I went to them, waited a moment in case they wanted to say something quick or send me somewhere, then sat on my heels beside Father. They were going to revenge Andriki, Father told me, and they wanted me to lead them to the Ilasi. Then I was happy! "This is very good, Father. I will go with you," I said.

"Yes, my son," said Father. "You must lead us there.

And you must show us where Andriki lies. We will bury him. But first you must tell us again how your woman's people killed him."

So I told them everything I knew, and I described everything I had seen about the little bird-spears. In the dust I drew one of them. With a narrow branch from our firewood, I made something like it.

"Were they like the little spear we found at Uske's Spring?" asked Father.

"They were the same," I answered.

"Where did they spear Andriki?" asked Marten.

"Once in the throat and once in the chest," I answered.

"How did the things pierce him if they were wooden?" asked Kida.

"They were pointed with bone," I said.

"Even with a bone point, this thing could not be thrown hard enough to pierce someone's skin," said Maral, taking up my copy. "How did they kill a man with a little stick like this?"

Sad to say, I had no answer. I had seen a thing I didn't understand.

Taking Andriki's sleeping-skin and necklace with us, we made the trip quickly, but found the cave empty and the Ilasi gone. They had known we would come, we reasoned, but not how many of us they would have to fight, although they could have known from Muskrat that we outnumbered them. So they would have known that when we found them, many of them would die, no matter what they threw at us. At any rate, they had left the bearskin, which told us that they had gone in a hurry. The cold, scattered ashes of their fire and the burned, mouse-gnawed bones told us that they had gone days before. But the flayed corpse of Father's wolf pup told us nothing. Why the people had killed him, we had no idea, unless they had left the corpse as a message to Father. If so, their message was wasted, and the pup too, since we didn't understand.

The Ilasi had hidden their tracks so well that we didn't try to follow. Instead we looked around until we found one of the broken bird-spears that I thought had killed Andriki. We looked at it as carefully as we could, fitting the broken ends together. Still we couldn't understand its strength.

Then we went back to where I had left Andriki's body, bent double from riding my shoulder. I don't like to remember finding him again so long after death. We all were unhappy and uneasy, although Father praised me for having hidden him so well. Insects had eaten him, but not animals. I had risked my life to do this for him, Father reminded the other men. We cut digging sticks for ourselves and dug a big hole. Then we found a redbush, cut strips of its slippery bark, and used it to tie Andriki's arms and legs against his body. I will always remember his hair, the only thing about him that still looked as it had in life—I remember his two yellow braids and, between them, his pale scalp showing.

When Andriki's body was ready, we lifted him into the hole, broke the string of the necklace we had brought, scattered the beads over him, and covered him with his sleeping-skin. Then we pushed the earth around him and packed it tight. We took out our knives, bared our arms, and cut ourselves so that our blood ran down on the fresh grave. "We are late, my brother," said Father, weeping. "Yet we have not forgotten you."

"Hona," said we all.

Then we covered the grave with stones so animals wouldn't dig him out. And then we went home.

As for Muskrat, her people never came back, and I never saw her again. I never saw our son either, although while I went with Father and the other men on our useless trip for vengeance, I had a wildly happy feeling that I would find him, grab him up in my arms, and bring him home, even without Muskrat. He was to Pinesinger's son what Andriki had been to Father. In a strange way, having him back would have been like having someone in Andriki's place again.

Yet that was not to be. Instead I began to dream of Muskrat's son. Each year in my dreams he grows older. It is as if the Woman Ohun wants me to remember him, since She knows he is mine in spite of everything. I wonder if he dreams of me.

Of course, Pinesinger's oldest child is also mine. In truth, I can't forget this, although during the winter that followed Andriki's death I might have liked to. Each day Pinesinger's pregnant belly grew, and the time of the birth of Father's child got nearer. Meanwhile she was trying hard to feed my blue-eyed son. She complained that her breasts grew small, but in this she was no different from any other woman trying to nurse a child in winter.

The winter was no easier than any other. We killed a bear, the one Andriki and I had seen crossing the plain. We treated him just as Father had told us to—we did not crack his bones for marrow and we left his head where it lay, with fat between his teeth. Even so, during the Lodge Moon and the Hunger Moon the deer left the forest and two tigers came, the Lily and a wife he had brought from somewhere, so all of us knew hunger.

Then one day, when the Moon of Roaring was new, Pinesinger said that she was cold and wanted firewood. She left the lodge, and when she came back she was no longer pregnant. Nor was she carrying any baby except my blue-eyed son. What had happened? No one asked her. Nor should anyone have asked her. Her milk could hardly feed one child. She had simply chosen to feed her older child, the child who had already proved he could live through a winter, the child she knew. I for one didn't like to imagine what might have happened to the new baby out in the snow. I tried to forget that anything had happened, although that child would have been to me as Andriki had been to Father. Everyone was unhappy, but so it was to be.

That same winter Pinesinger's blue-eyed son learned to walk, in a way. In spring he was given his name, perhaps the strongest any man can be given, since the name honored the Bear. It was I who chose the name, on a fresh spring morning at Father's lodge, just before we went to the Hair River.

Pinesinger and I were filling a waterskin by the lake, one of Muskrat's old tasks. I had given the boy my birchbark dipper and was showing him how to scoop up the water. "See how well he does that," said Pinesinger. "He can walk. He knows me. He could have a name."

"It's true," I said. "He could." Then I drew a deep breath and looked at the forest around me. On the tops of the trees the spruce needles shone in the morning sun. In the grass by the lake a spider's web shone all beaded with dew. And the water shone. Wind in the night had blown the broken ice to the far end of the lake, and the water rose and fell in front of us like someone breathing freely, glittering, breaking in tiny waves against the mossy stones at our feet. Now and then, from somewhere deep in the spruce woods, came the creaking, singsong voice of a tree. Summer, the time of plenty, was near. Once again we had lived through a winter. Once again the Bear had sent us animals to hunt and had not killed us. Instead, once again He was showing us the open water, letting us feel the spring sunlight there by the lakeshore, in the cloud of scent and pollen from the pines.

I watched my tiny son, who, no taller than my knee-high moccasin, was sitting on his heels on a rock just as I was sitting, but with his two hands, strong and clumsy, grasping the dipper. Here was a hunter whom the Bear would favor. I felt grateful to the Bear, but to name a child Bear would be out of the question. Yet as certain tigers have names that hide their real name, so do bears. "Call him Brown," I said.

"Yes, that's good," said his mother. And she did.

When Father began to hear Pinesinger's child called by a name, he brought her into his bed again. Then I thought that Father would be happy. At last, it seemed, he was going to have what he had always wanted—a child from the lineage of Sali, the great shaman from the Fire River whom Father so much admired. But Pinesinger didn't become pregnant by Father until the fall of that year.

She was still pregnant in the summer of the following year, when almost all the people who had kin at the Fire

River went to visit them. I didn't go, because of the mammoths. There had been very little snow in winter, and by early summer the meltwater pools on the plains went dry and the mammoths seemed ready to drink from the river. So we hunted them. I'm glad I stayed—even without Andriki we killed a young male mammoth who knew no better than to use the steep trail down to the water. We ate like lions, and my share of the hunt was part of a tusk, a piece longer than my arm and so heavy that I could hardly lift it. If I had gone to visit Mother, I would have gotten none.

When the others reached the Fire River without me, my mother was very disappointed. Yet she was so taken with Brown that I wonder if she would have noticed me. She told everyone that having him there was like having me as a child again, because he looked exactly like me when I had been his age. She told everyone that the first time she saw him, she thought he was me turned back into a child by the Woman Ohun. She said she couldn't remember that he wasn't her grandchild, since he looked as if he should be her grandchild. By mistake, more or less, instead of calling him Nephew, as she would call almost any child, or Stepchild, as she might have done, since she and his mother had both been wives of the same man, she kept calling him Grandson. I was told that many people laughed privately at this, so I was glad I hadn't been there to see it. Most of all, though, I was glad Father hadn't seen it. It was just like my mother to say unexpected things and to embarrass the greatest number of people, especially Father's people. Andriki once said that she had been a meddling old in-law even when she was beautiful and young.

The people who visited the Fire River were Yoi and pregnant Pinesinger; their kinswomen, Teal and Meri; Meri's husband, White Fox; Graylag's son, Elho; Graylag's stepson, the Stick; and the wives of these men. All but Elho's wife had kin there. The visitors left the Hair in single file very early one morning, disappearing into a heavy mist that lay on the plain.

For all Father seemed to ignore his women, he began at once to speak of the time when his wives would return. In fact, he spoke of them every day very fondly, as if he had never known anything but happiness from either of them. In the evenings he carved jewelry for them from his share of the ivory. By the time they were expected back, he had made two beautiful pendants, one for each, neither larger nor better than the other.

At last, one evening in the Moon of Fires, a line of people was seen gently swaying in the red grass far away. Father thought his wives had come, and he hurried out to meet them. To his great disappointment, he found everyone except Yoi and Pinesinger. These two had stayed behind. Father tried hard to hide his feelings, but from the way his eyes closed and his voice grew quiet, we knew that they were strong.

That evening, as we sat in his cave around the two fires, the men at one, the women at the other, hearing the travelers tell of their visit and their journey, I happened to hear him whispering over his shoulder to Teal, who sat back to back with him. He asked where his women were and why they hadn't come home. In her strong voice, Teal answered. As soon as their group had reached the Fire River, Teal explained, Father's two wives had become good friends. Both of them had stayed with Pinesinger's mother, Eider, who was related to Yoi in the same way that Teal was related to Yoi—their mothers had been sisters. So the women were lineage cousins. But there was more. Because Yoi's dead sister and Eider had been close in age, Yoi looked up to Eider as to an elder sister.

Warmed by Eider's joy in them, Yoi and Pinesinger had found it hard to remember why they had ever disliked each other. As a result, the two co-wives had begun to call each other Sister. Pinesinger had shared Brown with Yoi, and by the end of summer the boy hadn't known which woman to call Mama. That was as it should be with the children of co-wives. Anyway, as long as Yoi and Pinesinger were at the Fire River, Eider had not allowed any trouble between them, or allowed them to stay anywhere except together at her fireside with her.

Yoi and Pinesinger had been so happy to be in their childhood home, so free and comfortable among the members of their lineage, that their kin had easily persuaded them to stay for the rest of the year. Someone would walk them to the Hair someday, their relatives had promised. More likely, though, people had said, their husband would miss them so much he would come for them himself. He would want to get his child, born to him from the lineage of the famous shaman Sali. Ah yes, a little boy had been born to Pinesinger in the company of Eider, Yoi, Teal, and Meri, one mild evening in the Moon of Grass—more often called the Moon of Foals by the people at the Fire River.

In case Father came for his wives and infant, Uncle Bala had sent a message. He wanted Father to remember that gifts were still owed for three of his wives—for Pinesinger, of course, but also for Yoi and even for Mother. Now that I was married to Frogga, Bala thought that the question of Mother's ivory necklace could be raised again. There seemed little chance that Mother would return it, Bala said, so perhaps Father should stop asking for it and let it become one of the gifts given to my lineage by my wife's kin. Bala wanted to remind us that he often thought of Father as Frogga's father's brother. Yet even if Father was just a half-brother, he was a headman, so people expected a gift. "A big gift" is what Bala meant. The necklace would help people remember Father for his giving, not just for the women he had taken away with him, Bala said.

"Didn't I say this would happen?" Father asked me late that night at the men's fire. He was still trying to hide his disappointment over his missing wives. "Didn't I say that your mother would allow any marriage if she could keep the necklace? Was I right?"

This was where Andriki would have agreed strongly with Father, adding a few words of his own against Mother as well. At the men's fire we held our breath, as if in the dark, in the flickering shadows, we might yet hear Andriki speaking.

Then it began to hurt me that we were waiting for his voice, even if we didn't mean to, so I answered heartily. "Hi! You spoke of that necklace when I first came here, Father. I didn't think Mother would be so greedy, but you know her. Is she keeping the necklace? Let her! There's enough ivory by our camps each summer for all the relatives of all the Fire River women. The women know it, and their relatives know it. And if the mammoths learn about the trail, we'll find another way to hunt them. We will! It's in our nature. Right now at the Fire River the people are talking about us, our strength, our mammoths, our hunting lands, our ivory. Aren't we feeders of foxes and killers of meat?"

"We are!" answered most of the men.

SOURCES AND ACKNOWLEDGMENTS

Long ago in Asia and across the northern part of the New World, the story of an animal wife was apparently popular. It occurred in many places in slightly different forms, as the quotes that open this book are meant to show. The story is about a man and a woman who is really an animal in human form. In China and Japan the woman is a fox, but on our side of the Bering Strait the woman can be other animals too. The theme, however, is very much the same wherever the story is told: a man finds a woman with something unusual about her—she's alone in the woods, perhaps. Ignoring any suggestion that she is not quite what she appears to be, the man falls in love with her. She becomes his housekeeper or his wife. Although in most stories she keeps her animal skin somewhere on the premises (an ominous gesture that the man prefers to overlook), the man is happy with her because of her helpfulness and beauty. Sooner or later, though, he unwittingly does something wrong. In response, the woman puts on her animal skin, resumes her animal self, and vanishes into the woods (if she is a mammal) or into the air (if she is a bird). If she and the man have had children together, she takes them.

The animal wife stories seem always to be told from the man's point of view—they are ostensibly stories of a man having a strange or disappointing experience—and consequently they never end happily, because the wife is really an animal disguised as a woman, not a woman disguised as an animal, and once she leaves she never comes back. In contrast are "The Frog Prince" and related stories, popular in European folklore, in which a man who has been malevolently converted into an animal is rescued by a woman from the misery of his base, bestial state. Frog prince stories have happy endings.

This novel is a companion piece to an earlier novel, *Reindeer Moon,* for which I am indebted to a number of very helpful sources. These are listed in *Reindeer Moon.* In addition, however, I used the following works. For translation from the Russian I would like to thank my husband, Stephen Thomas.

Chard, C. S. 1974. Northeast Asia in prehistory. Madison and London. U. of Wisconsin Press.

Giterman, R. E. 1968. The main developmental stages of vegetation in northern Asia in the quaternary. Transactions of the Geological Institute, Academy of Sciences, vol. 177. Nauka Press. Moscow. In Russian.

Johnson, C. W. 1985. Bogs of the northeast. Hanover and London. University Press of New England.

Kynstautas, A. 1987. The natural history of the USSR. New York. McGraw-Hill.

Tilson, R. L. and U. S. Seal, eds. 1987. Tigers of the world: the biology, biopolitics, management, and conservation of an endangered species. Park Ridge, N.J. Noyes.

As in *Reindeer Moon,* the economy and physical environment of the people in this novel are loosely based on those of the Ju/wa Bushmen of Nyae Nyae in Namibia, in the days when the economy of the Ju/wasi was that of hunting and gathering. The cold savanna of the Siberian Paleolithic was interestingly similar to the African savanna, with a vaguely similar terrain and a similar fauna, although the latter was obviously adapted for heat instead of cold. The personalities, material possessions, culture, religious life, and social life of the people in this novel are entirely fictional and bear no resemblance to the Ju/wasi now or ever.

Few if any of the above bibliographical sources list the tiger as present in central Siberia during the Anthropogene. Siberia's version of the sabertooth, the homotherium, is another matter, but that animal was long gone by the time my story takes place. I include a tiger for three reasons. First, in a countryside so vast yet so lightly touched by paleozoology, the fact that no tiger's bones have been discovered doesn't necessarily mean that tigers weren't there. Second, the bones of a tiger, if found, could have been mistaken for bones of a cave lion, since the ubiquitous cave lions were very similar in size and build to the massive northern race of tiger, the fluffy *Panthera tigris altaica,* also known as *P. t. longipilis.* Third, I see no reason that the range of these magnificent animals could not have extended almost any distance along the forested hills and river valleys. Until quite recently the east-west spread of the tiger was extensive, from the Caucasus Mountains to the Sikhote-Alin Mountains, due north of Japan, where a few insufficiently protected wild tigers still cling to life today. A line drawn between these places would cross the site of my imaginary landscape. In this novel February, the Storm Moon, is also called the Moon of Roaring, after the tigers' rut season.

I took a liberty with the mention of a bobcat, since the bobcat is, strictly speaking, a New World creature. I used its name in place of another cat, the European wildcat, since for obvious reasons the words "European" and "wild" would not fit in this novel. After all, a bobcat can almost be called a thicket-dwelling, bird-hunting version of the lynx, which is found throughout the Holarctic region.

I did not take a liberty with the animal called tai tibi, except that its name is, so to speak, a translation into the imaginary Ilasi language of what in English is a household word. This familiar animal, which has inhabited Asia since the Upper Miocene, was domesticated long ago and today is found in every barnyard. Even so, it never inhabited tundra or cold savannas but preferred broadleaf forests and slightly milder climates to the fictional climate imagined here. Therefore, the only fictional thing about this remarkable creature is the name.

Many of the winter scenes in this novel derive from a midwinter visit to one of the most beautiful and interesting places in Europe, the ancient forest of Varrio above the Arctic Circle in northern Finland. Through the kindness of the Finnish publishers of *Reindeer Moon* I was able to travel to Varrio. For this I would like to thank Olli Arrakoski and Sirkka Kurki-Suonio of Helsinki, and Kaarlo Koskinen, Merja Saariniemi, Markku Kuusiniemi, and Juha Niemela of the Varrio Subarctic Research Station of the University of Helsinki. I am also very grateful to Björn Kurtén for much insight into the animal life of Paleolithic times—life that in a number of ways was possibly very different from that of today.

For her critical reading of this manuscript, I would like to thank Sy Montgomery. For the time of quiet concentration in which I was able to complete this novel, I would like to thank Myra Sklarew and the Yaddo Corporation.

Peterborough, N.H.
January 1990

Books by Elizabeth Marshall Thomas

The Animal Wife*
Reindeer Moon*
The Harmless People
Warrior Herdsmen

*Published by POCKET BOOKS

PRAISE FOR

THE ANIMAL WIFE

"Light-years separate Thomas's intelligent, literate fiction from most other novels set in prehistoric times. . . . Thomas has a magical feel for the patterns of the natural world integral to the hunter-gatherer culture. . . . Exuding authenticity and distinguished by resonant language, *THE ANIMAL WIFE* . . . is psychologically acute and soaringly imaginative."

—Publishers Weekly

"A . . . profound portrait of human culture in the Paleolithic period . . . Ms. Thomas is a brilliant and restrained stylist . . . she says powerful things about gender without a hint of ideology, and handles the violence and beauty of primitive life with all the narrative verve and none of the sentimentality of Jack London."

—The New Yorker

"Her rhythms are deep and long; they power *THE ANIMAL WIFE* with the mythic force of life in nature, evoking the deep cyclic mysteries of the universal pulse that moved the primitive people and all of us. . . ."

—Boston Globe

"A fascinating portrait of the early life of our species . . . *THE ANIMAL WIFE* dares to strip away any sentimental notion we might have about so-called primitive human beings."

—Chicago Tribune

"In Ms. Thomas's spare, evocative prose is much wisdom about men and women and the limits of our understanding of each other." *—The New York Times Book Review*

A Literary Guild Alternate Selection